Cherokee Talisman

Cherokee Talisman

A NOVEL BY

DAVID-MICHAEL HARDING

2/2018

Cherokee Talisman

Copyright © 2012 by David Harding

All Rights Reserved
A
Q&CY
BOOK

Cover photograph by Nina Fussing © 2012
www.wheelingit.wordpress.com

Drawing of 'Dragging Canoe – Cherokee War Chief'
by Mike Smith © 1991. All rights reserved.
Prints available at www.draysmith.com

Photograph of the author by
William Tillis and Harold Hutchinson © 2011

Cover by Kerwin Designs

DavidMichaelHarding.com

Printed in the United States of America
October 2012
First Edition

1 3 5 7 9 10 8 6 4 2

ISBN-10 0615652530
ISBN-13 978-0615652535
Library of Congress Catalog Number: 2012910304

For
Chris

A son-in-law through Courtney's choice
A son through ours

FOREWORD

There are few places more beautiful than the Cherokee homeland in the fall of the year. It is during the fall that our Creator paints the leaves on the maples and oaks, making the forests a colorful display of beauty. It was also in these same forests that many Cherokees lived, loved, and died. Our history as a people was so affected by the Trail of Tears that many historians begin the telling of our story at the Trail of Tears moving forward, and those who walked through those forests of maples and oaks are all but forgotten.

David-Michael Harding, in his novel *Cherokee Talisman*, takes the reader to our homeland in the fall of the year, in such a way that the reader can almost smell the earth and see the beautiful colors of the leaves. It is a glimpse of oneness with the land that Harding conveys to the reader so that the love of our homeland, and the desire to protect it, can be felt by the human spirit and understood. *Cherokee Talisman* brings to life characters from our history and through a flare for fiction and historical research, Harding tells their story. Cherokees that might be painted by racist misconceptions as blood thirsty savages are humanized by Harding, making them heroes of a very real time in our history forgotten by man, and preserved by few. History is written by the victorious, but when almost forgotten historical characters are brought to life, and their stories told, they are preserved for the ages, and in this preservation David-Michael Harding has succeeded.

Cherokee Nation Principal Chief Bill John Baker

Tahlequah, OK
November 2012

"Dragging Canoe"
Cherokee War Chief

PREFACE

Tsi'yugunsini ("Dragging Canoe") was one of the greatest Native Americans to have ever lived. His home was in the Smoky Mountains of current-day Eastern Tennessee. He was a highly skilled Cherokee war chief who lived, loved, fought, and died during a time when the United States was still struggling in its infancy. We look back at our nation's history during the latter part of the eighteenth century as a time of expansion, perseverance, and strength of American character. Tsi'yugunsini looked at the colonials as invaders, thieves, and terrorists.

Britain's King George was an invader as well, but he was four thousand miles away while the American settlers were pushing for expansion into Cherokee territory. When the Revolutionary War broke out in earnest Tsi'yugunsini sided with the British, choosing the devil at a distance over the one at his door. This may explain why he is not remembered and how victor's justice has clouded our past.

Tecumseh, another tremendous Native American, from the Shawnee Nation, also sided with the British, most predominantly in the War of 1812. For reasons as simple as timing and the sound and spelling of their names or as complex as their travels and influence, Tecumseh is recognized and commercialized while Tsi'yugunsini is less than a footnote. In the years following the Revolution the two men fought together against the new Americans in the Chickamauga Wars. They believed the total unification of all Native American nations against the new country was the only way to salvage their unique way of life. They were right, and Tecumseh championed the philosophy until he died in battle in 1813. His dream never came to be. If it had, a map of the United States may look decisively different.

However, over two hundred years after Tsi'yugunsini's death, one notion of the great chief remains. It is well documented from the 1775 treaty negotiations at Sycamore Shoals that Tsi'yugunsini, in absolute opposition to any land succession, boldly proclaimed that the names of the indigenous nations and their people would be forgotten or mispronounced by the expansion-minded colonies and their history. Today, of the over five hundred distinct nations that once comprised the United States, less than a handful are remembered. The same holds true for the men and women of those lands who served their people with distinction.

Interestingly, a vast number of our states, cities, and rivers still carry Native American names and while these are repeated countless times a day, the pronunciation is often scrambled and the origin forgotten, just as the great chief predicted. His own home region of Tennessee is derived from the Cherokee word *tanase*. Even the most widely visited national park in the United States, The Great Smoky Mountains, owes its name to the Cherokee who referred to the range as *shaconage* (shă–con–ă–gee) "place of blue smoke." Perhaps a greater, and sadder, testament to his tremendous foresight is that his declaration applies to his own name.

The chief's name has been written several ways — each one of which impacts its spelling and pronunciation for English speakers.

I have attempted to present the Cherokee (*Tsa-la-gi*) names as accurately as possible and suggest the English reader sound them out as written. The historical representations are accurate as a reflection of recorded history; however, there are gaps filled from my own pen as is the nature of historical fiction. I am certain my adaptation is consistent with the time, events, intent, and outcome. My respect for the Tsalagi nation and others referenced in this novel are such that I sincerely apologize if I have unintentionally misrepresented any person or event.

I would like to credit the *Cherokee-English Dictionary* by Feeling, Pulte, and Cowen, © 1975 by the Cherokee Nation of Oklahoma, and *Sacred Formulas of the Cherokees* and *Myths of the Cherokee* by James Mooney from his material collected in the late nineteenth century originally published by the Bureau of American Ethnology in 1891 and 1900.

Wa-do.

David-Michael Harding
November 2012

Note: Pitch and emphasis are important elements in the Cherokee language. The "ts" sound might be described as a blur between the English sharp "ch" and soft "j."

Tsalagi (Tsă-lă-gee') Cherokee
Tsi'yugunsini (Tsĭ'-u-gŭnsĭ'-nĭ) Dragging Canoe or Dragon
Totsuhwa (To-tsooh-wă) Redbird
Ama Giga (Ă-mă Gĭ-gă) Bloody Water, Totsuhwa's grandmother
Galegi (Gă'-lĕ-gee) Blacksnake, Totsuhwa's wife
ahwi (ăh'-wĭ) deer
osiyo/siyo (sĭ'-yō) hello
wado (wă'-dō) thank you

CONTENTS

PROLOGUE

Autumn comes late in the Carolinas. Summer willfully drags her feet which pleases some and riles not but a few, including the trees which are anxious to change their hues, rid themselves of summer's trappings and rest in the coolness of the fall. Flies are permitted by the lingering summer heat to continue harassing the horses and livestock who have waited out the long season in anticipation of the cold that will drive the insects into hiding. The whitetail deer, browsing beneath the impatient trees, are also tormented by the flies and without the long tails of their domesticated neighbors are given to sprints through the thick brush to escape. These rushes and the pestering insects can give way to doom as the deer's concentration on the flies and escape coax their senses away from high alert. Then a hunter, his body wrapped in the tanned hide of his quarry, slips on silent feet through the disgruntled trees. His black hair hangs loose around his cinnamon brown face shielding it from the flies like a horse's mane. When the breeze is right, when the distance is right, he sends an arrow carefully honed under his own hand from a bow that was his father's into the deer's distracted heart.

The flies that gather gorge themselves on the blood that is pulled by gravity alone down the quiet deer's side. The heart is still. The hunter comes upon the body and sits several feet away watching for signs of life. When there are none he moves to the deer and rests his bow across the soft brown hair of this animal that has given the hunter's family continued life. He crouches at the deer's head and cups his hand under the dead mouth. Water from a leather bag pours into the hunter's hand and to the deer's lips.

"Thank you, my friend," he says tenderly. "This will help you on your journey." And the flies walk across the hunter's hands leaving the blood that has collected on their feet.

1775   1790   1806   1814   1818   1821

T he murmur was low and soft. Its belly was formed of quiet words passed from mouth to ear and accentuated by subtle gestures with black eyes and russet hands that only the Cherokee picked up and understood. The broad meeting room encompassed the entire building and needed two fireplaces to ward off the cold in winter. Tonight both burned small fires more for light than heat. Contentious words would soon raise the temperature while smoke from the fireplaces masked the woodsy smells of men who had traveled far. The room itself glowed as countless candles and lamps struggled to drive away the darkness. More than usual were present as the murmurs continued to banter about the offers and terms of the treaty. Tsi'yu-gunsini, translated by the English speakers as "Dragging Canoe," looked into the abundant flames and thought them wasteful. His adversaries — Richard Henderson who represented the Transylvania Land Company, John Sevier from the government, and Col. Daniel Boone, the mediator for hire — enjoyed the light. Sevier himself had directed the extra lamps into place.

"I want to see their faces," he had said.

The light did what it could, but the beams were generally ineffectual in aiding the cause of the white men seated around the long, rough-hewn benches and dining tables. But a single match would have shed enough light on the face of Dragging Canoe to indicate his thoughts on yet another treaty. The Cherokee, known to themselves and other Indian nations as the Tsalagi, were being asked to make land concessions again.

Dragging Canoe was a powerful man, strong in body and even stronger of mind. His name had been given him because of his rugged determination. As a small boy he had struggled to drag a long, heavy war canoe to the river intent on following his father, Attakullakulla, and other warriors into a battle. Since that day his battles had been many and his name became Tsi'yugunsini – "the canoe, he is dragging it". Most Cherokee names evolved. His was no different. Adversaries played on the name "Dragging," and modified it to "Dragon." A war cry from the Dragon's mouth resembled a fiery burst and meant a brutal death to any within reach of his weapons. The skill that laid waste to many lives over the years had vaulted Dragging Canoe to the level he now maintained. All chiefs envied his command and prowess at war but some chided him for not making peace when the battles were going to the enemy. Regardless of the attitude of his peers, his warriors followed him with a fervor few other leaders, red or white, would ever enjoy.

Another young chief, Doublehead, a distant cousin of Tsi'yugunsini's, was six years younger and also opposed the selling of more land. Doublehead had a growing power base in his own village as did most localized chieftains consistent with the governing style of the nation. His older brother, Utsi'dsata or "Old Tassel," was a powerful leader, close in stature to Tsi'yugunsini's father, Attakullakulla. Yet Attakullakulla was "Uka," the First Beloved Man of the Nation and as such held a delicate sway over all the chiefs present.

Doublehead's opposition was not as vehement as Dragon's or as violent. On another day when it would profit him more directly Doublehead might not speak out against the process of deeding land to the whites, but today he would support his relative's attempt to rally the chiefs in the room against the signing. Tomorrow might find the two at cross-purposes. Tonight however, they would be shoulder-to-shoulder though Dragon would take the lead.

Irrespective of their enthusiasm both men stood at odds with the senior ranking members of their families as well as most of the other influential chiefs in the brightly lit murmuring room. Attakullakulla, referred to by whites as "Little Carpenter" for his slight frame as he was much smaller than his son and also for his ability to craft treaties, was cautiously supportive yet came to the discussion with his own agenda. He had been a sound fighter in his younger years but from his earliest days he measured his accomplishments against his political aspirations. Over time, victories and losses alike enticed him to seek trade and compromise with the men of light skin with wide eyes who came over the mountains. Unlike many others he had learned to speak their language and welcomed the unique trade goods they carried, especially their weapons. During better days he had been courted by the arriving peoples and burdened with presents. But time eroded the esteem in which the white men had once held Little Carpenter and protection of the British king gradually waned until he was left to deal with land-hungry men and out and out butchers. Attakullakulla made these things known to his son, his triumphs and his tragedies, and thus shaped the young chief's mind.

Tsi'yugunsini's lessons did not lead to a direct hate of the white men who encroached on the land but rather the results that followed their intrusion. A cycle quickly began, wrought by Dragon and his warriors which brought destruction to the settlers despite the earlier intentions of either group. Through the years Dragon had fought side by side with a great many men — red, white, and black. And though he did not attack the colonists who came in the first days, instead learning the art of trade from his father, their increasing number and abuse of the land and his people distilled itself to a hatred of the constant flow. Soon that hatred began to spill from him with the cut of every worthless treaty. A paper line would be established — a boundary no colonist could cross. But the lines quickly blurred. Then the numbers outweighed the names on the paper and a new treaty with more land was requested. Refusals had resulted in wars — wars the numbered white people, better armed and supplied, would invariably win. So a new pact was signed in an attempt to save the heart of the nation from the interlopers. And this is how it had gone. Today was just another knot in the rope that Dragon felt tightening around the throat of the Cherokee.

As a champion for the nation, his passion was for his people, not against the men who now tried to see his face in the fire and candlelight. If he had indeed felt a rage against them, their scalps would be hanging from his lance by morning. But through his father he had come to grasp their purpose and learned it best to follow and understand their devious intentions than to be blindly led. And on those days when Dragon's pursuit of understanding frustrated him and begged him to pick up his gun, Attakullakulla had tempered his fire. But the peaceful chief, currently dressed in white to symbolize the same, was losing ground to the son who would much rather don the red robes of a war chief and advance on this enemy who professed to be a friend.

Dragon had been witness to a number of these treaties through the years. As a boy and later a young man he had accompanied his father to many such meetings. On the heels of the signed documents he had watched white settlers creep into Cherokee hunting territories and multiply until they were like locusts. They took game off the land in huge numbers and cleared the trees for their farms. A single cabin grew into a town and quickly sucked the Cherokee lifeblood out of the forests. The white-skinned people trapped incessantly, robbing furs from the villages of Cherokee. They stole trade and stole outright. They took much and brought little. And what they did bring into the lush valleys were notions peculiar to him. The strongest of which was the purpose of this latest meeting and the meal laid out before him — ownership of the land.

White people claimed to have ownership of the land, as if they held dominion over it. He had abandoned any measure of comprehending this peculiar white-way years before. Even now as the thought seeped through his mind again, Dragon smiled slightly at the absurd notion. The land could not be owned. Does anyone own the sky? Do they pretend to own the water that flows? The wind? The rain? Trees? Stones? The soil? No one can own the land. The Tsalagi understood that the earth was provided for them. If they took care with it, it would support them. The ground would give enough of the Three Sisters to feed the people. The revered

Sisters — beans, corn, and squash — would spring from the dirt each year and there would be plenty for all. And then the ground would rest and the people would dance on its back and sing songs of praise and thanksgiving for the Three Sisters and the land that had provided them.

In the cool forest the land gave life to deer, bear, and elk. The wolf hunted there alongside the Cherokee. Each took only what they needed. When they had, they gave thanks to the deer that would feed his family — be they wolf pups or Tsalagi babies with black hair and dark eyes. By feeding the deer and harboring its young, the land provided meat to the nation. Do we own the deer? The grasses they eat? The land beneath their hooves? Dragon no longer smiled. These men were strange — strange and selfish. And stupid for thinking they could own the land. But own it or not, they had come and continued to come and the numbers grew with each season.

He stepped away from the soft conversations of his brethren and walked to the log wall. He squatted down, his back to the wall, feet flat on the floor, his knees high in front of him. This had always been a more comfortable way to sit than on the chairs and benches the whites favored. He lifted a hand and stroked his lips gently as his mind raced on ahead of the negotiations that whirled around his father and continued in lesser stages at lesser levels on the outlying tables.

With his finger, graced by a scar and hard yellow at the knuckles, he caressed the deep pockmarks on his cheek. Many years before an evil spirit had infected him and he had nearly died. Thousands around him had perished. Their skin had blistered and they were torched with fever. Dragon understood little of this evil spirit apart from knowing that the shamans who had kept the tribes healthy from the time the Great Sprit had given them life now failed. Since the arrival of the whites the Cherokee had been decimated by sicknesses the plants in their forests could not or would not defeat. Dragon considered that the guardian spirits who had protected the nation and given it many tremendous victories over their enemies, were now punishing the Cherokee for these treaties that allowed the whites onto land meant for Cherokee. On bad days, he often thought that it wasn't just the trading of their ground that had angered the spirits, but that the anger was brought on by the mere presence of the white people. This was land the Creator had meant for Tsalagi feet to tread. No white feet were intended for these woods, mountains, and valleys. The Cherokee should have driven them off or killed them outright when they first appeared. Yes, on bad days he felt this way. And today was a bad day.

Dragon stood slowly and slipped along the wall to the door. John Sevier and Richard Henderson, making their rounds, encouraging the Cherokee chiefs with each step, were in his path.

Sevier stuck his hand out across Dragon's chest. "Where are you going, Tsi'yugunsini? There is rum left to drink!"

Dragon dismissed the arm with only his eyes. "I have had enough to drink."

"Then stay and talk some more," Henderson said as he leaped into the conversation.

"I have had enough talk as well."

With that Dragon stepped away. Sevier grabbed his arm, something Henderson would have liked to have done, but fear stopped him.

"Listen, my good friend," Sevier continued in a hushed voice. "These things will happen. It's up to us to make the best treaty we can for your people."

"Do you truly care for my people?"

Sevier looked at Henderson before his shifting eyes returned to Dragon. "Of course I do."

"If that is so do not promote this treaty. Or any other."

"Now hold on," Henderson said. "This is a good deal for the Indian. There's silver, horses, and land for everybody."

"The Tsalagi do not need your silver or your horses."

"Maybe," Sevier continued. "But we do need that land." He paused and measured the ensemble around him and the safety it could afford against the Dragon. "And we'll have it."

Dragon watched Henderson for a moment to gauge his reaction before looking back sternly to Sevier. Again the eyes of the chief pushed away the white man's hand.

"That tongue of yours will one day betray you," Dragon said quietly.

Henderson realized that his partner had stepped too near the flame. "Look," he said with a nervous smile over feet that began to shuffle. "I'm sorry. What John means is that it appears the treaty will come to fruition — in one form or the other. The Transylvania Land Company is not here to cheat you. I want to make the best deal for both parties. I want everyone to leave Sycamore Shoals a winner. You can help make that happen."

Dragon's eyes left the white face and peered out over the men in the room. They settled on his father as Henderson continued.

"Dragging Canoe is a great chief. His people respect and admire his words, as do we. Tell us what we can do and we'll do our utmost to accommodate you."

Dragon spoke. The words were meant for Henderson, but also for Sevier and his role in the treachery. "You can leave these valleys and not return."

At that Dragon stepped toward the door. His movement caught the notice of most of the men in the ongoing meeting. He made eye contact with none, but the sentiments of his soul were scribed in the taut muscles of his scarred face. Henderson and Sevier, as well as those Cherokee who, plied by rum and gifts, favored the treaty, were pleased when Dragon opened the door and was swallowed by the night outside. Boone was pleased as well.

As a mediator Boone realized that now there would be one less dissenting voice and a strong one at that. Just as surely, the opposite side felt their case weaken as the door closed behind the disgruntled chief.

The moonlight replaced the flames of the oil lamps and glistened across Dragon's black eyes as he moved hurriedly away from the light in the doorway. He paused beneath the overhang at the corner of the building as his sharp eyes adjusted and scanned the village. Dark shadows moved occasionally from here to there, militia making their rounds and others supporting the feast inside. Against the moonlit sky were the trails of smoke spewing lazily from the many fireplaces burning throughout the complex. If there were Shawnee nearby, they could find this town with ease, Dragon thought, and shook his head at the indiscretion of the settlers.

Habit forced Dragon to lean around the corner of the cabin and glance down its long side. There was no real reason to be on alert apart from being in the company of white men, but Dragon's nature and his experiences seemed to always find him not far from preparation for combat. His senses had rewarded him many, many times and tonight proved no exception. Against the wall of the meetinghouse cabin was a figure peering in and about the clapboards of a closed window.

Dragon was absorbed by the darkness away from the cabin and effortlessly glided through the night until he was silently positioned twenty feet behind the voyeur. The figure was thin and short, perhaps five feet tall at best. In all likelihood this was just a nosy woman. The warrior relaxed, thinking himself unnoticed and moved to slip away, his departure as secretive as his arrival, but the figure spoke and the words halted him.

"Don't mark it," the figure whispered.

Stayed by a frail voice and surprised he had been found out, Dragon listened in the dark for his next direction as his hand instinctively felt for the knife at his hip. But as the words themselves sunk beyond the knife and his surprise, he realized that words such as these could not come from the mouth of an enemy. A moment more passed and no further orders were issued. Dragon eased closer to the shape against the window.

"Please don't do it," the form suddenly whispered again.

Again the voice brought Dragon up short. But here, closer, his ears told him the voice was young. Careful examination by the pale light also showed the powerful chief that the speaker was even shorter than originally considered. And most surprising, the words were apparently not meant for him — at least not meant to be heard.

Leaning against the building was a young boy about seven winters old. Dragon's whispering orator was perched on a teetering box struggling to see through the cracks of the rough shutters that comprised the window. The boy spoke to the cracks in unheard whispers sent to the Cherokee chiefs reclining at the tables. "No. Don't do it," the boy breathed again.

The boy was so intent on his spying mission he did not hear the soft soles of Dragon's moccasins as he stepped up from behind. The chief was displeased that anyone would eavesdrop on the meeting he had abruptly abandoned, regardless of the message in the child's hushed tone. Dragon reached out with his foot and deftly kicked the box from beneath the boy. The scattering box made little sound as it tumbled across the grass. So dulling was the grass that the men inside were uninterrupted. The boy however, was ready to suffer a harsh fall. A single hand snapped out and clutched the boy's bare arm before he had fallen a few inches.

"Yuh-wa da-nv-ta! I'm sor-" the boy began to yell until Dragon's free hand clasped over his mouth. Both of the child's hands jumped instinctually to Dragon's hand covering his mouth. The warrior did not tell the boy to remain still with a word but instead tightened both hands and shook the boy slightly as the youngster dangled in mid-air.

The lithe body went limp and his hands dropped away from Dragon's. The man shook the boy once more but less so in order to insure understanding. The boy shook his head yes beneath the powerful hand.

Dragon slowly removed his hand from the boy's mouth as he lowered the child to the ground.

"Ga-dode-tsa do? What is your name?" Dragon asked forcibly.

The boy was still reeling and frightened by the big man in the dark.

"I have spoken to you. Why do you not answer me?"

"I am sorry," the boy replied, all the while still searching for courage amid the answer to the question. "Da-qua-dov...Da-qua-dov To-tsu-hwa. My name is...My name is Redbird."

"Of what clan are you, Totsuhwa?"

"Paint."

"That is a good family. Why does a Paint sneak through the dark and spy on his chiefs?"

"I was trying to see the meeting."

Dragon took the boy's shoulder and walked with him toward the front of the cabin. When Dragon stepped into the light of the moon Totsuhwa realized under whose hand he had fallen and he shuddered.

"Are you cold, Totsuhwa?"

"N-no, great chief."

Dragon stopped. "You know me?"

The boy was nearly afraid to acknowledge that which had already slipped from his tongue. "Yes."

"Who am I?"

"You are Tsi'yugunsini, great chief of the Tsalagi."

"Is that who you say I am?"

Encouraged and emboldened by his conversation with the warrior, Totsuhwa forgot himself. "Yes! You have fought many battles to defend our people. You have killed many Chickasaw and Creek and Shawnee. Now you kill the whites! That is why they call you 'The Dragon!'"

Dragon patted Totsuhwa's shoulder as he began to walk again. "You do not like the whites."

"No. They lie and steal."

Dragon smiled in the dim light of the moon. "Your father has raised you well."

"My father is dead."

"Which battle?" Dragon asked as though the cause of death was a foregone conclusion, as indeed it was.

"My mother told me a place called Oldfields."

"The Chickasaw."

"Yes."

"Your mother has given you your history then."

"She used to, but now she is asleep in the Darkening Land to the West. I stay with my grandmother and her people."

"Where was your mother taken?"

"A spirit made her very hot and her skin break. Our shaman could not keep her from the West."

"I know this spirit. He rested on me, but I was strong and drove him away. And still he left his tracks on my face like a deer in the snow. When he comes to me he sees his mark and remembers that he cannot defeat me. Now I can walk among the dying and he dares not touch Tsi'yugunsini. This I have done."

"I would like to defeat the whites like you defeated the spirit."

Dragon stopped walking away from the cabin. "Why do you say this, Totsuhwa? Have they harmed you?"

"I see them in the woods near our village. They take many deer my grandmother says the Creator sent for Cherokee arrows."

"That is why you asked the chiefs to not mark the leaves, the things they call 'paper?'"

"Yes. And when we play away from the village they chase us and throw rocks. Some friends have gone to the forest and not returned."

"Are you afraid of the white men?"

Totsuhwa dropped his eyes from the warrior for the first time in several minutes. "They have frightened me many times."

"Do you run from them?"

The boy's chin stayed tucked. He wanted to lie but could not. "I have done so."

Dragon looked around the dirt courtyard of the village square. Not seeing anyone close by he squatted down in front of Totsuhwa and lifted the boy's chin.

"Totsuhwa," he said as he pointed to the boy's skinny chest. "Rabbits grow to become panthers. The whites know nothing of this magic. The rabbit sneaks through the dark and whispers cunning thoughts to his friends," Dragon said as he now pointed back to the cabin window. "And they learn and grow strong. When the rabbit grows into a panther he will not run. Understand?"

Totsuhwa nodded in the darkness. "I think so, but I hope there are deer in the forest for the panther to hunt when it is grown."

Dragon looked away, beyond the boy back toward the cabin. He rose to his full height still staring down the meetinghouse and without another word walked away from his audience of one with a stride that was deliberate.

"Are you going back into the meeting, Tsi'yu-gunsini?"

"Yes," Dragon answered without stopping.

Totsuhwa's chest began to swell. The great chief had walked with him and spoken his name. Now he was going to defeat the white men for him.

From the edge of the dim light near the cabin door, Dragon stopped and turned back to the boy. "Why are you not beside me?"

The question perked Totsuhwa's ears, but his feet didn't know what to do.

Dragon held out his hand and motioned quickly just once. "Are you still a timid rabbit?"

The boy shuffled hurriedly up near the warrior who had stepped away at the first movement of the small feet. Totsuhwa did not speak to Dragon again but heard the great chief declare as he opened the door to the meetinghouse, "You should have ahwi, the deer, you were meant to eat."

Most eyes ran to the door as Dragon walked inside. The eyes stayed with him and failed to notice Totsuhwa in his shadow. Henderson and Sevier had rejoined Boone at the front of the room. Dragon walked back to the side of the few dissenters and sat in the odd chairs. Totsuhwa took up a slight position along the wall behind Dragon but had hardly been in place before an attendant to another chieftain took his arm and urged him toward the door.

"This is not a place for you. You are bold to come here, but that boldness will serve you better on another day. Return to your mother and tell her to keep you in the fields until you are ready."

Totsuhwa's eyes were wide as they jumped from the would-be sergeant-at-arms to his guardian, but he made no attempt to move.

The warrior looked down at the boy as his own face measured the surprise of Totsuhwa standing as before. "Has the turtle taken hold of your feet?"

Still Totsuhwa moved nothing save his eyes which continued to dance around Dragon.

"Or have the worms filled your ears?"

Totsuhwa pointed weakly at Dragon's back as he spoke to the evictor. "Tsi'yugunsini..."

The word was only strong enough to gently tap the great chief on the shoulder. Dragon turned slightly in the awkward chair and nodded to the attendant. The acknowledging nod was returned and a comforting hand replaced the one that would have shown Totsuhwa out.

"You have powerful friends, little one. You will stay, but be still like the eyes of a snake. Your friend has taken the talking stick and is rising."

What talk had lingered in the room now ceased. Dragon was standing proudly and allowed his eyes to make contact with every face in the room as he gently held the elaborate stick decorated with beads and color-stained thin leather fringe that symbolized that he alone could speak. His eyes made no distinction from face to face, white to red, ally to traitor. They asked only to be heard. When he had visited upon each face in the room he looked behind him at Totsuhwa. There was no smile and little sense of recognition, only the same request that he be heard — heard and remembered.

"A-na-da-nv-tli. Brothers," Dragon began as he turned to face the assembly. "Listen to my words. We have seen whole Indian nations melt away like snow in the sun before the white man. They leave scarcely a name of our people except those wrongly recorded by their destroyers. Where are the Delawares? They have been reduced to a shadow of their former greatness.

"There was a season when we had hoped that the white men would not be willing to travel beyond the mountains. Now that hope is gone. They have passed the mountains and have settled in land the Cherokee have called home. Now they wish to have that action approved by treaty. When that much has been gained, the same spirit that carried them over the mountains will lead them upon other land of the Cherokee. New lands will be asked for. New concessions will be forced and coerced by gold and treachery. Finally the whole country which the Cherokee and their fathers have so long occupied will be demanded and the last of the Ani-Yunwiya, The Real People, once so great and strong, will be made to seek shelter in some distant wilderness.

"My dreams whisper that once there, the nation will be permitted to stay only a short while until they again see the advancing banners of the same greedy host that courts us now. And then, not being able to point out any further retreat for the miserable Cherokee, the extinction of the whole race will be proclaimed."

Dragon allowed his words to reach into the hearts of all. He calculated the next words and weighed them against the outcome. In the end, Totsuhwa's deer tipped the scales and the war chief continued.

"Should we not take all risks and suffer all consequences rather than allow further loss of our country? All risks, all consequences to insure that Cherokee deer remain in Cherokee land to feed Cherokee children? Such treaties as you speak of may be all right for those of you who are too old to hunt or too old to fight. As for me, I have my young warriors about me. We will have our lands. A-waninski. I have spoken."

The threat was thinly veiled. The "consequences" was war with the white men.

When Dragon had finished he signaled by laying the talking stick on the table in front of him. He turned away without looking down and walked defiantly again to the door. As before, all eyes followed his step. Totsuhwa, unsure of what to do but certain he did not wish to remain in the cabin minus his guardian, walked behind his chief.

Sevier motioned after Totsuhwa. "Let the children follow him and his ideals." He smiled and whispered to Henderson, "Silver and horses will work on men."

But as Dragon neared the door, other chiefs, taking a cue from Totsuhwa, stood and fell in behind the boy. As Dragon and Totsuhwa cleared the building, every Cherokee, including Attakullakulla, followed. In moments, Henderson, Sevier, and Boone and were alone in the cabin.

"Yes, Sevier," Boone said. "Children follow him and great chiefs as well."

"But perhaps not that far," Henderson finished. "I will talk to Attakullakulla tonight. He knows that what we are trying to negotiate is right."

Sevier was annoyed. "Right? I don't give a goddamn about what's right! Colonel Boone? First thing tomorrow morning, you go fetch some rum from the quartermaster. Start handing it out for breakfast. Then we'll meet here tomorrow for supper. By God we need this treaty!"

"We'll have it before we're through," Henderson said as he continued staring at the door. "We'll have it."

"You're damn right we'll have it," Sevier said as he began scraping his papers from the table. Then he paused and looked at Colonel Boone. "Why are you still here? Shouldn't you be out there plying the vote? Christ, what do we pay you for? Go on!"

Boone moved as close to Sevier as Dragon had been less than an hour before. His words were different but came from the same part of a not so dissimilar heart. "John, I suggest that you not push these people. You'll do what you want. But now I'm telling you. Don't push me. You've got all the cards. I know it. You know it. And the Indians know it. I'm just bringing together the inevitable. But me? You don't know a damn thing about me. So don't try me. Don't try me."

The colonel walked away leaving only two men from the mass and mix that had been present minutes before. He moved slowly. The disrespect he'd been shown was difficult to swallow, but it was washed down by the knowledge that horses and gold would be its chaser and that soon he would venture west, away from his own trespassing kind and all manner of treaty talk.

When Boone had gone Henderson turned to Sevier. "You'd better lighten up on him, John. I wouldn't test him or these people."

"To hell with him and to hell with these people. You think I care about him? I don't give a good goddamn about him or those savages. And neither do you so save your care and concern. Okay, Richard?"

Henderson didn't hesitate long. Sevier had known his intent from the start. "You're right. I don't care what happens to them - after we get this treaty signed. But right now Colonel Boone is all we've got."

"And rum," Sevier laughed cynically.

"That's true. But since we are in agreement about these savages I need to assume that we are also in agreement on the present condition of our scalps. If you want to keep yours where it is and I know I wish to retain mine, I say again, let's not insult these people. There wasn't a one in this room tonight who wouldn't take our hair if it profited him. I'm certain that Attakullakulla can be included in that group and I wouldn't put it past Boone to take a white man's scalp if he had a mind to."

Now Sevier smiled outright. "Probably so. He's been so long in the wilderness he can't remember what side he's on. And how about the Transylvania Land Company? How do you suppose they feel about the Indians?"

Henderson hesitated over his own papers but smiled through the side of his mouth. "We'd kill every one for a single acre of land just to have them out of our way."

"I believe you would, Henderson. I believe you would."

"You've killed plenty of Indians haven't you, John?"

"I've killed a share in my time. And if you're asking me if I'd kill them over this land the answer is hell yes. I've killed them for less. It's for the good of the country."

"Good? This has got nothing to do with good. It's about land."

"I realize that, Richard."

"Land equals money. When this is said and done it's about money. Good or bad. Right or wrong is immaterial to me. And you."

"Don't lecture me, Henderson. I've fought these people. I've seen what they do. They're animals. And yes, when it's done we'll have your precious land, but it is and always has been about good and bad. We've got to drive these savages out and make way for civilization. Sooner the better and the more completely we drive them out the better."

"By 'completely,' you no doubt mean annihilation?"

Sevier paused only a moment. "Preferably."

Henderson shook his head in faint disgust and finished with his own papers in a huff then stomped off toward the cabin door.

"Would that bother you, Henderson?" Sevier called after him.

Henderson did not hesitate or pause to answer until he had already opened the door. Only then did he look back over his shoulder. "No. No it wouldn't," he said before walking out and leaving the door open.

Sevier watched him go and began shuffling his papers again. "I thought so."

The small town had already absorbed the Indians by the time Henderson and Sevier parted company. A few lingered in collecting shadows and were already cornered under the tongue of Colonel Boone. The colonel was less impassioned than his Cherokee counterparts and much less well received. He spoke respectfully and was listened to, but he soon left the Indians to the darkness and retired.

Dragon had not lingered for the others. He marched away from the enclave to a patch of woods several hundred yards distant. Totsuhwa mirrored his steps and walked alongside his chief through the dark. Neither stopped nor spoke until they had arrived at Dragon's camp. A number of young men lingered about the site and drifted close to hear their leader. But they would be disappointed as his first words were not meant for them.

"Totsuhwa. Tsa-li-si, grandmother, will be searching the settlement for you."

"She thinks I am asleep with the ponies."

"Do you wish to deceive your grandmother?"

"No."

"Then you must go."

"Yes, my chief."

The boy moved with no small measure of reluctance and despite the lack of light Dragon could see his disappointment. The chief allowed a few slow steps before his voice reached out.

"Totsuhwa. Come."

The boy did as he was instructed. He was a little afraid, but interest, respect, and absolute awe outweighed it.

"Totsuhwa. The rabbit has begun to die. The panther has begun its birth. Do you understand these things?"

The small naked chest swelled up. "Yes, I do."

Dragon motioned to another warrior as he addressed Totsuhwa. "Where does tsalisi sleep?"

Though the darkness prevented the others from seeing exactly where he was pointing, Totsuhwa raised his hand and pointed toward the buildings. "The Paint have a camp on the far side. We have traveled with them."

"How is tsalisi called?"

"She is A-ma Gi-ga."

"I know of her and her medicine. Your grandmother is powerful. She is very wise. Peace and war chiefs alike travel across the nation to take counsel from her. They have heard of Ama Giga's strong relationship with the Spirit. They say He speaks to her often and directs her steps."

"She teaches me."

"You will be wise to listen, Totsuhwa. You will be wise to listen."

A young man had come up beside Totsuhwa during the exchange. Dragon addressed him over the amazed face of the boy.

"Go to Ama Giga and tell her that Totsuhwa sleeps beneath the trees of Tsi'yugunsini."

The young man sprinted off into the night without a word. Dragon walked a short distance to a dying fire and squatted beside it. As he began tending the flames, sticks of wood were placed within his reach by the attending warriors. As the flames grew higher, the circle of light spread out on the men around it. The circle was deep. Totsuhwa wondered at the many men who seemed to materialize from nowhere as they crowded tighter around the fire. Dragon poked the sparking branches and began to address them.

"Tonight, even now as we sit here, these trees are being taken from us. Sevier and Boone will promise horses and gold," he threw another stick into the fire, "silver and whiskey provided by Henderson. Minds will grow weak with the whiskey and tomorrow there will be many to mark the white man's leaves."

"That is true, my son," came the voice of Attakullakulla buried behind the crowd. Dragon's eyes diverted from the flames only enough to find his father as the elder walked through the parting warriors with his own entourage. Doublehead was beside him.

The two men joined Dragon beside the fire and sat in silence. Totsuhwa sat wide-eyed in the growing flames across the fire pit from Dragon and watched as the three chiefs sat adjusting burning tree limbs in the fire for no reason. Attakullakulla stared through the flames over to the boy his son had brought into the circle then his eyes drifted upward until his head was leaning back and he was staring nearly straight up into the rising smoke. While seemingly looking for an answer in the twinkling embers floating up into the night sky, Attakullakulla began to sing softly to himself.

It was a song Totsuhwa did not know. The voice never rose above a whisper, but it captivated all the men and the one boy in the circle. The old chief chanted for a few minutes then the song fell away from his lips and he brought his eyes back down to the fire. Once again he was staring through the flames at Totsuhwa.

"The Everywhere Spirit has whispered to me. He knows the plight of the Tsalagi and has given me an answer." Then Attakullakulla turned to his son. "You cannot stop the treaty for the land."

Reverence for the First Beloved Man of the Nation caused the men nearby to bite their tongues. Dragon was hardest pressed, but he offered no rebuttal.

The elder then stood over aching knees using Dragon's shoulder for support. "Tonight I will sleep in the arms of the Everywhere Spirit and He will clear the answer He has provided. When the sun wakes we three will go to water and I will relay to you the Spirit's voice. Let there be no more talk of these things tonight."

Attakullakulla patted his son's shoulder then stepped away from the circle, his son, Doublehead, and their warriors. He was escorted by several men for some distance and then he drifted further into the trees away from all the warriors and there, in the forest of the Cherokee, slept the sleep of those who wait on the Spirit.

Dragon stood abruptly as did Doublehead. "Totsuhwa. Why are you not at my side?" he said with a smile as he reached out as though to put his hands on the shoulders of the boy.

Totsuhwa scrambled around the fire and jumped in front of the man most feared by the settlers not far away. As Totsuhwa waited, a log popped behind him and a spark landed on his arm. The slight burn made him jump instinctively and brush at his bare skin. Around him, Doublehead and the warriors laughed slightly. Dragon looked at them smiling and at the boy.

"Standing alongside Tsi'yugunsini places you near the flame." Dragon patted the men's shoulders nearest him. "These warriors already know this. Now you know it, Totsuhwa. And still you wish to remain?"

"I do."

"Good," Dragon said as he now put both of his hands on the skinny shoulders in front of him. "The rabbit continues to die. Come and rest. Tomorrow I will meet with my father while the ones below sleep with their whiskey."

Without another word the warriors moved from the fire and began slipping to the ground beneath their blankets. Dragon and Doublehead walked some distance from the flames and were taken in by the trees. They stopped near a small pile of provisions. Each man unfolded a few blankets on the ground in no apparent fashion. Dragon handed a few to Totsuhwa as he stretched out on his blanket bed. As the chief unfurled a heavy blanket and let it fall over himself he allowed his body to relax and closed his eyes. Doublehead had done the same.

Totsuhwa wrapped himself in the blankets while still standing then lay down alongside Dragon's feet. While his mind raced with the events of the night and the words he had listened to, he heard the great chief's breathing grow deep. He thought that he would not sleep, that his eyes would be held open by the presence of the Dragon, but seemingly in a single moment Totsuhwa was stirred by low voices and the crackling of a fire. The blankets Dragon had used were folded haphazardly and stacked except the heavy one which had been thrown over Totsuhwa, but Dragon and Doublehead were nowhere in sight. The boy knew instantly that the men had gone to water as Attakullakulla had directed the night before.

Going to water — quiet baths in the cold water of early morning — was a tradition among Totsuhwa's people. He knew from Ama Giga that it was a ritual done to purify the mind and body before a ceremony or other special event. As a boy he would not be permitted unless he was sick; perhaps this was why Dragon had allowed him to sleep. Whatever the reason Totsuhwa knew that Attakullakulla, Dragging Canoe, and Doublehead were somewhere in the river — called the Long Man by the Tsalagi — preparing themselves for something unusual.

Earlier that morning after going to water Dragging Canoe and Doublehead had listened reverently to Attakullakulla speak about the treaty that would be placed on the table that evening.

"The Spirit has once again given you tremendous wisdom," Doublehead said.

Doublehead was instantly disappointed in himself for answering so quickly. Quiet thought was an admirable trait among men. He had gained some respect in his village, but he was also known for being harsh and making rash decisions as he had just demonstrated, as well as decisions that suited himself rather than the people. He wanted the loyalty Dragging Canoe commanded. Attakullakulla wanted it for him as well which is why the old chief often called the two young men together and looked for his son's strengths to influence the younger Doublehead. So far it hadn't worked and upcoming events would prove it fruitless.

Dragging Canoe had heard the same words that morning from his father but made no offer of acceptance or denial. Instead he watched the water flow in front of him. He gently dipped his hands and stared as the droplets formed and ran from his skin. Attakullakulla gave his son ample time as a show of respect due a growing war chief. The water on his hands was nearly dry when Dragging Canoe replied to the divine strategy Attakullakulla had delivered.

"The words of the Everywhere Spirit are undeniable. I am a lowly warrior, Father. I will speak out no more against the treaty as you have proposed here this morning. Yet, though my lips will seal themselves off from the words within, through me those words will grow strong. And should the white men abandon their leaves or beseech of us more land I will no longer feel the restraining arms of the Spirit's words to you. And when my last words have settled on their ears I will send my warriors' arrows into their hearts and with my knife I will lift their hair."

"It is right to be watchful of the whites," Attakullakulla said. "When my days as a warrior are past you two will lead our people. During those days you will find it difficult to battle a foe so many and so strong. I pray the Spirit guides you then as He has guided me.

"The words I will speak are done to protect our people alone. The ways of those beyond the Cherokee Nation are not our ways. This treaty will cause trouble for many but not the Tsalagi. It will send the settlers to the north, away from the heart of our homes.

"Doublehead, go to the town and tell those that attend Judge Richard Henderson that I wish to see him."

Doublehead rose from the water's edge with the understanding that conversation between father and son would continue in his absence. "Do I request Sevier and Boone?"

"No. Sevier is a butcher who disguises himself as the government and Boone is nothing to us. He will war with the highest bidder then go the way of the wind."

"I will find Henderson though I am sure he is still sleeping like an old woman."

"Wake him but be civil. He is a part of our protection though he does not realize it is so."

Doublehead left without looking again at Dragging Canoe. He was only a few feet out of earshot when Attakullakulla stood and looked down at his son. But the son out raced the father to words.

"Do you understand, Father, deep within your heart, in the furthest part where your blood mixes with our ancestors and our heritage, free from any influence of the whites, that this treaty and the Spirit's plan, will not hold back the white men for long?"

It was the son who was now obliged to wait. The depth of respect, for both his father and the position he held in the nation would have bid the young chief to wait for a very long time, but it wasn't necessary. The answer was near the elder's lips as it had been from the moment the Spirit had whispered to his mind.

"These things I know."

"And when the future holds hands with the past? What will you have me do?"

"That which is necessary for the good of the people. Tsi'yugunsini, the time is come when the good of the nation does not mean warfare. You have seen that through my eyes today."

"Yes, Father. I have seen."

"Know this thing as well. A man such as you, a Tsalagi chief, the proud son of Attakullakulla, must also do that which your own spirit requires of you."

Dragging Canoe smiled as he looked up at his father. "You know where my spirit leads."

"I know," the old chief said as he likewise smiled. "And in that doing you will become renowned throughout the nation and beyond. Men will fear the whisper of your name."

The smile faded but the words did not. "My son, the Spirit has given me many visions. Last night was just the brush of His hand. Of all the things I have taught you remember this above all - the battle against the white man is lost even now.

"We will make peace, make treaties. We will fight. But the Everywhere Spirit has told me many things. He has said that the way of the Tsalagi is hard. The stones beneath our feet will become our beds.

"The Spirit has opened my eyes. Through the flames I see the white men driving the Indians of all nations like cattle. The old cows and the calves are weak and stumble. The strong young bulls turn and gore the white men, but they are too many. In my vision the white men carry whips that are made of the snake that makes noise with its tail. I have seen them bite the bulls and they die. The ground swallows them and the white men pass over their bones. There is no one to mourn the dead bull when he walks to the Darkening Land because the others have been driven on.

"These things I have seen. You must remember them. Remember them in all that you do. They will not lessen the strength of your bow or dampen the powder in your long gun, but remember them still. And when you have remembered them — have them safely in your thoughts — pass them on to another. Have you heard my vision?"

"I have heard."

"That will be enough."

Henderson was not dressed when an aide advised him that Attakullakulla wanted to see him to discuss the terms of the treaty. As he hurriedly stomped into his boots and stuffed his shirt into his trousers, the chief waited in an outer room. When the land contractor entered he was pulling his suspenders over his shoulders.

"Good morning, Chief Attakullakulla."

Attakullakulla looked at the man as if it were he who had asked to see the chief. This blank stare born out of a fierce countenance brought out a fear in the white man. Perhaps Boone had been right. Perhaps these savages had been pushed too far. The anxiousness was reflected in his voice.

"Was there something I could do for you?"

The Cherokee chief stood straight and spoke very deliberately. "You wish for land."

There was a pause that Henderson thought the chief would fill. When he did not, Henderson proceeded cautiously. "Yes. That's correct."

"The Cherokee control land from the Iroquois in the north to the Seminole in the south."

There was another gap in the conversation and again Henderson tried to fill it. "Yours is a tremendous nation."

Attakullakulla still had not moved but continued describing the wherewithal of his people. "The land reaches from the great waters where the sun is born to the Creek Nation and the wide water over which the sun sleeps."

"Yes, I know. You have plenty of land. Surely what we have discussed is paltry in compare—"

"You will have land," Attakullakulla said to Henderson's disbelief. "I will speak to the others and they will hear my words."

Henderson was flabbergasted. He dragged a chair out from a simple table and plopped down, one arm hooked over the back. "You're not going to oppose the treaty?"

"No."

"And your chiefs?"

"Tsi'yugunsini will not make his mark, but the treaty will be marked by others."

"Including you?"

"I have said."

Henderson was speechless. He rubbed his chin and ran his fingers through his hair as he sought for reason in his guest's early morning proposal. After another moment of consideration he asked outright. "May I inquire as to what brought about this change in my good fortune?"

Attakullakulla was annoyed but compelled to answer. "I have seen the outcome. I want the best for my people, as I always have. The allegiance of my son is not so easily gained. He has been raised to defend his nation. This is what makes him a fine leader. Not today, but time will bring Doublehead and others to your tables. This will not be true for Tsi'yugunsini. I have little doubt that you will have to deal with him for many years. And despite what we do today my heart will ride with him."

Henderson ignored the warning the chief had just given him. "Fine then! Fine! Now, have you considered the parcel?"

"I have."

The land trader was out of his chair. He hurriedly unrolled maps, some rough, others quite detailed and spread them on a wide table across the room. His pointed finger danced and skated from line to boundary and back again, points that carried limited meaning to Attakullakulla. "Now, here are my thoughts," Henderson continued. "This is essentially the border of Carolina. I would like to see us come to terms with this parcel west to northwest of that break. We've discussed this piece in the—"

Attakullakulla stretched his hand over the map and covered the area Henderson had indicated. The chief's free hand drew a large circle around a stretch of land further north. "This is what we will give."

Henderson chinked his neck and contorted his body around to see the piece Attakullakulla had shown. "All right," he said slowly as he examined the map. "Now which river basin are you indicating, specifically?"

It was Attakullakulla's turn to point. "This is where we stand?"

"Yes."

Attakullakulla's finger ran across the paper to the map's north. There, three fingers spread out until they directed to three distinct lines on the page beneath his hand. "The land that surrounds these long waters."

Henderson looked again almost in disbelief. The land under the chief's worn fingers was intertwined by three major rivers — the Ohio, the Kentucky, and the Cumberland — each one an excellent territory. "How far up the basin are you considering?" he asked.

"Your leaves are not enough. The land will run the back of the long waters to my brothers the Iroquois in the north."

Henderson stared down at the maps in wonder. From quick calculations drawn on a pad to the side of the maps, Henderson determined the grant neared five million acres. The figures turned into dollar signs right before his eyes. With the chief's mark on the treaty, Judge Richard Henderson, primary stockholder of the Transylvania Land Company would be wealthy beyond measure.

"Your face is pleased," Attakullakulla said.

"Well, yes. I am pleased. I'm happy to have this negotiation process behind us so both our nations can move on in harmony."

"The payment will be as offered last night. Also, you will relieve any debts my people have with the traders who wait at this place for payment. They know you are about to buy land so they circle like vultures. You will do this?"

"Done."

"And this land is sizable. You will encroach no further. Those words will go on your talking leaves."

"Of course. I will draw them up myself."

"Tonight I will present this to the chiefs at your treaty council. They will agree, except my son, and your treaty will be marked."

"Thank you very, very much, Chief Attakullakulla. This is a wonderful day for the Chero—"

"Awaninski," Attakullakulla said absently as he headed to the door.

"Well, thank you. Thank you very much," Henderson said repeatedly though the last words were spoken to an empty room. "Thank you very much."

While Attakullakulla had been speaking to the land buyer, Totsuhwa returned to his grandmother with the news of his sleeping at the feet of the great chief, Tsi'yugunsini.

"I have heard," Ama Giga said as she busied herself around the temporary camp. "You are a chief now I suppose."

"No," the boy answered.

"Then perhaps a warrior."

"Not yet. But one day!"

"Is that day today?"

"I don't think so."

"That is a fine thing because the fire requires wood and I dare not ask a warrior to fetch sticks."

Totsuhwa looked at the dwindling fire and watched a few weary sparks jump meagerly from the slowly dying bed of coals.

"Tsalisi? What is fire?"

"It is a friend to the Tsalagi people."

"But what is it? How does it come to be?"

"How do birds fly?"

"They move their wings," Totsuhwa answered, still staring at the cooling fire bed.

"And so it is with the fire. It flaps its wings around the wood you bring to it and makes us warm and cooks our meat."

"It is not the same. If I put water on the fire it will stop moving its wings."

"Do you think the bird would not stop moving its wings if you put him under the Long Man? The bird would die like the fire dies."

"But the fire returns. From where?"

Ama Giga ceased her toiling and lowered her aching bones to the ground. She sat low and held her arms up. "Come to me, Totsuhwa."

Her request tore him away from the coals. When he reached her she rubbed his arms before slipping her hands around his waist. "You are a fine boy, Totsuhwa. And you will be a fine man. Today you are still a boy, but one night in the camp of Tsi'yugunsini has opened your eyes to the world around you. It is good that you ask these things.

"The fire is a gift from the Creator. He gave it to Water Spider when the Tsalagi were young. You see, the Creator had the Thunderers send down lightning into a hollow tree on an island. Many animals who could swim or fly tried to bring the fire back to the Tsalagi on dry land. Many tried and many failed. But Water Spider walked across the water unafraid. She made a woven basket for her back and placed a single coal in it. This she brought back to our ancestors.

"The flames from a single cooking pit may die, but we will always have the fire because it was a gift from the Creator."

"Thank you, grandmother. You are wise."

"It is a story from our heritage. It is not mine. You must tell it to your children one day."

"Ama Giga? Is the land a gift from the Creator too?"

"Yes. The grandest!"

"And like the fire, we will always have it?"

"It will always be ours to use as long as the people take care of it and the animals who share it with us. The Creator has made it so."

"The white men will not take it?"

"The white men are plentiful now, like locust in a time of sorrow for the corn sister. But the locusts go. They die from eating too much and go back to the earth. So it will be with the white men. They will eat too much of the land and it will kill them. Then the Tsalagi will reap the harvest once more."

The boy's face demonstrated his relief. Ama Giga noticed it and hugged him. "You have been listening to the talk of the chiefs. You have been troubled by it."

"Tsi'yugunsini has talked about the white men. Last night Attakullakulla received an answer from the Everywhere Spirit. This morning Attakullakulla, Tsi'yugunsini, and Doublehead went to water to talk on the vision the Spirit gave through the fire."

"Attakullakulla is a fine chief. The fire will have given him much."

"The fire is our friend."

"Yes."

"The Spirit comes to us through it."

"It may, but not if you let it go out. Now go. Collect the wood the forest has left on the ground for you. Go!"

The old woman sat on the ground and watched her orphaned grandson disappear in glimpses as he dashed through the trees. He would have to venture far to find kindling as the settlement had depleted anything nearby. But Ama Giga no longer worried for him. In his questions and on his face she had seen that he had the invitation of the Spirit and hence, its protection. She wondered if Tsi'yugunsini had seen the same.

When the wood had been collected for the fire and the ponies had been staked over fresh grass, Totsuhwa wandered back toward the camp of Tsi'yugunsini. Doublehead was there holding court with a few braves. He was extolling the benefits of the treaty and in doing so drew a harsh stare from Totsuhwa. The boy looked through the camp, anxious to see the reaction when the Great Dragging Canoe heard Doublehead promoting the treaty within the tree-lined walls of his camp.

"He has gone hunting," Doublehead suddenly said to him.

"Wado. Thank you. Do you know where?"

"Only the deer know for certain. Tsi'yugunsini is a skillful hunter, almost as good as myself." Doublehead laughed and pushed the warrior nearest him. "The deer do not hide from us as they know the deed is done as soon as we pick up our bows in the camp." The other men shook their heads. "It is true!"

The laughter gently subsided. Doublehead looked at the sky and measured the sun on the horizon. "The deer wait for him in the mountains where the sun will sleep tonight. I would go there if you wish to find him."

"Wado."

"But do not go into the mountains looking like a deer or Tsi'yugunsini may split your back with his flint!"

That was a troubling thought to the boy and he did not reply as he moved away from the camp to the west.

The sun had crested and dropped the width of his hand before Totsuhwa considered that he might be moving in on Dragging Canoe. The boy had discovered a well-worn deer trail some time before and had begun mirroring it from the side. After each set of ten steps Totsuhwa stopped to listen and look at the forest. He could hear the light quick jumps of squirrels among the litter and the occasional crackling of a bird warning of his approach. His ears directed his eyes and he located the offending sentry in the canopy.

"Shhh," he said to himself and the bird. "I mean no harm to your friends, but if you cry out Tsi'yugunsini will think me a poor hunter. Ho-wa-tsu. Please."

The bird fluttered from branch to branch to see the boy more clearly. It watched him as he bid for its silence. This was no threat and the bird was compelled to be quiet, but the damage had been done. The Dragon was moving at the bird's first warning.

The warrior understood that the cry from the bird would have gone up because a perceived threat was in the woods. It could be a man and the presence of so many whites near the village meant that the trespasser would likely have fair skin. Dragon adjusted his thinking further still and thought that perhaps due to his stance on the treaty it was he who was now the hunted.

Totsuhwa moved methodically from beneath the irksome bird. He continued mirroring the trail, stopping periodically to listen. His steps were now as light as falling snow. There was a sense in him that he was nearing his quarry.

Dragon sprinted hard through the trees but scarcely made a sound. His strides brought him in a wide arc until he was back near the game trail. He hid himself behind a large tree and waited. When his acute ears brought him the soft sounds of a step he deftly loaded an arrow and pulled back on the bow. Shadowed movement brought his hands, eyes and the meticulously honed jasper red flint point together on a slight break in the trees three steps ahead of his pursuer.

Back at the settlement, Henderson had summoned Sevier moments after Attakullakulla left. "We've got it! We've got over five million acres! Attakullakulla just walked in and said yes. Just like he did it every day. And it amounts to pennies."

"What parcel?"

The maps came into play again as Henderson spun them around on the table. "I haven't drawn up the papers yet, but according to the chief we're talking about all three river valleys — the Kentucky, Ohio, and Cumberland. All to the north."

"I thought you wanted this section?" Sevier questioned as he pointed to a stretch of land between South Carolina to the southeast and the proposed tract to the northwest.

"I did — that is, I do, but I'm not going to look a gift horse in the mouth. That parcel is minuscule compared to what I've got. I'll get this section to the northwest then parlay this smaller tract into it. You'll see."

"Christ, Richard. That is a lot of land. Hell, it runs clear to the Iroquois territory up north."

"Damn right it's a lot of land! And that means a lot of money. The Transylvania Land Company will be selling off land grants for fifty years behind this deal."

"Transylvania Land Company, my ass," Sevier said laughing. "That company is you and you know it."

"Well, I've got some partners to think about."

"Bullshit, Richard. You're the same as me. You'll take care of you and that's about the extent of it."

"Be that as it may, John. When that treaty gets signed tonight all of us are instantly wealthy. I'll see you get your share as long as you keep the British off my ass until I can turn the green in those valleys into gold."

"I'll hold up my end, but it won't be easy. There's a lot of talk about a revolt against the king. These damn colonists are a heady bunch."

"They'll calm down when they find there's five million more acres to settle. All those revolutionary types will move west into this newest frontier. Hell, we'll sponsor Colonel Boone to lead the way!"

"Well, let's get the thing signed first before you give that Boone any more money. I don't think he's done a damn thing for us."

"Boone's all right. He's ready for a new frontier, that's all. He's just the man to pave the way into this settlement for us."

"True. And works for a beaver pelt! Doesn't much like the Indians any more than we do. I'll bet that son of a bitch Dragon doesn't have many more scalps than our Colonel Daniel Boone!"

Dragon's tally was about to increase by one. He had held the powerful bow taut for nearly a minute as he waited for his prey to clear its cover. The arrow left Dragon's release hand as the boy began his step into the break in the trees. The recognition of Totsuhwa came in that fraction of a second between the release of the arrow and the arrow's clearing of the bow. In that beat of a hummingbird's wings Dragon jerked the bow with his lead hand and affected the weapon's flight.

Totsuhwa froze as did the warrior's heart in the instant before the arrow stung a tree inches in front of the boy's chest. The shaft of the arrow was still quivering in the tree when Totsuhwa's wide eyes followed its embedded flint to its fletching, the nock and beyond. The arrow was pointing from its mark in the tree backward to the man who had propelled it. Totsuhwa's grandmother had been right about the Spirit's intervention in the boy's life.

Tsi'yugunsini's hands were as they had been the moment he had sent the arrow. The release hand still rested by his cheek and the bow was still held out in front of him, shielding himself from Totsuhwa's trembling face.

The bow eased down and Totsuhwa found himself staring into the fierce eyes of the Dragon. The boy's own eyes had remained wide open and had yet to blink. A sizable portion of Totsuhwa's mind and body told him to run. He may have angered the mighty chief and he could slip a second arrow from its quiver in a breath. If he had not upset the war chief, he had certainly embarrassed himself for stumbling within range without notice. Uncertainty reigned until Dragon's arrow draw hand motioned for Totsuhwa to come.

The youngster's bare feet had just begun to move when Dragon held up his hand to stop. Totsuhwa did and waited for his next direction. When it came it was that same hand pointing to the arrow in the tree. The boy understood. Arrows that flew straight and true, crafted by the archer himself, were valuable. Totsuhwa began wrenching the shaft of the arrow back and forth in an intensive effort to free it. The flint had bit deep and releasing it without snapping the shaft was difficult for the boy's small hands. Afraid of failing while his chief watched, Totsuhwa dug at the bark around the point with his fingers until small pieces gave way. After considerable effort the arrow followed.

Totsuhwa held the arrow triumphantly over his head in both hands while a broad smile beamed from below. Dragon nodded then gracefully padded his hand up and down for the boy to approach quietly. Totsuhwa carried the arrow in front of his naked chest and looked around him as if suddenly conscious that there was still a hunt afoot.

Dragon watched the boy approach and took notice that he took great pains with the arrow, carrying it in both hands as if a slight bump could shatter it. When Totsuhwa was close Dragon held out his hand and received the arrow. It was an old one, still ramrod straight with tight feathers and a sharp point. He examined it for damage. Arrows were difficult and time consuming to make. Ones as right as this old friend were treasures. The hunter opened his quiver and carefully slipped the arrow inside with its brothers. Only then did he begin to walk deeper into the woods speaking softly to Totsuhwa as he tagged along.

"Thank you for bringing the arrow," Dragon said behind a faint smile. "I left it in that tree near you. It was lucky for me you stumbled upon it."

Totsuhwa's face flashed ashen as he recalled the strike of the arrow. "Lucky for me too."

Dragon didn't miss a stride but slipped his arm around the boy's shoulder. "Yes, lucky for us both."

The walk through the woods seemed to move away from a hunt for some time. Dragon was taking in the sights and sounds of this forest that he realized would soon be lost to his people. Totsuhwa simply delighted in being by the great chief's side. In time the hunter returned and began to walk lighter and with more purpose. The boy mimicked his every move as he fell in behind. Not many steps had passed before Dragon brought the pair up on the ledge of a narrow wooded gully. He motioned Totsuhwa to the ground behind a rotting stump that was perched on the ledge. Totsuhwa was instructed with a hand signal to be still. Dragon crouched for a few quiet minutes and surveyed the small ravine before lowering himself to the ground beside the waiting boy.

"You did well to track Tsi'yugunsini," Dragon said in a hushed voice. "Many have tried to do so and have not been as successful."

"Probably some of those that did find you wished they had not," Totsuhwa said as he remembered the arrow striking the tree.

Dragon smiled broadly. "I imagine that is true."

The boy lowered his chin slightly, but his eyes stayed on the master. "Did I ruin your hunt?"

"No, ahwi will always wait for the arrows of Tsi'yugunsini. This is a good place. They will come if we do not think strongly of them."

"Think strongly of them?" Totsuhwa echoed.

"Yes. If you concentrate on the deer they can hear your thoughts and will shy away. They will give themselves to us for our needs, but we cannot insult them by telling them what they must do. Rather, we must hunt them skillfully for they are born of these woods as are the Tsalagi. Keep your thoughts clear."

Totsuhwa closed his eyes and leaned his head back against the stump. His brow furrowed after a short while. He opened his eyes, dropped his head and looked up at Dragon. "It is hard to not think."

The Dragon smiled again. "Relax and think of Ama Giga and the things she has taught you."

Totsuhwa remembered the conversation with his grandmother from that morning. It wasn't long before Dragon touched his arm.

When Totsuhwa opened his eyes he saw Dragon slipping the old arrow he had wrestled out of the tree from the quiver. The practiced hands loaded the weapon and moved in absolute silence around to the side of the stump.

Totsuhwa listened intently, making sure not to move unless directed. He heard a light step in the old leaves that lined the gully. It was a deer. But as quickly as the thought came he dismissed it with remembrances of his grandmother. Dragon looked over his shoulder, smiled, and nodded as though he had seen into Totsuhwa's mind and witnessed the quick exchange.

Then the teacher pointed with his eyes and a slight motion of his head for Totsuhwa to look into the ravine. The boy moved like molasses until he'd turned and just his eyes cleared the jagged dark brown top of the stump. There in the small gorge below them was a fine buck weaving slowly toward the hunters. Its steps were dainty among the debris of a hundred seasons and its nose nudged the ground as it walked. The brown and white tail flipped back and forth lazily much like the deer's carefree ears. There was no alarm in the air, no dangerous scent in its nostrils, no reason to be afraid.

The hunters watched the animal browsing through the tiny valley, each step bringing it nearer to the arrow being drawn back. Totsuhwa's eyes darted from the deer to the bow and back. He didn't know when the release would come and wanted to be certain to witness the hit. Had he been older and more familiar with the hunting ways of the Real People, he would have been signaled by Tsi'yugunsini's whispered words.

"Yuhwa danvta. I'm sorry." And the arrow silently exploded from the bow. Totsuhwa saw the arrow slam into the deer's side just behind the animal's shoulder. He also heard it hit. There was a resounding thud that stunned the animal before any realization of pain struck it. The blow staggered the deer to the side, but it recovered in a flurry of scattering spindle-like legs. When the feet were collected the mortally wounded animal began a sprint; however, it was short lived. The run through the trees snapped the protruding shaft off the arrow and wrenched the flint point deep in the deer's heart causing more damage. In mere moments the loss of blood dropped the animal to its knees to rest, but the rest would be an eternal one. The deer would rise and race no more. Before the hunters reached it the deer was dead.

The exuberance of youth had propelled Totsuhwa over the stump and down into the gully before the deer had regained its footing. The dying animal had taken no notice of the boy, but Totsuhwa was on its blood trail like a hound. Dragon followed but at a leisurely pace. He knew he had hit the mark. The deer would not go far and the blood would lead him there quickly enough.

When Totsuhwa came upon the deer he stopped. He looked for signs of life as he purposely shied away from the head. Though the buck had only velvet covered nubs for antlers at this time of year, he did not want the animal to see him if it were still able to jump and run. But the deer would never run again and it took only a few minutes of observation for Totsuhwa to see that was the case.

Dragon came upon the animal as the boy was considering getting closer though he had yet to move. The bow and quiver were carefully set aside before Dragon pulled a small animal-skin water bag from around his back. He walked to the dead deer and crouched low by its head. Totsuhwa followed him and knelt alongside examining the deer and watching the chief.

"We must give ahwi water for his journey to the Darkening Land," Dragon said as he poured a small amount of water into his cupped hand beneath the deer's mouth. "It is right. We thank you, friend. You will feed many Cherokee for many days. Perhaps a baby will be kept warm by your coat. You are a fine friend and we thank you."

"And the Creator who sent us ahwi?" Totsuhwa offered.

"Yes, and we thank the Creator of all things who has given us this meat for our food and this hide for our clothes." Dragon stroked the deer's face with the water that remained in his hand. "To-hi-du. Good peace."

When the deer had been sent to the Darkening Land, Dragon retrieved his weapons and handed them to the boy. "Look along the trail for the shaft. It has been a fine arrow. The feathers may still be of use."

Totsuhwa carefully held the chief's prized weapons and walked gingerly back into the gully looking from side to side for the splintered arrow. Behind him Dragon hefted the deer onto his shoulders. With the legs together across his chest he began walking down through the mountains toward his camp.

After some effort the broken arrow was discovered. Totsuhwa was anxious to catch up to the Dragon, but the weight of the chief's bow in his hands was too tempting. When he slid the pointless shaft into the quiver he exchanged it for a complete arrow, handcrafted by the great Tsalagi war chief. Fingers never meant to do so notched the arrow in the strong bow. He spied a nearby tree and held the bow out before his face. Totsuhwa pulled on the arrow, but the sinewy cord and the tightness of the bow proved too much — he could scarcely budge it. A few more meager attempts were enough. He had held the powerful weapon that had killed many times. That would have to do.

Totsuhwa caught up to Dragon in the foothills before the encampment. He only nodded to the chief when he caught his eye, much like Dragon had done to him, to signify that he had found the broken shaft. There was no conversation but the boy was beaming when they strode into the Dragon's camp.

Doublehead was still sitting around a crackling fire with a group of other braves. "You went to the woods empty-handed and have returned with a deer and a cub!"

"The deer you have seen," Dragon said. "But you mistake a cub for a panther. This one has tracked me in the forest when you yourself have failed to do so many times."

"And for being a great warrior he is rewarded by toting your bow?"

"Again you do not understand what your eyes see. Our game is so heavy it takes both my hands to carry it. Totsuhwa has the bow to protect us from a marauding bear or lazy Cherokee like you who sit and talk instead of hunt. You might try to steal the meat we have earned and then Totsuhwa would have to shoot you with our arrows."

"I see then. But we are yet rewarded, are we not, my brothers?" Doublehead said to those around him. "We sit and discuss the future of our nation and the food comes to us."

Dragon had not stopped walking. He, with Totsuhwa following, was nearing the far side of his camp. "As so many times it has happened. You are wrong again, this time on two charges. This meat does not come for you. It is for the lodge of Ama Giga. And you are not discussing the future of the people. You are discussing treason. Enjoy the grasses you pick for your meal and the white man's silver in your pockets. Perhaps if you beg Sevier he will trade you some meat for it."

Dragon laughed as he walked away from the men. A few of the warriors stood and looked longingly after the deer. "Do you suppose Ama Giga will feed two hungry hunters?" Dragon asked the boy.

"Oh, yes! We have few to hunt for us. She will welcome our fine friend," Totsuhwa said as he patted the dangling leg of the deer.

Ama Giga waded into the carcass even while she continued to thank Tsi'yugunsini. She and her sisters in the Paint clan began skinning and carving up the deer with quick well-practiced cuts seasoned with an air of celebration. Though the task could have been accomplished in several minutes due to the clan's experience and skill, the women lingered over the deer for two hours or longer, relishing the coming together.

Dragon stayed only long enough for the women to sever the deer's hindquarters. He asked for half of the rump and was promptly given it. With the leg and attached meat slung over his shoulder, Dragon picked up his bow and quiver to head back to his camp. Totsuhwa was watching the women do their cutting and the chief at the same time.

"Doublehead will cry if I leave him hungry," Dragon said.

"He might," the boy laughed.

"More importantly, I need my warriors to eat meat. They must have their strength. We do not know yet what tomorrow will bring."

The comment brought both the chief and the little boy back to the realization that the laughter of the day would soon be overshadowed. The sojourn into the hills had been a pleasant respite from the concerns over the treaty, but when the mountains had given way to the town, the white men and their wants were still there.

"Help Ama Giga with her work, Totsuhwa. And thank you for your company on the hunt. You did well."

The war chief left with the meat for his men and Totsuhwa saddled up near his grandmother and waited for her instructions as he continued watching the matriarch of the clan dive her hand into the belly of the deer. She fumbled around blindly before withdrawing her bloody hand which she immediately held out to Totsuhwa.

"Here, my son. Tsi'yugunsini will have need of this. Clean it well and take it to him."

The boy looked in his hand and saw the flint point that had nearly taken his life and had captured the deer's. He clutched it tightly in his fist and sprinted off to the long water.

The cool water rinsed away the blood and hair from the arrowhead as well as from Totsuhwa's hands. In the shallows where he squatted the water was running slow and was only about a hand deep. Totsuhwa laid the arrow point on the bed of the river and took his hands away but kept them coiled in case the current might try to steal the chief's possession. The reddish jasper color of the flint stood out from the gray stones of the river bottom. The arrowhead had a hundred sides, the result of the flaking and chipping that had formed it, whereas the river stones were smooth and round from years of being caressed by the flow. The flint was hard-edged and sharp, the river stones soft-edged and dull. One could never be mistaken for the other nor could one fit in the other's world.

"Could a river stone be an arrowhead?" Totsuhwa thought to himself. "And how long would a flint arrowhead survive in the Long Man before its edges were worn down?" These were things he must remember to ask Ama Giga.

The water had done its job nicely. The arrowhead was clean and fairly shined. Totsuhwa fingered it over and over and thought about how Tsi'yugunsini must have fashioned it — flaking the reddish stone with repeated well-placed chips, cracks, and strikes.

Then the boy's thoughts raced on to the enemies it may have struck down for the war chief. Considerable death had been carried on the wings of this piece of flint, but Totsuhwa could only suppose how much. In his imagination an interest that bordered fear came out as a slight tremble in his hand. He suddenly looked around the riverbank as he imagined the appearance of those lives claimed by the glistening stone. It was time to return the arrowhead to its owner.

When a sprinting and gasping Totsuhwa broke into Dragon's camp he drew no attention. Not that his running and panting would not normally have done so, but rather because there was no one there to see him. It seemed that Dragon, Doublehead, and the other men had gone to the settlement. The treaty process was underway. As soon as the realization came to him, Totsuhwa dashed off again, though his breath had yet to recover from the race away from the ghosts at the river.

The treaty meeting had begun as a feast of sorts. There was a considerable amount of food, but the primary article on the menu was liquor. Henderson wanted to insure the signatures Attakullakulla had promised made their way to the parchment and thought of no better way to lower the resistance of the Indians than by lowering their sensibilities. Primed by rum, any resisters would quickly give way to pledges of silver and horses.

Dragon had known since the early morning conversation with his father that the treaty would be approved, but he was prepared to argue against it for principal and to insure the men in the room — white and red — knew his heart. His father's plan, provided by the Spirit and laid out to Henderson, would sway the others, this much he clearly understood. On another occasion, with less at stake, even he would have found himself aligned with his father's strategy, but Dragon understood that it was temporary at best and at worse would ignite a firestorm of war and bloodshed that would rain down on the Cherokee people for years to come. Attakullakulla's proposed land grant to Henderson included little of the Cherokee's truly sacred homeland. Though a small portion was a far-reaching Cherokee hunting territory, the vast millions of acres the crafty chief was about to sell to the Transylvania Land Company were occupied by the Shawnee Indian Nation, a fact Attakullakulla knew very well. Little Carpenter had once again skillfully reinforced his name as the crafter of treaties.

"My friends," Richard Henderson began as he stretched out his hands in an attempt to qualm the boisterous collection of men. "The great chief, Attakullakulla, has brought a proposal to the table that is most accommodating. The land suggested will satisfy the colonists of this nation that grows around you for many, many years. In exchange, the Cherokee people will be paid handsomely and can be assured of the protection of their sacred homelands. As a bonus, Attakullakulla and I have agreed that the Transylvania Land Company will assume any outstanding debts you and your people may owe to the traders who frequent this post and other Cherokee land."

There was a favorable murmur through the throng.

"I have taken the liberty of preparing the necessary documents. They are here before me and await the marks of the leaders of the great Cherokee Nation."

Henderson offered a quill to Attakullakulla who was seated nearby. The chief took the feather but laid it on the table in exchange for the talking stick. The chief stood and held the ceremonial piece close in front of his waist as he addressed the assembly. Though he spoke English, these words were in his native tongue and he spoke quickly so as to confuse Boone and others who knew some of the language.

"My brothers. Doublehead or myself have spoken to each of you concerning this leaf waiting for our marks. You know the terms we have agreed to. You know the land we speak of and its owners."

Boone had understood this much and thought the chief meant himself and his people. He was confused when catcalls and war yelps went up from the warriors in the room who had fought the Shawnee many times.

Distracted by the outburst, no one took notice of Totsuhwa as he crept into the room and around the wall until he was behind Dragon. The room was crowded and the walls nearly full, but he found a quiet spot where he could watch the red and white faces and nervously cradle the arrowhead in his hands.

The eruption subsided and Attakullakulla continued, now speaking even quicker. "This treaty will pit two enemies of the Cherokee against each other and move them away from warring with us."

Henderson grabbed Boone's arm. "What's he saying?"

"Something about getting away from war."

"Good. That's good."

Attakullakulla kept on. "They will have only energy and weapons and hate for each other and will leave the Cherokee in peace."

Henderson and Sevier both looked to Boone. He whispered to Henderson who in turn whispered to Sevier, "They want peace. This gives the Cherokee peace."

"The leaf will keep the white men to the north, away from land the Creator has provided the Cherokee. It will give them land for a hundred years. Granting our nation one hundred years of peace."

Boone leaned to Henderson's ear. "He says the treaty will give the Cherokee a hundred years of peace."

"Great!" Henderson said softly before repeating what Boone had told him to Sevier. "I love this man, even if he is an Indian."

"I will put my mark to this leaf," Attakullakulla said. "For all the nation to see that today we insure the land that our fathers hunted will remain."

The crowd voiced their approval as Attakullakulla exchanged the talking stick for the quill but grew eerily still as Dragon rose to his feet.

"That son of a bitch!" Sevier whispered to Henderson as the talking stick was handed around the tables to Dragon.

"Relax, John. We've got Attakullakulla. That's enough. Let the Dragon have the floor for a few minutes and pound his chest. He's just a brute, a relic, a throwback to the past. Fortunately for us, his father sees the future more clearly."

"The great Attakullakulla has spoken," Dragon began when the baton reached him. He spoke slower than his father had, both willing and anxious to have his words translated. "We all know him to be a champion for the people. He is a fearless warrior and leader of brave men. Tonight however, the wise eye of Chief Attakullakulla does not see. The peace we seek through these leaves will not last. It will not last the hundred years. It will not last ten. It will not last one."

Boone scratched his chin and squinted as he struggled with the Tsalagi language. He leaned toward Henderson but was met by his hand.

"I don't give a damn what that savage says," Henderson said with a sly smile. "He won't stop the treaty. You can keep his Indian gibberish to yourself."

The colonel leaned back into his own chair and picked up a piece of beef with his fingers, successfully tuning out anything the Dragon might say.

"Those who are caretakers of the land will rise up. They will fight the settlers, yes, but will also hold the Cherokee responsible for what we do today. Would we not do the same if another nation gave away our land?

"And the greatest concern is not the nations who live in these lands now, but those that will. These wide eyes will...not...stop!" Dragon said as he pointed fiercely at Henderson and Sevier. "They will not be content until their people sleep in every Cherokee village and the Cherokee are forced to sleep with the dogs if we are allowed to sleep at all!

"I respect my father. I respect my chief. I will say no more on this treaty for that respect, but Tsi'yugunsini will not place his mark alongside that of his father's. Awaninski."

The talking stick was passed back to Attakullakulla who took it but immediately set it aside for the quill. He dipped the quill in a small bottle of ink and proceeded to make his mark on the treaty papers. When he had done so, he purposely spilled a small amount of ink on the table. Then he stood as other chiefs approached.

Some touched their thumbs to the ink and then to the paper near Attakullakulla's mark while others made their own distinct marks or copies of a few letters as their name. Dragon remained seated and noted each face. There would be no retribution against the signers. Perhaps the day would come and Dragon knew it would, when they would regret the decision they had made.

But tonight the agreement had been reached and the past, regardless of how recent, could not be undone. Dragon would have to let the night pass and several others after. He was certain he was right about the Shawnee and the unending thirst of the white men, but he could do nothing more tonight.

Henderson had gotten the last mark necessary on his documents. He was beaming as he blew across the parchments to dry the inkblots from the Indian's thumbs.

"Well, Colonel Boone," Sevier said as he leaned back in his chair. "That's another one down. How many more to go before we own the whole damn thing?"

"Can't say. Reckon it depends how big the parcels are."

"How big the parcels are," Sevier laughed. "I think we ought to get Henderson to make a few changes in that paper he's got right there. Hell, I'd make it read for all the land from Canada to Mexico and call it legal."

"The Spaniards and the French might have something to say about that."

"To hell with the Spaniards and French. And to hell with these cursed Indians too!" Sevier dropped his chair forward to the floor. He leaned heavily on the table across in front of Henderson. "Mark my words, Colonel. Before this is over, we'll have it all. We'll have it all! There won't be a Spaniard, a Frenchy, or an Indian left. You'll see. Know how I know? Because of men like this fellow right here." Sevier pointed painstakingly at Henderson who was rolling up the treaty for safekeeping.

"Men like this are going to insure that every clump of dirt between Canada and Mexico, and the ocean and the Mississippi River, gets sold. And before they can sell it, they gotta steal it. Got to get that precious treaty paper. And you know what, Boone? I'm with 'em. I threw my lot in with those boys long ago, and I'm not ashamed to say so. I've made money and there's a lot more to be made. To hell with these savages. And the Spaniards. And the French."

Sevier mumbled on over another glass of rum he partially spilled while pouring. Boone said nothing but continued to eat and drink, unconcerned about this treaty or any other.

The rest of the men in the room were returning to their meat and drinks as well. Dragon was sitting almost alone, the chiefs on either side having turned their chairs slightly away in order to engage those nearest in more pleasant conversation. They wanted to talk of the money, the hapless Shawnee and the hundred years of peace, not the bleak future Dragon suggested.

Totsuhwa saw this and brought himself up to the side of the great warrior. The arrowhead clenched in his hand would be his inroad. "Great Tsi'yugunsini," he said softly as though waking someone from sleep.

The chief moved only his head and looked at the boy. A little hand came up and opened, revealing the freshly scrubbed flint point.

"Ama Giga said you will have need of this."

Dragon looked at the arrowhead and nodded. "Yes. Ama Giga is right." Then he looked across the tables to the gathering celebration of white faces. "I will have need of it and many like it, I believe. Many, many like it."

Totsuhwa remained at the Dragon's side, his hand still open holding the arrowhead. When Dragon's attention broke from the white men, he saw that he had left the boy standing. His own hand covered Totsuhwa's and closed the small fingers around the piece of flint.

"That is for you to keep. For you to remember this day," he said sadly before adding with a smile. "And our successful hunt together."

A few loud yells went up from the rum collected in the bellies of men relieved to have the treaty process complete.

"This is no place for warriors such as us, Totsuhwa. It is time to pack our camp and leave this place."

Dragon was beaten to movement by Henderson who stood and raised his hands again to quell the crowd. "Friends! Friends! May I have your attention please?" Caught off guard, Boone choked down another mouthful with a belt of whiskey and translated reasonably well for the men present.

The room continued to rumble for another minute before Henderson's pleas restrained it. "Friends, before we continue to enjoy the fruits of our labors tonight, there is one small order of business I wish to address." Henderson unrolled a second set of documents as he continued. "The land we've discussed this evening will do everything the great Chief Attakullakulla has said it will. However, one indisputable fact remains — this section is an island to the Transylvania Land Company. It's far to the north and does not border any of our existing claims. As it stands I will have to walk across the ground of my brother, the Cherokee, to reach this new land."

The blood in Dragon's body ran cold. He knew where Henderson was headed, several did, but it seemed only Dragon cared, or cared so deeply that the icy blood quickly turned and began to boil. Totsuhwa witnessed the change in the countenance of his chief. He held the arrowhead gift tightly and unconsciously took a few steps back. There had been much compassion in the words from the man to the boy, but words would not shelter him if Dragon flew into a rage.

"What I propose to my brothers is a bridge — a bridge of continued peace, a land bridge from my holdings that surround us to this new territory in the north. I am prepared to pay handsomely in order to insure the peace we have made here today."

Dragon leaped to his feet. He stomped the floor in defiance of what he was hearing. There was no more fierce and deadly a look as Dragon put forth at that moment. "We have given you this!" the lethal warrior screamed. "Why do you ask for more? Will you never be satisfied?" Dragon brought his fist down hard on the table. If he hadn't captured everyone's ear beforehand he had it now.

"You have bought a fair land. When you have this you have all! No more. No more! The Cherokee will sell no more land!" Dragon pointed ominously at his father. "You see, Attakullakulla? One hundred years? The ink is not yet dry on your treaty and they are after more land. They will not be content until they have driven us beneath the earth as they have the elk." Dragon motioned around the room to his people. "We all know that there is no more game left between the Watauga and the Cumberland. They have driven it out or killed everything sent there to live."

Now Dragon returned his attention to the white men, Henderson in particular and pointed with a hard hand at the marked sheaf of papers that constituted the neatly rolled and tied treaty. "When you venture into that land you will find its settlement dark and bloody."

The war chief spun away from the table. Tested warriors parted like children before him as he stormed out of the meeting. This time no one followed. Even Totsuhwa hesitated to go after his chief; afraid that to follow too closely on the heels of a man such as Dragon caught in a tempest might be perilous. So he waited, shrinking back against the wall and listened to Henderson and Boone apply salve to the wounds ripped open by the tirade. The words were more silver and more promises exchanged for more land, the "bridge of peace".

Totsuhwa held the arrowhead of the chief and understood each translated word. From the wall, small and unnoticed, the rabbit moved ever closer to death while Totsuhwa wondered if he alone had heard the Dragon's predictions as the second treaty was ratified.

While the boy held his spot at the wall, Tsi'yugunsini held court with his warriors a short distance away. Only a small number were present at their temporary camp. Others had not made the journey and still others reveled in the food and drink at the town. Dragon would not admonish them tonight for he knew their hearts. The young men would take drink and meat where they could but when Dragon gave the call to arms each one would be present and ready to kill the white hand that had poured the whiskey.

Dragon's words were succinct. "When the sun wakes we will leave this place." With that, he moved away from the continually burning fire and threw his blankets across the ground.

Some time later Totsuhwa slipped into the camp. He did not see Dragon's face among those at the dwindling fire so he walked to the spot where he had slept at the Dragon's feet the night before. There he found his chief beneath a pile of blankets, sleeping. He would venture no further tonight. Tomorrow he knew the camp would be broken and the warriors would melt into the forest. In the move back to their villages, Totsuhwa understood that he might not see the great war chief again. From the last outburst at the treaty council he knew the Dragon would likely be at war with the white men, though the remainder of the chiefs would not follow. All but alone in his absolute defiance even the great Tsi'yugunsini would be vulnerable.

Totsuhwa slept alongside his grandmother that night, the chief's arrowhead clutched in his hand. When she stirred at first light the boy rose with her. He hurriedly rekindled the morning fire then sprinted off in the hopes of seeing his new friend before the mountains had swallowed him. He was disappointed when he reached the temporary campsite and found it abandoned. Without hesitating, Totsuhwa jutted back and forth through the camp checking the ground like a dog circling for the scent of a rabbit. There were fresh tracks leading to the settlement. Perhaps the boy would catch the warrior band there.

The town was up early. Several Indians were squinting hard against the light, their heads wracked by the effects of the rum and whiskey from the night before, but all were moving. With the treaty process completed there was little reason to be here, for the Cherokee or the land traders. Each was anxious to get home and enjoy the spoils the preceding days had brought.

Richard Henderson, John Sevier, and Colonel Boone were collected on the stoop in front of Henderson's quarters. When Dragon and two additional warriors entered the complex the white men caught sight of them. Dragon's companions left the chief after a brief conversation and went to a trading post to secure provisions. Dragon had seen the white men as soon as his foot touched the ground inside the confines of the village square. He knew they were watching and in all likelihood plotting. Dragon was correct.

"We ought to have him thrown into irons right now," Sevier said with a tight jaw.

"On what charge?" Henderson quipped.

"Disrupting the public peace. Threatening an officer. Drunk and disorderly. Treason. Hell, I don't care. That son of a bitch is going to cause a lot of trouble."

"Treason?" Boone asked.

"I said I didn't care for what. He's holding back the growth of a nation. That's plain enough. I call that treason."

"The growth of your nation or his?"

Henderson laughed. "Relax. We've got our treaty. We've got the land. And speaking of that land, Colonel Boone, I'd like to offer you a commission to lead a group of settlers up there."

"I might be convinced to head up that way for a spell."

"Fine. Draw up a manifest of provisions, etc., and I'll present it to the board of the land company. I'd like to see you get underway as soon as possible. Some decent maps of the place would go a long way. It'll speed the sale of farm parcels. Also adds some credibility to the place. Makes it appear more inviting to settlers if they think roads and towns are coming along right behind them."

"I reckon you've got it all figured out, eh, Henderson?" Boone smiled.

"Well, I hope we got a lot of it figured out. We've done this once or twice before and that's generally how it goes."

"I'll tell you something, Richard," Sevier thrust into the conversation. "You'd better have a plan in mind for that goddamn Dragon over there. Mark my words, that son of a bitch is going to be a thorn in our side until the day he dies."

"Well, John, if we're lucky some unfortunate accident may befall the great chief."

"And remove the thorn," Boone added.

"Exactly," Sevier echoed. "And remove the thorn."

Totsuhwa hit the square just as the trio finished their declaration. He saw Tsi'yugunsini right away and beyond him the source of his consternation. Dragon started to walk toward the three white men and their unheard discussion of him as Totsuhwa trailed to the side. As Dragon reached the group Totsuhwa set himself up in a dark shadow beside the stoop so he could hear and see without being seen himself. As ever, the arrowhead danced in his hand.

"Good morning, Chief Dragging Canoe," Henderson offered profusely. "What a wonderful day, is it not?"

"The sun is warming, but it is not a good day," Dragon answered.

"No?"

"No. It is a sad day for my nation." Dragon looked around and caught sight of a pair of half-drunken Indians staggering onto the unmarked village square. "Though not all of its people can see it."

Henderson smiled broadly and stepped down to the chief. "What if," he began, "now just what if you are wrong? What if Chief Dragging Canoe is the only one out of thousands of Cherokee who is against the settlement of this land because he is wrong?"

"I am not wrong."

"Yes, but what if? What if you could see the future and in it you saw this countryside awash in quaint villages. Schools for children. Churches to worship God. Fields of corn waiting to be harvested."

"These things I have seen, but it is not the future. It is the past. There have always been villages in this land. Cherokee villages. Where the Spirit speaks to us. Where our children learn. Where our corn grows. But you have burned our fields, ridiculed our Spirit, and killed our children."

"Now hold on there, Mister all high and mighty," Sevier threatened.

With Sevier's step, Dragon's hand slipped to his knife.

Boone tightened and reached for his own.

Henderson stuck his arms out across the chests of the white men. "Hold it! Hold it. Everybody relax. Just relax. John, Chief Dragging Canoe is still our guest. A little decorum if you please. We may not agree with him, but he deserves his say."

"He's had enough say."

"Not now, John," Henderson said. "Now is not the time. We've had a good night. No sense spoiling everything we've worked for. Don't want a martyr now, do we?

"Chief Dragging Canoe," Henderson continued loudly. "I welcome the great chief's opinions — though I do not share them, nor apparently does his father and rest of his nation. I welcome them nonetheless.

"Are you headed home, Chief? Don't let us keep you. Thanks for stopping by."

Henderson retreated back toward his rooms, gently nudging Sevier ahead of him and pulling Boone along behind. "You'll have to excuse us, Chief. We are preparing to outfit Colonel Boone here for an expedition into our newly acquired territory. We've a great deal to do. Please excuse us."

Totsuhwa moved a few steps to watch the white men as they neared the door. To his surprise he heard Tsi'yugunsini laugh. The sound stopped all three men on the porch as surely as a rifle report. As all three turned back to Dragon, the chief shook his finger at them lazily.

"You have purchased much good land." He laughed cynically. "But I am afraid you will have trouble if you try to live there."

Dragon turned away smiling and immediately held out his arm toward Totsuhwa. The boy jumped out of the shadow and the chief placed a hand on his skinny shoulder as they walked away from the bewildered men and the treaty.

When their steps cleared the town Totsuhwa looked up at the Dragon. "You saw me in the shadow from the start?"

"From the start."

"You have good eyes."

"I do."

A few short steps passed and Dragon still smiled the smile he had gained at Henderson's door.

Totsuhwa inadvertently washed it away in an instant. "Tomorrow we will fight the white men?"

"Tomorrow we will fight the white men."

"Then you will need this," Totsuhwa said as he held up the precious arrowhead.

Tsi'yugunsini glanced down without stopping. "Yes, thank you," he said though he made no move to take the point. "Its brothers will take many whites off the land, but my warriors and I also have the white man's guns. Even now, my men trade for more rifles, shot, and powder with silver given by Henderson. We will use their own weapons against them."

Tsi'yugunsini motioned to the arrowhead. "It is a powerful weapon. Many have felt its cut." The chief's words affirmed
Totsuhwa's ghosts by the water but he was not done. "Remember,
it is yours now. A reminder of our fine hunt."

The boy had no words but stared at the gift, unable to banish
from his imagination its violent history.

Tsi'yugunsini stopped and put one hand on the boy's shoulder
as he pointed more deliberately to the arrowhead. "Do not be afraid
of this stone," Dragon said as though he had read Totsuhwa's mind
yet again. "It is strong but you are its master now. It contains great
power of life and death. To our enemies it is death. To our children
it is the life that comes with the food it brings. Carry it with you
and it will protect you with these powers. Its time as a weapon has
past. It is a talisman now to your spirit. Take Tsi'yugunsini with
you and take what Ama Giga teaches and you will be a powerful
warrior and shaman to our people." Dragon hesitated and looked
with gentler eyes at the boy. "We will go separate paths, little panther. This is your protector and a reminder of our hunt and perhaps
a reminder of Tsi'yugunsini."

It was true that the fight would begin before long. Within days
Tsi'yugunsini's tomahawk would be deep red to the handle in white
blood. Hair that was once near blonde and light brown would hang
in mats of dried black blood from his belt. Totsuhwa would not
see these things. Reluctantly he followed Tsi'yugunsini's orders and
stayed with Ama Giga. They both understood that there was much
for him to learn from his wise and experienced grandmother and
also much growing that needed to be accomplished before he could
ride with the war chief against the invaders.

Between now and that day, Totsuhwa would learn the mys-
tical ways of a shaman priest, a Tsalagi medicine man, and carry
the spirituality of Ama Giga and the Real People to the next generation. The day would eventually come when he would take his
place alongside Tsi'yugunsini as one of the premier warriors in the
Cherokee Nation and yet his knowledge of the ancient medicines
and mythology of the people would always overshadow his much-
heralded skill in combat.

In the days when Totsuhwa's training took root beneath Ama Giga's hand, the fledgling collection of colonies up and down the land collected themselves and waged war against their British masters. Dragon had been at war against the colonists and any other white faces that had the misfortune of crossing his path since the day he and his band rode away from the Treaty of Sycamore Shoals and Henderson's promises. The war chief would find a willing ally in the British who responded by supplying him with guns and ammunition to be used against the settlers seeking autonomy from King George. This support temporarily stymied the Dragon's attacks against British outposts and saved the lives of many unknowing and unwary red-coated soldiers who drifted too near Dragon's weapons. The new Americans however, would not fare so well.

Fueled by his growing hatred of all things white, Dragon ravaged homesteads and travelers with heartless, bloodletting abandon. His war cry froze gun-toting long hunters and made grizzled mountain men cower to their knees like frightened children. The answer to their pleas would be the wrenching of his tomahawk from their split skulls and an unceremonious wiping of their brains on the grass. With a deft cut around the head of his victims the Dragon would scalp both soldiers and civilians. Men, women, and children alike fell under his knife and reaffirmed with frightening intensity the name the whites had hung on him.

Though it was he himself who made no distinction between soldiers and children, justifying to his heart and to any critics that no whites had ever given Cherokee babies quarter, the red coat officers who gave him gunpowder also gave him still more incentive with active trade for the hair of colonists. This bounty drove settlers into a frenzied fear for their lives, which the British hoped would in turn drive them to the king for protection and end the colonial rebellion. By supporting Dragon and his ruthless war parties operating out of the Chickamauga River Valley, the men from across the sea used him as both an executioner and as a wedge of fear between colonists and the new United States government.

Ironically, Dragon and his men found themselves aligned with the Shawnee from the northwest for the first time in either nation's history. As a consequence of Attakullakulla's deception of Henderson and Boone's subsequent attempts to settle the land, the Shawnee raised up against the colonists. When the British Empire began returning the fight against its revolting colonies, the Shawnee Nation welcomed the advance. Later, when Dragon's warring Cherokee met their Shawnee compatriots for the first time along a skirmish line fighting for the British and them all aligned against the American colonists, each party would eye the other nearly as often as they did the overt enemy. Only when the Shawnee leaders discovered that the Cherokee chief was Tsi'yugunsini, who did not sign the treaty at Sycamore Shoals, did they allow the continuing uneasy truce.

Many years later, when they were abandoned by the British, the nations continued to war together against the new Americans. It was then that a young Shawnee chief, Tecumseh, studied the ways of battle with the great Tsi'yugunsini and, after forging a friendship that would endure through their violent lifetimes, took his knowledge back to his own people to form one of the most powerful Indian nations on the continent.

While the Shawnee accepted Dragon and his barbarous warfare, his own people suffered as a result of it. When the American Revolution broke out in earnest, the Cherokee had sought to remain neutral. Attakullakulla had no fight with either tribe — the blue coats or the red. He wished only to have his nation left in peace. But the actions of the Shawnee and Dragon's Chickamauga raids on the part of the British caused the warring colonists to paint with broad brushes.

John Sevier was in South Carolina pounding on Richard Henderson's desk as each man reiterated the troubles of the colonies as they saw it.

"Damn it, Richard! Have you heard a word I've said? The British are pushing us from the east, the goddamn Shawnee are raising hell from the west, and that son of a bitch Dragon is massacring anything that moves!"

"I heard you, John! Christ, I heard you! But there isn't a damn thing I can do about any of it. Jesus, I'm fighting for my life here!"

"Fighting for your life? Do you hear what you're saying? The Shawnee are attacking daily. They outflank us, outrun us, outmaneuver us. They say it's like chasing smoke out there. And your old friend Dragon? He's literally butchering children!"

"You think I don't hear the reports, John? But how am I supposed to stop him?"

"You're not. You can't. But Christ, I expect a little more support."

"John. Now it's your turn. Listen to me closely. It is my firm belief that the colonies will win out over Britain. The king just cannot successfully manage a war from England. It's too far. Logistics favor the colonials. They are dug in deep and will triumph, I'm certain of it. When that happens they will turn all their attention to the Indian problem and it too will be eradicated. Now here's the part that's killing me — the goddamn government here, that you are begging me to help salvage, is on the verge of taking away the assets of the Transylvania Land Company. Do you understand where I'm going here? All that land we suffered over to get is about to be stripped away."

Sevier was taken back. "How?"

"The legislature is saying that individuals and private companies cannot buy tracts from the Indians. Simple as that. It all has to be done by the weak and struggling government of the colonies. Goddamn it."

"That sets your finances back a bit, doesn't it, Richard?"

"Don't be flippant, John. I lose, you lose."

"Well there's a lot of land to be taken up one way or the other. By legal means or whatever and it'll all need development, exploration, and surveying. So there's a lot of money to be made still. But these savages have got to be run off it or buried under it first."

"You and your Indians. Why do you hate them so?"

"They're animals. They dance around fires like devils. They talk gibberish you can't understand."

"As do the Spanish and French."

"And they'll scalp you quick as look at you."

"A trick they learned from us, I believe."

"You talk like you give a damn. And there you sit — you robbed them of millions of acres of land and I dare say never lost a night's sleep."

"They were always paid following extensive negotiations."

"Keep telling yourself that, Richard. But in the meantime, I'm pulling together a group of regulars and we're headed west into the Cherokee Nation."

"What for? The Cherokee are neutral."

"That son of a bitch Dragon sure as hell isn't neutral. We're going down there to set things right."

"You're not going to find Dragging Canoe in the nation. He's down warring out of the Chickamauga River area. The Cherokee have all but cut him off."

"It doesn't much matter who we find. There'll be a whole lot less Indians to worry about by the time we get back."

"John, let me say this again - the Cherokee are neutral."

"An Indian is an Indian."

"Go after the Shawnee."

"Let ME say this again, Richard — an Indian is an Indian."

"The Cherokee are not hostiles!"

"I don't care! They're closer and easier to find..."

And so it began.

———————————

The horse snickered and shook its head at a scent on the breeze. The horse alongside picked up the same scent and neighed in reply to its familiarity while the two riders in the party sat comfortably on their backs, oblivious to that which the animals had become aware.

The high canopy of the forest looked down with filtered light on the backs of the men and the horses as they moved along at a leisurely pace. In the movement through the trees the sun seemed to flicker casually across the two white faces and the brown leather of their saddles. The day was warm and invited no rush, but had the riders seen what the trees had witnessed and what their horses had sensed, their spurs would have been dripping with the blood of their mounts.

"Andrew, that is a helluva good looking parcel," Clooney said. "Can it be bought right?"

"You mean cheap?"

"I do indeed."

"Of course. Were that not the case, I wouldn't have troubled either one of us to ride all the way out here."

"Can you get terms?"

"I can."

"Buyers?"

"Stacked up like cord wood."

"Very good, Mr. Jackson," Clooney laughed. "As has become your custom, I am dutifully impressed."

"We will be able to section off and sell individual grants outright, then use the money generated to make the rather genteel monthly payments to the present owner. Our expenditures will be limited to the first surveying costs and I've got somebody lined up for that who will take payment in acreage."

"Who's that?"

"John Sevier."

"I thought he's been commissioned to hunt down Indian renegades."

"He has. I think he might be a colonel now, but John's never been averse to making money, especially with land. He's had his fingers in more deals than you or I will ever see. I've my doubts he'll do the surveying himself — probably can make more in Indian scalps — but it'll get done and it won't cost us one red cent."

Andrew Jackson, in the role of young land speculator, was about to succeed again. The ink on his juris doctorate degree was hardly dry when he ventured into the land business. There was money to be made as there had been fifteen years earlier when Richard Henderson had negotiated his famous treaties, but he was dead now and hindsight coupled with history to demonstrate to Jackson that the grants had to be made with other white men or via the new government. The United States had been born of blood, but laws now dictated that individuals and private enterprise could not negotiate treaties in any form with the remaining indigenous peoples, just as Richard Henderson had predicted. Therefore, Jackson sought out early settlers who had claims to large tracts of land and Revolutionary War veterans who took their pay in westward territories. He was able to wheel and deal with these men free from governmental interference.

"Well, Andrew, I'm not against making money either but the way you've got it set up I don't think you need me."

"That's where you're wrong. The landowners want to see that I have the wherewithal to make the payments. And truth be told, I don't. I'm relying on the quick turnover of the properties to make the subsequent payments."

"I follow."

"What I need is someone to partner up with me. Someone who'll go the down payments and provide proof of solvency before the sellers will consummate the deal. Still follow?"

"Better than ever."

"I need a partner. You want in?"

A lead ball hit Clooney beneath his left eye before he could answer. At the same time the sound of the report made the horses bolt. A second shot came. Blood spurted from the hole in the wounded man's face as the second ball whistled by Jackson's head. Clooney fell backward from his frenzied animal, dead before he hit the ground with a sickening thud. His horse, pulled to the rear by the reins twisted in its dead rider's hand, stepped backward onto the lifeless body snapping bones beneath its hooves.

Jackson didn't have time to scream his would-be partner's name. He fought to regain control of his frightened horse. In the harried movements of the stammering animal, three Cherokee painted arrows whizzed by, severing the small branches off trees that hung nearby.

Safety lay straight ahead in the direction the shots had come from, but the shooters would be reloading. Jackson looked back in a spilt second at Clooney splayed on the ground with his horse trampling him, still tied to the dead hand. He saw his limits in that fraction of a moment and buried his spurs in his horse's ribs.

Jackson and his horse crushed through the trees. Totsuhwa saw him coming and quickly set his rifle down and sprinted to intercept him. Dragon saw his adopted son's intentions but continued reloading his long gun.

When Jackson saw the painted warrior dashing through the woods toward an intersecting point ahead he knew what would happen. His spurs raked the sides of the animal again, but he would not beat the Indian who seemed to be flying low across the ground. Fortunately the forest and his horse cooperated and provided an escape.

Jackson drove the animal through a break in the trees hard away from the racing Indian. Totsuhwa saw the move and pushed to compensate for the change in the direction of the chase but was out maneuvered by the speed of the horse. In seconds the fleet-footed Indian was outdistanced by the scrambling charger and its flailing rider.

Dragon set the primer in his flintlock and brought his rifle to the ready, but the trees again protected the fleeing white man. With no chance of a shot, Dragon ran to his own horse tied nearby and swept his worn body onto its back. As he did, Totsuhwa, strong and exuberant in the prime of his life, flew back through the trees and leaped onto his own horse, his rifle back in his hand. Dragon had the lead as both men urged their animals after Andrew Jackson.

Behind them, other warriors descended on Clooney's body. Like wolves pouncing for the kill they drove their knives into the corpse to insure the death and satisfy their bloodlust. One took the startled horse and ripped the twisted reins from the dead man's hand while another sought to free the hair from his head.

An Indian brave ripped Clooney's head backward, pointing the corpse's open dead eyes to the clouds. The chasm beneath the left eye dripped blood that was drawn out by movement and gravity alone as the heart had ceased to beat moments after the bullet struck. With a fist full of hair, the brave made one long slicing cut from just above one of the dead man's ears around through the forehead to the top of the other ear. He pulled the scalp free with a sound of wet cloth tearing. Still holding the partially detached scalp in one hand, the warring Indian put a foot on Clooney's shoulder and pushed his body forward. With the hair drawn tight away from the head, the warrior made a single slash through the scalp at what had been the back of the dead man's head. The gruesome procedure was accomplished so quickly it was nearly bloodless. Two cuts in the space of a second and the trophy was hoisted in the air with a resounding triumphant cry.

While the prize was being raised, other men were running for their horses, mounting and galloping off in search of Totsuhwa and Dragon. The leaders of the band were easy to trace. The sounds of their horses careening through the trees helped signal the way for the trailing warriors. Dragon's war whoops echoed through the forest as well as he continued to threaten the terrified Jackson. The heart-pounding, mind-choking scream meant death was at hand and was the last sound a great many white men had heard since Dragon had ridden out of Sycamore Shoals fifteen years before.

The killings and raiding had come in spurts. There were some quiet days at the onset as the treaty settled into the minds of those involved and even after as the Cherokee returned to the way of life they had enjoyed for centuries. But when the Shawnee attacked Daniel Boone and the first settlers, the peace that Attakullakulla had promised would last a hundred years began to unravel.

Eventually Henderson realized the extent of the Cherokee deception but was loath to let on for fear the revelation would further incriminate his already dwindling hold on the land. Before it was over, the government would commandeer the vast bulk of the parcel that changed hands in the Treaty of Sycamore Shoals. Henderson would be given a token tract of land for his time, trouble, and role in the intended deception of the Cherokee.

When the Shawnee land was discovered to be not as welcoming as had been thought, colonists pushed elsewhere for land, just as Dragon had predicted. Settlers and soldiers alike were tracked and hunted by Dragon and a seemingly ever-changing array of faces around him. Warriors came and went over the years and battles. Some were lost to the guns of the ever-encroaching enemy but not many. This was a testament to Dragon's skill in preparing both his men and the attacks. However, disease or the calling needs of their villages took other men down. But when one left for home or for the Darkening Land another rose to take his place. As the years passed and the Dragon's reputation grew with the colonial thirst for land, the new recruits were often Shawnee and even Chickasaw.

This is how it was when Dragon and his raiders came within two days' ride of Totsuhwa's village almost ten years earlier. Several months prior, Totsuhwa, as a burgeoning young shaman, had officiated over the funeral of Ama Giga. With her movement to the Darkening Land, Totsuhwa was without family. So the sixteen-year-old boy put the few possessions he owned — some unique herbs, tubers, and leaves, a few small clay pots of Ama Giga's, and

Tsi'yugunsini's arrowhead, into a fawn-skin medicine satchel and slung it and a smallish bow and quiver over his shoulders. Then, with the promise that he would return and bless the village of his birth and training, he rode into the forest of his ancestors in search of the great Tsi'yugunsini.

When the young man and his brief mentor of so many years before met again, timeliness cemented the old relationship. Dragon's pack was fresh from killing but had suffered injuries in the skirmish. Two warriors had been hit by gunshot and a third had been slashed with a saber. The wounds were painful if not immediately life threatening. As always, lack of attention could claim lives days or weeks later. Worse than the wounds was a stomach illness that catapulted through the band as a result of drinking contaminated water. In the rapid retreat from the battle, dry-mouthed warriors sought to ease the pain of their wounded and their own thirst by drinking from a pool they would normally have passed by. The predictable results were debilitating cramps and diarrhea.

The raiders had stumbled their way back into their river valley region for safety, seclusion, and rest. Fresh water did little to ease their malady. When a lookout saw the young man riding upon their hideout, studying the ground as he rode, he wished the rider were a Cherokee shaman. As he realized it was a boy, he cursed. But the curse would not take. In its stead, the wish had been granted and soon the lookout, along with the rest of the men, would glory in the arrival of young Totsuhwa.

Dragon did not recognize the young man at first, but as soon as he was invited to speak, the great chief went to Totsuhwa and put his arms around him. Dragon then held him out in front of him at arm's length and studied the slender frame.

"Totsuhwa. The one who gives counsel at windows. You have grown from a twig into a fine young tree."

"And from a rabbit into a panther," Totsuhwa offered.

The words made Dragon remember and in the remembering there was a smile. "And into a panther."

The two shared the smile for a moment as they looked each other up and down. In the looking, Dragon took note of Totsuhwa's horse and the lone satchel slung over the young man's shoulder. "You have traveled light, Totsuhwa."

"Yes, I took my provisions from the land."

"With this child's bow?" Dragon teased.

"It is the only one I have, but it is good for small game and my arrows are true."

"Yes, but the prey we seek is larger than your rabbits and birds. If you are here to hunt with us you will need a stronger weapon."

"I carry much strength," Totsuhwa said as he pointed to his head then to the satchel.

"Yes, I recall that now. You have been studying with a master. How is the great Ama Giga? Does the Spirit still speak to her often?"

"I believe He does, Tsi'yugunsini. But the words are clearer for her. She sleeps in the Darkening Land for five moons now. There the Spirit can talk to her without the sounds of this world interfering. It was His wish to be able to do so. That is why He called her to Him."

Dragon put his arm over the young man's shoulder and led him deeper into the campsite. "Ama Giga has trained you well. And you have listened to her I see. It can be heard in your words."

"Thank you. But I carry your words as well. That is why I have come. I am here to fight with you."

The walk took the two through a maze of warriors hunched against rocks and nursing themselves in shadowed crevices of the mountain.

"Thank you for coming to fight, Totsuhwa. The Shawnee has sent members of their nation as well. Some from other nations join us daily. We have a strange force, young Totsuhwa." The Dragon smiled slightly and shook his head. "The enemy that encroaches on us all makes old enemies fight shoulder to shoulder. We take arms and powder from the British, the French, and even the Spaniards.

"You are brave, young panther. I know that. But there may be a more useful enemy you can battle for me." Dragon stopped and motioned to his men. "My warriors are taken with a demon. It was asleep in the still water. My wounded woke it in their thirst.

Perhaps you could ask the Spirit to strengthen them once more. Our nation has need of them."

Totsuhwa slipped his arm out of the child-sized bow and looked to set it and the accompanying quiver aside. Dragon interceded and took the small weapon delicately. With his hands free to rummage through the satchel, Totsuhwa moved quickly toward the nearest prone member of the beleaguered troupe. As he did, Dragon turned away, carrying the small bow and arrows with points knapped for birds and rabbits.

The ancient remedies in the satchel began the healing process for the small tribe immediately. Totsuhwa made a foray into the woods and returned with other offerings he mixed, cooked, and prayed over until even the most severely wounded raider was resting comfortably. Only then did Totsuhwa go in search of Dragon once more.

He found the war chief sitting on a rocky outcrop with a young man. Tsi'yugunsini was working a long piece of wood with a sharpened stone. "Your warriors are resting," Totsuhwa said.

Dragon neither looked up nor answered as his hands continued to labor over the wood. Totsuhwa would not insult himself or the chief by repeating the words. Rather, he sat down on a slightly lower ledge nearby and watched the war chief's hands work the stone and wood. He looked hard but discreetly at the other young man who was not much older than himself. He was Shawnee.

After a few moments, Dragon spoke without looking at either young man. "You have not lost your ability to track me. The white hunters and John Sevier, they have been tracking Tsi'yugunsini for fifteen winters. Still they come only close enough to die. But you have ridden for two days and walked through the front door of my lodge. You have the same gift you used that day when we took the deer near Sycamore Shoals."

"Wado, Chief Tsi'yugunsini."

"This young warrior," Dragon said as he scarcely motioned to the man beside him. "You know his people?"

"I do," Totsuhwa answered as he now openly eyed the young man with suspicion.

Again it seemed Dragon did not divert his attention from the wood in his hands. "Allow the distrust to slip from your eyes, Totsuhwa. And do so now. This is Tecumseh — a young warrior of the Shawnee who shares our hearts. Today he becomes your brother as he is mine. He shares your desire to learn and your desire to fight. I have made it known that should I fall in battle, Young Tassel, who is called John Watts, will wear my blanket. But Tecumseh and his brother will lead the Shawnee in the fight from the north."

Then Dragon motioned toward the medicine bag. "And you have other talents now. You are a gift to your people."

"I am still young in the ways. But Ama Giga gave me her gifts. I have used them on the men."

Dragon reached down and patted Totsuhwa's shoulder then resumed his work on what would become a strong bow for his returning young friend. "They are not my warriors any longer, Totsuhwa. They are ours. You are our shaman."

It was thus that Totsuhwa took his first steps into the council of chiefs. Dragon took the skills of Ama Giga, deeply set in Totsuhwa's life, and added everything a war leader could.

Years later, now in the woods pursuing Andrew Jackson with a body that had grown from a sapling to an oak, Totsuhwa was both a respected shaman and a feared warrior. No trace of the rabbit remained.

Dragon's shrieks pierced Jackson's ears as the white racer whipped his horse into a lather. The warriors, better mounted and better riders, were closing. The chase through the trees had been a long one and both Jackson and his horse were winded. At last the pair broke from the wood line into the open fields that buttressed a small town. The collection of houses and outlying farms would provide a measure of protection if Jackson could reach them. What he didn't realize was that the devil-may-care attitude of Dragon would permit him to ride full bore into the settlement on Jackson's heels and cut the white man down right in the street. Though he didn't know this reckless part of Dragon's plan, Jackson did glance over his shoulder enough to see the Indian fifty yards behind pushing hard. Totsuhwa, riding like the wind himself, was now three lengths behind his mentor.

The pounding of the horses' hooves and the screams from both red and white men caught the attention of the people in and about the settlement. Out of concerned habit, most of the faces that appeared carried a long gun. When the vicious parade approaching the buildings became evident each collected gun drew down across the field in the direction of Dragon and Totsuhwa. Though both warriors were intent on Jackson, the ducking white faces beyond and the gathering guns did not go unnoticed. Reluctantly, they reined in their mounts as a shot erupted from the corner of a far-away building.

Dragon judged the distance as he eased his horse to a stop just as Totsuhwa pulled up alongside. Neither expressed a concern over the gunshot, though Dragon leaned heavily into his horse and breathed quickly.

"They waste their lead," he snorted as he gasped for his own breath along with the winded animal beneath him.

"They do, but that one," Totsuhwa said as he pointed to Jackson jumping from his horse and sprinting into the nearest house. "That one will not venture into the forest again soon."

Dragon laughed as he pulled his horse around and began walking it back to the woods, still breathing heavily. "I believe you are right," he wheezed. "Did you see how he flailed at the animal? Begging for faster feet? I saw him look back at us. His eyes were big, like this!" Dragon made a contorted face and held his eyes wide open with his fingers. "The eyes filled his face!"

Totsuhwa laughed with him, as much at the face Dragon made as the notion of the frightened white man. The laughter quieted over the heavy breathing of the horses as the animals' sides continued to heave. The two would walk easily for some time.

"Totsuhwa," Dragon began after several minutes. "How long have you been with me?"

"Many winters."

"And have I not taught you well?"

"Yes, Tsi'yugunsini. You have taught me many things."

"Perhaps I am a poor teacher."

"No, my chief. You have instructed me in a great many things," Totsuhwa said with growing concern. "Things I use every day. If

I fail it is because I am a poor student, not that you are a poor teacher."

"Hmmm..."

"Why does the great Tsi'yugunsini say these things?"

There was hesitation in the chief's voice. "I am wondering how you happened to miss your shot back in the woods." Then Dragon could not hide a mischievous grin.

Totsuhwa scowled. "I missed because you shot early."

"My man lies dead in the trees while yours enjoys a cold drink of water. How is it I failed?"

"Because you shot early. We were supposed to fire at once, on a count. You shot early and caused the horses to bolt from under my rifle. It was not my mistake."

Dragon only grunted but after a few strides of the horses, he began to look in front of and behind and around Totsuhwa. The younger man looked down at himself, following Dragon's eyes around the horse.

"What is it? What do you see?"

"Nothing. I was looking to see where the scalp is hanging from the mistake you did not make."

Totsuhwa bristled then the two laughed again as Dragon reached across both horses and punched Totsuhwa's shoulder.

"I see no scalp on your belt, Tsi'yugunsini," Totsuhwa laughed.

"It comes to me. See?"

Sure enough, the other members of the raiding party were waiting in the woods. When the two men pulled up in their midst, the brave who had scalped Clooney walked up to them holding the hair up to both of them. His eyes and those of the others looked from Tsi'yugunsini to Totsuhwa and back again to see who would take the scalp and claim the coup. When Dragon reached forward the warriors all voiced their approval. Then the man who had just handed Dragon the scalp looked around Totsuhwa's mount for the scalp the men believed the young shaman would bear. When they saw none, their eyes again looked back and forth between the two men.

Dragon smiled slightly. "He had a good horse."

The band smiled and laughed together as though sharing a good joke and not the missed chance at killing a man. Soon the throng was absorbed by the trees and vanished with no sense of urgency. Experience had taught Dragon that the white settlers would brace for an attack at their homes and would not venture into the Cherokee's forested lair. Later that night the group daw-dled around a low, nearly smokeless fire.

"When the sun wakes we must head to the southwest," Dragon began. "We will find the Spaniards there. It is time for them to fill our powder horns."

A sly laugh filtered through the men. The Spanish had sev-eral ongoing land disputes with the newly minted government of the United States of America. The conflicts often resulted in bloodshed. Dragon, in a constant state of war against the latest Americans, welcomed the offers of the Spanish ammunition and weapons. He had put them to good use, much to the delight of Spain.

"Tsi'yugunsini," Totsuhwa said. "If Spain defeats the Americans, they will turn on us as the Americans and British have done."

"That is true, but for now we take our weapons where we can and use them against the present enemy."

A young warrior chuckled. "Perhaps we should bury the bullets the Spaniards give us. We can dig them up to use on them if they win their wars."

The snickers that followed were more sinister than humorous. If the Spanish ever took up a side against the Cherokee, the war-riors would attack with no thought to the previous aid Spain had rendered.

However, before thoughts of warring against Spain took hold, Totsuhwa stepped in. "But I do not believe the Spanish will defeat the settlers. Britain could not and they are stronger than Spain. The red coats have shown us that no power can win a war from across the seas. Invaders are repelled when they have no foothold in the land. And men fight strongest when the ground beneath their feet cradles their fathers and mothers. That is why the homeland of the Tsalagi will always remain with the Tsalagi."

"That is so," Dragon said. "The Creator meant for no feet other than Tsalagi to walk through it. No other feet."

The conversation melted away with the dying embers. One by one the crouching men moved to the ground and gave way to sleep. When the last man was still, Dragon called to Totsuhwa.

"Do you sleep, my son?"

"No, Tsi'yugunsini. I am awake."

"Come to me."

Totsuhwa stood from his place on the ground and walked over to the chief who remained prone near the fire bed. The young shaman knelt beside his teacher and waited. In a few moments Dragon reached up and took Totsuhwa's hand. In the dim light of the fire, the young shaman saw that the hand, like the warrior who possessed it, was wrinkled and worn. Dragon pulled Totsuhwa's hand to his chest and held it against his heart.

"My son, I come looking for the shaman. Is he here?"

Totsuhwa smiled. "I am here."

"Shaman, today when I chased the man through the trees I had great pain in here."

"Sometimes the Spirit puts a burden on our hearts that we must wrestle. The pain-"

"No, shaman. This is a true pain, not a pain of the soul. That pain I know well too. I felt it grip my heart when Attakullakulla moved to the West.

"This pain was in my body and came up my neck. It was as though a stone lay across me and I could not breathe."

Dragon lay quiet for a short time before he spoke again. "That is why I could not catch the white rider for you. My arms were too weak to drive my horse or raise my rifle. Yuhwa danvta. I am sorry."

It was the first time Totsuhwa had seen any frailty in his life-long hero. The grasp of it was overpowering and made something within him not recognize the truth for what it was.

"You have chased hard today, Tsi'yugunsini. And you have not had meat for several days. We have moved often. These things have tired you. I feel these things myself as do all the men. Tonight we will rest and tomorrow you will lead us to the Spaniards."

"Perhaps the great shaman is right."

"Yes. Listen to your shaman."

"I will listen."

Dragon lay quietly and Totsuhwa slipped his hand off of the man's chest. He stood as his teacher rolled over to his side. The aging chief pulled a blanket over his tired shoulders and tried to sleep.

The shaman returned to his own bundle but knelt only to retrieve a peculiar dried root from his bag. When he crouched again by his mentor, the elder turned his head and asked with his eyes why he had returned. The shaman held out the root near Tsi'yugunsini's mouth.

"Here, my father. Chew this slowly. It will help you sleep and ease the stone off of your chest."

Dragon fumbled for the tuber and took it but dropped it just as quickly. His hand stayed by his mouth as his eyes sought out the safety of his son's face. Totsuhwa immediately caught the root and brought it to the older man's mouth. Dragon curled his lips around the bulb and pulled it into his mouth. He began massaging it with his tongue and nodded an acknowledgment to the shaman.

Totsuhwa gently patted his father's shoulder, stood, and returned again to his temporary bed this time to try and sleep. But the arms of sleep would take their time encircling him on this night. The change in Tsi'yugunsini was dramatic and sudden. As Totsuhwa lay in the flickering low light of the fire he searched his mind for changes in his chief that perhaps he had not noticed or acknowledged. There were none. Dragon's strength and personal command had drawn a veil over any weakness that might have shown itself. If he had experienced these pains before, Totsuhwa had not seen them. He had been with the man every day, nearly every moment for the past seven years and to him, a gifted shaman, there had been no sign.

Totsuhwa raised up from his blankets enough to see the dark silhouette on the ground that was the feared Dragon. If indeed the Spirit was calling for the chief, Totsuhwa would have to stay closer than ever before and use all his skill to ward off the Raven Mocker.

He was not prepared to release the hand that had befriended him, taught him much, and become his family. Selfishly, he had no desire to be left alone again.

The next morning the sun's rays ran out ahead as the sun approached the horizon, foretelling the coming of another day. Brilliant reds, oranges, and yellows splashed across a cloudless blue morning sky and rewarded the eyes that peeked through the gritty deposits of the night's sleep.

The men staggered and stumbled to their feet around the dead fire. On rising nearly all immediately made way for the edges of the circle and urinated. Totsuhwa called to them from his bed.

"Bring wood."

The young men returning to the makeshift camp brought relieved faces and handfuls of kindling for a new fire.

Dragon was sitting up with his blanket draped over his shoulders. The cloth that covered him was heavy and had once been bright but now it was dirty and ragged at the edges, worn down by travel and use, not unlike the man it protected. The colorful pattern that remained signified to any who might approach that the bearer of the blanket was a ranking chief. The geometric design and hues painted a picture of authority endowed by the people. No warrior, regardless of how brave and revered in battle, could toss this mantle over his back. Even at times when the accompanying weather would not request the employ of a cover, the chiefs would often drape their special blankets across their shoulders. The purpose served was like that of the gold braid that set apart the white man's generals. And also like the generals, the chiefs had other blankets, other uniforms, plain ones for day-to-day use. But for Dragon, his constant travel necessitated few possessions and also made the ground beneath his feet home. As such the revered blanket was always with him as it was this morning as he watched his warriors collecting for the day.

"We have no need of a fire. The sun will soon warm you if you are cold."

The men stopped and awkwardly held their gathered twigs. Totsuhwa stood and began retrieving the pieces from the men and placing them in the previous night's fire pit. "You are right, Tsi'yugunsini, but I have need of a small fire. I must prepare a medicine."

"Is one of our number sick?" Dragon muttered.

"No, but there are magics I must have with me."

"Prepare your fire, shaman. We will wait."

The foot soldiers relaxed again and settled back around the ring of the fire pit. They each pulled berries, fruits, dried corn, and venison from their bundles and nibbled their breakfast as they watched the smokeless fire grow beneath Totsuhwa's hands.

The shaman pulled odd leaves from his bag and crushed them with tubers and bulbs that were stranger still. The men shrugged their shoulders at one another, admitting with gestures that none recognized the plants. Totsuhwa put the dried pulp into a small clay bowl and set it on a flat rock near the fire. He added enough water to the pot to nearly fill it and then left the mixture to heat. Occasionally, Totsuhwa would drop in another leaf or a bit of unrecognizable oil, sap, or dust and stir the brew. When the mixture began to set off steam Totsuhwa moved it from the fire with two sticks acting as pinchers on the pot. Then he left the concoction alone to steep.

Dragon lingered by the fire as the others busied themselves with the horses and rolling up their beds. Totsuhwa came and sat near his leader.

"How much longer will the Spanish provide us with weapons, Father?"

"Only the Spirit knows for certain. As I slept, He spoke to me. You are right. They will not beat the settlers."

"When our powder horns grow empty, it will be more difficult to wage our battles."

"It is difficult enough now, is it not, my son?"

"It is."

Dragon looked up into the bright sun now two hands above the mountains. "How are the people?"

"They support us as best they can. It is hard. The colonists and American soldiers attack often. Even the Creek to the west. The Tsalagi have few allies."

"You are a wise man, Totsuhwa. Tell me. Do I make it better for them or worse with what I do?"

There was only a slight pause, but in it Dragon took a complete answer. Totsuhwa saw the expression flash over Dragon's face and answered hurriedly but too late to stop what the silence had loosened.

"Were it not for you, the whites would have overrun every town in the nation. They would have dug holes and planted their forts and settlements along every league of hunting territory many, many winters ago. You have prevented this when others would have meekly traded it away."

"Do we bring hardship to the people?"

"No. We have stopped more attacks on our villages than we have ever invited. Far more. You know this to be true in your heart."

"Yes, but then tell me, shaman. Why does my heart ache?"

"You are tired. When we have reached the Spaniards you will be rested." Totsuhwa stood and as he did he surreptitiously picked up Dragon's water gourd. The young shaman secretively cradled the gourd and walked to his blanket roll which he picked up along with his satchels. Then he retrieved the cooling clay pot and walked into the woods unnoticed by all but Dragon.

Once sheltered by the trees Totsuhwa put the water from Dragon's urn into another and poured the warm contents of the clay pot into the empty gourd. He forced a tight-fitting stick into the opening then pulled it back out a very little bit so it would not be too snug. Then he concealed it once more and returned to the dying fire.

The warriors had collected the horses and were mounting. Totsuhwa and Dragon's horses were brought for them, befitting their stature. When they had climbed aboard the animals Dragon motioned to the west of camp and the warriors fell in line and moved off. As his adoptive father came within reach Totsuhwa handed him the medicine-filled gourd.

"Your water, my chief."

Dragon took it and nodded knowingly. No one else paid attention to the pass. Totsuhwa would not embarrass his father. There was no need for any of the others to know their leader was failing.

The next several days passed in comparative quiet for the band of raiders. Totsuhwa was grateful that their scouts, riding on ahead and to the far sides, had not located any settlements or travelers. Dragon rode quietly and sipped from his water gourd on occasion and in the evening he chewed the roots Totsuhwa placed near him. A week into the journey he was stronger. The timing was good.

The line of slow-moving horses and riders heard the sounds of another horse trotting through the trees toward them. As one, the group pulled up and watched the forest ahead, fingers itching across the triggers of long guns and the notches of arrows. The flash of brown skin over the color of a recognized horse eased away the anxious fingers as one of the scouts came into their midst.

"Soldiers."

Dragon did not ask how many soldiers had unknowingly shown themselves to the outrider. He asked only how far as he pushed his horse to an easy gallop. The distance and location would dictate Dragon's strategy in the attack — the number of enemy meant little if anything. If what lay ahead was a full regimental column, Dragon would split his force and attack with a small party from the rear side where his men would be facing the sun. When the soldiers reacted to the attack and form up, the larger group of Dragon's raiders would attack from behind the muster lines, blinding the soldiers with the sun. The soldiers' officers would be behind their men, closer to the second attacking wave. They would be the first to be killed and the regiment's plan would die with them.

An attack on such a large force would be quick, unlike the raids on colonial outposts that often turned into a siege. There, Dragon would move his men often and have them show themselves to the white eyes inside the post. He even had the men appear with and without shirts, partially covered with blankets, with their hair pulled back, with it loose, and every variation and combination thereof, in order to convince those inside that the warriors at their door were huge in number. Then the Dragon would attack at night and diminish the foe's strength. Finally, when he had parried enough to weaken the enemy through lack of food and water, he would set the buildings on fire. Driven out by the heat and flames, the terrified white faces rushed from misery to death.

On this particular day the half dozen soldiers about to meet the Dragon were accompanying an equal number of hunters and trappers. Each group had set out to forage for game. When the parties met in the mountains they merged for a time to trade tales and news and maybe a little tobacco.

The scout escorted Dragon to within sound of the men who were ambling along on horseback, trailing two riderless horses they would use to pack home the game they hoped to kill. The warriors dismounted and crept along silently until they could easily see their prey. Dragon judged the sun, the terrain, and the direction the hunters were headed then turned back into the deep woods.

His war party counted ten strong. Other days it might be many more, some days less, but it always proved to be big enough. The men were well armed and excellent shots. Dragon elected to divide his small band and attack.

While Totsuhwa left with four braves to circle around the pursued soldiers and their temporary companions, Dragon and his group tied up their horses and sprinted through the trees to catch the slow moving hunters. Near the end of the run, Dragon felt the Spirit tightening in his chest.

Totsuhwa's men completed their circling maneuver and left their horses. They too raced through the trees on silent feet until they had caught the travelers. The warriors on either side of the soldiers and hunters strained to see their counterparts in the woods across the way, but neither was successful. Totsuhwa eased his men along through the woods, mirroring the riders but staying very low so as not to be caught with a wayward round from the opening volley.

The shaman had told his band to use their guns for one shot then revert to the faster-loading bows. All of this would come after Dragon had attacked and in the process drawn the backs of the soldiers around beneath the sites of Totsuhwa's guns. Neither expected much trouble dispatching the dozen trespassers on Cherokee land.

Without a signal to his son, Dragon opened fire on the small column of men. His own shot buried itself deep in the brain of the first man to die. The rifles of the warriors on either side of Dragon killed the men on either side of Dragon's target. Other men were hit by lead following those first reports but were still alive enough to scramble for cover.

The training of the soldiers in the group drove them off their horses and into a skirmish line, rifles trained on the smoke that lingered from Dragon's guns. His men had jumped to other cover as soon as they had fired knowing the smoke would betray them. They pulled up their bows as the soldiers' guns fired into the arms of the trees and hit nothing.

The civilian hunters in the party, lacking military bearing, spurred their horses to flee rather than fight. The dropping dead and dismounting soldiers hindered their escape as did the sudden rain of Cherokee arrows from Dragon's side. Several white men felt flint tear their tissue and splinter their bones. A few fell immediately while others spurred their horses or staggered off to die slowly from blood trickling out of their bodies no one could stop.

Totsuhwa watched the backs of the soldiers turn toward him as they took up positions in their attempt to repel Dragon's attack. He would have waited a moment longer, but a settler had escaped the initial onslaught and was whipping his horse over the gathering of dead and dying at the animal's feet. Pressed into early action, Totsuhwa stepped from the safety of the trees and pulled up his rifle. He lined up his sights on the leather-covered broad back of the hunter and a lead ball took flight. It bore deep into the man's spine. Instant numbness caused the rider's hands to fall from the reins and he tumbled headlong from his horse. The animal scampered away, driven by the sounds of Totsuhwa's men firing into the dusty blue backs of the kneeling soldiers.

All but a few members of the hunting party were dead or nearly so. Those that remained trembled as they fumbled to reload their cumbersome rifles. Totsuhwa's band, closer to the men who now spun to face them, leaped from the cover of the trees and sprang onto the hapless soldiers. The speed with which they moved was only equaled by the ferocity in which they swung their tomahawks and war clubs. Hardened soldiers, grown men, screamed like frightened children as the Cherokee, who seemed to be a hundred in number, swarmed out of the trees. In a single heartbeat they were on the men.

Totsuhwa hurriedly set down his rifle after his only shot. He jumped like the others toward the collection of dead, dying, and men about to be so. In the move he saw the man he had just shot trying to pull himself away using one arm. Totsuhwa started for him but nearly ran into a rifle muzzle coming up to fire. He caught the barrel of the gun with the head of his war club and wrenched it up sharply where it discharged harmlessly into the air. Without breaking the stride of the weapon, Totsuhwa brought the club down into the head of the gun bearer while the barrel still pointed skyward. A sickening crunch and moan erupted simultaneously from the stricken hunter just ahead of a splash of blood, brain, and bone. Like his war club, Totsuhwa did not lose a step as he continued on toward the man who was struggling to crawl.

At the moment he reached the desperate man, the cripple struggled to look up from the ground. The sight that loomed above him was terrifying. The lower half of Totsuhwa's face was painted with jet black charcoal. From his eyes upward into the scalp his skin was colored deep burnt sienna made from clay. His long black hair was tied with a piece of dangling sinew in a crude top knot that left the hair flailing wildly as he moved. He was bare breasted, having removed his loose deerskin shirt to prevent it from being grabbed, torn, or bloodied in the fighting. Two wide handprints were on his chest, placed there with the excess colors from his face. The rest of his upper body glistened with a light sweat.

On each arm was a narrow rawhide strap tied just below his shoulders. Under one Totsuhwa had tucked a few sprigs of fresh growth from the trees he had run through – a symbol of life; his. Under the other were three fallen maple leaves gathered from the forest floor – for death; the trespassers'.

There was a wide light colored scar that came around the front of his right shoulder, compliments of a militia bayonet years before. Since then he had mastered his teacher's use of his weapons. Now Totsuhwa often cruelly smiled in the middle of a fight when the arrogance of his enemies at fighting an undisciplined savage was replaced by the shock that this savage could thrust and parry with a wooden war club as well as an English nobleman could with a saber.

Over it all were Totsuhwa's eyes. There was an intensity in them that even startled the hardened men in his band. Whether it was the color on his face or something deeper inside his soul, the eyes appeared to blacken so deeply on the precipice of battle that they looked to be empty holes that led to a deep dark place unknown. They did not blink. And the blackness spread to his face. This is what nightmares were made of.

As the wounded man wrenched himself on the ground to see who had shot him and who would kill him, his legs, useless from the lead ball in his back, twisted below him. Totsuhwa looked into the sweating face of the man beneath him. The trapper trembled as his jaw fidgeted in fear. Sweat rolled down his forehead into his eyes and dripped off his nose into the coarse hair of a scruffy mustache and beard. In short jerky movements the man wiped his eyes with his only working hand.

Screams came from behind as Totsuhwa's warriors descended with a fury on the remaining white men. The eyes of the stricken man darted behind his executioner and saw the carnage that was about to overtake him. Two braves held a wounded soldier up on his knees, three arrows piercing his chest. One steadied the dying man and the other sliced his neck from ear to ear while pulling back on his hair. The gaping wound spurted puffs and bubbles of blood as the dying man breathed his last through the slash across his throat.

Totsuhwa took no notice of the killing behind him. His icy eyes stayed locked on the man at his feet. In a blur he raised his war club to end the man's torment. But when the hunter raised his own good arm above his head to instinctively ward off the blow, something tied to the man's belt caught Totsuhwa's hollow eyes.

Next to the brown, dirty and stained deerskin coat, tucked in a tattered leather belt, was a mass of matted black hair. Totsuhwa immediately recognized it as a scalp, perhaps two or more. Scalps alone would not have riled a vicious interest from Totsuhwa as he knew they could be Creek, an enemy he might himself kill on another day. However, stuck in the dried bloody mess was a short string of what first appeared to be beads. Beads in the hair would have caused only a momentary delay in the war club crashing through the upraised arm and into the man's skull, but these were not beads at all — they were seeds.

As Totsuhwa became more aware of the seeds strung as they were, he lowered the war club. He cocked his head first to one side then the other as he struggled to peer into the dried bloodied tangle of hair. The hunter spied the Indian above him looking at his waist belt. His own eyes ran to the belt as best they could and realized it was the scalps that were captivating his murderous host. As hurriedly as he could, the man ripped the scalps from his waist and held them in a quivering hand out to Totsuhwa.

"Here! Take 'em! I give 'em to you!"

Totsuhwa stared through the scalps to the string of seeds nearly covered in dried blood dangling from the hair and said nothing.

"HERE!" the man bellowed as he shook the scalps.

Totsuhwa reached for them. With great tenderness he slipped his hand beneath the scalps. The hunter released them quickly and withdrew his own hand in a flash.

"There now," he said somewhat more relaxed but still sweating and nervous in the numbness that held the bulk of his body. "A gift! We're friends. See there?"

Totsuhwa put the war club beneath his arm and used both hands to delicately clean the seeded string in the hair. When he had done so he saw clearly that the string was made up of alternating seeds of corn, bean, and squash carefully woven into the hair. The shaman spoke in reverent tones to no one but the seeds themselves.

"You are the Three Sisters. You have danced in the decorated hair of the one who tended to you. She planted you in the belly of our mother and with the help of her hand, you have fed my people. She was a caretaker, a worker in the fields. A woman who hurt no one."

The wounded man lay very still while Totsuhwa spoke to the Three Sisters. The man's reaction was quick however, when Totsuhwa snatched the war club from beneath his arm and brought it thundering down. The shaman's aim was for the defending arm he knew would come up. The thick round wooden head of the club struck the forearm with such force it continued on and

bounced off the man's chest. The break and contortion of the forearm was unnatural and ghastly. It had given way easily, removing
the last vestige of a token defense. The numbness helped alleviate
the pain, but the sight of the mangled arm made the man scream
in horror.

Completely unable to offer resistance, the hunter lay sweating,
trembling, and shrieking. Totsuhwa tucked the scalps into his belt
and dropped the war club alongside the prostrate man. The shaman
then slipped his knife from its sheath at his waist and grabbed the
scraggly hair of the hunter. With the man's head twisted back and
screams spewing from his bearded mouth, Totsuhwa scalped him
with two rapid cuts.

The sight and sounds of the screaming hairless man brought a
temporary halt to anything else that was occurring at that moment.
All the warriors stared in disbelief at the man, still living with
blood trickling down his face from the hair being ripped from his
head. Even Dragon paused over a dead soldier to watch his son
as he threw the man's hair to the side, picked up his war club
and stomped away, leaving the man very much alive, screeching
insanely from the pain.

The man continued to shriek until an annoyed warrior rushed
at him with his knife, intent on silencing him forever. The hunter
looked through the blood and tears in his eyes at the onrushing
brave and welcomed the knife in his hand.

But Totsuhwa would prolong his misery. "No!" he ordered.
"Leave him."

The warrior did as he was directed and backed away from the
hairless, blood-soaked scalper of women.

The trapper screamed. "Kill me! Kill me! Please!"

But the war party turned their backs. The man continued to
scream until the pain and exhaustion overtook him. Still alive, he
lay back and moaned, occasionally trying to wipe the blood out of
his eyes with his mangled arm.

By now the other members of the man's party were all dead.
Scalps were being stolen from their heads along with what weap-
ons they carried, many of which were locked in the grip of death.
Whatever might be useful, easy to trade, and easy to carry would be

taken. A few trinkets, such as a chain, a pocket watch, or even shiny buttons, would be taken as souvenirs of the raid for the warriors or one day given to their families as gifts. More likely, the pieces would be gambled with and lost and won.

The horses that had not been shot or injured had their saddles loosened then were tied in a line. The first horse was bundled up with what supplies the hunters had carried. It and the others, along with all the tack, would be sold or traded to the Spaniards. Horses that were injured in the fighting were unsaddled and had their bridles removed. They were left to wander and survive or die at the discretion of the Spirit who looked over all things.

The group lingered over the tasks. The stealing was done at leisure and there was no bickering over the items taken from the dead. Over the course of the next several days and weeks, thanks to gambling around a dying fire pit, most of the items taken after the killings would trade hands several times. This was understood, so any piece that sparked an interest in one eye would be duly noted as to who carried it away from the bloody scene that had been the hunting party. When the gambling reached a fever pitch, the piece would be asked for or emerge of its own accord. So it was that buttons and coins, buckles and papers, knives and even a small spyglass entered into the Cherokee economy.

It was several hours before Dragon and Totsuhwa made any move to leave. Totsuhwa had cleaned his knife and war club, but he never again looked in the direction of the man who still, hours later, unwillingly clung to life. Dragon had rested beneath a tree and consigned his warriors to the tasks and pleasures. When a scalp was offered to him he waved it away bestowing it on the bearer. The brave yelped happily knowing the hair would fetch a price from the Spaniards.

When the jobs were completed and the bodies stripped of anything of value, the horses were sent for. On their arrival, the Cherokee horses whinnied at the fresh animals. When they passed close, a blur of kicking feet or a flash of teeth demonstrated the disdain the animals felt for the unusual scent of their brethren. It was as though each band of horses were mimicking the attitude of their owners, but unlike their riders, when the horses had moved together for a while their smells mingled and nearly all animosity dissipated. The riders would never be that forgiving. As Tsi'yugunsini led the group away, Totsuhwa's battered victim still struggled agonizingly for death.

At the same time Dragon's raid had begun on the hunting party, another attack, equal or surpassing in its brutality was commencing two days ride to the southeast. Colonel John Sevier and a rag-tag group of misfits and mercenaries had, with the help of Creek scouts, located a small Cherokee village. All told, the inhabitants numbered about thirty with only a few men of fighting age. When Sevier rode out of the burning village several hours later, the dead Cherokee also numbered about thirty. No one was left to tell the story of the massacre firsthand, but the footprints scattered throughout the smoky embers of the camp spoke volumes. The horses' hoof prints showed metal horseshoes and the riders, running through the lodges with firebrands or rifles, had worn heeled boots. These were white men and white men's horses.

Sevier's renegades numbered nearly seventy. They banded together when Sevier commanded and rode hard until the deeds were done. Then they went back to their homes, barrooms, and brothels carrying the black mementos of their killings dangling from their belts. On this day they would net many scalps, though several would have to be tied together to make one of adult size.

Unscrupulous traders were known to split the scalps of warriors and then claim they were the result of two separate kills. This occasional practice of halving made the trophies small, so when a child-sized scalp was placed on the trading block it was viewed with much suspicion. If it were sold or bounty collected honestly as a child's, it brought less money but with no more disdain at having been wrenched from the head of a child than an adult.

One of those Cherokee children was hanging from the crook of Sevier's elbow as the colonel tightened his chokehold and lifted the four-year-old off the ground. Little hands and fingernails clutched at his jacket sleeve. The rail-thin little girl was so light that when Sevier spun around, the child's body sailed out like a thin leafy branch in a brisk wind. He laughed over the screams of the girl's mother who was being dragged into a nearby lodge. The girl could not breathe so she uttered no sounds, but tears were able to break from her eyes before being whipped from her cheeks by the violent spinning.

Sevier stopped as roughly as he'd begun and the skinny body flapped from his arm like a flag in a dying breeze. The screams from the lodge were silenced just as quickly while around the village sporadic gunfire and the crackling of growing flames continued. Occasional cries from women splayed on the grass or dirt next to their dead husbands and children came and went as the mercenaries raped their way to murder. Stripped of their last thread of respect and void of any further use, the battered women were strangled, stabbed, and shot until the last of them, once a pretty wife and doting mother but now unrecognizable following the effects of a dozen men, was scalped as she lay nearly naked, covered with dirt and blood. Her body convulsed against the pain and her face scraped the ground. Pieces of torn-up grass stuck to her thighs, held in place by the sweat of others and her own blood. She continued to shake as the blood seeped from her head but no mercy came to touch her until it came disguised as Death.

Sevier heard the quieting of the camp around him. "Any left?" he asked loudly.

"Not a soul," came a reply.

"Not a soul," Sevier said to himself and the dangling child. "Never was a soul in this godforsaken place. Indians don't have souls.

"Do you?" he said to the little girl in the chokehold. "You're just like animals — dogs and pigs."

As he spoke a few of his men gathered. They looked at each other and laughed at their commander's words.

"They're animals!" Sevier laughed loudly as he again flung the girl around.

"That one you got there's a touch young, John. Might fetch a dollar on the block. Make a nice belly warmer in a few years though."

As the group laughed Sevier tightened his hold and the child's face reddened deeply. Spots of red broke the surface of her eyes as blood pushed to the surface. Her tiny fingers and nails clawed again at Sevier's coat sleeve but accomplished nothing. While her bare feet twitched in the air, Sevier grabbed his own fist and crushed his arm around the child's throat. In a few seconds the lithe girl relaxed into unconsciousness and as the others stared, Sevier squeezed harder, sending the youngster to the Darkening Land.

Abruptly, Sevier released his grip entirely and the girl's body fell to the dirt by his feet.

"Damn, John! You are one son of a bitch. That was a little one, that was!"

Sevier nudged the tiny corpse with the toe of his boot. "Nits make lice, my friends. Don't forget that. Best to kill them when they're small. It's easier. They don't have time to make trouble or make others like themselves. Yes, men, nits make lice. That's all there is to it. Let's go."

The men cinched up their pants, tied down the scalps and rode away as though they'd done nothing worse than butcher a hog. A straggler in the group, scurrying around the burning lodges for keepsakes and booty, came upon Sevier's dead girl. He nudged her as Sevier had before. When death prevented a reply he yanked his knife from its sheath and crudely lifted the fine black hair from the little head. With the final cut, the body fell back to the ground in a puff of dust. The treasure hunter raised the scalp as though he had claimed a prize following a valiant battle then looked around and noticed he was alone with thirty butchered corpses.

He scrambled to his horse, but the quickness of his feet frightened the animal and it tried to pull away. The man looked over his shoulder at the dead scattered around the burning village and felt nothing but cold from the growing fires. The horse attempted to rear and the butcher lunged for the horn of his saddle. The bloody scalp in his hand prevented a solid grip and his fingers slipped. The reins were now wet and sticky with the girl's blood and they slipped easily through the man's fingers. He leaped after the horse but only served to scare it more. With a jumping spin the horse wheeled on its hind legs and bolted from the village after the others. The man, still clutching the tiny scalp, fresh sweat streaming down his face, sprinted after it, leaving heeled boot prints on the dusty ground of the camp turned slaughterhouse.

Dragon and Totsuhwa took their band to southwest. The new horses captured in the raid on the hunting party held skirmishes of less and less ferocity with the Indian ponies until the walk became quiet. When a temporary camp had been established, the warriors' excitement with the day and their own massacre of the soldiers and hunters grew along with the fire.

Increasing numbers of dead logs were tossed upon one another until the cooking fire resembled an inferno. Victory yells and yelps sang out in earnest as the warriors danced. They stomped their feet and displayed the trophies from the day. As sparks and floating embers lit the dark sky, the men kicked, spun, and whirled around the fire. They waved the soldiers' scalps at the moon and shook the confiscated weapons in the air in thanks to the Spirit.

Dragon and Totsuhwa sat outside the ring of dancers and watched. Like their warriors, they too were very pleased with the fight, the petulant captured horses, the scalps, and most of all the deaths of the white men. The guns they'd taken from the dead hands would be that many less to fire upon Cherokee villages and the men themselves would be that many feet that would never walk on ground the Creator had not meant for them. Their stores would now nourish Indian bellies and those waiting for the hunting party's return would go hungry. Ahwi would wait in the forest for Cherokee arrows as it was meant to be. It had been a good day.

"Will you dance, my son?" Tsi'yugunsini asked his second.

"No, Father."

"We have reason to celebrate."

"We do."

"And yet?"

"I will not dance so I may grieve for the woman with the Three Sisters in her hair."

"It is right for you to do so."

The pair sat and watched the growing jubilation before them. Each was drawn to the fire. Their eyes locked on the dancing flames behind and about the dancing men. Tsi'yugunsini breathed deeply and brought his son's attention to him.

"Are you resting well, Father?"

"Yes. You have learned the lessons well. Your medicines are powerful. Ama Giga is smiling and proud."

"She was a wise woman."

"She was," Dragon said rather abruptly as he reached into his bedroll and produced his pipe. "And so I will honor her and this day with a smoke."

Totsuhwa smiled and returned his attention to the fire.

As Tsi'yugunsini prepared his pipe he spoke casually, looking up at the dancers and the flames from time to time. "The fire is a gift to us, Totsuhwa. The Spirit gave us the fire to keep us warm, to cook our food, to burn the fields to make the Sisters grow. In the fire I see a reminder of the Spirit. He loves the Tsalagi people. Our dance is to honor the Spirit, the Creator of all life."

"Yes, Father."

"I have heard the white men talk. They see fire and think of a demon. Why is that, my shaman?"

Totsuhwa thought only a moment. He had heard the stories before from Ama Giga and white traders. "They believe if you are a bad man, when you die you go to a bad village. It is a place where fire burns always and scorches the flesh of those who must live there. They are burned yet do not die. They are only tortured."

"That is a bad place."

"It is only a story told to make white children obey their mothers."

"Probably so," Dragon grunted.

"That is why the whites do not see glory in dancing with the fire. We honor our Creator. They see it as honoring this burning place of theirs."

"They understand nothing."

"They are a different people, Father. They do not understand Tsalagi ways."

"They are ignorant and foolish."

"They are. They take always and give back never. The Spirit will call them to answer one day for their misuse of His gifts."

"It is my prayer to the Spirit that He does this soon, while there are Tsalagi left to see it."

"The Tsalagi people will always be here, Father. We are caretakers of the Spirit's creation and He has made us a strong people. We will not be driven out."

Dragon puffed his pipe to life then handed it to his son. When Totsuhwa reached for it Dragon clasped his hands. "Totsuhwa, will you make an oath to me - a solemn promise to an old man?"

"Yes, but you are not—"

"You will not leave our land. Don't let them drive you from the mountains and valleys given us. In the fire the Spirit has shown me many things. Beyond our mountains is the Darkening Land of our people. Beyond our mountains is the death of our nation. Tell me you will not leave our mountains. Never let anything take your steps onto the flat land to the West, toward the Darkening Land. As long as one Tsalagi who has your spirit remains on the land of our ancestors, the spirit of our people will live through that one. Will you do this for me? Will you not leave our land?"

Totsuhwa stared hard at his father and gripped the hand that covered his. "This thing I will do."

"Good. Good. Thank you, shaman. Should the Spirit call me I can sleep in peace."

Totsuhwa held the pipe now and drew on it. He waved the smoke from the bowl across his face with his hand. The smell was rich and warm. He breathed deeply and listened to the cries of the dancers. He puffed several times then handed the pipe back to Tsi'yugunsini. He stood and felt for the black hair hanging from his belt.

"I am returning this woman to the earth."

"As it should be," Dragon said as he drew on his pipe before laying it aside. "While you take this woman to the Spirit, I will dance for her and others like her."

Totsuhwa moved away from the fire pit and disappeared into the woods. He moved deep into the trees carrying the scalp with the seeds tied in it and also his medicine pouch. Dragon meanwhile, began dancing, easily at first but increasing in speed and intensity every few minutes with the encouragement of his men.

Far away from the roaring light of the fire and the noise and commotion of the dancers, Totsuhwa drifted across the forest floor.

He used the moon and his sharp eyes to find a peaceful spot in a small clearing. The opening allowed the moonlight to broach the treetops and brighten the ground at the shaman's feet. He turned and looked up at the glowing disc and followed its light back to the earth. With tremendous care he knelt down and tugged away the grass and its roots and formed a small divot. Totsuhwa set the sod to the side and continued to dig out a small hole. In Totsuhwa's hands a stubborn rock became a small pick and transformed itself from obstruction to tool before being placed alongside the grass to await its return to the miniscule grave.

He pulled a scrap of deerskin slightly larger than his hand from his pouch and spread it out near the hole. Using both hands for gentleness, he eased the woman's scalp from his waist and slipped it onto the deerskin. Then his hands returned to the pouch and retrieved a mixture of herbs and seeds from within. He placed these on the deerskin shroud and then folded the hide over itself.

A prayer escaped his lips as Totsuhwa moved the deerskin and its precious contents into the ground. The prayers continued as the loose earth was replaced along with the stone pick and finally the sod. When the job was done, the shaman ran his fingers through the grass to blend it back in with its surroundings. The light from the moon could do little to discern where the grave was. This was how Totsuhwa wished it to be. But while the young Cherokee leader lingered at considerable length in a quiet song over the site, the ferocity of Dragon's dance began to rival his warriors'.

Tsi'yugunsini's knees pumped up and down - high to his bent chest, his head bowed low to the ground and his arms waving around him like the wings of a soaring eagle. The entire entourage of dancers swayed in a line like a writhing serpent as they weaved their way around the fire. The yells were sporadic, crested above and below by songs and prayers of thankfulness to the Spirit for His intervention during the raid. Weapons were again held aloft in muscled hands as chants filtered up around them and on to the heavens. The prayers thanked the Creator's hands that had guided their bullets and arrows and thanked Him for protecting each man under Dragon's command. Driving the prayers was the seemingly fitful dance that matured into a frenzy of thanksgiving.

The fire and the Spirit within bathed their sweating bodies in its changing light as an acknowledgment for their gratitude.

The pitch and timing of the singing and the steps rose and fell like waves against a shore. In the ebb of the boisterous but prayerful celebration the men caught their breath and brushed the sweat from their eyes. Though the spring night was cooling, the fire and exertion, coupled with the increasing duration of the dancing petition, drove all the warriors to exhaustion. After a momentary slowing of feet and calming of chants, the flow came upon the men once more and their fervor again approached a pinnacle an outsider might have viewed as madness.

The night embraced the feverish dancers and the quiet shaman still on his knees in the forest. It passed silently as it listened to the soulful prayers of one man and the triumphant songs of others. Totsuhwa asked the Spirit and Ama Giga to welcome the woman who had braided the Three Sisters into her hair. He lobbied his grandmother to find the woman and show her the way to the Darkening Land. Totsuhwa did not wish her spirit to be left wandering, shocked by her early and violent death into not understanding the way. His appeals were long and mournful as the night eavesdropped around him.

The fire snapped at the feet of Tsi'yugunsini and the ground recoiled with his stomp, but the night came only so close to the dancers, held back by the light of the flames. The darkness understood it would eventually win out as the fire and the dancers tired, but tonight it would spend considerable effort in the waiting as the warriors' festive mood carried them to the early hours of the morning.

The earth beneath Totsuhwa had given up the dampness in its grasses to the shaman's knees. He stood and waited for his body to shake off the stiffness wrought on by the hours he had labored for the woman of the Three Sisters. When the ache left him he returned to the camp. There he found the fire dying, the night enjoying its anticipated victory, and Tsi'yugunsini breathing rapidly, lying on his bedroll. Rather than peer down at his chief, he knelt and felt again the stiffness that had secretly remained in his legs.

"Your festival has lasted long, Father."

"As it should. This was a good day for the Tsalagi. Guns and horses have exchanged their loyalties today." The chief smiled through his sweat-covered face. "The Spirit has shown them their errors..." His voice and smile trailed off.

"You have danced much, my Father. Now you will rest."

"I will rest, e-tsi, Mother," and he found another brief smile for his doting son. There was a quiet between the two men for a time. He was loathe to ask but protected by the son before him, Dragon made a request of the medicine man.

"Shaman? Would you have your roots for me? I am afraid my dancing has not pleased the Spirit. He sits on my chest and makes it hard to breathe."

Totsuhwa immediately reached for his bag. He produced a few tubers and placed them on the blanket. "These will lift the Spirit. I will make some drink as well." Before the shaman could rise, Dragon touched his leg and stopped him. It was a moment before he spoke.

"When the whites first came and the people began marking the white leaves to give away the land, there came great sickness among our people. The Spirit brought the sickness to punish the people for betraying the gift the Creator had given." Dragon's finger crept up and touched the pockmarks on his own cheeks. "The evil spirit left these tracks on me so he would remember he could not kill me." Dragon's eyes eased shut and he smiled. "I have told this story."

He took a shallow breath and the smile faded as before. "This pain in me, the weakness has come many times since the last snows. Tonight it is strong. I believe I have offended the Spirit, and He has put this pain in my chest." The powerful chief slowly opened his eyes. "Tell me, Totsuhwa, you are a wise priest of the Tsalagi people — what is it I have done?"

"Nothing, my chief. You have done nothing. You are a hero to your people. Tomorrow you will lead us and for many seasons to come. You will—"

Dragon's fingers moved from his own face to his son's lips. "Shhh... Do not let the rabbit sneak back into your mind, my son. Listen for the Spirit with the panther's ears. Let the rabbit play with the children you will one day father. Tell me what the Spirit whispers to you. For me, I hear Him call. His voice is in the pain that walks through my shoulder and down my arm." Dragon breathed deeply and painfully. "If He wants me, I will go. If I am to be punished, I will accept the punishment."

Totsuhwa collected himself in the eyes of his father. He spoke clearly and slowly, mindful of the words and the teachings behind them. Over them all were the words of the Spirit, channeled through the shaman. "There has been no wrong committed in your heart."

The pause that followed lasted over a minute.

"I have killed many, many times," Tsi'yugunsini said.

"You have protected your people and the land and sought to recoup with death for the lives of Tsalagi men, women, and children lost to the swords and bullets of our enemies."

"So the Spirit does not seek to punish me?"

"No," Totsuhwa said as he picked up a root and pressed it into Dragon's tired hand. "If it is time for you to walk to the West, it is to go accept the reward for all you have done for our people."

"This you know to be true?"

"It is true."

"You have spoken with the Spirit of this?"

"I have."

"You have said it then. I can accept the fate that comes to me." Tsi'yugunsini grimaced, breathed sharply, and then held it for a moment or more. When he breathed again he pressed the plant between his lips and began to rub his arm.

"Are you cold, Father?"

"No. The Spirit is calling."

Totsuhwa began to rise again and placed his hand on his father's. "I will make the drink."

Dragon gripped his son's sleeve as tightly as he could and held him down. "Remember your words to me, Totsuhwa. Remember your pledge. One must remain. Do not leave our land. Not for a single breathe of time. If you do, the people and the land will be lost."

"I will not leave it, Father. A-waninski. I have spoken."

Tsi'yugunsini released his grip and replaced it with a gentle pat. He nodded his head as a thank you as Totsuhwa moved away to prepare the mixture that would ease his father's pain.

The preparation was the same as before but was slowed some by the night, which was winning its battle with the drowsy fire. Yet the fire was awake enough to heat the small clay basin and its elixir. Totsuhwa waited for it and in the waiting sought answers for his chief and his people in the Spirit of the calming fire. He saw that the fight against the whites would not continue many more seasons. The enemy was strong and plentiful. What they lacked in compassion for the land and knowledge, they sought to overcome with voluminous numbers.

The Spirit of the once-roaring inferno now crackled softly in Totsuhwa's ear that the camps of the Spaniards would wane and the Cherokee would be alone again to face the leviathan intruder. The resting blaze also permitted the shaman to envision people in the flames, each walking toward the Darkening Land to the West. And he dreamed there were cries of dying children in the snapping embers.

Totsuhwa literally shook his head at the visions in an attempt to clarify them and show them to be something other than what they were. It was possible that he sought simply to drive them from his mind. Though he had always embraced the revelations granted by the smoke and fire, tonight he secretly hoped he was seeing things brought on by the late hour and the weariness of a long, battle-tried, and blood-soaked day. When Tsi'yugunsini had drank his special tea and strength had returned to his body, Totsuhwa would ask him about the things the Spirit had just shared with him. Between the two of them they would understand better and decide the meaning of the manifestations for the people.

The brew was warm. The fire had completed its last task before surrendering to the hour. Totsuhwa pulled his hand up into the sleeve of his rough shirt and gripped the small pot with deerskin-covered fingers. He carried it to his chief slowly and carefully, moving it in a tiny circle to stir the contents. When he got to his adoptive father, Totsuhwa touched his own lips to the top of the clay and sipped at the tea to check it. It was hot but not unbearably so.

He blew across the top of the mixture and the steam melted away in the dark night. Then he crouched again beside the resting chief.

"Father. This will ease the burden."

The great Dragon drank the warm medicine but did not answer.

The morning sun had breached the faraway horizon and was beginning its time-worn ascent over Shaconage (Sha-con-a-gee), the Land of Blue Smoke, the Cherokee mountains. In the valleys the mist that gave the mountains their name was placidly rolling. Totsuhwa had remained by his father's bed throughout what remained of the night. By the time the sleeping warriors, scattered around the camp where they had fallen from their dance, began to stir in earnest, the sun was well above the mountains. The previous day's battle and late night dancing had drained them all and they had each pulled their blankets over their heads to ward off the sun of the new day. Those who thought at all believed Dragon must have done the same, as he had not roused them from their temporary beds. But now in their rising, they came to realize something was wrong.

Totsuhwa was crouching beside their chief. This was not unusual, but from his mouth was coming the soft yet unmistakable tones of a requiem for the dead. A few warriors, still clouded by their dancing and reverie, had staggered off to urinate before stumbling back into the camp. Only then did they hear the gentle lament streaming from the shaman. Now each follower of Tsi'yugunsini knew he was dead.

The first tears on Totsuhwa's cheeks had dried several hours before. He had long ago brushed away the itch they had left in their drying tracks. From the onset he had sung the songs that would alert those in the Darkening Land of the Dead that Tsi'yugunsini was coming. The songs were also meant to tell the Creator that a warrior who had served Him well was crossing over to the other world. Scattered through the songs were chants of encouragement to his father to walk on with courage and pride in his step.

All the excitement and thrill of the day and night before was gone from the faces of the men who gathered around their chief's body. Some sang with Totsuhwa while others quietly crouched nearby. When the last refrain was lofted heavenward, Totsuhwa stood and directed the affairs of the funeral.

Four men began digging nearby. The hole would be about five feet deep and nearly round, perhaps only two feet across. It would be opened at one side to allow for the digging itself and the placing of the body. The preparation of the burial chamber was time-consuming and difficult. Their hands, sharpened sticks, knives, and rocks were the only tools. Before it was completed, every member of the band would have dirt from the grave embedded under his fingernails.

The shadows of the day were growing long again before the crypt was ready. Totsuhwa had gone to the woods and collected strips of tender birch bark and a fistful of maple twigs, which he had placed along with small piles of corn and tobacco carefully resting on large leaves near the gravesite. He had also gently rolled Dragon's body onto its side and pushed his knees up to his chest. The chief's arms were folded in front of his knees and he was completely covered with a deerskin.

Once the time for interment had come, stiffness had also come to the Dragon's corpse. Four men lifted his body as Totsuhwa draped and tucked the deer hide around him. Tsi'yugunsini was carried to the grave and very gently eased into it so his body sat upright with his legs and arms folded in front of him. He faced west into the setting sun. The warriors stepped back slightly and made room for the shaman.

Totsuhwa squatted by the tomb, uncovered Dragon's head from the deerskin and prepared a small fire of the birch and maple. As he quoted chants learned from Ama Giga, he sprinkled tobacco on the tiny flames. The hymns attached themselves to the light smoke from the fire and rode up to the heavens carrying Tsi'yugunsini's spirit on their wings. The incantations were lengthy — commensurate with the rank of such a powerful chief. In the moments between the narration, Dragon's bow and quiver were placed in the grave with him along with his pipe and his few personal effects.

An underling placed a few more twigs on the small funeral pyre as Totsuhwa wrapped up the corn in its leaf. "This will feed you on your journey," he said as he carefully placed the tiny package in the grave. He did the same with the tobacco as he said softly, "For your pipe."

Finally, Totsuhwa pulled the deerskin back over his father. "When the Spirit greets you, He will see ahwi's skin across your back and know that you are Tsalagi. Then He will welcome you for He will know you for what you are, for who you are."

All that remained beside the tomb was the dying fire and Dragon's chief's blanket. Totsuhwa stood slowly and picked up the blanket as he rose. Then he reached into his medicine pouch and produced the flint arrowhead he had taken from the deer the Dragon had killed with him long ago. He slowly weighed the mantle in one extended hand while the other vigorously rubbed the old arrowhead. He held both talismans as he peered down at his father.

"Thank you, Tsi'yugunsini. For these gifts and all the other gifts you have given me..." His voice cracked only a fraction but he felt it giving way beneath the weight of his father's death. A hard swallow followed, and Totsuhwa's black eyes turned fierce and skirted across the faces of those nearest him. Like scolded children, every warrior dropped his face away from the man who was fighting back tears. Each one turned away from the funeral and moved to the far reaches of the camp or tended the horses or just vanished into the forest to contemplate their own loss while their new leader dealt privately with his.

"When no mother was there, you took me into your family. When I had no father, you schooled me. The seeds of Ama Giga, you tended..." Tears began to run from the corners of his eyes as Totsuhwa remembered all those he had loved and lost.

"I would like to have these days again, Father. But I would have them without the battles. I enjoyed being by your side in each one. It was there that I saw your triumphs over many enemies and it was there that I learned the ways of a warrior, a chief, and a man. But, my Father, I would have enjoyed more the quiet days to come when we would have hunted together, searched the mountains and land together, sang and smoked as one. These are days taken from me now. They are days taken from the grandchildren you have yet to know."

The tears ran unabated now and Totsuhwa lifted his face to the sky to slow them, but only their direction changed and they ran in a constant stream to his black hair. He felt them move deeper through his scalp and let them run out their course. Though the tears were unstoppable, he did manage to hold back the crying gasps for breath his lungs screamed out for.

"The Spirit has called and like a true Tsalagi warrior, you have listened. Your pain is silent now. No more will the white man hunt your steps and haunt your dreams. Now in the West you will know things that have been and things yet to come. Whisper to me, Tsi'yugunsini. Whisper to me in my sleep and in my wakening. Tell me the things I need to know to help our people. Live on through me and help me be a better shaman, a better man."

The proud head came forward until the chin rested sadly on the strong chest. "There was love between us, my Father. Men such as we do not speak of such things to one another, but I say these words now. I love you, Tsi'yugunsini. I should have said these words to your ears before they slept. The chance is lost. Please hear me. I love you. I love you."

Totsuhwa held a silent vigil over the grave for some time. He slipped down and sat in the style of his father as he sang again, whispered again, and cried again. Behind him, the warriors tried to busy themselves doing nothing while each and every one snuck a peek at Totsuhwa every few minutes. At long last, a young brave approached the grave reverently. When he was acknowledged by the slight turn of his shaman's head he asked if they should break the camp.

"No," Totsuhwa said softly. "We will stay in this place to celebrate and mourn Tsi'yugunsini's walk to the Darkening Land of the Dead. When his scent no longer lingers on the ground we will find the Spaniards."

"Yes, Totsuhwa."

The young man hesitated but did not stumble over his next words. "Do you wish us to cover Chief Tsi'yugunsini?"

Now it was Totsuhwa who hesitated. "Yes," he said after several moments. And he turned away.

Throughout the next several days the things that passed as conversation were glances, grunts, and nods of the head. A gloom had settled over the wild band and stretched from the sun's rise to its setting. The men were not anxious to leave the grave and held on longer than was necessary or customary. Each knew that Tsi'yugunsini was not in the ground, but rather that he had walked on to the land of the dead. Yet still they lingered, feeling more attachment to the material body than the spiritual one. Even Totsuhwa loitered. And he might have stayed even longer had he not thought the horses were staring at him one morning, wonder on their long faces as to why they had remained tied and hobbled in one place for so long. Only after looking hard in the faces of the animals did Totsuhwa quietly direct his men to break the camp. Certainly it was time and long since in keeping with their ways and methods of comings and goings. The warriors had the wondering horses loaded and were on their backs in the few minutes it took their new chief to say goodbye again to their old one.

The ride west to the Spaniards was accomplished in decreasing degrees of silence. Each step of the horses, each measured stride, placed an increasing distance between the men and Tsi'yugunsini's grave. With the gap came the beginnings of an expected detachment that would permit the warriors to again concentrate on life unhampered by the thoughts of death. Until Dragon's death had run its course through their minds, made its remembering mark and settled into the far reaches, the men were not safe. Once time had worked its magic, the memories could be recalled on quiet nights around ceremonial fires when stories of great chiefs were relayed to children. For Totsuhwa the time would be measured in years. All the while, loneliness and sadness caused brittle fissures to open in his mind.

Stripped by Dragon of the ability to concentrate, he lumbered along on his horse oblivious at times to the world around him. The impact was so marked it clouded his mind and judgment. While the other raiders were drawn away from the death by the passing of mountain ranges, Totsuhwa was caught so deeply in its web it would take stumbling into the camp of the Spaniards to rouse him. Even then, the awakening would not be complete.

Those warriors who had traveled to the Spaniards before recognized immediately that something about the Spanish encampment was different. In his mourning, Totsuhwa did not see it at first but came upon it gradually as he spoke with a man he had dealt with in the company of Dragon many times before.

"Where's the Dragon?" the Spanish soldier asked as he looked through the deep tan colored faces around him, all still on their horses.

Totsuhwa did not balk. "He waits in the hills." It was not a lie. "What for?"

"The bounty on his head is strong. I am here to smell the cheese."

The soldier laughed. "Go on now, Totsuhwa! We've supported you and Dragon for years now. Our people are friends." He motioned around the camp with both hands. "There's no trap here. Send one of your riders up to get Dragon. It's important that we talk. Much has happened."

Totsuhwa was not ready to have word of Dragon's death spread through the white world. He had long been aware that the title they had hung on the great chief had brought him much renown and struck fear in white hearts. Having the white soldiers and men like Sevier pursuing a literal ghost would be good for a while longer. It would tax their resources. More importantly, it would keep them awake at night and reaching for their rifles when the wolves howled.

Totsuhwa smiled to himself. For most white settlers, the dark of night was not a necessary element in their fear of the Dragon. When an unseen bird chirped harmlessly under the sun, grizzled hunters and frontiersmen snatched their rifles, hearing instead Dragon and a raiding party just beyond the trees ready to spring and lift their hair with two quick cuts. Now Totsuhwa's smile spilled out onto his face.

"You and I will talk. You can tell me what has happened."

The soldier hardly noticed the first smile to cross Totsuhwa's face in several weeks. He merely shrugged his shoulders and turned to lead the way to a pitched tent. "Suit yourself."

When Totsuhwa dismounted and followed the soldier, the rest of the band slipped from their horses as well. They stretched a tie line and fastened all their ponies to it then began setting about to find the best trades they could for the scalps and trinkets from their conquests. All the while they were vigilant, taking stock of the Spanish camp that seemed less active than normal.

In the tent Totsuhwa and his host began traversing the details of recent events. "Well, amigo, I tell you. Spain and the United States have come to terms."

"A treaty?"

"Yes, a treaty. There are no more disputes over territory and boundaries. Everything's been settled. There's no more war between them and us. Same is true for British and French, from what I hear."

"They will break any treaty they sign," Totsuhwa said resolutely.

"Maybe. Maybe not. It's not for me to say. All I have are my orders. We are to stop all engagements against the United States. And that includes supplying the Cherokee."

"The treaty will not bind them. They only know lies. You should strike them first while they gloat and plan their assaults against you."

"I can't do that, Totsuhwa. You know that."

"Even now I say they are moving against you."

"Listen a minute. What I am going to say isn't meant to be taken personally. I think it's just a fact of life. I know they have made and broken a number of treaties with your people. But... I don't think that will happen with us."

The soldier looked at the open well-worn grassy floor of the tent and it fell to Totsuhwa to spur the rest of his ideas from him. "What gives this thought to you?"

The soldier's face came up but he talked softly, trying to lessen the sting of his words. "Because we are like them. We live as they live. We are white, not Indian, Totsuhwa. Because we are white."

The shaman immediately felt the impact of the words. There was a truth in them he could not deny. It was a moment more before he would react but when it came it was only a silent nodding of his head.

"Take what I've said to Dragging Canoe, amigo. He will understand. And tell him one thing more for me. He too should make peace with the United States."

"Tsi'yugunsini has tried to make such peace. He and his father before him. But there is no iron in the words of these white men or in the white man's talking leaves. We want to live in peace. It is the white man who pushes us, who lies and steals from us. When he feels guilty he puts together a treaty and asks us to put our marks on it. When we do, he is satisfied for a short time but it does not last."

The Spanish soldier lowered his head again. "I know. But I'm telling you as plainly as I can, if you don't seek a peace with them, they will hunt you down. They won't stop until all the Cherokee are dead."

Totsuhwa shook his head. "Yes, I see this. But I think it may be true whether we make a peace or not."

The two men sat quietly for a few more minutes. Totsuhwa rose first. "I am thankful for the trade you have given us in the past. And for the gunpowder. We have put it to good use," he said.

"I'm sure you have. One more thing. I can give you what supplies I can before you go but it is doubtful we will meet again. I am going back to Spain. Back to my home."

"That is a good thing for a man to do."

"Why don't you go home, Totsuhwa?"

The answer took its time making its way up the shaman's throat. "Perhaps I will."

When Totsuhwa emerged from the tent, his men had already learned the sad truth from what few soldiers remained at the site. The warriors had exchanged and bartered for what they could. Some were pleased but most were disappointed as the value of colonial scalps had taken a drastic downturn. Still, the Spaniard was good to his word and gave the men gunpowder, cap and ball, and a few blankets without charge. Totsuhwa thanked him again, shook his hand in the customary fashion of white people and rode into the trees, this time back to where the sun was born each day.

His braves spoke softly from horse to horse as the travelers stretched out in a winding line. Totsuhwa was at the lead, moving with no haste whatsoever. He was as uncertain of where to go as he was of what to do. In short order his leader, mentor, chief, and father had been taken from him along with the lifeline of munitions they had come to rely on. Totsuhwa could continue to fight the settlers without Tsi'yugunsini, but he could not fight, not for long, without the support of the Spaniards, especially with the British and French gone as well.

As the ride east grew into days, Totsuhwa weighed his choices and the probable outcomes. Most reflected death nearby. Perhaps the Spaniard was right. Perhaps he should go home. Unsure even where that might be, he quizzed his men as to their villages and found as many homes in as many directions as there were points on the white man's compass. Without fanfare, he dismissed the warriors. They would fight no more. They would go home.

Moving on alone, Totsuhwa continued east. He had not ridden by himself since he came to Tsi'yugunsini. He patted his horse's neck as a gentle thank you for the animal's company and began singing a quiet song of praise to the Spirit for keeping him alive to see this day.

After Totsuhwa had seen the moon come and go twice since leaving the Spaniards, Chief James Vann, carrying the white name of his father but the lineage of his Cherokee mother, began another journey with a band of armed warriors. One of Totsuhwa's men had met Chief Vann and his company in the mountains of the south as he had been making his way home. He shared the news of Tsi'yugunsini's death. The troupe stopped and sang songs for the great chief and danced around a monstrous fire, not unlike the one on Dragon's last night, as they praised his courage and strength and urged his spirit westward.

Unlike Totsuhwa, who continued to meander to the northeast alone, Chief Vann rode with several attendants in keeping with his rank. He had parlayed his white father's connections into thriving businesses of trade and ferry boats throughout the nation but remained true to the upbringing at the hands of his mother. As such, his fair treatment, fair prices, and Cherokee blood combined with the white world to make him not only wealthy by any standard but, more importantly, respected and trusted by the people. Today he rode with a war party — an extension of Tsi'yugunsini's Chickamauga Cherokee renegades. Their intent was to meet others and form a massive band that would attack the Western settlements. In another day they were joined by Doublehead and his own band of raiders.

The members of Doublehead's pack mixed easily with those who rode with Chief Vann. The news of Dragon's death was shared as they rode along in solemn silence, but within a few days each group spoke and laughed as they exchanged insults. Doublehead ignored everyone except Vann. He rode up too close to him, and his horse bumped the younger, more prosperous chief.

"O-si-yo. Hello, Chief James Vann."

"Doublehead," Vann said as he pushed the horse away with his foot. "Your horse does not mind you."

"Perhaps he does," Doublehead said with a laugh as he reined his horse hard into Vann again.

Two warriors rode quickly toward the jostling horse, but Vann held out his hand and stopped them.

"Do not be troubled, brothers. Doublehead's horse is just a fool. He has learned much from his master."

The men laughed as Vann pushed away the horse yet again. But the laughter quickly perished under the harsh eyes of Doublehead.

"You mock me in front of the people," he said. "You have been too long from battle to remember the taste of blood in your mouth."

Vann all but ignored him. "You are an old man. You are a shadow of Tsi'yugunsini. I think often of him. The people will speak of him forever. You, they have forgotten already."

Another snicker ran through the group and Doublehead turned quickly to confront the transgressors. Unrewarded, he spun back to Vann.

"Chief James Vann," Doublehead said matter-of-factly as his tone suddenly changed. "When you have a son beside you — another half-breed — you will make him a farmer of pigs, like you?"

"Go in peace, Doublehead, but leave us. Ride on another path. Take those foolish enough to follow you into another valley."

"A half-breed who raises pigs does not tell great warriors to come and go."

"We are different men, Doublehead. Both with Tsalagi blood, but your spirit is twisted." At that, Vann urged his horse ahead and away from his tormenter.

"My spirit is twisted, you say, Vann?" Doublehead shouted after him as he reined in his mount. "You would have me leave and divide our force. You are no warrior. You are no chief. You are the twisted one!"

Chief Vann didn't look back but that night around the fire the challenge wasn't far from his mind.

As the burning logs popped and snapped, punctuation for his words, Vann crouched on the ground and laid out the next day's plan. "The scouts tell me that in a day's ride, when the sun is highest, we will come to a white settlement. We will show ourselves and they will hide in the cabins. Then we will conceal ourselves, sheltered from their guns. We will negotiate their surrender. No harm will come to them if they do so. When they come out we will send them back to the east and burn the cabins to the ground."

Several of the men, from Vann and Doublehead's bands, exchanged glances. Before their eyes stopped moving, Doublehead was on his feet. "No scalps?"

"No," Vann said. "There is no need. That is only a cry for more soldiers. Better to have the land than beg for more enemy."

"You said my spirit is twisted. Your mind is twisted! You will have them by the throat and release them so they can come back. Kill them all. We will trade the scalps for powder and shot."

"Trade with who? The British are defeated and have moved across the water. The French have retreated north into the snow country. And the Spaniards have gone home. No, we do it this way."

"Tsi'yugunsini would spare no lives."

"That is true, Doublehead, but I have asked the Spirit for guidance on these things each night. With our supplies low and our allies gone, we are not to invite the soldiers with our raids. Burning their cabins and pushing them east will do."

"Not for me."

"You have decided to ride with me, my old friend, and you will follow."

"Are you sick with the fever, Vann? The men you free, they will be back before a moon has passed and you will fight them to the death. Many of our men may die. Warriors we cannot spare to lose."

"We will lose more if the soldiers come. We burn the settlements. That is all."

"No slaves?"

"No. We protect the land. That is enough."

"Your father's blood shows in you. This is white man's thinking. They will come back and kill our women and burn our crops. Our children will starve, Vann. We must kill them all and take their scalps for trade, wherever we can find it. Kill them. They have broken the treaty."

"Each treaty. I agree," Vann conceded.

"Then they all die for all the promises broken."

Chief Vann looked ahead stoically, instantly removed from the conversation. "They did keep one promise."

"None," Doublehead protested.

"No. One. They promised to take our land and they did."

There was a still minute before Doublehead confirmed his intent. "Yes, and for that they all die."

"No. They walk to the east. We put their homes to the torch and take their stock and supplies. No more. Awaninski."

Vann rose and walked away from the fire. His men followed him a short distance and began dropping to the ground to make their beds. Others lingered and looked to Doublehead for direction.

"When the cabins are reached, follow my war club with yours," Doublehead whispered. "These women may busy themselves with a stolen cow, but our knives will shine in the blood of our enemies."

Another day passed in relative calm. Throughout, the horses enforced their private hierarchy with snapping hooves and flashing teeth set on bare flanks as the warriors chided one another with verbal assaults and their own coarse fun. As the men rolled their blankets and unhobbled the horses the following morning, a single Cherokee rider appeared in the trees and rode up to Chief Vann, who squatted near the calm smokeless fire.

"In the forked valley. Two ranges south on the water," the rider said to Vann without pointing.

The chief nodded then asked a question with only his eyes and a slight tilt of his head. The answer was immediate.

"The rising sun sits on the mountain's shoulder behind the cabins and the Long Man."

"Good," Vann replied as he squinted into the early sun. "We will take our next meal by that water. Tell the others to prepare."

In quiet minutes all were packed and mounted. Vann and the reporting scout casually led the party away from the camp and on to the forked valley. All conversation dropped away before the cabin top appeared. Doublehead did not look at his conspirators. He had said all that needed saying. Rather than dismount and use stealth to their advantage, Chief Vann led the band to the edge of the river some distance from the cabin but in clear view. Men began slipping from their horses to take water, eyeing the building and grounds for signs of life.

The cabin was a simple four-walled log box, but large enough for several families staking a claim together before building their own homes nearby. There was no additional protective wall or buttress surrounding it. The sole window was a leather-hinged heavy shutter with a cross cut through it for maneuvering rifle barrels. The door was the same. The roof was bark and sod. The cabin was stark but functional and stout. Nearby was a crude fence of saplings bound to rough posts with leather straps. It made a rough corral. Inside it was a pair of oxen, two cows, a yearling steer, and three aging horses. All the animals were at the rail sniffing the air of the Cherokee horses and watching. The white eyes inside the house were watching too.

From their place by the river, the Cherokee couldn't hear the scrambling and frantic words inside the cabin. Five men, three women, and three children rechecked the door and window bindings as well as their rifles. In minutes, barrels poked through the windows and took aim on the Cherokee though they were beyond effective range.

Vann caught the movement at the windows but took little notice as he rode slowly into the nearby woods with three attendants. The quartet circled through the trees and dismounted a considerable distance from the cabin. They tied their horses up silently and moved toward the guns on foot. In a few minutes they were at the tree line. By the time they were in place, the main band had melted into the safety of the forest.

"IN THE CABIN!" Chief Vann yelled in halting English. "You are on Cherokee land by the treaties. You go!"

A quick rifle shot was the answer. The bullet snapped through the trees many yards away and high. Vann didn't flinch.

He shouldered his rifle as did his escorts — two to his left and one to his right. "The window," he directed to the two over his shoulder. "The door," he said to the other. "Follow with two arrows. Save your powder."

The four men took easy aim. The rifles cracked fractions of seconds apart. The wood of the window and door recoiled splinters as the bullets struck. Nearly before the wood chips hit the ground a hail of arrows began to strike. Four bit the door in rapid succession. Three cracked into the window shutter, while a single slightly errant bolt lodged in the wall of the cabin.

Inside, the women dove to the floor on top of the children while the men crouched and cringed along the interior front wall and listened to the thumps of the arrows. Frightened eyes darted around the single room over the dirt floor. Questions in their eyes and on hushed lips asked each other what to do and what would become of them. There were false words of strength for the benefit of the women and the children, and perhaps the men themselves, but it was clearly just bravado. The men sitting closest to one another along the wall whispered that they would all be scalped as certain as the sun would set. The crash of the arrowheads into the cabin and the reports of the Cherokee rifles still echoed, and their knocking on the house seemed to indicate over a hundred men waited outside and would be prepared to wait them out or rush the cabin as they saw fit.

The senior man in the group stood abruptly and moved to the door. "We have to try for terms."

"Terms? Terms of surrender? With these bloodthirsty savages? There'll be scant terms with these animals."

"Unlikely. They know we'd get a few of them. The Chickamauga Wars cost them a bunch of men. Did you hear that English? These are Cherokee, like as not. They don't have much fight left. This little band is trying to flex its muscle."

"By lifting our hair."

"Hush!" a woman cried out as she clutched two boys, each around five years old.

"Hush up like she says. We'll get outa here minus an axe and a metal pot or two."

"They'll take it all after we're outa the way!"

"Naw. This frontier has growed up a lot. Them fellas know if anything happens to us, the militia will be here in a month and burn this valley to the bare earth. We'll get out alright. The sooner the better."

Across the open glade there was no such urgency in Chief Vann's thoughts. He dropped to one knee and exchanged the bow in his hand for his rifle that rested against the tree he had used as a shield. Vann started to reload it slowly as his men mirrored him. "I wonder," he said calmly, "what does a man feel when, as warriors, two men shoot lead and arrows at each other in battle? It must make some tremble."

His men slowed until their movements were barely visible. The pair over his shoulder exchanged puzzled looks before one asked hesitantly, "Chief Vann. You have seen men in battles as we all have. What do you mean?"

"That I have seen a new thing today."

"Tell us so we can see too."

"Many times I have watched strong men whither like a vine that needs water as smoke from gunpowder fills the air. Fear of another man's bullet coming at them makes them shake and shoot into the ground or sky. But today I saw a piece of wood make a skillful hunter shake like a snake's tail."

"Where did you see this?"

Vann motioned to the cabin window and the single arrow lodged in the log wall next to it as he laughing looked at the man who had fired from his left.

"You missed the window! The wooden window scared you!"

Vann and the other two warriors laughed out loud and couldn't stop.

Inside the cabin, the settlers' faces tightened. "It's some kind of war cry..."

The warrior who had missed his mark stared intently and squinted to better see the errant arrow. "That is not my arrow. Mine are in the window wood."

Between rolls of laughter, Vann choked out an answer. "You lie as good as you shoot! I see your markings from here!" And the laughter grew louder.

Embarrassed and as though to redeem himself, the archer quickly finished loading his rifle, took fast but careful aim, and fired into the shutter of the window again. As before, he followed with two arrows in rapid succession, but this time each hit the window cleanly. Satisfied, he nodded at Vann and motioned to the cabin with his bow. The men just laughed harder.

The window under assault opened slightly, and half a white face peeked out through the arrows. "OUTSIDE THERE! We're leavin'. Don't shoot!"

Chief Vann immediately broke from his laughter. He made a snap hand gesture and one of the men darted into the trees to bring up the rest of the band.

The cabin door cracked open. "Hello! I'm comin' on out! Don't shoot!"

"Come!" Vann echoed. "No shooting!"

"No shooting!" the cabin itself seemed to echo in return.

Chief Vann stepped out from the tree line rather brazenly. He was covered by the two remaining rifles behind him. The leader of the group in the cabin eked the door open enough to inch out but kept one hand on the doorframe to propel himself back inside at the first sign of trouble. As the man emerged, Vann strode across the cleared ground until they were near enough to talk without shouting.

"Name's Tucker."

"I am Blue Knife," Vann lied. "Take up your people and go to the east."

"We will do just that. Gonna take some time to get packed up and all."

"We have no time for you. Take up your people and go to the east. Go east now."

"We need to pack food and such. We have young-uns in here."

Vann was patient, but others were coming up behind him leading their horses and were less so. "The little ones will make good captives," Doublehead blurted out as if it were a foregone conclusion.

"No," Vann countered. "We want them out of our mountains and away from our waters. They will all go as I have said."

Now Vann shouted at the cabin, Doublehead having provoked him. "Load your backs with three days' food. Come out and put your long guns in the ground. Take one for the hunt. Leave them. Leave the most of the long guns."

"How about my stock?" Tucker said as he motioned to the corral.

"Stock? The cattle and horse? They are payment for breaking the treaties. Leave them. Pack and go. Quickly. No harm will come but do it now."

Tucker retreated inside the door. "Pack up what you can."

There was a short scramble in the cabin as provisions were hastily thrown together.

"I ain't givin' up my rifle!"

"Rather give up your hair? Pack up but quick. I'll stall 'em some."

As the race continued behind him, Tucker popped back out the door. This time he had his rifle in his hand but was holding it loosely by the barrel out away from his body. The sight of the white man carrying a rifle brought twenty guns and half as many bows up to firing positions. Tucker abruptly tossed the rifle aside.

"See there?" he said. "Holdin' up my end of the terms. No gun. Leavin' her right there for you."

Emboldened, a few warriors stepped away from the trees toward the cabin. Tucker took several hesitant steps as if to meet them. Behind him, the rough-hewn door opened and the others in the cabin trickled out. The men came first, carrying their rifles as had Tucker, with slings of whatever food and supplies they could carry slung across their backs and held in their free hands. The women were tight behind them holding the shoulders and hands of the three children.

Vann stepped out further into the glade and pointed with his rifle. "Go east. Stop when you are wet in the big water of King George!"

The Cherokee who understood some English began to laugh. Others, joining their friends, laughed along, though they didn't understand Vann's English. Doublehead looked at them all as though he were the brunt of the joke.

"Fools," he said as he ripped the reins of his horse from an attendant.

The old warrior bounded onto the horse's back like a man half his age, but before he could wheel his horse toward the cabin, Vann had snatched another mount nearby. The two men were an instant apart in their actions — the second reading the intent of the first as they moved like trailing ripples on water.

Doublehead's horse spun toward the cabin as Vann broke behind him. Nearly every man in the war party began their own pursuit of the racing horses as Vann's joking words instantly melted away in their ears. They were filled by the "Ka-la-la!" war cry that exploded from Doublehead as his horse bolted toward Tucker. For his part, the white man stared with a look torn between wonder and shock. In seconds his face caught the hard cherry wooden ball of Doublehead's war club, and the look shattered under the blow.

As Tucker crumbled dead on his feet, Doublehead cocked his arm as his wide eyes caught the nearest man. The horse had not broken its stride and was on the others in an instant. The trespassing settler who wanted both his scalp and his rifle now raised his gun, but the horse was too fast and he was too slow. As the rifle came up, the war club came down. In a heartbeat of time that separated living from dead, Vann's horse rammed into Doublehead's, sending the horse, Doublehead, and intended victim sprawling in a ball of dust, horsehide, and deerskin.

Chief Vann stepped his horse toward the cabin and screamed at the remaining white faces, each paler by what had just occurred. "Go! GO! Leave this place!"

As the small group started to hurriedly shuffle along the cabin, huddling for the protection that came at the hands of the man screaming from horseback, a single arrow whistled by Vann's leg and pierced the nearest woman's cheek. The flint sliced her face with ease, like a thin stick pushed into soft mud. It stopped when it passed through her throat and hit the back of her skull. The woman's hands fell away from the children they had clutched, and she dropped to the ground twitching, the fletchings of the arrow quivering with her body.

Vann traced the path of the arrow back to one of Doublehead's men. He and others were notching more arrows and shouldering rifles.

"No! No!" Vann waved wildly like a man gone mad while behind him a more frightening sight was coming up from the dust cloud of the horse and men Vann had barreled into. Doublehead had never left his horse's back, and as the animal scrambled to its feet, Doublehead came up with it, like an apparition appearing out of the fog of dust.

Vann wheeled his mount once more between the rising horse and the terrified settlers. He reached down and plucked a boy from the melee as freshly launched arrows struck new targets. The boy landed in a tangle of arms and legs across the chief's lap. Vann's horse spun away from the whistling arrows and presented the boy's head as the perfect target to Doublehead as his own horse reached its full height. As before, Doublehead cocked his war club and delivered a snapping crush down on the child's skull. Vann felt the crunch travel the length of the recoiling boy's body followed by the slump of instant death. In its blind search for more death, Doublehead's bloody club was pulled back across its master's chest and took aim at the nearest possible victim — Vann, but this time it was undone by Vann's reaction. The young chief grabbed the back of the dead boy and threw him with one hand at Doublehead and his club.

"What's happened to you, old man?"

As the boy's body fell away, Doublehead glared as an answer. If there was another reply coming, Vann wasn't waiting. He raked the sides of his horse and the animal charged toward the fleeing settlers. The warriors who were hot on their heels were nearly run over. Others who were reloading their weapons stopped for fear of hitting the chief as he purposely placed himself again between the scattering whites and the Cherokee. As quickly as the killing began it was over.

Vann urged the settlers away and corralled the fiery warriors, several of whom were already rifling through the cabin along with Doublehead. Vann didn't look twice at the cabin but repeatedly glanced over his shoulder at the drifting whites.

"They are not to be trailed. I have given my words to this."

"You have given words to a trespassing white man," came Doublehead's voice as he emerged from the cabin. "It means nothing."

For the third time in nearly as many minutes Vann's horse raced across in front of the cabin. He reined in in front of Doublehead.

"My words are strong whoever I give them to. You have allowed yourself to become as bad as the whites. You are no different. Take your men and leave us. I have no time to watch over you and keep you free from briars. You were a good warrior once, Doublehead, but that man has died. You are a baby killer."

"He was a dog!" Doublehead screamed.

"You are nothing to me and nothing to the people. You are not even Doublehead. You are Baby Killer. Now, leave this place."

"I'll leave you women to your chores, but we'll meet again, Vann."

"We will, and I look forward to that day."

1775　　1790　　**1806**　　1814　　1818　　1821

"My banished brother, the one you called 'the Dragon,' has been dead now for many, many years," Doublehead said with disregard for Tsi'yugunsini's memory. "Those of us who remain do not threaten the white man. We have lived in peace. This will continue. You have nothing to fear from the Cherokee. Do the Cherokee have any reason to fear you?"

The white faces in the room only smiled disarmingly. Doublehead noticed the changes in countenance, the sly sideways smiles, but dismissed them as easily and quickly as he dismissed the memory of Tsi'yugunsini. "No matter," the chief said offhandedly. "Show me your talking leaves. I will make my mark."

In the years since Tsi'yugunsini's death, Doublehead had labored to position himself in the hierarchy of the nation. He didn't have the wealth of Vann but was a chief in his own region of the nation and was filling a vacuum wrought on by death and political dissension. Chief Vann had been right in that Doublehead had been a fierce fighter in earlier days, so fierce he had been known to cannibalize his victims to gain their power and show his own. Now, free from the shadow of Attakullakulla and the Dragon, Doublehead parlayed his brutal talent into a posture where he felt he could speak for many. White treaty negotiators had supported and promoted his personal esteem and welcomed him to the table. Once there, Doublehead had become selfish and oblivious to the needs of what he claimed to be his people. He disguised his greed as the inevitability of white progression, and he allowed numbers to grow on the papers he signed. Today would be the last.

A white hand slipped a paper beneath the chief's as Doublehead dipped a ragged, short quill into an indigo well. He scratched his mark on the coarse parchment and laid the quill aside. "It is done."

Pale hands hurried the paper away. It left the room and was followed by most of the white men as Doublehead and his few attendants waited for their payment. It would come as metal axes and knives, guns, horses, whiskey, and promises but mostly silver. When the trade had been consummated Doublehead would leave with his bounty but would leave behind ten million acres of Cherokee land.

News of the land cession was slow in reaching the Cherokee towns. The peace chiefs of small Cherokee villages who had become aware spread the message and assembled to give voice to their dissatisfaction in larger groups in larger towns. When the hierarchy of the nation had thus been informed and settled into their places, two chiefs emerged to lead. One was a fine young chief called "The Ridge" and the other was Doublehead's nemesis, now an older, wiser, wealthier, and more powerful James Vann.

The Ridge was almost full-blood Cherokee. His mother had a white Scottish father. With a Cherokee matrilineal line, Ridge enjoyed a childhood filled with nights of sleep collected in the arms of the forest and days of hunting. Only later in life did he actively seek out the advantages thought to be gained from the white man's language and education. Though often in the presence of the white world that had encroached upon his people, Ridge had continued to reject those things that seemed to foreshadow the extinction of the Cherokee Nation. This included the selling of land.

Both Vann and Ridge were dressed as every other chief in the room, the mixture of white and red culture reflected in their clothes — combinations of deerskin and woven cloth. Several years of comparative peace had fostered trading between the new and the old Americans giving each group the things they needed or wanted. Cherokee desired the metal tools, knives, axes, and sewing needles the colonists utilized with regularity, and the settlers wanted the deerskins and beaver pelts the Cherokee skillfully hunted and trapped. The relationship of trade soon grew cyclic as the demand for hides pressed the settlers to offer guns and metal traps in order to increase productivity. But providing the Cherokee with more weapons did not sit well with those whites whose ears, even fifteen years later, still rang with the battle cries of the Dragon.

While Vann had become a chief by earning his rank, others in the room, like Ridge, were chiefs in their own regions due to lineage or accomplishments in battle. Each man was subject, in his mind, to no one — so much so that Doublehead did not attend the council. Perhaps it was just as well as he was the subject of the discussion.

When it came to the selling of ten million acres of Cherokee land, someone would have to be held accountable and someone would have to take the lead. It fell to Vann and Ridge to preside over the rowdy chieftains and somehow restore order to both the meeting and, more importantly, the nation. It would not be an easy task. Many considered the two men half-breeds. Totsuhwa, now in his late thirties and the prominent shaman in the entire nation, felt this way but did not make it known. Nor did he participate in the clamoring that filled the room.

"Brothers! Brothers!" Ridge said at the top of his voice. The noise settled only slightly. "Let us remember who we are!" At those words the noise dropped considerably. "Let us remember what we are." And the room was quieter still. "Save your voices for your war cries." Suddenly the room was like a grave. There were many who thought the statement was the lead in of a call for war, which was welcomed by some, feared by many. Men of both inclinations were instantly riveted.

"My brothers. We are the chiefs of a great nation. We have never spoken out so in council. Remember the talking stick and the ways of our fathers."

Chief Vann interjected. "Our fathers did not have to deal with treachery coming from our own people." The words brought up a swell of soft rumblings from the group as Totsuhwa remembered the signing away of land when he was a boy at Sycamore Shoals and Dragon's opposition to it even then.

"That is true," Ridge said. "But they dealt with treachery from many other quarters. This is perhaps only a new form. They dealt with theirs, now we must deal with ours."

Vann sprang to his feet and whipped his knife from his belt. "This is how we should deal with ours!" And the men in the room brought their voices up to greet him.

Ridge let the wave crest before he spoke. When the tide of encouragement settled back, he continued. "I cannot say I disagree, Chief Vann. Yet now, today, there are other issues to consider. First and foremost, we must agree — each man in this room, each man he meets on the way back to his village, and each man under his control and every chief of any power within the Tsalagi Nation — we must agree that there can be no more selling of the land."

"Ridge, there is no argument there. Our council has come together to stop the desires of one when he has put to the knife the desires of many. Tell us, can this paper of Doublehead's be reversed?"

"I've spoken with the white chiefs. They have already released the land to new settlers. If—"

"We can drive them out!" a voice cried out forcibly.

Ridge continued. "If we attempt to engage them we will find ourselves where we were before — killing and being killed. And, trust me brothers, this time the white men will not be stopped by a treaty. They will advance on us with the slightest provocation and will not stop until every Cherokee is dead."

"So," Vann asked. "What do you suggest? How do we put iron in our decision?"

The Ridge held out over his answer for a long moment. When he spoke again his voice was steely calm. "If a Tsalagi sells any land, anything from a hundred million acres down to the spot covered by the shade of a single tree, it will be considered a capital offense against the nation, and he shall be put to death for his crime."

James Vann was still standing. He began to nod his head. Others around him looked up at him and at Ridge. Finally, Vann relaxed. "It is a good law," he said and quietly sat down.

Totsuhwa spoke from his place along the wall and put words to the thoughts of many. "Does this new law apply to those who supplied the reason for its passing?"

The phrase was gilded and protected on many sides, but all understood what was being asked and what the answer would mean to Doublehead's health. The Ridge looked to Vann for a moment, as did all the men in the room, but it was Ridge who would answer.

"We have made this law today, not yesterday," was all he said and it was enough. Even as the words settled in the minds of the chiefs of the Tsalagi people, Totsuhwa allowed the tiniest of smiles to skate across his lips. Ridge was protected from promoting or condoning retaliation on Doublehead for what he had done but Totsuhwa knew his people and their ways. The same protection Ridge had found behind his words would not extend over Doublehead. Someone in the nation would enact the required vengeance. It might even be him, Totsuhwa thought.

The gathering would continue for several more hours. Many of the Cherokee leaders had come far and it would be months or years before they were all together again. The Ridge understood this clearly and used the time to plant seeds of change and adaptation that would germinate in the minds of the attendees then repeat the growing process in those men, women, boys, and girls under each individual chief's care. If the chiefs could come together as one mind today, he believed the nation would profit long after the gavel had fallen on the meeting.

The front of the room served as a staging area for Ridge's proposals, and he paced back and forth as each was presented. The pacing helped to diffuse the anxiousness he felt over what he was compelled to say. In his heart he firmly believed the recommendations he offered would be the salvation of the nation. Without them, he feared nothing would remain of the Cherokee in the tracks left by the white man's wagons and their stiff boots.

"My mother was born in the mountains of the Tsalagi," he began. "She was Tsalagi. So I am Tsalagi. I will always be this. My wife is Tsalagi, so my children will be as well." He paused and registered with each face. "I want them to have a nation of their own. I want them to grow and live and die in peace.

"There are those among us here today who have fought against every white man's step on Cherokee soil." He looked earnestly at Totsuhwa as he continued. "Many of you have battled alongside the greatest warriors our people have ever known. They lived their lives to free us from the tyranny of the whites. Their fight was long and often glorious, and through their conquests we have gained time to prepare. Those who have gone to the West have given us time to see the future. Have you seen it?" He held on Totsuhwa for a moment longer, asking the question to the single man before he moved on from the stoic face.

"Have you seen it?" he asked again to the group. "I have. And I believe many of you have seen it too."

"What have you seen, Ridge?" Chief Vann blurted out. "What is it you want us to see with your eyes?"

Ridge moved into the room and bent toward the chief with heart, eyes, and hands full of sincerity. "The future of our people if we do not adapt to the white man's world. That is what I have seen."

Vann looked back and reflected the sincerity. "What face does tomorrow wear, Ridge?"

The young leader straightened as though it pained him. He walked back to the front of the room as if exhausted. The words that tumbled from him were labored and heavy. "We, as a nation, must become more like the white people." A low rumbling returned to the throng, but Ridge continued to venture into the deep water. "Our clothes," he said as he plucked at his shirt. "The way we govern ourselves," he said as he motioned around at the group of men and the building that held them. "Our towns. And the way we teach our children."

"No!" The strong voice belonged to Chief John Brown. Like Ridge and Vann and so many others in the room, Brown took the name of his white father along with his blood, but unlike others,

Brown rejected all things that spoke of assimilation. "Why must it be the Cherokee who change? Ours is a good life! It was the way of our mothers and their mothers. Ridge, were the people of your village, your family, were they not happy in the days when you fetched wood for your grandmother's cooking fire?"

"We were happy," Ridge said reverently as his face reflected the pleasant memories in his mind.

"So why must we change?" Brown repeated. "The ways of the Tsalagi are good ways. We should not change them. Let the whites change for us."

"They cannot, will not, change," Ridge said clearly. "And we cannot force them to or even invite them to. They are too many and they are too strong."

"I will not lead my villages down a path that turns them white," Brown commanded.

"Why?" The Ridge said as he settled back onto a bench seat and leaned forward, his arms resting on his knees. "Why do you protest so? Do you not see the shirt that covers your back? Have you forgotten since you put it on this morning that it is made of the white man's cloth? And that knife on your belt. Was it not made in the white man's fires?"

"I know what I have, Ridge," Brown said harshly. "I have made trade with whites, and I do not say we should stop. But we are Cherokee first. We are not like the whites. And we should not try to be. They disgrace the land. They kill game for sport and people for no reason at all."

James Vann spoke up. "These things Chief Brown says, they are true. The white people who come into our valleys are not clever or worthy. I am not certain it is a good thing to copy these people. If we hunt ahwi, the deer, we do not copy the ways of a pig, do we? No, we are silent and still like a panther. Pigs cannot take a deer. Panthers can. If we are to remain at peace with the land we must stay Cherokee. Copy our fathers, not these who trample on our fathers' graves."

The Ridge stretched then leaned forward again. His temperament was getting hot, but he restrained his words out of respect for the chief's stature. "We will remain Cherokee, true to our fathers.

I can scarcely believe my own words, but I know they are right. We must embrace the white world that is all around us or we will lose ourselves. Please understand this. We have little option. We can make a decision ourselves now. Or we can wait and have that decision made for us. Only then the decision will be harder because it will not have been ours to make. We will be turned into our graves by the white man's plows or chased from our mountains entirely."

Chief Vann was calm and in his voice was the echo of a despair that would never be resolved. "I dream sometimes that the land cannot hold many more Tsalagi bodies." The others were covered in silent respect and let the powerful chief's words rule, words that sank into every heart — those for and against Ridge's proposal. Vann's eyes moved around the room and he was forced to turn awkwardly in his seat to find Totsuhwa.

"Tell me, shaman of the Real People. What do your dreams whisper to you? I have spoken of mine. And Ridge has told us he has seen the future. Will you tell us what the Spirit has told you through the fire?"

Throughout the meeting Totsuhwa had been crouched along the wall, sitting in his customary fashion. He did not rise at first but spoke from the comfort of the wall. "I have fasted many times as I thought on the white men in our land. Each time, I ask the Spirit for guidance I can bring to the people. Each time I have seen the same things."

Totsuhwa stood but did not parade about the room. Rather, he held his spot, standing ramrod straight with his eyes almost glazed as he looked out over the heads of the chiefs of the troubled nation.

"In the vision, waves of locusts come over our mountains and eat all the people's corn, beans, and squash, and we starve. The locusts grow fat on the Three Sisters taken from us. The Cherokee die and the wind blows away our bones until there is no trace we ever lived in these lands."

No one had heard these words from the shaman before and the men were struck dumb. The jaws of the regal chiefs around the room went slack; their mouths open in shock and surprise. Men whose faces had been hardened by years of gory fighting didn't notice the countenances that draped across their faces until they were left staring at the shaman like children who first notice the stars. Totsuhwa was revered, almost glorified, and his words taken as though they were coming from the mouth of the Spirit itself, as they were. Even so, it took several minutes for men to understand the weighted words completely.

The pronouncement had come into the room like a vulture settling on carrion. Chief Vann could smell the stench of the bird in his nostrils and instantly knew that Totsuhwa's dream outweighed his own and that the ground would be forced to take in more Cherokee corpses, many more. He was the first to react to the shaman's words, but the response came only as the dropping of his head in resignation of what he deemed was now the inevitable.

The Ridge heard the words as well. He was the first to see the reaction of the tribal leaders and understood that Totsuhwa's words, true or not, inevitable or not, would turn the men in a direction that would have no direction at all. The vision would set the nation adrift. It would flounder, waiting with resolute patience for the prophecy to come to fruition. While Ridge's mind and eyes darted around the room, seeking a way to steer a nation whose rudder was being cut away by the words of the shaman, Totsuhwa settled back to the floor.

The Ridge slipped from his seat and struggled to appear resolute in his move to the center of the room, trying to draw the group back and with an unseen hand, ease the gapping mouths closed around him. "Totsuhwa, I thank you for your vision. But let us not lose sight of ourselves. Though there is great truth in all the shaman's words, we do not know how many seasons must pass before these things may come."

Vann interrupted curtly. "Totsuhwa. When do the locusts come?"

"They are here now."

"Yes, but—" Ridge tried.

"And they are the white men?" Vann continued.

"It is so."

"And when will the Three Sisters be taken from us?"

Totsuhwa stood again and pointed calmly at the door. "There is a house for trade up the road there. The white government runs this thing. It is called a factory — a word I do not know well. I see the people go there to buy food instead of growing it in the ground or taking it from the forest. A Tsalagi man comes away from that place with food for his family. His hands stay clean of dirt and blood. He has neither to hunt or plant or work to eat. How can this be a good thing? Chief Vann, I see the Three Sisters slipping away as we speak."

"Your words are true, Totsuhwa," Vann said softly. "Your words are true."

"Yes," Ridge said as he jumped into the fray. "But to leave the place with food or a metal knife one must take a hide or pelt in for trade. My hands are bloodied after the skinning. To take a pelt is good work, Totsuhwa. Don't dismiss the trapping so easily."

"To trap for the use of your family is good. Do'-ya, the beaver, offers himself to us for our needs with a glad heart, but we cannot trap and trap and trap him; kill him and all his family so we can trade his children's skin for corn we could grow ourselves. Listen closely — not to me, my brothers, but to the Spirit who speaks through me — do'ya will leave this place forever if we do these things. And when he leaves, ahwi will follow him. And when ahwi is no more, the Cherokee will be no more."

Chief Vann breathed deeply, and most of the room followed. Again Ridge saw the room slipping away, driven on by the gloom spreading from Totsuhwa's visions. He had to stem the tide and thought of only one card strong enough to play.

"Brothers, I do not question Totsuhwa. His medicine is powerful and he has fought bravely for our people. He is known throughout the nation to be wise and well versed in the ways of the ancients." He hesitated to let the compliments soften the coming blow. "But we have seen our shamans falter in the past. In the days of my mother's youth, and even my own, the sickness spread through our people like a wildfire and they could do nothing to stop it. I remember those times and my mother's memories. Do you? Do you, Chief Vann, recall the days when our medicine, our fasting, and our visions meant nothing to the sickness?"

"I do."

"Remember them and remember how we thought we would all be stricken and die. Yet," Ridge held out his arms wide and smiled pleasantly. "Here we are. The Raven Mockers did not overtake us." Ridge hesitated and spoke softly to ease the words into minds that would not take them easily. "The shamans were wrong." Then he whispered for effect. "They were wrong."

The faces listened and understood then turned as one to Totsuhwa for his rebuttal but their watch would be in vain. The shaman knew what The Ridge was trying to accomplish. Totsuhwa would let it pass, bearing instead the burden himself. He would not defend his profession, the past, or even his dreams. However, he did send a tight look to The Ridge. Without words and suffering no affront, Totsuhwa told Ridge that he could not deter the message of the Spirit. The other chiefs recognized the silent reply for what it was as well and Totsuhwa gained another measure of respect.

In order to free the room Totsuhwa spoke briefly and moved the thoughts in another direction. "Do not allow your efforts to betray the nation. To all who do they should know that they, their children, and their children's children, will be held accountable."

Ridge countered tenuously. "This is what we have agreed to already this day."

"Remember your words," Totsuhwa said and he let his gaze slip away.

"But there is no punishment for children, Redbird. Not among our people," Ridge said, cautiously smiling as he looked around the council for support.

Totsuhwa had never cared for the English version of his name. He knew Ridge had used it with purpose. He hesitated and let Ridge have his way before he answered.

"The punishment for our children is not there in your knife or in the white rifles. It is not losing their lives. It is losing their way of life."

Ridge moved back to the front of the room and fumbled for the reins that would bring the meeting back beneath his control. He would not engage Totsuhwa again. The shaman's perspective was rooted in the past and he would not be swayed. To try would only bring others to his side.

"Brothers," The Ridge said again. "There are steps to be taken, things to be done in the movement of our nation. Nothing needs be done today or tomorrow. But encourage your people to move toward the white world. Do not instill fear in them or hate. Welcome the changes yourselves and the people will follow. In doing so you lead them to life."

"What do you ask of us?" Vann questioned.

"There are two areas that, when we have grasped them, will help us as a nation move closer to the whites than any others. They are education and farming." The second notion made more than a few faces grimace.

"We must educate ourselves and our people in the English they speak. Without it, we cannot understand and speak freely. This cuts us off from them. With their language comes their formal education. They see value in education, as do I, the maturity and discipline it teaches." Ridge heard the unvoiced objections. "I know. I know. We teach our sons and daughters discipline, and it is a good way. But remember, what we are doing now is adapting to a new way — not better or worse — only different and one that will insure the longevity of our people." He continued to purposely avoid any eye contact with Totsuhwa, who still stood.

"I will go to the white government and ask for help in setting up their schools for our children. Our children will then be able to use both languages to their own betterment."

There was only a small amount of discussion in the room following his remarks and he let the talk settle before he moved on.

"The second is farming," he continued. "We must move further in that direction."

"What do you mean?" Chief Brown asked, somewhat perturbed.

"We have to farm more extensively, more completely. Grow more crops. Raise cattle and pigs."

"We do these things now."

"On a bigger scale. We must grow enough so we can sell the surplus and use the silver for other things we need. We should grow grains for livestock and use that for our meat. Then we would not have to rely on hunting for food."

Chief Brown stood up. "That is the end. We have hunted our land since it was given to us. Now you say we must stop?"

"No," Ridge said emphatically. "Of course not. But I am suggesting that one of the ways to place us closer with the whites is to not depend on hunting. Hunt for meat, yes, but rely more on growing our beef and pork. It is their way and becoming more so with each season."

"This is not right," Chief Brown said as he shook his head. "It cannot be right. My uncle pulled me from my mother's breast and placed a bow in my hands. Ahwi gave himself to me and came beneath my arrow when I was not long removed from my mother's belly. I teach the sons of my village these same lessons. Now you tell me I have to stop hunting and instead must throw husks of corn over a fence to pigs?"

"I didn't say that," Ridge offered meekly.

"Totsuhwa," Chief Brown continued unabated. "You speak for the Tsalagi more than these half-breeds. What does the Spirit tell you about our hunting?"

The word caused a rumble through the council. Totsuhwa did not want to undermine the already feeble leadership Ridge and Vann were trying to establish but his heart was true to the people and the Spirit's voice had been strong in him since birth. "Hunting brings a balance between us and the land."

"We never said not to hunt!" Ridge said loudly, his temperament coming out. "You can hunt all you want! Teach your children to hunt! But if you want them to live on this land, if you want them to live at all, you had also better teach them to farm!"

"Women farm!" Brown screamed back. "Warriors hunt!" He stomped into the center of the room and motioned wildly to everyone present. "I have hunted far to the West where the sun sleeps. It was not the mountains of my father or his before him, as are these mountains, but no white man can be found there. The land is beneath the feet of the Osage. Some of you know them. They are a welcoming people. I will take my villages and go there."

"Welcoming perhaps to a hunter," Ridge said. "But that is all. They will see your villages as an invasion, the way you see the white settlements."

"Then we will fight! As our fathers have done. We will not lie down like a beaten dog. We will live without change, without fear, without the white man, and without their farming."

"Do not do this thing, John Brown," Chief Vann asked gently.

"Why? Better to live as the people we are in another land than to live as what we are not in our own."

Totsuhwa did not move from the wall but spoke clearly. "If you split the tree you will weaken it, Chief John Brown."

"Then let us not talk of splitting the tree. Let the whole tree move to the West and away from the locusts that come over the land."

"Chief Brown," Ridge said firmly. "Those are words from a child. We will not leave our land."

"Why do you say so with such reverence for it? It does not bother you to sell our fathers' graves, why should it bother you to abandon them for the sake of their grandchildren?"

"No," Vann said with an unyielding tone. "We do not leave the land of our fathers. This was given to us. We should not move from it. I put it to our shaman. Totsuhwa?"

"I was born in this land. I will die here. My pledge has been made to Tsi'yugunsini, my father. I will not leave these mountains for any reason."

"Ah, the white man's Dragon," Chief Vann said. "He wore the red robe well." A moment was allowed to pass in reverence to the name.

"I shall stay," Vann picked up and a chorus of agreement ascended from the room. "If you, The Ridge," Vann continued, "say we must make changes to live on our land in peace, then we will make them. I will raise my sons in two worlds. They will learn the white words and what the white men see in their talking leaves. I will teach them to hunt and the ways of my father, but I will also teach them to grow cattle and hoe beans and corn." The chief smiled and turned to those nearest him. "I may have to send him to his mother for that." And a welcome release of laughter filled the room.

Totsuhwa smiled along with the others and watched as the revered leaders chided one another about becoming pig farmers.

The laughter was easy but beneath it there was a current of disdain and fear that it might become far too real. Shucking corn for hogs seemed a long fall from wearing the red cloak of a Cherokee war chief.

The only man who did not join in the joking was Chief John Brown. "When you pig herders are finished laughing I will tell you goodbye. But I ask you. Tell your people there is one chief of the nation who will not lay down to the white world. Tell them if you dare. And tell them that they are welcome in my villages no matter their clan. They can travel to the West with my people."

"To the West lies the Darkening Land of the Dead," Chief Vann said as the last smiles vanished.

John Brown moved toward the door. He slipped through the crowd and touched no one. Each warrior moved only as much as was necessary to allow his passing. He paused at the door and looked back into the room. "And death is here as well. You should listen to Totsuhwa. The Spirit speaks through him. I believe his vision."

Chief Brown looked around the room and saw many faces for what would be the last time. "Before the next moon," he said with one hand on the door. "The valleys that cradle my villages will be empty. You can graze your pigs there." And he walked out, leaving the door open behind him.

Someone eased the door closed on Chief Brown's shadow and every man in the room felt a tug in their hearts — some born out of a want to join the splinter of the tree in its walk to the West, but most felt the pangs of a nation whose breaking point had come. The departing Cherokee would number less than a thousand but the precedent would reach into the minds of every man, woman, and child of the Real People. The Ridge and James Van would talk on about their plans but their efforts on behalf of the nation would be forever overshadowed in the minds of those chiefs that remained in the room by the sight of Chief Brown's back.

Vann himself said little more yet wondered to himself and those nearest him in life if Chief Brown had turned his back on the people or had merely turned his back to a cold wind to protect those beneath his care.

Totsuhwa knew the answer but he had also made a promise to Tsi'yugunsini, a promise he would not abandon.

No one else left the meeting until the sketch for the revised nation had been carefully laid out and understood. Those who ran the white schools would be invited into the villages and their teachings welcomed. Everything from dress to trade and commerce would be affected by the cultural changes suggested and sworn to. There would be much balking before all of the plans were embraced but the way had been cleared. Ridge's final announcement, however, was met with wild, unmitigated enthusiasm.

"There we are, my brothers. The path of our fathers has become a cleared road. It is a new road leading to peace on the land for our people." There was little in acknowledgment from the attending warriors apart from movement to collect their things and relieve cramped muscles and minds.

"One last thing," he continued, and the men settled back in anticipation of another placation of their heritage disguised as a move to the white world. "As we are all together to consider these things we have discussed, it is a good time to make a notice to all within the sound of my voice. Go back to your villages with these things for our future and let them rest on our people's minds and be talked about around the fires for two moons. Then collect all the people, collect all who can travel, and bring them to the place of the central fire," he hesitated. "For the grandest ball game we have enjoyed in years!"

For the first time in hours the roof was pushed up by wondrous cheers instead of thick thoughts of disheartened oppression and concern. Immediately the chiefs began to chide one another on the strengths and weaknesses of their respective teams. As quickly as the first barbs were placed, the language of gambling broke over the men and anything The Ridge may have wished to say in closing was drowned away in a sea of wagers.

"I have seen your men run. They limp along like hobbled cows!"

"Yes, your warriors know how to run better than mine."

"They do. And the nation will think more of you for admitting your weakness."

"Yes. They run well. I saw them do so when the Shawnee lances fell close!"

The chiefs nearby roared in laughter.

"Totsuhwa! Put a curse on the legs of his men for insulting my warriors!"

Totsuhwa laughed along with the others as he worked through the room toward the door. "No curse," he smiled.

"A blessing then for my runners."

"And seek out the shamans of your villages for your blessings." Then a feeling of responsibility pinched him and he stopped at the door as Chief John Brown had earlier. His smile remained but his advice was to be taken to heart. "Have your warriors eat no rabbit. Tsisdu is very quick but he runs in no direction because he frightens easily and becomes confused. This will happen to your ball players if they eat him before the game."

"That is true," many said in unison. "My father spoke of this. Totsuhwa knows the ways."

The chiefs nodded their thanks to the shaman while he looked to the front of the room and The Ridge. Like the collected chiefs, Totsuhwa dipped his head as a thank you to him for his efforts on behalf of the nation. The plans were difficult to savor for most, Totsuhwa included, but he could not help but agree that without the changes the Cherokee might be pushed to extinction. Even with the proposals the locusts would still triumph. The visions had told him so and his faith in them was strong. No words could alter them.

Totsuhwa left the building and the council behind. He walked several hundred yards along a trail that was larger than a path but smaller than a road until he came to the place he had slept for the last several days. His horse was hobbled and grazing nearby. His few belongings were as he had left them, neatly wrapped and rolled beneath a tree. Next to the blanket rolls were a few large pouches and bags that held several smaller ones which in turn held the remedies, medicines, potions, and history of the Cherokee Nation.

He moved to his horse, which did not shy away. He knelt and removed the hobbles from its feet and repositioned a loose braided rope from its neck to its lip then led the animal to the tree. In a few minutes, the horse was loaded and Totsuhwa swung onto its back. The journey to this meeting had taken ten days. The return trip would be accomplished no quicker. The days leading back to his village might even seem longer as his mind was already racing on ahead to his home — a simple cabin tucked on the far distant fringe of the homes that comprised the town. But more than the warmth and familiarity of his hearth, a woman with soft hands and black eyes over high cinnamon cheekbones, framed by waist length pitch-black straight hair, was waiting.

As a girl she was often seen climbing trees. Her hair — long, straight, and deep black — waving from side to side as she climbed made her family think of a black snake slithering into the trees. So she came to be called Ga-le-gi, after the blacksnake. This is how she introduced herself to Totsuhwa at the Green Corn Dance.

During the days of dancing and celebration, tradition carried that all sins and wrongs committed during the preceding year be forgiven; however, the transgressor must have sought peace and forgiveness through fasting and prayer. Totsuhwa held court over the most heinous transgressions and, with the advice and counsel of the attending chiefs and mothers of the villages of the guilty party, rendered the forgiveness of the people. This was the arena in which Galegi and Totsuhwa first met. She had come to argue for a youth in her village and he had been there to listen.

Galegi had warm eyes but her features could be tight and harsh, especially when arguing as she was before the council at the Green Corn Dance. She was attractive though few counted her among the many beautiful women of the nation. And while her friends had been married for years and had become mothers, some many times over, Galegi had not yet taken a husband. Instead she concerned herself with the affairs of her village, called everyone her children, and had risen to become First Woman of her town as her mother before her.

During the quiet years that settled around her village she dispensed her dominion over the people under her care with an unusual gentleness. But when war and raiding brought bound captives into the town, she cut off their fingers and scalded them on their way to death. Youngsters, however, she released to the care and upbringing of families in the village. Once assured of their safety and rights, as though they had been born into the family, these captives were considered her children as much as any other. It was just such a captive-turned-child that Galegi was defending when she and Totsuhwa first came to face each other.

"What has this boy done that he stands before us?" Totsuhwa asked somewhat surprised as he stared down at the rail-thin waif of a boy scarcely six winters old.

Galegi stood behind the boy and placed her hands on his shoulders. "He took—"

"Can he not speak for himself?" Totsuhwa asked.

"He can, but he is Seminole and there are words of ours that he does not—"

"Our words are close enough," Totsuhwa interrupted again, which irked Galegi considerably. Her stature in her village did not lend itself to being interrupted and questioned and she found herself instantly disliking the famous and powerful shaman.

"Boy," Totsuhwa said loudly as he leaned toward the nervous youngster. "What is your crime?"

"I...," he stammered before looking up at Galegi who urged him on. "I ate the corn."

Totsuhwa turned his palms up and gestured as to what crime that could be.

Galegi had the answer but withheld it until it was requested of her.

"Explain to me what crime there is in this boy eating corn."

"You wish me to speak now?" Galegi asked in a voice that was falsely demure.

"I do," Totsuhwa said, both annoyed and intrigued by the tone of the petitioner before him.

"He took the seven ears our village had saved from last year's harvest."

Now Totsuhwa was more interested. "Boy. The corn you took, do you understand what fates you tempt?"

Again the boy looked up to Galegi, and she in turn looked to Totsuhwa. "He understands now but did not understand then."

Totsuhwa took it upon himself to insure the child's education. "Boy. Each year when the harvest is gathered, we collect seven prime ears of corn and hold them in the villages. When new corn is planted the next growing season, the new corn will know to come to the old we have saved. If we do not save the old harvest the new corn may not find its way to our fields. Do you understand this?"

"Yes," the boy answered timidly.

"Without corn our people will starve to death. Do you, as Seminole, want the Tsalagi people to die?"

"No."

"How do I know you are not trying to starve my people?"

Galegi was becoming perturbed. "He was only hungry. He knows nothing of treason."

"He is Seminole. Is that not enough to know of treason and treachery?"

"And all Tsalagi are delights."

"Enough! Your tongue is sharp, woman. The boy does well to have you accompany him, but still the crime remains."

"Totsuhwa, you are a great shaman to our people. Your wisdom walks ahead of you into every village. Surely you must see that the corn has come this season. See that we are here for the Green Corn Dance. If the boy's actions had frightened away the new corn or it had lost its way we would not be here. Is that not so?"

"That is so."

"The people and children of our village have treated him poorly for his crime. He was brought here from the faraway south as a captive. Being so young, he did not understand our ways. He thought he would be a slave like those with dark skin who run from the white men to his own people in the south. He did not understand that we would not enslave him. He thought he would not be fed. So he took what food he could find. He took the seven ears of corn. He is here for the forgiveness of the nation always granted at the Green Corn Ceremony. Please grant it to him."

Totsuhwa gave the words consideration before he rendered his decision. "What is this boy called?"

"He has been called Gi-tli, the dog, by the people in our village because of what he has done."

Totsuhwa waved his hand as the declaration. "No more. You will be Gi-yu-ga, the ground squirrel, until you have become a man. The ground squirrel takes away the corn but only to survive, as you thought you must. Now it will be a reminder to you of your crime but a reminder to your village only that you will survive. Nothing more will be said or done against this child. When you are a man, you will receive a new name that fits your courage and cunning. Does Giyuga have a family?"

"Yes. Chief Vann has agreed to take him into his own."

"That will be a good family. Chief Vann has many new ways to teach him and his own as well. You have placed this young plant in fertile soil."

Galegi thanked the shaman and urged the boy away but was halted by Totsuhwa's words. "And you. What is your clan?"

"I am of the Wolf clan."

"It is a good clan."

"We are a strong people. Of good stock."

"This I have seen. In the past and today. The boy has a name but you, how are you called?"

"I am Galegi."

Now Totsuhwa, astride his horse headed home from the council, smiled at the memory and coaxed his horse forward. The sweet memories begged him to ride a little harder. He could ride longer days on the way home and rest less often. Perhaps if he pushed he could make it in eight days rather than ten. Totsuhwa needed to be home for the comfort Galegi's hand would give him but more so for the comfort he might be able to offer her. Galegi was carrying their baby and was nearly ready to drop the child.

When the thoughts of home and his wife took themselves away from his mind far enough to enable him to see the present clearly again, Totsuhwa found he was riding past the government trading house. He saw the metal equipment meant to ease work and increase production. As he had so many times, he wondered if either was a good thing for the Cherokee or for any people. Leaning against the outside wall behind the metal plowshares and farming stuffs was a bolt of bright red cloth. It pleased the eye and Totsuhwa knew of a face that would brighten beyond the hue of the cloth when she saw it. He pulled his horse around in front of the store and slipped from its back.

The store owner knew Totsuhwa immediately. The tall Cherokee with the muscular arms was nearly as well known in the white world as his own. Certainly any white man who lived in the blurring line between the two nations knew of Totsuhwa — Redbird, the great medicine man. The owner was surprised to look up and see the warrior filling his doorway. He understood that Redbird had little use for the things that filled the tiny government factory store.

Totsuhwa drifted in slowly and waited for his keen eyes to adjust to the light. The smells of the store were a strange mixture. There was a greasy smell, then after two steps, something sweet. Another step and another scent — some fresh, some stale. There were soaps and foodstuffs and smells from woods and herbs, each one meant to tickle the nose or eye and loosen purse strings. Totsuhwa passed them by, though he did enjoy the aromas — so many, so different in one small place. His mind was locked on the red cloth, but he knew the traders well enough to understand that his interest must appear passing or the price would go up like sap in a tree when the cold weather fades.

"Can I show you something?" the seller asked rather timidly.

At the remark a comb and looking glass fell beneath Totsuhwa's eyes. He did not answer the man but merely pointed to the pieces. The man sprang to the display case and produced a fine-toothed comb carved of dark wood and a round hand mirror, half the size of Totsuhwa's hand. The mirror had a polished beveled edge and a handle that, along with the frame, was fashioned from the same dark wood.

"Beautiful set there," the trader said as he handed the pieces to his customer.

Totsuhwa held the comb in one hand and the mirror in the other as though weighing them. He could see the wood was from the rhododendron and had been neatly carved.

"They're made from rhododendron," the man blurted out, trying to impress. "The best wood. Real nice fine grain for pieces such a manner as this here."

"I know the wood. What is the trade?"

"Well now," the trader said cautiously as he first eyed the horse outside then Totsuhwa up and down before settling on the large pouch slung over his shoulder. "What do you bring? I don't see no pelts on your horse yonder."

"I have no pelts."

There was a lag in conversation and Totsuhwa gently laid the fine pieces on the rough counter, but he had seen the white eyes prying to see into his pouch.

"Well sir, most trading is pulled off with pelts and furs — hides and such a manner. But maybe you got a little gold dust or a nugget or two in that pouch a your'n."

Totsuhwa tightened his arm on the bag and adjusted the strap tighter to his shoulder. He had no gold, but the increased security concerning the bag whetted the trader's appetite.

"Or maybe, you bein' a medicine man and all, you got some 'sang in there?"

Totsuhwa did have 'sang, ginseng root, and knew it to be highly prized by the traders. The long hunters and mountain men coveted the herb the Cherokee casually called "the mountain climber." Totsuhwa used the herb in many remedies, referring to it as Yunwi-Usdi, Little Man, because of the roots often being shaped like a human body. It was indeed valuable, and though he was reluctant to trade away what the earth had given him, Totsuhwa weighed it against the pleasure his wife brought to his life and the baby she was about to produce.

"I have your 'sang."

"Oh, now we can do us some bartering," the man said excitedly as he rubbed his hands together vigorously then placed his palms down on the counter. "Let's see how much ya got."

Totsuhwa snapped his hands down on the counter on top of the trader's. The man tried to pull his hands out from beneath the powerful tanned palms but couldn't budge them. His eyes were wide as Totsuhwa leaned across the counter.

"No see. What amount on your scale for the comb and looking glass?"

"Well... see that depends on the quality of—"

Totsuhwa pushed down slightly on top of the pinned hands.

"Or what I mean to say is...I'm sure it is the finest quality. Is it ground powder or still root?"

"Powder."

"Good. See, that's good. Worth more like that."

"I know."

"All righty now. Let's see. Them there two pieces ought to fetch..." The man's eyes jumped from the comb and mirror to Totsuhwa's stern face. "I figure 'bout...oh, let's start off with—" The pressure increased on his hands. "Er...I mean, five ounces. Five ounces. That's my best price. Five ounces of 'sang and ya got yourself a fine comb and mirror there."

"Two."

"TWO! By God they'd arrest ya for stealing if I sold you them pieces for two ounces a 'sang!"

"Two."

"Here now," the man said as tried to gently slip his hands out from beneath Totsuhwa's again but found them still fixed to the counter top. "Tell ya what I'm a gonna do. I'll trade ya them there pieces for four ounces a 'sang, and I'll toss in some mighty fine tobacco. Now, how's that sound?"

"Your tobacco is no good."

"No good! It's the finest they is! The seed come over on a boat clean from the Indies, I think England maybe."

"Your tobacco is for women to smoke. My tobacco comes from the forests of my fathers."

"I know, but ain't ya game for trying something new?"

The pressure increased again on the hands.

"Okay, okay. Forget the tobacco. How 'bout some..." The man stopped and looked beyond Totsuhwa to the open doorway. Now he whispered. "How 'bout some whiskey? You know, I ain't supposed to trade Indians fer it, but I keeps me a stash tucked away fer special customers. What'd ya say to that? I know ya likes your strong drink."

Totsuhwa lifted his hands from the counter, and the trader left his in place a moment, surprised by the sudden removal of his bonds. Then he began to rub the blood back into them.

"We got us a deal then?"

Totsuhwa shook his head no. "Two for the pieces there and one more for the red cloth," the shaman said as he pointed to the front of the store.

"How much red cloth?"

"Enough for a woman's skirt."

"Oh, that's a powerful lot of red cloth. I'd sooner—"

"Three for the pieces and the red cloth. And do not trade the whiskey to my warriors. If news of you trading whiskey to my people reaches across the land to this ear," Totsuhwa said as he pointed to his right ear. "I will come back to this place when only the moon will see." The shaman spoke leisurely, with great clarity so there could be no mistake made. "You will feel a blade touch your throat, and that is all you will feel. Do we...'got us a deal then?'"

The man pushed the comb and mirror across the counter and nodded his understanding without words. While Totsuhwa pulled his pouch to the front and began rummaging for the ginseng, the trader walked to the front of the store and picked up the bolt of material. He returned and unfurled it over the counter. The trader spread it smooth with his hands and picked up a pair of scissors. As the scissors touched the cloth edge they were stopped by Totsuhwa's outstretched hand. The warrior eased the scissors and the seller's hand further down the counter, another foot or so, increasing the size of the purchased cloth.

"She is quite tall," Totsuhwa said with a smile.

"Figures." And the scissors were pushed across the cloth making a clean cut.

Totsuhwa pulled the comb and mirror from beneath the fabric and placed them on top of it. He very gingerly began wrapping the pieces in the bright red cloth and then wrapped the material on itself until it formed a small bundle that fit neatly in his bag. Only then did he pick up the ginseng.

As Totsuhwa slipped open his pouch, the dealer produced a set of scales from beneath the counter. Totsuhwa watched him closely as he handed the man the purse and the trader began spilling the powdered root onto the weighing tray. Though Totsuhwa did not fully understand the mechanism, he masked the fact by his keen attention. When the scale balanced itself even slightly, Totsuhwa clasped the merchant's hand over the bag. "That is enough." And the trader could not disagree.

The patient horse took Totsuhwa's weight easily as the warrior swung onto its back. The shaman would not push the animal too hard and the trip home would take the standard time. Along the way Totsuhwa stopped only long enough to set a few snares for squirrels before retiring. In the morning he checked his simple traps and cooked what he caught for the day's ride. Several times throughout the days he chose to walk and the horse was grateful for the rest. Over the course of the trip the medicine pouch with its special cargo rode carefully on his hip. Always watchful over it, the presence of the mirror inside made Totsuhwa especially careful and he guarded the bag against tree limbs, jostling, and bumps.

Three days into the journey, Totsuhwa began to fast. The minor pains of hunger reminded him to pray and sing. He recited many prayers and incantations he had not used in some time, being careful to leave out a phrase or begin with a word of practice so the Spirit would not be called upon only to discover that there was no patient or necessity for His arrival. Rather than spend the mornings cooking his meals, Totsuhwa smoked and drank his herbal mixtures as he refreshed his mind and body for the day ahead. The self-denial was meant to be a reminder of the many things he had learned but he also wanted to be fresh of body and spirit when the day of his child's birth came upon him. He went so far as to practice the sing-songs which would hasten the baby's arrival.

"Little boy! Hurry! Come out! Come out! Little boy! A bow! A bow! Let's see who'll get it! Let's see who'll get it!

"Little girl! Hurry! Come out! Come Out! Little girl! A sifter! A sifter! Let's see who'll get it! Let's see who'll get it!"

The thoughts of his baby brought a broad smile to his face. The smile faded as Totsuhwa looked down at his horse as though startled. He quickly turned and looked at the horse's rump then back to its head. "Do you have a baby in you that is going to jump down now? That song was not meant for you, my friend. Another time," he said smiling again as he roughly stroked the animal's neck. "I will sing for you another time."

The fasting continued for five days. Totsuhwa rode and walked quietly, smoked occasionally, sipped his mixtures, and prayed often over the affairs of the nation and those of his growing family. On the third and fourth days of the fast he spoke not a word either in song or to his horse, but was consumed with visions and dreams in the night and throughout the day. By the fifth day he was speaking again but ignored the horse. His words were direct answers to questions posed by the Spirit which had come to visit him. In the questions and revelations Totsuhwa saw many things and heard many voices from the Tsalagi past. Some came as apparitions of animals and events not readily understood. On these, Totsuhwa would reflect and look for clarification and understanding through other as yet undreamed dreams.

One reverie had become as clear as settled water, made so by its constant repetition. It was the vision he had spoken of at the council. In its heart the locusts flowed over the mountains — first as a single insect. Then a few became a trickle. The stream rapidly grew to a torrent and soon the mountains themselves began to crumple under the weight of their number.

The Cherokee picked the first pests off the stalks of corn and crushed them between their fingers. When more appeared, the children were given the task of picking them and crushing them into baskets they carried. In a breath the baskets were too heavy for the children to carry and the swarm began pulling the children into the ground with their weight. All the while the Cherokee crops withered until there was nothing left.

The locusts began to consume the homes of the Cherokee and their animals when the crops had been eaten. Then the Cherokee people themselves were devoured by the flood of insects and soon all the ground became a mass of the bugs and nothing else. At this point the vision always ended and Totsuhwa's eyes cleared. He was again in the safety of his forest. The only insects were the flies that followed his scent and that of his horse. These he brushed away and swatted, waving his hand in rhythm with his horse's tail.

That night Totsuhwa set traps again. He built a small fire for the first time in several days and watched the flames lick away at the tinder. Lack of food and the persistent travel had made the shaman tired. The horse nibbled greens from the forest floor nearby while its master felt his head and shoulders growing heavy. In time Totsuhwa laid down to rest his body. In his sleep the vision came again.

Frantic, he leaped for his son's hand as the youngster was being pulled into the ground by the heavy weight of the boy's locust-filled basket. Totsuhwa sliced the cord that held the bin to his son and it sank in the earth as the boy leaped into his father's arms. They turned toward the cornfield as Totsuhwa held the child aloft, high above the swarming insects. The two watched, trembling, as Galegi, racing toward them, was overcome with the pests in a wave that consumed her in a blink of an eye.

Her screams shook Totsuhwa from his dream and he sat up with a brutal start, his wife's screams echoing in his ears. The commotion was so intense that Totsuhwa's horse, still browsing nearby, jumped with such a sudden fright that it tripped in its hobbles and fell. The clatter of the stumbling horse confused the rattled shaman even more. Totsuhwa was caught in the dreamy world between sleep and wakening. He inadvertently spun on the ground and twisted his blanket around his legs. Trapped, he lunged for his rifle, rolled with the blanket trailing his legs, and came up with the weapon at the ready, prepared to fire upon the mass of tumbling beast in the dark that was his hapless horse. Only at the last possible moment did the fog lift from his senses enough to show him what he was about to do. As quickly as the gun had come up, he brought it down.

He relaxed slightly as he came to be fully awake. The horse continued to flail until it found its feet and stood up. It shook slightly, still frightened by the freakish movement of its normally calm rider and by the fall it could do nothing to prevent. Totsuhwa was shaking as well. He breathed deeply as his eyes darted through the darkness for familiar things. The fire had been reduced to a glowing bed of coals but it gave enough light to show Totsuhwa his rolled bundles and medicine pouch. That was enough to prove to him that he was again in the right world and he unwound the blanket from his legs and returned to his sleeping place by the fire. But sleep was slow in returning as Totsuhwa wrestled with the dream he had been entrusted to interpret for the nation. Now he had to do the same for himself as he pondered the role his family had come to play in the most recent version of the nightmare.

The thing that kept sleep at bay was the simplicity of this newest vision. He understood clearly the Spirit's manifestation of the white men as locusts and what they would do to the Cherokee. The representation of his son nearly being lost to them and his wife being taken did not require a gift or any prayerful consideration. The cure, the saving, or the bending of the dream to save them, however, would require much.

In the gray that came with the first light of morning, a squirrel chased a potential mate up and down and around a narrow pine. Haste and passion blinded the courting pair and the male drove his mate headlong into a snare Totsuhwa had fastened against the tree. The skillful snare worked to perfection and closed around the victim's neck, tightened, and the squirrel flipped against the restraint until she choked herself to death.

While her suitor skated over, under, and around her on the tree, alarmed by her thrashing and mid-air dangling, the female strangled. In less than a minute it was over.

The male was overcome with curiosity and ventured closer. He sniffed the air, smelled the hormones that had invited him in the first place and breathed in the growing odor of death. He retreated in a gray blur to the safety of the treetops.

Totsuhwa had been awakened by the same sun that crept down the pine tree and eventually shone on the hanging squirrel. The hunter rose and found his trap. He slipped the noose from the squirrel's neck and held the body under his arm as he put a finger to his water bag and shook it. The drops that settled around his finger were transferred to the tiny gray mouth as the hunter gave thanks. As he did so, Totsuhwa heard the chatter of the male squirrel high above. He looked up and searched through the canopy until he found the male squatting on a lofty branch, screaming at the killer.

"I am sorry for your loss, sa-lo-li, but be saddened for only a short time. She will wait for you in the West. Until then go run through the trees and find another mate."

As the body was carried off and prepared, the male followed in the trees. He continued to harass Totsuhwa for some time then returned to his own territory to mourn and try to understand what had occurred.

Totsuhwa finished the first meal he had eaten in five days. There was nothing left to waste. The tiny hide and tail was cleaned then rolled up to be dealt with later. Totsuhwa wanted to get home to Galegi and the unborn baby he now felt, as a result of his dream, would be a son. As he bounced onto his horse he thought of the boy and the dream and was instantly troubled by the dual worlds he would be brought into. He forced the trouble back down the throat of his mind by thoughts of what the child would be like and what he might be called. Much would depend on the conditions of his birth and his actions as a child. But like the thoughts of the locusts before, these considerations were pushed aside by something new.

If the boy was to be reared in both worlds for his insured survival, his name must be English like the whites and like the young leaders of the nation. Ridge. James Vann. These men had Cherokee names as well, but in their dealings with the locusts they used their white names to assure themselves a place at the white man's table. Perhaps the boy should have another name as well — something that would ease his steps into the world that was coming.

This thought occupied Totsuhwa's mind for the bulk of the ride home. A name was an important part of a Cherokee he reminded himself. The name would reveal part of the boy's personality or become a part of him as much as his hand. The name could be injured or offended if not chosen with great care and attended to. If poorly treated the name might not respond when called, such as when a chant or remedy was delivered. It might be difficult to find a white name that carried the weight for a Cherokee that Totsuhwa demanded.

He ran through lists of every name of a white person he knew but each time was left with a lingering trace of the original owner which discouraged him. Then he broadened his scope and recalled the king, George, but considered that it was a name that carried a uniqueness which should be available only to the chiefs of that nation. There were other less lofty dignitaries he recalled. There were princes and dukes, bishops and high sheriffs. He had heard white traders talk of them and even stories from the old Cherokee chiefs who had traveled across the wide water to talk with the king.

One of those chiefs, he now remembered, spoke of a chancellor. Totsuhwa was unsure whether "chancellor" was a name or a title, but it rang well in his mind's ear. He tested it on his tongue. "Chancellor." It sounded good to him. Perhaps not as good as "King," but that would be like naming the boy "Chief." Totsuhwa laughed at himself for the notion and repeated the name.

"Chancellor. Chancellor. That is a good name."

The boy must have two white names, Totsuhwa thought to himself. "All the white men do." But one at a time. Perhaps Galegi would have a second name. That thought stopped him.

Galegi would not have a second name as she would be hard pressed to recognize the first. She would call the baby "Usdi," as all Tsalagi babies are called until a Cherokee name for a growing child presented itself. Totsuhwa understood this and would offer no argument. His wife was more steadfast against the white ways than any man in the room at the council meeting. She would accept Totsuhwa's white name for the boy as a right of the father but he was unsure she would ever use it with regularity. These were the things in Totsuhwa's mind as the final days passed on his trip home.

Two more days' ride found Totsuhwa within sight of the last mountain range between him and the woman he loved. He had been gone almost a month, and knew the changes in his wife would be pronounced. Her belly would be swollen to bursting and the baby would be ready to drop down. He gently squeezed the bundle wrapped in his satchel as a test to see if the mirror was intact. It was, as near as he could tell, and the picture in his mind of Galegi's face when he gave it to her caused him to spur the horse with his leather-covered heels and move the animal into an effortless gliding lope.

The horse crossed the top of the last mountain with relative ease. When the mount and rider cleared the range, a lush valley opened up before them. They began to walk and take in the sights that were home to both. The animal whinnied at the familiar smells and if he could have, Totsuhwa would have whinnied as well. There was great comfort here — in the smells of the trees and brush lands and the crops growing in their patchwork greens further up the valley. Some distance away Totsuhwa could see a faint plume of smoke rising from the main section of the village. It would be the combination of several cooking fires coming together above the town.

Totsuhwa's own home fire would be burning further to the north, far out of sight, a distance that set the shaman well apart from the village proper. He liked the distance, the cushion between his family and the rest of the world. Visitors came well announced and not often. Any that crept close without calling out would not be welcomed. If the couple's dogs did not repel the rude guest or blatant enemy, Totsuhwa and Galegi, she as hard as he, would. The simple cabin was a private place where the couple lived and studied, laughed and loved, and now would raise a family.

Totsuhwa found himself concentrating on the feelings and trying to memorialize the thoughts for a future date. When he caught himself, his chin dropped a degree and he sighed. He knew immediately why he wanted to capture the sentiment. Around these pleasant musings of a man coming home there rode the specter of a warrior who was constantly moving and struggling against the very bindings Totsuhwa now longed for. From his earliest days as he'd sprinted out of Ama Giga's camp after his chores were done, he had felt the wanderlust and detachment rise up in him. He had recognized in his dreams and with Ama Giga's guidance that the longing was his own spirit looking for the mother and father who had gone to the West and left him alone.

With his grandmother's death, Totsuhwa's spirit was again sent to wandering. It was then that he had found his teacher. The days with Tsi'yugunsini had found him the most at ease with his spirit. The men were almost constantly moving — searching for enemies, for supplies, and for cover. It had suited him more than he realized. But as with his other loves, the Dragon had gone and

Totsuhwa was left alone again. So he had resumed his search for the thing that would fill the hole in him.

Redemption came in Galegi and ran deep and seemed complete, but after a few months in the cabin he inevitably would feel the tug of the forest. The feeling had an easy escape. The nation needed its principal shaman or a highly skilled warrior. Treks were required to gain the medicinal fruits of the woods or dream quests to fill the spiritual reservoir inside him. Though he cuddled his bride and nuzzled her neck as a goodbye, there was always a deep breath that filled him as he rode into the hills. As strong as Totsuhwa was as a man, a physician to his people and a fighter, he found a weakness in his heart that whispered the insecurities of abandonment — real or imagined. The shock of a child whose father had been killed took root in a young mind when fever claimed his mother. Others in his life, drawn to death by disease or battle, both common occurrences in his world, left other smaller scars until Ama Giga walked West and the gap widened to the hole that grew rock walls when his mentor drifted to sleep after the night of celebration.

So now, as he rode into his valley, the excitement and anticipation was tempered by the sense that in a month, maybe more, a whisper would tug at his mind that to linger meant hurt would ride in one day and leave him alone. Though he knew this, he wondered how many times he could withstand a loss. His answer was self-imposed distance, and he knew he would find a reason to escape to the comfort of his mountains once again.

Horse and rider's ears picked up the sound of a creek ahead. The animal had smelled the water before the sound reached its twitching ears and though it was not burdened by thirst it would dip its head when it reached the creek. Totsuhwa would do the same. In a few more steps he slid from the horse's back without pulling the animal up. While neither missed a step the pair continued walking to the water. Here the brook was narrow, little more than four strides wide.

The horse nuzzled the water and blew its nose into it. Totsuhwa knelt beside the creek and put the reins under his knee to keep his partner in tow. With both hands now free he took off his shirt and began to bathe himself in the shallow water. A small quiet pool before him acted as a reflecting glass and he examined what he saw. He pushed his damp black hair back away and turned his face from side to side looking for dirt but also checking his features. Totsuhwa had seen nearly forty winters come and go yet thought himself still a young man. Galegi was a few winters younger but much prettier. They would make a beautiful baby.

"Come along, friend," Totsuhwa said as he stood and wiped the water off his face and body. "Let's go see our chief." He slung the shirt over his shoulder and urged the horse through the ankle-deep water and up the gradual bank on the other side and on toward home.

They had not gone far before the easy breeze brought the sound of Galegi's singing to Totsuhwa's ears. The horse was stopped to clear the rustling of its steps from the shaman's keen senses. His own steps could be like a mouse but the horse was far clumsier. They held their ground for only a moment as Totsuhwa honed in on where the ringing voice was coming from. The horse meanwhile, only wondered why they were stopping when the comfort of home lay just ahead.

When the direction had been discovered, Totsuhwa took the hobbles from his pack and tied them to the horse's front feet. The animal would wander on toward home without its rider. Totsuhwa patted the horse's rump and walked off the trail toward the singing.

The voice became clearer with each step along the flowing stream. The water was vibrant, as was all moving water to the Cherokee. It spoke to those who would listen and carried wisdom and visions on its back. The Long Man brought healing from a great many maladies and blessings during times of celebration. When the baby was born Totsuhwa would bring him here to be welcomed and bathed by the Long Man. Today it was cradling his love.

When the stream came fully within sight, Totsuhwa crouched low to the ground and crept along like a panther. The babbling of the stream's voice mixed with Galegi's and brought a warm bud of a smile to the stalking hunter's face. The sight of his wife a moment later drew the smile into full bloom.

Here the brook was spread wider, nearly forty feet, and the flat water deepened and slowed. The lady was bathing waist deep in the stream three-quarters of the way across the creek from her unseen husband. Her cinnamon skin glistened with the dance of sunlight and water as the elements played across her shoulders. A cupped hand brought water to her face that trickled down her full breasts. Both hands dipped into the stream to shower her protruding stomach, spooning the cool water and rubbing it into her tight skin. The singing voice trailed on and off, varying from forceful notes full of raucous vigor to a soothing hum. Between the rise and fall Galegi spoke to her baby in tones that were as wide-ranging as her singing. She cooed reassuring words of a mother to her distended belly then turned into an encouraging teacher who admonished her pupil to learn, be brave, be honest, and true to the Tsalagi blood that nourished the tiny body.

When Galegi squatted and dipped her head back under water Totsuhwa jumped to the bank. He squatted and sat as he always did as he waited for his wife to surface. She did so with great ease and grace, letting the water and her hands push the long black hair that had given her her name back against her head. The water was still reeling from her eyes when her husband purposely startled her.

"Your belly will frighten away the fish, woman."

Galegi jerked toward the voice but in the same instant she recognized her husband and comfort draped over her like a soft robe from a buffalo calf.

"I see no one fishing." She smiled as she feigned to look around her.

"With reason. A woman with child should not enter the Long Man without a bark strip of walnut tied to her toe. Otherwise the fish—"

Galegi leaned back and let the water support her as her surfacing foot interrupted her lecturing husband. Tied to her big toe was a thin band of walnut bark.

"I have not lived in the house of a shaman this past year and learned nothing, oh wise one."

Totsuhwa nodded and smiled as if he had been gently scolded. "I think I should see your talisman closer to know you have chosen the right wood." And Totsuhwa held out his hand toward his wife.

She responded by lifting her foot again and holding it out toward him. "Here it is if you wish to see it."

"I should get wet in order to save you from the wrath of the fishermen?"

"A good husband would not think twice."

"I am a good husband."

"So you say."

The tender jab silenced Totsuhwa's words then raised Galegi's eyebrows as she continued to question him. "And still you are dry."

He dropped his knife and medicine pouch then immediately strode into the water, clothes and all. She laughed at him as he abandoned his cautious ways and tromped along much like his horse. The splashes were exaggerated and done for Galegi's benefit until a hurried misplaced step on the creek bottom caused Totsuhwa to stumble in earnest. While he floundered and went under, Galegi laughed. But when he failed to thrash back to surface, the laughter slowed and eventually stopped. A moment passed as the surface of the water settled back on itself until no sign of the falling man lingered.

Galegi took one step toward the spot and called her husband's name. When no movement in the water answered, she took another quicker step and called Totsuhwa's name a little louder. As the answer came back the same she trudged hurriedly to the spot she had seen her husband lose his feet, shouting his name as she did.

She reached the spot where he had gone under and ducked into the water to find him. However, as soon as she plunged into the water Totsuhwa's arms encircled her legs from behind. He exploded from the water, bringing a showering geyser and his wife up with him from the creek bottom.

Any anxiety Galegi had felt rising in her throat vanished beneath the touch of her husband's strong hands. His growl from the pretended attack was drowned out by her laughter and in a flash the sound was muzzled by the deep kiss that held them until the splash had long become a memory to the brook. The kiss held the couple fast by the lips until reassurance from each flooded through the mouth of the other and filled them both to bursting. They were together once again.

In the long embrace Totsuhwa felt the fullness of his wife's breasts and the pressure of her stomach against his. Reminded of his child, he eased slowly out of the kiss. He touched her naked belly with both his hands and moved them tenderly over the whole of it as though they were searching. His eyes followed his fingers through the gentle caress until they had touched and seen every inch of the baby's resting place. Only then did the hands move to Galegi's face and hold it as they kissed again.

As the kiss melted Totsuhwa spoke to his wife while his eyes darted to her stomach and back. "How are you?"

"Fine. Just fine," she said through another hug which made her words even more true.

"And our child?"

"Fine as well."

The father caressed the mother's abdomen once more. "He is fine," Totsuhwa said rather absently as he thought again of his dreams.

"He?" Galegi said dramatically as she tapped her fingers across her tummy. "Are you so certain this is a bow? It could be a sifter, you know."

"Yes, I am certain. Our child will be a bow. The cricket will cry because he will know our son will hunt him and practice shooting his tiny bow."

"A girl would help me grind the corn and sift it for our meals. She would carry my lineage through the line of the clan."

Totsuhwa hugged her and kissed her but this time only on the cheek. He smiled and carefully pushed his hips into hers. "We will make a sifter after the bow jumps down."

She playfully slapped him on the shoulder and he pretended to be hurt. "You know what you want to know. The baby will be what pleases the Spirit."

"That is true, Galegi. And it is the Spirit who has told me the child will be a boy. You will see."

"If you tell me this then I will expect a bow. And we will see about that girl." And she kissed his cheek in return.

The kiss on the cheek moved to Totsuhwa's lips. The thrill that had overcome them when they first touched in the water — the thrill of being in each other's arms once again — gave way to passion. Galegi wrapped her legs around her husband and he carried her to deeper water as the kisses deepened beneath gasps for air. The couple's hands raced over their faces, arms, and backs as though searching, as indeed they were, for the softest touch, the hardest touch — the touch that would both excite and satisfy. Her hands came to the front of his pants and fought with the wet and swollen leather ties. He stopped his own groping and held her out away from him.

"Are you sure? I do not want to frighten the boy."

"He is asleep," she said as she continued fumbling with the ties.

"We may wake him."

"Not if we are quiet," she said as the pants finally cooperated.

Totsuhwa smiled. "We are not good at being quiet. I can be but you cry out like a screaming eagle."

"Only to make you feel like a man. Were it left to me, I could sleep."

Now Totsuhwa laughed out loud. "You wiggle like the snake you were named for! If we were lying in hiding from our enemies a stone's throw away, you would still cry out, such is your pleasure."

"And that would be you — wanting to make a baby as we lay in hiding!"

The ribbing was soon supplanted by more kisses until, with the placid support of the water, they made love slowly and with great care.

Afterward, in the glow of a warm and drying fire, Totsuhwa pulled the presents from his pouch. Each one was answered with a flood of kisses.

"They are so beautiful," Galegi said as she stroked the comb and mirror.

He pointed into the mirror at her reflection. "No, this is beautiful."

Feeling that neither a confirmation nor denial would be appropriate, she fell again into her husband and kissed him with growing passion. The bright red cloth was in her hands and she used it to caress Totsuhwa's face.

"Do not wipe away your kisses," he teased.

"I do not. But feel how soft."

"It will make a nice dress."

Galegi pushed away and stood up awkwardly. She pressed the comb and mirror into her husband's hands for safe keeping and unfurled the cloth down her body. She held it at her neck and waist and spun back and forth until the red cloth flew out away from her while her husband clapped his approval.

Many more days would pass before the baby was ready. Even then it delayed. Totsuhwa went into the cabin and entreated his wife to allow him to sing the songs that would make the boy jump down but Galegi would not permit it.

"The child will come when the Spirit says it is right," she quipped as she cut and sewed the bright red cloth. "Your songs are powerful and true, but we will listen for the Spirit's voice, not yours."

After more days had passed, with increasing discomfort for the would-be new mother, Totsuhwa tried again. This time the couple was outside. She sat on a large log rolled to the house for just that purpose as she worked the red cloth. He was wrapping wet leather around the flint of new arrows.

"Let me sing the magic songs. The boy will come, and you can sleep in peace."

"Listen, great shaman," she answered as she set her sewing in her lap, "Do not entice the boy with your promise of a bow and arrows. If he comes because of that, he may run for things that mean little his lifelong. Rather he is slow to come but wise and mindful and choosing of his own way."

Totsuhwa was slightly perturbed. "A bow does not mean little to a warrior. It belongs in the hands of a man."

"I apologize. I spoke without thinking, husband. A bow is a powerful thing in your hands. I meant that I do not want our son to rush for things. I want him to be cautious and pursue those things in life that mean most." She cupped his hand. "Things like a strong and devoted mate. Love of family and people. Concern for our land. Things that do not tease a baby from his mother."

Totsuhwa overtook his wife's hand and held it in his own. "I ask the Spirit to give our son your wisdom over mine, Galegi. You see things I do not."

"No, Totsuhwa, my little one. You are so wise in the ways of the people. And in that powerful chest there is a heart as big as a bear's. Our son will have the mind and arms of his father. Anything less and he will have been cheated."

Totsuhwa smiled but secretly hoped his boy would have a great many traits of his mother despite her kind words to the contrary. Galegi was a wonderful woman and a beautiful wife. She would make the perfect mother to their son.

"What is that smile?" Galegi asked.

As though caught in a bad act, the smile ran away. "Nothing," he said.

"Nothing?"

"Our boy. I am thinking of how he will look in his mother's arms."

"And his father's," she said as she struggled to stand then went to him with the red cloth held before her huge stomach. She handed him the red bundle then bid him help her get down to the log nearer him. When she was as comfortable as she could get, he handed her back the cloth so she could continue her work. She, however, pushed it back to him.

"No more today?" he asked.

"No more today or tomorrow. It is complete."

"Good! In a few days it will fit you again. Then we will dance and celebrate our new boy in your new dress." He paused only a moment. "And maybe make a sifter for you beneath it."

She pushed him away with a smile. "You are a bad man. I do not know why I make you gifts."

Totsuhwa looked around the front of the cabin. "Where is my gift?"

"In your hands, oh wise shaman."

"What do you mean?"

"For the greatest shaman of the Cherokee, you can be slow." She laughed but quickly added, "I still love you though."

"You have a sharp tongue for a woman who will not be able to move from that spot unless I help her."

She ignored him. "In your hands, Totsuhwa. The gift is the red cloth. Open it."

Confused, but following her directions, Totsuhwa unfolded the red cloth. It was not the shape he envisioned. Rather, it was a shirt, a large shirt, his size.

"What is this?"

"I did not need a dress. You needed a shirt for dancing."

"It is so bright and pretty." He stopped and lowered the shirt into his lap. "Can a warrior wear such a shirt?"

"He can."

"Then I will. But I meant the red cloth for you. It was a gift. You cannot give it back."

"The cloth was your gift to me. The shirt is my gift to you. They are not the same."

"You are the wise one or at least the crafty one, like a fox I think."

"Do you like it?"

"I will have it always."

"It is not for butchering deer."

"Yes, Mother."

"Only for dancing."

"Only for dancing, Mother," he said as he leaned forward and gave her a thank you kiss. Then he put the shirt around her shoulders and sealed it with his arms.

The couple sat that way, with all four hands resting on Galegi's stomach, until discomfort elbowed the very pregnant woman and made her move. Totsuhwa helped her to her feet then eased her back down on the log only to help her move again a few minutes later.

While the couple waited out their delinquent baby, the ball game proposed by The Ridge was coming together many days' ride away. Teams of players carrying their sticks and tossing balls back and forth, some for practice but most to relieve tension, filtered into the wide valley where the games would be held. Entire families joined in as the accompanying festival of cooking, eating, and gambling nearly overshadowed the games themselves. Small children mimicked the men and ran with little sticks styled after the warriors'. Fire pits raged everywhere on the valley floor, warming one meal or another, preparing a special treat for the children or stirring up a magic elixir for the players. All around the fire-dotted floor of the valley were impromptu practice games and planning sessions organized by informal coaches who doubled as players. Minor injuries were quickly rubbed away or covered with mud and soon lost to the growing fervor of the real games.

A secondary game was afoot as well. Commingled with the ball game preparation in the collecting crowds and even on the playing fields, the seeds planted by The Ridge were being spread, planted, and tended. Most Cherokee ears were receptive to the words of their chiefs and quickly came to understand the importance of adaptation as opposed to annihilation. Many had considered this long beforehand and had come to practice it without knowingly doing so. These constituted the comfortable majority and would convert most of the others in short order. Before the first official game was begun and without a shot being fired or a treaty drawn, the bulk of the Cherokee Nation had quietly aligned itself with the colonial government.

People moved in groups of twos and threes, fours, fives, and tens in ebbs and flows around the ball field. Some searched for a better position to see the action while others were hunting for better places to be seen. And one man was just hunting. His name was Bone Polisher.

Laughter and strategy for the games flowed through the crowds around the hunter. Stern looks shot from one team to another and back again with equal ferocity as game time approached. These passed over Bone Polisher's head as unseen as a summer breeze. His face was intense beyond the look of competition. The fever for the contest was building with the approaching hour but paled in comparison to what Bone Polisher secretly carried in his heart.

As his wanderings continued, all but unnoticed by the collecting masses, other Cherokee chiefs and their entourages settled in around the field. Doublehead had arrived the night before and had taken up a prime spot near the centerfield line. He was lounging with a small group of loyal braves, each taking their turn at easing pleasure from a whiskey bottle. Doublehead laughed too loudly and his remarks were biting, to both those who came within earshot and his own men. His men laughed with him regardless and washed away any concern with more whiskey. Others who wandered too near quickly changed direction under a lash from Doublehead's tongue. The exception came when a moderate-sized group of slow-moving warriors worked their way close as they circumnavigated the entire field. They were led by Chief James Vann.

The chief had been one of the hardest laboring converts following the convention, which was now two moons past. He had worked his own villages tirelessly and continued to promote the changes tendered by The Ridge at the ball game. Meeting little opposition, Vann and others, including Ridge, worked through the collected nation, thanking them for their support of the changes and encouraging those who might falter. The easygoing acceptance and excitement at the impending games were halted instantly when Chief Vann laid eyes on Doublehead.

"Osiyo, Baby Killer," Chief Vann said as though Doublehead had been called by that name his entire life.

The words stopped the traveling group behind the speaker and eased the whiskey away from the mouths that reclined on the grass.

"Mind your tongue," Doublehead said. He raised a hand slowly before him and turned it over and over again as he spoke. "A wave of this hand and my warriors will carve your heart out and hand it to me while it still beats."

The Vann contingency outnumbered Doublehead's men three to one and all of the latter group were spread out on the grass and deep in the arms of the whiskey, which made them more inclined to fight but less capable of doing so. Still, The Ridge and a few others nearby came closer and drew up tight around Chief Vann. He brushed them away and stepped brazenly over the prostrate drinking warriors at his feet. As he waded through the men, closer to Doublehead, he occasionally leaned on the reclining warriors for unneeded balance. None resisted.

"I think not, Baby Killer. These men are fine Cherokee. They are blinded temporarily by your gifts," Vann said as he reached low and slipped a whiskey bottle from a young warrior's hand. The chief took a big swig from the bottle and handed it back to the young man.

"Good whiskey, Baby Killer. It is not worth ten million acres of our hunting grounds but it is good whiskey."

"I told you not to play here, half-breed. You may think these wolves will not bite you, but you know I will."

"I know Baby Killer may bite, but a warrior is not afraid."

"You have never been a warrior. Your arms are weak from trading with the white men. My arms are strong from battle."

"It takes no strength to make a mark on the leaves, Baby Killer."

"That is not my name!" Doublehead yelled as he sprang to his feet. A half-dozen men, Ridge among them, surrounded Vann and pulled him back into the tight group. A few hands reached up to meekly restrain Doublehead, but he slapped them aside then shook his finger at Chief Vann.

"Go, Vann! Hide behind that other half-breed who calls himself our leader!"

Vann struggled against those that held him. "I am here, Baby Killer! I do not run from you! Let go, Ridge. I have heard enough from this traitor!"

"Traitor?" Doublehead echoed. "How do you call Doublehead a traitor while a real traitor ties your hands and prevents you from being a man?"

"That is enough, Doublehead," Ridge said forcibly.

"Do not speak to me, dog. No half-breed will ever tell Doublehead what to do!"

"Go back to your bottle, Doublehead. Be glad you still live. And leave the rest of the nation alone."

"I will do as I please."

"Then do so!" Ridge shouted as he released Vann and focused on Doublehead. "Tell more lies and sell more land. You know the law now. Go sell more land and the first Cherokee warrior you meet will have your blood on his blade!"

"What if that first warrior is you, Ridge? Your blade is rusty from sitting in the white man's schools. You two are no more Cherokee than that white pup of Vann's whose head I crushed."

The hands that held Chief Vann felt the muscles tighten but then quickly relax. He was too smart to be goaded into the fight.

The Ridge, however, was not so immediately concerned with wisdom. Vann watched as others moved in to restrain Ridge as he charged.

"Let him come!" Doublehead screamed. "I will do the people a justice by killing this half-breed who would hand us over to the white way."

Ridge was nearly lifted off the ground in his men's attempt to hold him back. "Justice? The people? You know nothing of either! You are concerned only with what profits you. You would trade every Cherokee child for a single ounce of silver."

"I am weary of listening to the words of a half-breed. Fight me now or go off with the women and cook my meal."

Ridge struggled again to get at Doublehead, but the struggling only increased the rapidity with which Vann and the others moved him away from Doublehead's clutch of men.

Chief Vann shouted back to the pacing Doublehead. "Thank you for the drink, Baby Killer."

Doublehead grew bolder as the stoic chief and the volatile Ridge moved further away. "Neither of you fools have ever learned the true ways of the Tsalagi!"

Vann stopped only for a moment then moved away after Ridge whose struggle was slowly dying. "We have learned the ways, Baby Killer. They are of acceptance and change. Of education and growth. We have other battles to fight and win. We do not need to battle each other."

"You are a coward."

Vann neither turned nor answered.

"You are a coward, James Vann!"

The words reached deep into the chief's ears and plucked at his mind but could not get inside. Integrity and quiet valor drove them away as he moved on after the fuming Ridge. However, just as he reached the men, shouts from behind him stopped the entire assembly and brought them around as one.

"I am no coward, Doublehead, or is it Baby Killer, as the great Chief Vann has renamed you?"

The voice belonged to Bone Polisher. He had tracked his quarry and was prepared to take him down.

"Say those words again, Bone Polisher, and they will be the last you ever speak," Doublehead said.

Bone Polisher slipped his tomahawk from his waist and spun it easily in his hand as he spoke the name over and over very slowly. "Ba-by...Kil-ler...Ba-by...Kil-ler."

Doublehead looked at him as though a bit puzzled. "Do I have a quarrel with you?"

"You do. With me and the entire nation."

"What is your claim?"

"You are a traitor, Doublehead — I mean, Baby Killer. You must answer for your betrayal of the people." The tomahawk ceased to spin. Bone Polisher hefted it up and down, adjusting his grip.

"Those words are your last!" Doublehead snarled as he ripped his knife from its sheath and began to circle his tormentor.

By now a crowd had gathered. The Ridge, Vann, and the others had hurried back and crowded in but they pushed back to form a ring when the knife blade flashed its teeth. Cheers and shouts began to well up from the younger of the spectators while the older chiefs watched over arms folded supremely on their chests. Ridge urged Bone Polisher on, as did everyone else. Doublehead had few supporters but needed none. He was older than his opponent yet still powerful and very skilled in the handling of his knife. Bone Polisher and the others in the circle eyed the blade and knew how deep its master would send it. Doublehead was not the type of man who would merely beat a man and slice him enough to end the fight. He would stop when the handle of his knife struck bone and could go no deeper. The only way to stop him would be to either kill him or wait for your own heart to cease pumping. When either occurred Doublehead would end his assault but not until.

All the men knew instantly that someone was about to die. Vann knew it along with the others and reached for Bone Polisher.

Ridge ripped his hand back. "Leave him to fight!"

"For what?"

"Because it is right! I should have fought him myself!"

"Ridge, we have laws!"

"Yes, and they demand Doublehead be punished!"

"We said the law would not be held against those who sold before the—"

"NO! We have other laws, maybe not spoken of so clearly, but laws that are as old as this valley. They say Doublehead must be punished." And Ridge turned again to face the fighting.

The two fighters were walking sideways in a narrowing circle. Bone Polisher watched the blade as it reflected the light while Doublehead watched only his opponent's eyes before stepping in and testing Bone Polisher's reflexes with a quick but harmless jab. Bone Polisher easily avoided the knife and jerked his tomahawk around to the front and waved it under Doublehead's face. The traitor to the nation merely smiled.

The deadly dance continued as that for nearly a minute — each man testing the other and gauging where to best attack. Doublehead's impatience drove him to strike before the preparation was complete and it cost him.

The knife attack was only a diversion. As Doublehead thrust the blade forward Bone Polisher stepped to the side, away from the menacing iron. In the step his eyes were glued to the knife and he did not notice the crashing punch until it was far too late to react. Doublehead's fist landed just behind Bone polisher's eye on the side of his head. It staggered him considerably and would likely have meant instant death on Doublehead's blade had not his own axe saved him.

Driven partly out of a last-minute reaction to the punch and perhaps more so by the momentum of his body reeling under the blow, Bone Polisher's tomahawk swung in front of him and caught Doublehead with a savage crack on his upper arm. The keen edge of the axe sliced through the muscle and laid it open. The gash was so deep that it hung a moment before it bled — seemingly surprised itself how badly it had been torn.

But the wound would be Bone Polisher's undoing. Doublehead ignored the blood streaming down his arm and instead found strength and intensity in the pain. Bone Polisher, still shaken by the punch to the head, saw the blood and jumped in on Doublehead for what he thought would be the kill. For his impetuousness Bone Polisher would pay with his life.

Doublehead recognized the look in Bone Polisher's eye as one he had seen many times in battle. Overconfidence was fatal. Doublehead dropped the torn arm as though it were nearly severed. He staggered backward as though about to stumble to the ground. His knife hung limply in the hand of the tattered arm. He even dropped his head as though he were fainting from the loss of blood. All this in the space of the time it took Bone Polisher to see the injury he had caused and prepare to relish in it.

But when Bone Polisher rushed in with his tomahawk overhead, ready to imbed it in Doublehead's skull, the knife came up smartly in a hardened fist. As the blade dove under Bone Polisher's ribs and bit his heart, Doublehead's free hand caught the wrist of the tomahawk-wielding hand. Bone Polisher's free hand came up slowly and settled calmly on Doublehead's shoulder. The fight was over.

Bone Polisher's eyes widened as Doublehead jerked hard on his knife and pierced deeper into the stricken heart. He wrenched the tomahawk down from overhead and it fell harmlessly to the men's feet. Now standing even closer, Doublehead leaned back and howled like an animal over his triumph. As he screamed, Bone Polisher collapsed against his chest. Doublehead held him there for the duration of yet another victorious scream then stepped back, withdrew his knife, and let Bone Polisher fall face first to the ground.

The defender of the people rolled over, never speaking or moaning through the span of a few breaths. He avoided the eyes peering down at him and looked instead up to the bright sky. In another quickening breath he looked up at Doublehead who was standing over him holding the knife. Bone Polisher's blood on the blade was mixing with Doublehead's own as it trickled down from his upper arm. The blood of both men dripped from the sharp tip of the knife to the ground.

Bone Polisher pointed weakly at Doublehead's bloodied arm. "You will remember me... I will be the witch in your arm...when the nights are cold."

Doublehead stared for a moment at his arm then shook his knife at Bone Polisher and splattered their combined blood across the dying man's face. "I have been cut worse by briars. You are nothing to me."

Doublehead turned and walked away as the last breath slipped out of Bone Polisher's chest. The men and women who had witnessed the killing stood silently for a moment as the realization that they had seen one Cherokee kill another settled in their minds. It was Chief Vann who broke the silence and gave the assembly its direction.

"It was a good fight. Two warriors have met and one has walked away. The other will wait for us in the West." He motioned to some of his men. "Tend to Bone Polisher." Then he addressed The Ridge. "Bring together your people for the ball play. This will not dampen our spirit. Play the games as you have planned."

Everyone in the crowd had seen the face of death more times than any could count. Even the children present had watched death steal in the cabins of the aged and sick and leave with a life. Most had seen warriors return from battle or hunting accidents with spilled innards and wrenched arms and legs only to die agonizingly in the villages of their birth. But again, this was Cherokee on Cherokee. Not totally unheard of but rare, made more so by the notion that Bone Polisher had represented the will of many. Still he had lost.

The Ridge looked down at the blood seeping across the fallen man's clothes. His eyes came away from the dead and looked for the living. In the distance he saw Doublehead walking slowly in the direction of a cabin at the far end of the valley.

Doublehead was wounded, more badly than he let on. Ridge could see it in the way he moved. Now would be the time to finish what Bone Polisher had begun. First however, the games would begin as Chief Vann had suggested. Then later, when the coolness of the night had stiffened Doublehead's injury, Ridge would visit him and settle the debt Doublehead the Baby Killer owed the nation.

The shock of Bone Polisher's death hung near the ball field but was kept at bay by the excitement of the event. The dead man's family mourned him properly and when they passed nearby received the graces of the others in the valley. Yet, when they had moved on, the dancing began again. Chiefs Vann and Ridge stoked the flames of the celebration as a welcoming to the way of life they were promoting and continued to foster the change in philosophy they hoped would be the saving grace of the nation.

While some mourned, some danced, some pressed politics, and others prepared for the ball play, Doublehead lay in a small barn near the cabin and wrestled to stop the bleeding. It would take some doing but with the help of a few reluctant attendants the bleeding was eventually stanched enough to allow him to rest. When night had encircled the valley he fell to sleep with the help of several long pulls on a whiskey bottle. As his breathing deepened, his attendants abandoned him for the fires of the dances that anointed the following day's games. And when the faces of Doublehead's warriors appeared in the glow of the fires, The Ridge slipped away into the dark.

A small fire was quietly snapping itself to sleep at the entrance to the barn where Chief Doublehead had sought to recover. The Ridge's feet moved like molasses, as slowly and as silent. They carried him around the fire into the barn and right up to Doublehead. He was sleeping. Fresh blood was working its way through the makeshift bandages tied around his upper arm. A great deal of blood was dried on the old warrior's lower arm and hand. His pants were also bloodied, as was his free hand from its struggle with the wound.

Ridge considered that Doublehead might yet die from the blow inflicted by Bone Polisher and considered slipping out of the barn and giving time a chance at the chief's scalp. That plan was rudely pushed aside by the sight of a near-empty whiskey bottle lying alongside the nation's betrayer. The bottle was partial payment for a sin committed against the people and Ridge had come to make it right. He raised his war club over his head as he measured the distance to Doublehead's skull. His own muscles tightened, coiling like a snake about to strike, but the club did not come crashing down. He held it overhead for another breath and then lowered it as silently as he'd raised it.

Ridge stepped back slightly and positioned himself at the man's feet. He tested the grip on both the war club and his knife then kicked the bottom of Doublehead's feet.

"Hey! Old man!"

Doublehead woke with a start and immediately pulled his knife more out of reflex than understanding. In his sleeping and wakening he had forgotten his injury until the pain in the arm and numbness in his hand reminded him. He began to grimace but caught himself and swallowed the pain as his eyes fought to pierce the haziness of wakening and the shadows of the barn.

"Who is that?" he demanded.

"Your executioner."

"So you say. I know that voice, Ridge."

The Ridge held his ground and watched as Doublehead gradually pulled his feet up under him. He understood that the wounded chief, once standing, would be on more equal ground but he let the advantage purposely slip away.

"You should have killed me in my sleep," Doublehead said as he continued to rise. "Not doing so was bad judgment. Now it is you that will sleep!"

Doublehead leaped from a partial crouch. Caught off guard, Ridge narrowly avoided the darkened blade but took the brunt of Doublehead's shoulder in the chest and was propelled backward to the floor. Doublehead landed on top of him thrashing with his fist and the menacing knife. Ridge dropped his own knife in favor of grabbing Doublehead's wrist and stopping the dried-blood-covered blade from driving into his own chest. His war club was temporarily useless as it was too close to gain the swing it needed. Instead Ridge punched with his fist as it gripped the handle.

A few inconsequential blows to the head and Ridge brought the handle and its punch down to the wound on Doublehead's arm. He struck as hard as he could into the bloody rag bandage with the weight of the war club behind each blow. Meanwhile his other hand was losing its battle with the menacing knife.

Being on top gave Doublehead the advantage of using his weight to drive the knife down. His other hand was snarled around Ridge's throat, brutally squeezing the air and blood from what he immediately thought would be his second victim of the day. Ridge locked his arm in place to prevent being stabbed but was fading already to Doublehead's superior size, weight, and strength. Though badly injured, the war chief was formidable. His choke-hold, even one-handed, was incredibly tight. He had fought count-less more battles than Ridge had ever seen and had taken hundreds of scalps, many after hand-to-hand combat such as this.

As the knife began to press against Ridge's skin, Doublehead tried to knee him in the groin. In the convulsive thrust of his leg, Doublehead inadvertently eased himself to the side, pressing the knife point to break skin but moving his wounded arm away from Ridge's club. This gave the war club the room it needed to swing.

Ridge felt the shifting weight immediately and responded by swinging the club to the side and up across Doublehead's back. The first blow cracked Doublehead squarely in the back of his skull. Stunned by the weight of the polished wooden head of the club, Doublehead froze. Another blow and another came in rapid-fire suc-cession. The third blow made a cracking sound when it struck and Doublehead went limp. His knife lay down on Ridge's chest more gently than had he laid it beside a dinner plate and the gripping hand at Ridge's throat eased away like water over a smooth stone in a creek.

Ridge did not rely on what he saw. He scampered from beneath Doublehead's relaxing figure and got up on his knees. He brought the war club up over his head as he had done earlier but this time it came down in an anxious flash as Ridge sought to insure that Doublehead's knife would remain quiet. The blows, now driven by both of Ridge's hands on the handle, continued to rain down until the club was whipping blood, hair, and brain high into the rafters of the barn with each swing. The pummeling did not stop until Ridge's arms were tired. Only then did he look down clearly into the misshapen mass of crushed tissue and bone.

Exhaustion and the release of tension pulled the bloody war club from Ridge's hands. It settled on the ground beside him and rested against his leg. Ridge looked at his handiwork and breathed deeply several times to calm his heaving chest. When he'd recovered enough to stand he bent stiffly to pick up his war club and knife then walked calmly out of the barn. He stepped around the drowsy fire and into the darkness, not looking back or saying a word to Doublehead's dead ears.

Another sleepy fire, this one outside of Totsuhwa's cabin, was being encouraged back to life with tinder and dried sticks. Totsuhwa had brought wood, several arms full, too much for the handful of women who were watching over Galegi inside where yet another fire burned in the gray stone pit. The baby was jumping down amid the attentive hands of the women while Totsuhwa reclined against the outside of the cabin a short distance away.

Two women braced Galegi's back as she sat nearly upright, holding herself just above the ground with her hands as she pushed with each contraction. Another woman wiped her face with cool water and adjusted the leather strap in Galegi's teeth when she needed to swallow. The time for the baby's birth was only minutes away now and Galegi bit down hard on the leather more than she swallowed so the woman just dabbed the sweat from her face. Others massaged the cramps in her legs and arms while the senior-most attendant crouched between Galegi's splayed legs and watched with the flames for the baby to appear.

Galegi's teeth pierced the leather and her arms shook from exhaustion with the passing of the baby's head. Wide eyes, a deep breath, and the pains of childbirth preceded the baby's shoulders. The worst was over.

Totsuhwa heard the strain in his wife's throat as she bit the strap and he saw the movement of the women as they craned to see the newest member of the Cherokee Nation. The child was wrapped in a soft hide and placed on Galegi's bare breast as she reclined in the light of the fire, the moonlight, and the stars shining in the open door. As she relaxed for the first time in several hours, one of the women went to Totsuhwa.

"Shaman?"

"Yes."

"Would you like to know if you have a bow or a sifter?"

"There is no need. I already know."

T he Long Man of the river was holding his breath. At least that was how it appeared to Totsuhwa as he listened to the roar of gunfire and cannons overwhelm any sounds that might be coming from the Tallapoosa River in front of him. The noise from the battle across the river was constant and the river did not have a chance to speak. The weapons were firing under the direction of Colonel Andrew Jackson as his troops attempted to lay siege to the last remaining Redstick Creek Indian stronghold.

Totsuhwa, Ridge, now a major in the colonial force, and John Ross, a young chief on the rise in the Cherokee Nation were on the riverbank along with five hundred other Cherokee men. The Tsalagi had sided, reluctantly, with the United States as the War of 1812 with the British continued to unfold.

When the Cherokee elders initially chose to remain neutral in the war, Major Ridge, who now took his military title as a name, induced hundreds of volunteers to fight for the United States government. Ridge, Ross, and others had feared that to remain neutral might weaken the new country or at the very least the Cherokee ties to it. They would not fight for the British but Ridge reasoned that to not fully support the country they were mimicking and struggling to be accepted by would be unwise. Bowing to the rationale behind it, the Cherokee hierarchy shifted their position and threw in with the United States against the British. So the men with Major Ridge increased in number until they were hundreds strong.

John Ross represented an even younger generation of men than Ridge. He was well educated and spoke both languages fluently. He had not waged war as Ridge had done but they were like minded. Ross settled in beneath Major Ridge's wing and was schooled in politics and maintaining the balance between two cultures. Ross was especially adept and fit in with both worlds. Cherokee via his mother's lineage, he was like all those deeply tanned and black-haired men around him but paler and he carried a trait that set him far apart from his Cherokee ancestry — his eyes were blue. With his unique blend, Colonel Jackson chose Ross as an administrative adjunct in his staff and a liaison to the Cherokee.

The Upper Creek Nation, in the northernmost regions of Alabama, had elected to side with the British. Had they not aligned themselves so, the Cherokee would not have felt compelled to defend their interests with their newfound governors. This thought crossed Totsuhwa's mind as he waited and listened on the riverbank and the thought caused him to shake his head and lower it slightly.

"Are you all right?" Ridge asked as he passed near and saw the regal chin of the great Cherokee shaman drop noticeably.

The handsome face, now forty-five winters old, came up and nodded with only his eyes.

"Good. If you are well then I know all is well with the people. You have the sense of the nation, Totsuhwa. I have seen it for many years. But do something for me."

"If I can."

"Come away from the river's edge. When Jackson drives into the encampment the Creek will try to flee—"

"Right into our guns," Totsuhwa interrupted.

"Exactly and there is no reason for you to be in the front line."

Totsuhwa motioned across the river to what was the backside of the Creek fort. "I know this land. The Creek have a strong position. The Long Man bends his arm around the land where they have made their stand. The river protects them well on three sides. On the open side where your colonel is, they have made a strong wall of timber. They can hold this position for a long time against your Colonel Jackson."

"You sound as though you favor the Creek's position."

"No. They are doomed."

"Well, good. I was beginning to think you didn't understand the power of Jackson's cannons," Ridge said almost as a joke.

"The cannons do not bring death to the Creek. They are valiant warriors. Only two moons ago I was near this place when they would have killed Jackson had we not saved him." The shaman paused and Ridge waited respectfully. "No," Totsuhwa continued as the gunfire did as well. "They will die because they are Creeks. The same as we will die."

Major Ridge did not grasp the shaman's message. He hadn't the time or desire as the battle was raging across the river. "Some of us may die today but it is important that we support the colonial army. Do you agree to this? It protects our future."

"It prolongs the inevitable, Ridge. Little more."

Again the sentiment was wasted.

"The Creek have joined hands with the British—"

"A thing we ourselves did not long ago."

"Yes, but now we are looking further ahead than tomorrow's trade of a deerskin or a beaver pelt. The Creek have sided with the British and made war on our allies — the United States men. So we fight alongside them."

Totsuhwa's attention veered away from the cannon fire across the Tallapoosa. "Ridge, my friend, you know that the Creek fight with the British hoping that a defeat of the colonials will mean the white men will leave their land."

"I do. They took the words of Tecumseh into their hearts."

The name brought about another pause in Totsuhwa's words and manner before he spoke. "He was a powerful leader for the Shawnee and had strong visions for all the nations."

"He did, but he's dead — died fighting against something you yourself have said cannot be stopped."

"That is true."

"So now," Ridge said as he placed his hand on Totsuhwa's shoulder, "we must do the very best we can for our people and part of that is swallowing the bitter medicine of life with the whites as friends and neighbors."

"It is bitter."

"Yes, but like medicine it will save the lives of our people."

Totsuhwa thought to say more — more about death being a part of life, that medicine and the shaman could keep the Raven Mockers from the door for a time though eventually the witches would eat the hearts of many dead like the white men ate up the land, but he kept still and returned his gaze across the Long Man.

"Do you see the many canoes at the water there, Ridge?"

Major Ridge squinted to see across the water and found a long row of canoes resting on the shore behind the Creek encampment. "I see them. They are for their escape should it come."

"If there were no canoes, there would be no escape."

"Of course."

"That is what you want, correct, Major Ridge?"

Ridge smiled. "It is indeed."

"Then we should cross the water and set the canoes adrift."

"Not we, Totsuhwa. Remember what I said. But I will send some men over straight away. Then the Creek will be trapped."

Totsuhwa didn't respond and felt a tearing in his chest. He had warred against the Creek for many years but always with clear reason. Now to fight them for the white men made him feel weak. Still, as the cannons continued to pound the fortification the Creek had erected, he realized that siding with the colonials, though providing only a temporary stay to what the Spirit had showed him, was perhaps the lesser of the bitter medicines before the people. But as Cherokee warriors collected at the river's edge to swim for the canoes, Totsuhwa wished he had not pointed them out.

As the men waded into the river, Colonel Jackson was laboring to have his cannons repositioned closer to the breastworks that were preventing him from entering the Creek fort. Inside, the Creek warriors, numbering nearly a thousand men fired upon the encroaching army through gun ports strategically cut into the timbers. Blasts from the cannons dotted the fortification but were having little impact.

"MOVE THOSE DAMN CANNON CLOSER!" Jackson screamed.

"Sir," his artillery officer answered. "We're only seventy-five yards out as it stands. Our gunners are already in range of their long arms."

"Get closer and knock that damn wall down and you won't have to worry about that, will you, Lieutenant?"

"No, sir. I suppose not."

"Then wheel those pieces closer!"

"Yes, sir!"

Jackson settled back on a hilly perch and watched the cannons creep up on the fort. The ground in front of the big barrels hopped as gunfire from the Creek struck the sod and showed that they were concentrating their fire on the heavy armaments.

"A little closer, Lieutenant," Jackson said to himself. "A little closer..."

When the cannons stopped and prepared to fire, Jackson huffed. "Could be closer."

The first blasts from the new positions struck the timbers of the wall but only pockmarked it as before.

"Damn it!" Jackson muttered. "Here I sit with two thousand soldiers ready to end this war and we're held back by a stack of trees."

Behind the Creek five hundred Cherokee watched a few dozen men as they snuck out of the river on the far side near the flotilla of Creek canoes. Totsuhwa was one of them. He had watched the warriors fording the river as he considered the plight of the Creek and his own people. Time would not stop what the Spirit had shown him, but time would give his son a chance to grow into a man. The type of world he would grow into would not be the one Totsuhwa, or Dragon before him, would have wanted, but if he could at least live in peace it would be a life worth living.

With revived enthusiasm and energy Totsuhwa plunged into the Tallapoosa and swam vigorously toward the Cherokee warriors who still straggled up on the far shore.

"What?" Ridge said to himself and anyone near him as he peered through the trees at the water's bank. He watched dumbfounded as

Totsuhwa's powerful stroke carried him gracefully through the current to the Creek side of the river. There he collected the warriors briefly then dispatched them with fistfuls of canoe lines back into the water. Totsuhwa himself hesitated on the Creek side only long enough to catch his breath. In a moment he was back in the river pulling a string of canoes directly toward the Cherokee and the much-bemused Major Ridge.

When the Cherokee who had been the first to reenter the river landed back on their own shore with the canoes in tow, Ridge met them with a single question.

"What are you doing?"

Most of the warriors merely pointed into the river at the swimming, canoe-towing shaman.

"Did not you receive your orders to set the canoes adrift?"

The men who had pointed to Totsuhwa now just looked to the canoes as they were being pulled onto the land.

A single warrior said simply, and not to Major Ridge specifically, "The shaman said to take the canoes here and wait for him."

When that fact had been made known a number of men immediately strode into the water to help with the canoes. Ridge could only stand aside in mild disgust and obvious wonder but little surprise that a Tsalagi shaman's request had outweighed the order of a United States Army major.

As the last of the canoes were placed on the dry land, Totsuhwa neared the shore. Again, a host of warriors quietly filtered into the water where they took the reins of the boats from Totsuhwa. He trudged ashore ahead of the last of the enemy's canoes and stood dripping and breathing heavily as Major Ridge clamored through the crowd.

Ridge was respectful but sharp in his questioning. The warriors thought him too sharp and physically moved around and behind their great shaman as the conversation unfolded, signifying whose orders they would follow.

"Totsuhwa, we discussed what we were to do, did we not?" Ridge asked, careful to avoid the word "order."

"We did."

Ridge found himself literally looking around for an answer. "And?"

"There has been a change," Totsuhwa said as he continued to catch his breath.

"A change."

"Yes. I know these Creek. Their gate will be strong. Your colonel's cannons will do little against it. Your ears can tell you this if not your eyes." Totsuhwa's purposeful pause was accepted and Ridge, along with all those within earshot of Totsuhwa's voice cocked their heads and listened to the continued bombardment of the Creek fortification.

"Your army has been using their cannons all morning and I still hear their fire. If they had broken down the wall do you think they would continue?" Totsuhwa waited for an answer but not for long. "Your colonel can not move through the wall like smoke. He is stopped. He wastes his ammunition and men against the front of the wall. I do not believe he is a good leader."

Major Ridge's eyebrows went up but he made no counter. Totsuhwa now pressed to the new strategy.

"We will use these fine canoes to land our warriors on the banks of the Creek. We will come at them from behind and pin them to the back of their own wall." Totsuhwa smiled broadly. "Then we will let your colonel in."

Laughter filtered through the hundreds of men who had gathered. Ridge was vastly outnumbered but compelled to present his side.

"By all estimates there are a thousand fighters in their encampment," he said as he pointed across the Tallapoosa in the direction of the shelling. "We have only about five hundred—"

"I will take only half of them."

"Half? That makes it four to one against us!"

Totsuhwa smiled again. "Four Creek dogs to one Cherokee warrior. That seems fair for them."

Again the men rallied in their laughter-filled support of their shaman.

Now Ridge objected. "Totsuhwa, you are a great shaman to our people, but you cannot do this. We have orders from—"

Totsuhwa was instantly stern, the easy laughter miles away. "YOU have orders, Major Ridge."

"We are all under orders as part of the United States Army."

"I am Tsalagi. These men around me are Tsalagi. You are Tsalagi." And he turned to move away. "We will attack."

Major Ridge was stymied. No one would take up his cause against the great shaman Totsuhwa. He had no recourse but to fall in line. Immediately he hustled back up to Totsuhwa and offered his support.

"If we are to do this, I suggest the entire force cross the river."

"That is not necessary. Half of the men will be enough. The other half will prepare themselves along the bank here as had been planned. They will strike those who attempt escape."

"Yes," Ridge protested. "But two hundred and fifty against a thousand."

"Will you tell the Creek our numbers?"

Ridge's face was confused.

"Then how will they know?" Another sly smile pierced Totsuhwa's lips. "When we reach the other shore we will leave the Creek their canoes. And when we attack, it will be from one side only. The Creek will see and hear the trap closing on their leg and will run to their canoes. If the canoes are gone they will have to turn and fight and we may lose many fine men, but instead they will find their canoes as they had prepared them and rush into the Tallapoosa's arms. Then you and your warriors will take them from the Long Man."

A strong wave of ready acceptance ran through the men nearby. Ridge heard it and had to agree. He did offer one last exception.

"All right. That is how it will be, but I ask you. Stay on this side of the river. There is no need for you to go into the bear's cave if he will be flushed out anyway."

"It is a thought," Totsuhwa said as he paused in preparing to launch a canoe. Other warriors nearby held up in their launchings as well. "But it is only a thought. You tend to the thoughts, Major Ridge. I will tend to the flushing of the bear." With that, Totsuhwa slung a quiver of arrows over his shoulder, picked up his rifle and the bow Dragon had made for him, and bounced into a canoe. Several others followed until it was full.

As the canoes filled with warriors and began crossing the river, Ridge took to his task of dispersing the remainder of his Cherokee along the bank as Totsuhwa had suggested. Then he settled on a good vantage point, watched, and waited.

The warriors reached the other side in short order. They aligned the canoes as they had been and filtered into the trees with Totsuhwa at the lead. Ridge watched the last of the party slip into the covering trees then looked away.

"Creator," he said. "Protect our protector."

Totsuhwa held up for the briefest of councils with his men then encouraged them on with a cautious blessing. "These men, these Creek. They are not the dogs I laughed about. They are valiant fighters prepared to die without a cry. Our plan will work. Believe in it, but those we meet will battle to the death. Move quickly among the trees. Give the appearance of swarming bees when we are only a small hive. Fire sparingly at good targets and reload with speed. Resort to your bows when time has stolen your rifles. When we reach the buttress we will open it for the white colonel and let his men flush the Creek to the river. Beware of the white soldiers. They are careless fighters. Show them an empty hand when they look to you. For them this means you bring no harm. Let us move now on silent feet until we have launched the first volley then stomp like a herd of buffalo and drive the Creek from their hole."

The warriors checked their weapons and were graceful in their vanishing. Totsuhwa and a small band quickly came upon the far reaches of the village where they discovered a few small outbuildings. Totsuhwa ordered them set afire then rushed off. The diversion would be useful.

Almost immediately on leaving the burning buildings Totsuhwa's men met the first Creeks. Surprised and unprepared for an attack from the rear, the Creeks were gunned down. The reports from the Cherokee weapons however, alerted the hundreds of other

Creek warriors who lined the main fortress wall. The gunshots also alerted Major Ridge that the Cherokee engagement had begun.

On the outside, Colonel Jackson's spotters called his attention to the smoke rising from the burning outbuildings. When the sounds of warfare from within the compound reached the colonel's staff only John Ross recognized it for what it was.

"My Tsalagi are attacking from the enemy's rear," he said.

"What was that?" Jackson questioned as he quickly looked from the rising smoke in the distance to Ross and back again.

"I believe the Cherokee have crossed the Tallapoosa and are attacking the Creek from their flanks."

"I gave no such order!"

"No, sir, I do not believe you did, but I hear Cherokee war cries between your cannon fire."

The Creek were hearing the screams as well and were responding. Hundreds jumped from their posts at the breastworks and turned to face the fire of the Cherokee. Left without cover, blanked against their own wall, the Creek warriors were being slaughtered while the Cherokee had the cover of the trees and the Creek's own homes.

Totsuhwa found himself bracing his shoulder against the outside wall of one such home as he leveled his rifle for a shot. The exploding report sent a ball into the chest of a Creek warrior and the man immediately crumpled to the ground. As the rifle came down to be reloaded a woman stepped from the open door of the small cabin and lashed at Totsuhwa with a short knife. He instinctively swung at her and clipped her in the jaw with his fist. She collapsed and fell backward into the doorway. Totsuhwa returned to his rifle and reloaded quickly as the firefight raged on around him.

Totsuhwa had gone only a few steps when he spied another Creek shooting arrow after arrow in rapid succession at the attacking Cherokee. Totsuhwa brought his rifle up and aimed quickly. Behind him a very young Creek boy emerged over his mother's semi-conscious form from the doorway of the cabin Totsuhwa had just abandoned. The boy carried a small bow suitable for crickets and tiny birds. Regardless, he pulled back on the gut-string and fired a short spindly arrow at Totsuhwa's back.

The arrow was poor and crooked and lacked a fine-pointed flint or enough weight to do much damage but it did nip Totsuhwa's thigh. The bite coupled with the sight of the arrow, any arrow, caused Totsuhwa to spin around with his rifle already cocked and ready. The sight of the trembling boy standing over his mother as he struggled with another worthless arrow halted Totsuhwa's trigger finger. He spun back to the real fighting and promptly killed the Creek with the fast bow. Then he lowered his gun again to reload. The boy in the doorway was still wrestling with his shaking hands to do the same.

Totsuhwa's eyes came away from his gun only long enough to see the boy load another arrow in the small bow. While the warrior watched the little fighter his hands continued loading the rifle.

"Get back in your house!" Totsuhwa screamed, but the little boy brought the bow up to his eye. Totsuhwa rammed the packing rod into his rifle as he marched at the child.

The boy fired and Totsuhwa deflected the small cumbersome arrow with the stock of his gun, never breaking stride. He reached the boy as the child fumbled another arrow to the ground. With one hand Totsuhwa took the boy by the arm and lifted him off the ground, throwing him into the cabin in one move. The boy tumbled like a ball but was unhurt. Totsuhwa stepped inside the cabin over the woman who was just beginning to stir and shouted again at the child.

"Stay in here!" Then he added, "Or you will die!"

Totsuhwa moved to rejoin the fighting and discovered the woman on her hands and knees groping blindly and confused out the cabin door. He reached down with one hand and grabbed her by an ankle and roughly dragged her back inside the cabin and across the dirt floor to her son. By the time the dragging had stopped the woman was wide awake again. She clutched her son and stared up at the fierce-looking Cherokee warrior above her.

"Stay inside with your boy. He is very brave but if you come out you will both be killed. Stay here." And Totsuhwa jumped toward the door and the battle.

"We will be killed anyway!" the woman screamed.

"No you will not," Totsuhwa comforted in a hurried voice.

"Yes we will! I know the way of your people. They are our ways too. But the white soldiers know nothing of this. If our warriors die outside we will be killed."

Suddenly she leaped across the floor and landed at Totsuhwa's feet. "Please! If you kill our men take my boy with you to your village!"

"No! I have a son! You will live. Now be quiet and stay inside!"

Totsuhwa jumped out of the door and ran toward the fighting, hearing the woman's pleas fading with each stride. In seconds he was embroiled in the battle. Real arrows erased the recent memory of play ones and the scream of passing bullets vanquished the cries of the woman in the cabin. Any remaining consideration for the woman and her child vanished from his mind as he drew down on another Creek warrior.

Though Colonel Jackson had not been responsible for the order he soon realized the value of the rear advance. The fire his men had been facing from the wall had been immediately eradicated as the Creeks sought cover and returned fire to the more pressing concerns within their own camp. Jackson quickly sent his troops against the fortifications and within minutes had gained access to the Creek stronghold.

Once inside, their superior numbers and guns drove the Creeks into early graves. No order followed to arrest the hostiles or provide them with quarter. The soldiers killed every man they found and a great many women and children who, like the two Totsuhwa had encountered, attacked with less than lethal weapons or their small empty fists. As the smoke from the guns cleared, hundreds upon hundreds of dead Creek littered the ground.

Totsuhwa was over a dying Creek brave swinging his war club violently when he came to realize there were no Creek left to kill. The man beneath his club did not moan or cry out. Totsuhwa stood up and wiped the splattered blood from his face and looked down at the warrior who had blood streaming from his nose, ears and head. The man did not move except his eyes. They came up to Totsuhwa and measured him from head to toe. Having found his killer to be a man of great strength, the Creek warrior nodded ever so slightly, an acknowledgment of a good fight and the accompanying good death. Then he closed his eyes and died.

Totsuhwa turned away from the dead man and began walking through the destruction. He could only venture a few steps before stepping over a fresh body. Far and away the majority were Creek. Now and again he happened on a white soldier. His concern for the dead varied only slightly but favored the dead Creek.

In his walking he discovered a few of his arrows with black and reddish crude paintings of snakes circling the shafts, stuck deep in the bodies of dead men. With less regard than if he had come upon an animal he had fallen, he pulled out the arrows. Where necessary he knelt and cut the arrow from the stubborn tissue, wiped his knife on the clothes of the dead man and moved on. As he squatted down over the last one he felt a mild stinging in his thigh, compliments of the Creek boy's tiny arrow. With it as a reminder, Totsuhwa moved off in search of the cabin.

Major Ridge and the remaining Cherokee had waited at the river's edge for stragglers from the fighting. Few materialized. The Creek were warlike into the depths of their hearts when their land and people were attacked. Most chose to die in battle, taking as many lives with them as they could. Those who had elected the Tallapoosa fared no better. They were killed before they were out of sight of their camp.

When the last bullets and arrows rested in trees, on the ground, or in still chests, the Creek Nation was nearly dead itself, such was the extent of the battle. Of the thousand Creek men who woke to the morning sun, less than fifty would be alive when it set. The Creek women and children in the fort fared only slightly better and many, like the woman and child who had come under the shaman's hand, had fared much worse.

Totsuhwa eventually found the cabin in the village of dead. As he got near he saw soldiers running from other roughhewn log houses carrying all manner of spoils and trinkets. No one came out of the cabin that held his attention and in a moment he knew why.

When he reached the cabin door he peered in cautiously, remembering the woman with the small knife and the boy with the tiny bow. Movement to the side of the single room captured his eye and he saw soldiers. One was going through the family's meager belongings and had already placed a decorative belt under his arm. A second was standing near the woman buckling his pants and refastening his suspenders. A third was still hunched over the woman between her legs. At the moment Totsuhwa understood, the third soldier raked his knife across the woman's throat. The gash was so deep it took a moment to fill with blood before it began running from her throat to the dirt beneath her.

The three soldiers were startled by Totsuhwa and the youngest, the pillager, was unsure if he were Creek or Cherokee. The second calmed him.

"He's one of ours," he said as he tucked in his shirt.

The soldiers then moved as if no one else were in the cabin. Totsuhwa was glued to the spilling blood. The woman did not cry out and was apparently unconscious from a beating. As the blood trickled to a stop Totsuhwa's eyes moved from the blood to the soldiers.

"There was a boy here," he said.

The soldiers looked at each other as though annoyed before the killer of them merely tossed his finger at a far corner of the room. Totsuhwa had been captivated by the soldiers and the woman and had not noticed the boy sitting upright in the corner. Totsuhwa took two steps toward the child but stopped when he saw the bloody damage on the boy's head. He was dead — struck in the face with a rifle butt. The sight stalled the great shaman and he breathed deep to regain himself. In the child's broken face, Totsuhwa saw the likeness of his own boy, Chancellor, home playing outside their own small cabin with another woman nearby who cared as deeply for her son as this dead woman had cared for hers.

Totsuhwa spun away and walked to the door. He hesitated and looked back at the three soldiers. The killer was now up and fixing his trousers. The second had joined the first in the robbing of the dead. Totsuhwa stared at them for a time, memorizing their faces.

"What are you lookin' at, Indian?" the killer asked.

The response was slow in coming and chilled the blood of the soldiers as it was meant to. "Dead men," Totsuhwa said as he again looked around the cabin. "Dead men." Then he moved out of the open doorway and away from the cabin.

He had not moved far when he began hastily snatching Creek arrows from the ground, the trees, and a few soldiers' bodies. He did this as surreptitiously as possible until he had eight or ten. Totsuhwa came across a broken Creek war club as well and slipped it under his arm. The arrows were tucked into his quiver with his own as he returned again to the dead boy's cabin.

As the last of the attempted escapees were felled in the Tallapoosa, Major Ridge crossed the river and took up a station with John Ross and Colonel Jackson to review the rout. When Jackson first saw Ridge he rushed in at him. His voice was excited and quivered as though there was a wavering between anger and satisfaction.

"That was a bold step, Major," Jackson said as he shook his finger at Ridge while a large company of men saddled up close around them. "I hesitate to dole out credit for the risk of life and limb, but in light of the outcome," he said as he looked away from Ridge at the bodies all around him, "I would say it was fairly well conceived." The colonel came up short of commending the major and quickly moved on, both in topic and physically, forcing Ridge to fall in behind him with Ross and several others.

"Do we have a body count yet?" Jackson asked an attendant.

"The numbers are still coming in, sir. I suspect the final tally to be about eight or nine hundred hostiles killed."

"And how about my own men? How many casualties did we incur because of this rabble?" To punctuate the question, Jackson weakly kicked a dead Creek's body as he walked.

"Surprisingly, Colonel, we only seem to have suffered the loss of twenty-three men."

The low number made the colonel stop. "Twenty-three?"

"Yes, sir. Twenty-three. And about eight hundred dead hostiles."

Jackson smiled broadly and puffed out his chest. "My my, boys. I would say that was quite a decisive victory, wouldn't you?"

Behind him there was laughter and glad-handing. Major Ridge was the reluctant recipient of a portion of the praise, much to the chagrin of Jackson. Ross meanwhile, eased himself away from it all and hovered at the fringe of the touring mob. He remained there until a soldier pushed through the crowd and whispered into an attendant's ear. As the whispers were passed, the soldier pointed away from the group in the direction of a number of cabins. Ross watched and wondered as the laughter of the other officers, none of whom took notice of the clandestine exchange, rose and fell around him.

When the silent message had been relayed the soldier melted into the crowd and was summarily snubbed for his lowly rank until he was outside the innermost circle of officers. Only then did Jackson's attendant move closer to the strutting colonel.

"Sir? Excuse me, sir. It seems our casualty total must be raised."

"Oh?" Jackson said as the laughter now died entirely.

"Yes, Colonel. It seems three more men have just been found in a cabin. Over that way, sir, if you'd care to investigate."

"Investigate? Investigate what?"

"Well, sir, it seems the men were... Begging the colonel's pardon, sir. I think we should take a look."

"Fine, fine, Lieutenant. Let's go."

As the group stepped toward the cabin, the lieutenant whispered as low as he could and still be heard by Jackson. "Sir, I think it's best that only a few of your officers accompany you. The men apparently died raping a woman."

Jackson's steps slowed considerably and the swagger left him. "I see," he whispered in return. "Gentleman," he now clamored. "Please conduct your business without me. Tend to your troops and any captives. I'll be with you shortly."

Then Jackson turned to his attendant. "Lieutenant. If you would." And the colonel stepped aside to have the junior officer lead the way.

"Yes, sir. I believe it to be the cabin straight ahead."

As the two men walked on toward the cabin, Totsuhwa was kneeling beside the Tallapoosa, rinsing his war club and washing blood from his face and hands. When the pinkish water stopped running from his hands he took a long drink and rested, squatting as he always sat, watching the Long Man flowing before him.

Occasionally a stray gunshot, killing a fleeing captive or a dying Creek warrior, punctuated a thought, but more likely it predicated a new one or drove the one in his mind into deeper recesses with its echo.

The river was murky, more gray than simply brown. It flowed quickly around the sharp bend, faster in the center than at the banks where the earth clawed at it with dirt and roots from trees that for some reason chose to grow too close to the water. Those trees, with their various shades of green and yellow leaves, would one day tumble into the Tallapoosa and be carried away. They would become fodder for the river itself, perhaps a place for fish to hide or merely a ripple that showed on the surface of the Long Man's back. These things were inevitable, Totsuhwa considered as he touched the coarse trunk of a tree nearby and thought about its descent down river. The inevitability of the battle that had occurred behind him was as sure as the chiseling away of the earth in the riverbank. And the tree's demise was as certain as the Creek's and soon, as the Spirit had shown, the Cherokee.

Unlike most days the water brought little comfort. Totsuhwa resolved to no longer fight for the white men. He would gather his few effects that had traveled with him to this place on the Horseshoe Bend, collect a few Creek ponies for his pay, and return to Galegi and Chancellor. He would teach his son and minister to his people. Working with the white men would be left to men like Major Ridge and John Ross, who were honorable in their endeavors but did not hear the voice of the Spirit as he did.

The shaman stood slowly and patted the trunk of the tree as a thank you for its company and shade. As he stood Totsuhwa again felt the slight sting of the cut on his thigh. He bent slightly and ran a finger into the dirt at the base of his friend the tree. With a quick spit the dirt became mud that he dabbed across the tiny cut.

Totsuhwa looked at the muck-covered wound and said clearly to it, "I hope you leave a scar, little cut. I wish to remember your brave maker."

Colonel Jackson's attendant was jogging through the Creek camp looking for Major Ridge. When he saw him standing with

John Ross discussing where the fight had placed the Cherokee politically, he hurried up to him.

"Major Ridge, sir? Excuse me, but the colonel has need of you forthwith."

"Is there trouble?"

"I can't really say, sir. The colonel just said to find you. He wants an Indian, er, I mean, a different perspective on what we've found."

"What did you find?" Ridge asked as he began moving along with the lieutenant, John Ross in tow.

"Bodies, sir."

"The battle is not more than an hour old, Lieutenant."

"Yes, sir, but there is something odd about these. The colonel wishes you to see them. Follow me, sir."

The three men appeared at the cabin doorway and saw Colonel Jackson squatted down inside looking closely at an arrow sticking in a dead soldier's chest.

"Come look at this, Ridge. What do you make of it?"

Ridge immediately went and knelt by the colonel. Ross, however, remained in the doorway and looked carefully around the one-room cabin.

Three soldiers were lying dead inside. Each one had his pants in various stages of being down or taken off. Their genitals had each been hacked severely. One had a crushing wound to the head which would seem to have been vicious enough to bring about immediate death Ross reasoned. The others had bloody noses, one obviously broken and displaced to the side. All three had arrows in their chests.

To one side of the room lay a dead Creek woman, her throat cut. In her hand was a Creek war club with a broken handle. Beyond her a small boy's dead body leaned against the wall. The child's face was a bloody pulp. In his lap was a tiny bow. Loaded in the small bow was a full-size Creek arrow. Two similar arrows rested at his side.

"See that arrow there, Ridge?" Jackson continued. "No blood at all. Looks like the savages shot him full of arrows after they killed him. Agreed?"

"Yes, sir."

"Oh, this is a bad bunch we've fallen into this time, Major."

"Colonel Jackson?" Ross said cautiously. "From the looks of this woman's skirt and her legs I would say these men were in the process of taking liberties with her."

"Probably so but they didn't get too damn far along with it. No man I know is going produce much of a pecker with a war club bashing into his skull."

"No, sir," Ross said. "But still, perhaps the woman and child fought back."

"You mean that little fellow over there?" Jackson said as he stood. "Hell, you think that little fellow and his ma killed three soldiers?"

"They are Creek arrows, sir."

"I can see that, Ross, but I'd sooner think some of their brethren interrupted the party and caught all our boys with their pants down, literally!"

"You are probably right, Colonel."

"Yes, I probably am. And what do you make of the boy in the corner with the big arrow?"

"Symbolic, sir," Ross said very reverently. "He no doubt tried to defend his mother. I suspect he was a very brave child."

"Indian mumbo-jumbo bullshit. Listen to me," Jackson continued. "Here's the riddle, gentlemen. Our boys didn't breech that wall until your tribe shook the Creek loose from it. And when we poured in there was plenty of fighting for everyone. Christ, there's a thousand dead Creek warriors scattered just outside that door!"

Jackson paused for a moment as his groundwork words became the foundation of his theory. "Now explain to me how the hell do three soldiers, in the middle of fighting for their lives, decide to test the fancy of this squaw while Creek warriors are still running around outside? Obviously the Creek had to be still raising hell or they wouldn't have stumbled in here and killed my soldiers. There now, Major Ridge. John Ross. Explain that to me." The colonel stood and folded his arms as he waited out the explanation.

Both men searched the dirt and the bodies for an answer. The lieutenant was as quiet as the others but shuffled his feet in sympathy for the unanswerable question posed. Ridge finally was obliged to speak.

"Colonel, they are your men. You know better than us why your people do what they do."

"Your people?" Jackson said methodically. "I thought my people were yours and so on and so forth."

"My people do not do things such as this."

"Oh, bullshit, Ridge! I've seen plenty of what your people can do. Hell, I've seen more women and children butchered with Cherokee knives than I can count! You've probably got a few blonde baby scalps hanging from your own lodge pole. So don't presume to tell me about your people. Know what I think, Ridge? I think a Cherokee did this. That's what I think."

Ridge stared at Jackson for a long minute.

"You've got something to say, say it, Major!" Jackson bellowed.

Major Ridge turned away from the gore of the cabin and stormed out pushing both Ross and the lieutenant aside as he did. Ross immediately stepped into the void and addressed the colonel soothingly.

"Sir? A few rogue Creek remained after the bulk of the fighting. They apparently came upon this... these men and killed them. It is important that an incident such as this, as we are unable to demonstrate the truth, should not come between us. Clearly, Colonel, these men were taking advantage of this woman and killed the innocent in the corner."

"Cherokee probably killed them too," Jackson muttered.

"Regardless," Ross said, "we cannot let this come between us. You have had a great victory. I would not want to see something like this take away from it."

The lieutenant chimed in and turned the tide once and for all. "Might I suggest to the colonel that these men be listed among the heroes who died here today and leave the dead to rest? It would prove unsightly for them, their families, and the military to bring all of this out for scrutiny. Sir, as Mr. Ross has pointed out, you have won a decisive battle here today. I'd hate to see it tainted by an investigation into the Cherokee or these men's behavior. I beg to say that it is unnecessary in light of the day's events."

Jackson looked over the dead once more then dismissed them all. "You're right, Lieutenant. Let's be done with it. Ross, tell Major Ridge to forget the entire affair. Lieutenant, list these boys as dead and missing then burn this place to the ground. Anyone who sees the corpses with their tallywhackers crushed and sliced up laying alongside a squaw with her throat cut and her dress up to her waist is going to know somebody was up to no good. Let the flames have them all. See to it." With that Jackson left the cabin and the affair quickly left his mind.

John Ross said nothing to the lieutenant and dismissed himself on the heels of the colonel but was certain to venture off in a completely different direction. Left to his own devices the lieutenant meandered through the maze of bodies. He graciously draped the woman's skirt down around her then unceremoniously went through the dead soldier's pockets. There was nothing else of value in the cabin but he was careful to find this out for himself. He glanced only in passing at the dead boy but then returned and picked up the tiny bow. "Nice little toy," he said as he swung it in his hand. "Make a cute present back East."

Those were the last words ever spoken in the cabin. The lieutenant took what kindling and tinder he could rummage from the house and placed it in one corner. He tore some pieces from the woman's skirt and a pile of rags and set them ablaze. When they were burning nicely he stuffed them under bigger pieces and stood back. As the dried wood began to catch in earnest he tossed larger and larger pieces on the fire. Soon the flames were licking the corner walls of the cabin itself.

Smoke filled the cabin from the open ceiling to the top of the door. This forced the lieutenant to crouch slightly as he picked up the few items he took as payment for the fire, including the small bow, and scampered out of the cabin and away from the growing fire.

No sooner had the lieutenant cleared the cabin than he literally ran into Major Ridge. When he raised his hands to prevent the collision the tiny bow lay across Ridge's chest. The lieutenant smelled strongly of smoke and the fire from the cabin was just beginning to show through the smoke-filled cabin door behind him.

"Is that from the boy?" Ridge asked harshly as he glanced at the tiny bow and back to the lieutenant.

The young officer was anxious but annoyed as he pulled the bow from Ridge's chest. "Sir, with all due respect to your rank, I took it as a trinket. Otherwise it would have burned up with—"

"With the bodies?" Ridge completed.

The lieutenant pulled away further. "I'm following orders, Major."

Ridge looked again at the small bow. "My people bury their warriors with their weapons, Lieutenant."

"Here then! Take it if you want it so bad!"

The Lieutenant tossed the bow at Ridge as he walked away in a huff, leaving the major to catch the small weapon as it slid down his shirt. Ridge examined it closely then carried it toward the fire that was beginning to roar. With one arm protecting his face, the major stepped as near the doorway as he could and tossed the bow through the door around to the far corner where he had last seen the boy's body. He had no way of knowing if the bow reached the little warrior but he did know it would be consumed with him and accompany him to the West as it should.

Meanwhile Totsuhwa had gathered a short string of four horses that had been raised as Creeks. He worked through the encampment, now littered with bodies and spotted with burning homes. He walked slowly, trying to ease the fears of the animals as they smelled the frightening combination of death and fire. As he and his train passed near the burning cabin that held the boy, he came within easy sight of Major Ridge.

Ridge saw him and recognized what he was doing. "So soon?" Ridge called out to which Totsuhwa only nodded. "There are other fights yet to fight. We can use your wisdom."

"Yes," Totsuhwa called back. "There are other fights but they are not here, not with these people. Their warriors will be few after this day. The back of the Creek is broken. Their chiefs will come to your colonel before another moon with their heads bowed low."

"And then?" Ridge shouted.

Totsuhwa stopped his horses and looked across the bodies and the smoke that filtered the space between the two men. "Then,"

Totsuhwa said calmly as he motioned with his damp war club to the dead between them. "Then your colonel will come for us."

A thick plume of smoke from the inferno that had been the cabin settled between the men as a benediction to Totsuhwa's words. When it cleared away Ridge could see only an empty space where the shaman and the horses had been.

The cleaning up of the battle of Horseshoe Bend took many days. The relatively few prisoners were transported to stockades until it could be decided what to do with them. The unfortunate ones were taken by the traders who tailed the army and sold into slavery. The lucky ones were held until, as Totsuhwa had predicted, the Creek chiefs came in for peace talks. When worthless treaties garnered the chiefs' marks, the prisoners were told they could reclaim their freedom for vowing allegiance to the United States. Though none understood, each took the vow or made a mark on the talking leaf of the white men and walked out of the stockades. But they walked into nothing — their families murdered, their homes put to the torch, and their livestock and crops destroyed or stolen.

Most moved further to the West to land the government had promised in exchange for their territorial heritage. Before another month had passed Jackson had obtained treaties that gave title to the whole of northern Alabama to the United States. As a consequence he also deeded the United States a sizeable portion of neighboring Cherokee land.

"Colonel Jackson!" John Ross protested. "I have examined the land treaties you have obtained from the Creek. Certainly you know full well that the tract of land which comprises the northeast corridor to Alabama is Cherokee land."

"I do," Jackson said nonchalantly.

"Then, sir, how do you so calmly lay claim to our land?"

"It is a necessary part of the Indian concession."

"Colonel, those are Creek concessions, not Cherokee."

Jackson slapped his hand hard on the table. "Indian concessions, Mr. Ross! The United States has need of that strip of land you claim to be Cherokee in order to properly access the land grant obtained through the war with the Creeks. Now, you will acknowledge and abide by it!"

Ross let the tension slip away a measured distance before he continued. "Colonel Jackson. My people fought bravely with you throughout this entire campaign. Many Cherokee men have been killed, far more in proportion to your own soldiers, in order for you to lay claim to that land. We supported you because we wished to be recognized as friends, as neighbors, your nation and mine. You cannot reward us by taking more of our land!"

Jackson stood up and leaned heavily across the desk at the much shorter Ross. "Let me tell you something, Chief John Ross. You sided with us because you know who's got the biggest army in this country. That's all. If it were the French or the British, you'd be sleeping with them to save your asses. But it's not them, is it? It's us. So you crawl in bed with me and hope for the best. Mister Chief John Ross of the Cherokee, the United States government has obtained INDIAN concessions, not Creek, not Cherokee." Jackson hesitated, leaned back off the desk and continued.

"Let me put it another way, Ross. I'll draw up a treaty annexing that strip of Cherokee land you claim to be yours to the United States. You can either see that it gets signed, and I don't give a good goddamn by who, or you can fight us. But remember Horseshoe Bend, Ross. The last Indians who took us on, didn't fare too good."

Ross could only stare at the man before him. He shook his head slightly then raised his finger and pointed squarely at Jackson. "Oh, I remember Horseshoe Bend. But it is you that should remember it. Without us, you would still be there or you'd be dead."

"Don't threaten me, Ross."

Now Ross's tone turned to almost pleading. "I am not threatening! I only wish you to see what you are doing! The Cherokee want to be friends with your people. We want to learn from you. Learn your ways of farming and government."

"Good!"

"But we want to learn these things on our own soil."

Jackson was quiet.

"On our own soil, Colonel," Ross repeated. "On our own soil."

Jackson stepped from behind the desk and placed his hand on Ross's shoulder. As he talked he steered the young chief to the door. "And so you shall, John. So you shall. Let's get this Creek business behind us. You have all the land you can use and more importantly, you have the unbounded friendship and thanks of the United States government. And that goes for me as well."

"But the land, Colonel—"

"One thing at a time, John," he said as he opened the door and escorted Ross out. "One thing at a time. Right now I have to attend to my surveyors. I'm sending a team out to survey the new land. Would you care to accompany them?"

"No thank you," Ross said with little thought and less enthusiasm.

"Suit yourself. But please do excuse me. Good day, Chief Ross." And Jackson closed the door.

Ross did not consider reentering the colonel's office. He knew that a portion of what Jackson had shouted had been true. So he walked away already searching his mind for ways to position the theft of more Cherokee land to his people. Despite this latest turn, he knew he must continue to inspire the confidence to evoke the changes he believed would save his nation.

In the weeks that followed, Totsuhwa worked his way west before turning toward home. He chose the longer route to purge himself of the sins he had committed at Horseshoe Bend. If he had stayed with the boy and his mother they likely would be alive. His horses listened to him for many days as he debated the choices he had made. Much better they give ear to him than Galegi, he thought, as the horses would be far less critical. Galegi was no lover of the Creek, but she despised the whites. Even if he told her of the battle he would not mention the boy with the tiny arrows. His wife would be unforgiving, but perhaps no more so than he would be to himself.

He vowed to neither speak nor ponder it again and let the little warrior rest, untroubled by Totsuhwa's cries for pardon. In spite of the decision, these things continued to weigh heavy on his brow as days turned into weeks of slow riding and makeshift camps filled with prayer. The sight of the woman and child continued to come to him, awake or asleep. The vision reminded him again of people who had stepped into his life and were taken. These Creeks weren't his blood, but in the final minutes of their lives they had reached out to the great shaman. He had not helped them, but he had avenged them. Now their spirits rode with him on his trek and whispered again of loss.

When the shaman deemed the journey west had cleansed as well as it could, the horses were packed and the small caravan moved back in the direction they had come. An equal number of weeks passed and found Totsuhwa near Horseshoe Bend and the horses again on their home range. The rider purposely steered the animals away from the scene of the battle and instead forded the Tallapoosa further to the north. As soon as the river had been crossed Totsuhwa's nose picked up the scent of a fire. The horses smelled it as well, but it was weak and they did not scare. Totsuhwa however, was instantly concerned.

If the fire was from the camp of what few Creek remained, they would not be welcoming to a Cherokee after what had occurred at the last confrontation. If it were a fire from an army contingency, he might fair only slightly better. Many soldiers could not, would not, recognize the difference between Indians. This was a sentiment that Totsuhwa and many others believed was purposely filtered down from the top of the military, namely Colonel Andrew Jackson.

The horses didn't care that the trip was halted and stood patiently as Totsuhwa tied the string of ponies to a tree. He checked the primer in his rifle and with it in one hand and his tomahawk in the other he slipped into the woods. The smell of the fire led the way. Totsuhwa worked his way as quietly as the smoke itself through the cover of the trees to the camp of the unknown.

The warrior was soon behind the cloak of a large clump of white birch trees. The camp was a bundle of boxes and cases, some of new light-colored wood and others dark and beaten from use. Several tripods of various sizes and descriptions leaned against the boxes. Weather-cracked leather straps wound tightly around the legs of the tripods and fashioned themselves into carrying handles that for the present lay limp.

A few white men, not in uniforms, moved around the camp. Some were searching the boxes, some were making marks on talking leaves, and others were finishing a late morning breakfast. There was no urgency in their steps or muffled voices and very few guns. Further away looked to be a small band of four soldiers — an escort, Totsuhwa reasoned, but they were laughing loudly, reminiscing over the tales of Horseshoe Bend, seemingly content that hostiles were, for the moment, far, far away.

An elderly man was sitting facing the hiding birch trees and blowing across a tin cup of coffee. The soft steam disappeared inches from the man's lips after framing a face that brought a resemblance to Totsuhwa's mind. The recollection brought both of Totsuhwa's eyes from around the friendly birch trees. He stared deeply into both the man's face and his own mind as he searched for the name or the place where the old man had left a footprint in Totsuhwa's memory. It was not easily forthcoming until a younger man in a well-worn and slightly dirty suit came near the old man and sat with his own tin cup.

"How's the coffee, Mr. Sevier?"

"Fine," the old man mumbled as the name pierced Totsuhwa's mind like a scalping knife.

When the blade of the knife withdrew it laid open a fold of memories in which a skinny boy balanced on a box and peered through a clap-board window. Of a strong catching hand that became a teacher and a father. And of a deceit played out against a nation forty years before.

John Sevier was the earliest name of a white man that he had come to know. Tsi'yugunsini had spit out his name many times and in an impressionable young man's mind the name came to be equated with bad things. As a growing shaman and warrior the name had burned itself into Totsuhwa like a brand, heard only when accompanied by the news of the destruction of yet another Cherokee village. Sevier was almost a curse word to him, a name and a thought to be avoided. But Totsuhwa could not avoid this. Here in front of him sat the man who had stole from so many and killed and burned with wanton disregard and brutality.

Totsuhwa turned his back to the tree and breathed deep. The shaman part of his spirit was trying to calm the warrior in his muscles and keep him from rushing through the trees and enacting revenge for the entire nation on Sevier and any others who happened in the way. He pressed his back hard into the tree and felt the tingling stabs of the ragged bark. "Not just now," he whispered to the warrior.

While Totsuhwa waited, settling his memories by the tree, Sevier drank his coffee.

"Which parcel will command our attention today, Mr. Sevier?" the young surveyor asked.

"Hummm?"

"I say, which parcel will command our attention today?"

Sevier had been contemplating other things. He was old. His bones ached. It used to be only in the morning on rising; now the discomfort seemed to last all day. There were pains in his chest when he exerted himself and he sometimes wondered, like now, how many years he had left to add to the fortunes he had gained and lost.

Chief among his losses was the Henderson Purchase back in seventy-five. He and Richard Henderson had orchestrated the deal so well they'd obtained millions of acres for pennies and positioned themselves to reap enormous profits for years to come. Then the goddamn governmental interference began. It started as a trickle of whispers that centered on private negotiations with those god-forsaken Indians. Before it ended, the trickle had become a torrent that washed away millions of dollars. The subsidy Sevier had ended up with was nothing compared to the potential and the bitter taste he came away with still circled his mouth. The few scraps the new country had thrown him — military appointments, rank, even governorships and the like — were paltry and taken as insults. This latest government job, the surveying of the land recently taken from the Creeks, was no different. Sevier cared little about it apart from the affront to his dignity, but the money was good. As head surveyor he could manipulate the invoices, time, and materials and come away with a handsome reward for his time spent in these woods. What he could not know was that the woods held something else besides trees and invisible boundaries drawn on maps and that the something else, the someone else, would never let him leave the woods alive.

Other woods embraced other men hundreds of miles to the southeast. A Seminole hunting party moved through a swamp in Florida checking a trotline, gathering eggs from nests, and spearing fish, frogs, and young alligators. They moved as silent and still as the black water in the marshes beneath their feet, looking for a prize in the form of a munching deer absorbed by the fresh green sprouts of grass and oblivious to their presence.

Noiseless hand signals replaced words as the troupe worked through the ankle deep water of the marsh. Even their spearing was quiet except for the occasional splash made by a dying fish's tail. To insulate the noise, the hunters held their barbed spears in the victim and the water until the struggling ceased. Then their knowing hands reached into the black mud and pulled up the trophy. Several of the hands that followed the spears into the sediment were as black as the mud that held the prey. This would be the excuse General Jackson, fresh from his new commission, needed as he searched for new lands, new conquests, new Indians to kill, and a few run-away slaves.

Sevier drained the tin cup and wiped his maw on the sleeve of his coat. The cup was tossed with little regard near the fire for one of the underlings to tend to then the old man picked up a note pad and wandered slowly away from the camp.

"I'll be following that creek in the valley. You young bucks can take the highlands," Sevier said humorlessly to the others as he passed by the surveyors finishing their meal. They barely acknowledged him and tended instead to their stomachs.

Totsuhwa however, noted his movements well. As Sevier melted into the woods, so did he.

Sevier drifted further into the forest in the direction of the creek and unknowingly deeper in the snare as the soldiers finished their paltry meal. The first to clean his plate set his utensils aside and pulled a jaw harp from his shirt pocket. He softly strummed a few notes as if to check its tune then launched into a slow, raspy melody.

"You'd better pick that tune up unless you're trying to put us back to sleep," one of his comrades said as the soldier tossed a piece of bark from a fallen tree at the musician.

Out of spite, the player continued with a disjointed waltz for another minute. Gradually he sped up until a rousing if not scattered collection of notes streamed into the forest. To accompany him, another soldier picked up his own used spoon as well as that of the musician, wiped them both on his shirt, then held them together and began clapping them against his thigh in time to the music. The third soldier began to whistle thru his teeth and clap the rhythm.

"Now that's more like it," he said.

The trees filtered the music until it reached Totsuhwa's ears as a slight rising and falling hum. Sevier's ears had become weak with age and did not hear the notes of the coarse music at all. Even had they been as keen as a deer's they would not have heard Totsuhwa's moccasins as they closed in. The feet were skating over the ground as feathers falling on powdered snow. They were quick but incredibly light and came to the earth with eyes of their own that steered them away from broken branches and twigs that could snap and sound the alarm. In another minute the soldiers could not be heard even by Totsuhwa's ears and in a few more strides the deadly war club was being raised in his white knuckled fist.

Sevier heard only the rush of wind, but it was enough. He had spent countless hours in the woodlands, encountered savages of all sorts, animal and human, and had come away with awareness. Just now, even if that awareness was wrinkled from age and disuse, Totsuhwa's movement sent a wave of wind and sound and feeling out in front of the club and it tapped Sevier on the shoulder. The old man turned into the feeling and saw the blur of the war club. His eyes widened in involuntary action as if disbelieving and trying to see more all at the same time.

It was something Totsuhwa had witnessed on the faces of those who were about to die many times in his life. He knew the hands would come up instinctually and he had learned to gauge the strike accordingly. But at the last possible moment, as Sevier's hands meekly came up to ward off a blow they could not, Totsuhwa purposely swung the war club high and let it pass within an inch of the old man's head.

If Sevier had realized he was still alive he might have reached beneath his coat for the pistol that rested there. Totsuhwa knew the gun would be under the coat, though he had never seen it, and thrust his hand beneath the garment and plucked out the pistol before Sevier could react to the war club or the grab. In the span of a breath, Totsuhwa was standing very close in front of Sevier holding the white man's weapon in one hand and his own in the other.

Sevier trembled and cowered, confused as to why his skull had not been caved in. He was so close he could smell the woodsy earth smells that covered Totsuhwa and blended him into the forest. He could also smell his own sweat as it ran freely down his face and stung his eyes. When he raised a hand to wipe them, the war club sprang up. Sevier immediately froze and quivered violently, but when the blow did not come for the second time in as many minutes, he peeked between his raised hands. As he watched, he moved his hands like slow-flowing molasses and brushed shakily at the corners of his eyes.

Totsuhwa watched as well and found real pleasure in seeing the old man tremble. He stepped back slightly in order to take in the sight more completely. The pistol was awkward in his hand. Its size made it only good for killing men. With no long barrel it was ill fashioned to bring down a deer or an elk, but it might be worth something to trade. He stuffed it in his belt behind his back, never taking his eyes off Sevier.

The old man now felt he understood. Though he was well past his prime, he considered that he was about to be taken prisoner to work as a slave or to be sold or tortured simply for being white. None of these conditions appealed to him, so he hastily chose to try and escape or reach the soldiers.

When Totsuhwa put the pistol behind his back, Sevier lunged forward and shoved him then began to run. Totsuhwa did not take flight after him for an instant; instead he continued to marvel and relish the old man's fear.

Sevier ran, stumbled and fell and rose to run again. The branches and briars Totsuhwa's feet had navigated so delicately snatched Sevier's boots with each step. When he fell a second time he realized Totsuhwa was not in pursuit. That and the comfort of a growing distance between the two adversaries gave Sevier the strength to yell.

"INDIANS!" he screamed like a frightened child. "HELP!"

In the temporary camp, the jaw harp wailed and the spoons rattled while every hand clapped the beat of a whimsical song never heard before or since.

"HEEELLPP!" Sevier bellowed, but by the time the contorted word reached the camp the music had drowned out the cry of the desperate man.

Totsuhwa walked the short distance Sevier had run and stood nearby, weighing his war club in his hand and studying it as though he were looking at it for the first time. His eyes moved to the man on the ground while Sevier's moved to the club.

The old man cried out again and again, but each time it was weaker as he realized no one was coming. His face was bathed in a fearful cold sweat and the length of him trembled. His own breath tasted putrid and the stench of fear rose off him like a mist. The heart in his chest beat so wildly as to burst. Pains began to radiate from it as Sevier gasped for air. In a sudden burst he clamored to his feet and began stumbling again through the forest.

The forest litter was an ally to the Cherokee shaman yet again, and soon Sevier was fumbling and falling. He rolled down a slight bank and lodged against an old tree. His coat had slipped down his back, nearly pinning his arms. Discarded trappings of the trees stuck in the sweat on his face and tangled themselves in his hair. When Totsuhwa came upon him he might have laughed at the sight had not the man been John Sevier.

Tightening pain was coursing down the old man's arms. Breath was hard to come by. His legs would not run another step. Sevier looked up through his misery.

"What...do you...want of me?" he sputtered.

Totsuhwa cocked his head from side to side, studying and enjoying the deteriorating condition before him. He was in no hurry.

"What do you want?" Sevier demanded in a bold rush.

As before, Totsuhwa did not answer the command directly. Instead he squatted down in his usual style and picked up a dried stick and a sprig of grass from the ground. "I want our land back, John Sevier."

The shock that was already present in the old man deepened and spilled out of his face. "You know my name?"

A splash of relief followed the phrase. Sevier thought for a moment that if he were known, he might be in the company of a savage, yes, but a savage friend. Then he recalled the swinging war club.

"How is it...you know me?"

"All Cherokee know of John Sevier — the white man who steals land with the talking leaves and burns villages."

"You're mistaken. I—"

"And kills women."

"That's not me!" Sevier said through a quivering smile. "My name is Harrelson, not Sevier."

"And butchers children."

"Why, I'm a friend to all Indians."

"And lies."

Sevier was quiet, but his heart was pounding. The savage knowing who he was would prove no relief; rather, it was his undoing. The sweat continued down his face, and the pressure was swelling in his neck. There was a tightness in his throat he recalled from other poor days, but even on those days it was not so painful as this. He breathed short quick breaths and felt as if he were trying to suck air down a rapidly shrinking pipe. Meanwhile Totsuhwa crouched nearby, patiently observing, not unlike a vulture waiting in a high tree for death to bring dinner.

"What do you want?" Sevier asked again.

"I told you."

Sevier searched the undersides of the treetops above him and the patches of blue sky peeking through for what the Indian had said. When he found it, his red, sweat-filled eyes returned to Totsuhwa.

"Land? You want land?"

"Yes."

"I can do that. I am...surveying for the government right now. If you live here I can parcel it off to you today. It's yours. It's that easy."

"Easy?"

"Yes. That easy." Sevier began to pull his sleepy legs up under him in an effort to stand. "Now, if you would just...help me back to my camp...I'll draw up the papers for you. How's that sound? Might even...have some whiskey there for you. I could use a shot or two myself. The old ticker just ain't—"

Totsuhwa stuck the head of the war club in Sevier's chest and easily held him on the ground.

"You will give me this land?" Totsuhwa laughed.

"Yes. It will be yours alone. No one can take it away from you."

The war club came away slowly, but suddenly Sevier knew better than to rise. It was less than a minute but Sevier felt it was an eternity as he studied the Indian.

"Why do you do these things?" Totsuhwa asked with real compassion in his voice.

"It's my job," answered a befuddled Sevier.

"It is your job to take what is not yours? And give things that are not yours to give?"

"Huh?" Sevier grunted, legitimately confused by the plain-stated honesty.

"This is Creek land. You cannot give it to me."

"No. You don't understand. It was the Creek's, but they sold it to us."

"You took it. They did not sell."

"We won it in battle!" Sevier blurted out, exasperated and tiring of the debate with a man whose people he despised.

Totsuhwa thought of the battles, the recent one at Horseshoe Bend, the little boy and his mother, and a hundred others. He considered who had begun the fight between the white army and the Creek and what it was over and the winners and the losers, but he let it go and merely shook his head at it all.

"You've been killing each other for years!" Sevier shouted before clenching his teeth against the rising pain.

Totsuhwa shoved the club against the old man's chest hard. "The Cherokee fight the Creek when we must. We fight to avenge a death, to make right a wrong. Not to steal land that even the Creek do not own!"

Sevier hit the club to knock it away, but Totsuhwa brought it back around and shoved it hard up under the old man's jaw, nearly lifting him off the ground.

"You filthy bastard," Sevier muttered.

"You promise me land that you do not own. Then you say no one will take it from me. These are words you have said many times, John Sevier, and each time they come out of your mouth, your words split like a snake's tongue. Tsi'yugunsini saw your lies when no one else could. He saw them and taught me much about the white man's words. But you will say them no more, John Sevier."

Totsuhwa dropped the club and wrenched his knife from his belt. He pressed the broad side of the blade against Sevier's lips until the point pushed tight beneath his eye and the handle creased his chin. "My knife will cut your tongue from your mouth, and I will hang it from my war club for all to see — Cherokee and Creek. Your talking leaves and that tongue will lie to us no more!"

Totsuhwa grabbed Sevier's hair and wrenched his head back. He would have sliced the old man's gullet with one stroke had not fear and desperation teamed up in Sevier to give him one more chance at life. With both hands he grabbed at the knife and caught Totsuhwa's wrist. He threw himself to the side and came out from beneath the knife and Totsuhwa all in one smooth roll that would have impressed any fighter.

Totsuhwa could have easily stabbed the old man in the back or raked the blade across the exposed throat as Sevier tumbled, but he was still not pressed to hurry as he might have been against a more agile and youthful opponent. As it was he was left with only a few strands of gray hair in his hand.

Sevier screamed louder than before as he awkwardly stumbled again through the trees. Totsuhwa scooped up his war club and trotted behind him, concerned only that he kill Sevier far enough from the camp to prevent doing battle with all of the surveying company at once. Totsuhwa could hear the music of the soldiers again. This was where Sevier must die.

With a practiced swing he caught Sevier's heel with the club head and sent him sprawling in a face-first tumble to the ground. Before Sevier had finished his fall Totsuhwa was on him. The knife blade was pressed against the wrinkled mouth again, and the war club was raised in preparation of a crushing blow. But Sevier's eyes, rolling back in his head, took on an evil appearance and Totsuhwa stopped.

The face of the thief turned the color of wood ashes and he breathed quicker than the snapping of a tent flap blowing in winter. His hands ignored the blade and the raised club and instead clutched his own chest and neck. The eyes rolled down again but clearly did not focus. The breathing that had been so shallow and rapid very abruptly stopped as the pallor of death poured over the old man as surely as a shadow races ahead of sunlight. Totsuhwa jumped to his feet, away from the sudden change.

The warrior had witnessed life being squeezed early from countless men but never had he seen one die by merely his touch and the threat of death. He stared in amazement as Sevier's body relaxed from its contortions and urine involuntarily spilled from it. As the body continued to settle Totsuhwa nudged it with the head of his club. It moved only with the weight of the weapon and relaxed again when the war club was pulled away. There was a thought of slicing the old man's throat against some trickery but the shaman knew the face of death and that it could not be faked. Instead he regained his composure from the surprise and spoke softly to the dead ears.

"Death has been stalking you, John Sevier. It was very close long before the Spirit brought me to you. The Raven Mocker was at the door waiting for a chance to slip in and take you in its claws. It wanted you like water to a dry mouth — so badly it could not wait for my knife to spill blood from your heart. You were a bad man, John Sevier, to excite Death this way. But now it is satisfied and you are where you should be. I will not lift your hair or cut your tongue out as I would have. Death had its own plan for you and I will not interfere.

"Go on now, John Sevier. Go and sleep in the coldest darkest part of the West. Go, as though you had a choice. I wish the seeds you planted, the talking leaves you held before the Cherokee for their marks, would be vanquished so easily."

Totsuhwa stepped backward. He slid the knife into its sheath and tucked the war club's handle into his belt. Purged of a great specter from his past, Totsuhwa walked away from the body and the memory of John Sevier. The faint music from the soldiers quickly faded but the talking leaves, the seeds of John Sevier, would continue to grow into thorns pressing against the feet of the Cherokee for generations.

The horses had waited and promptly fell in line as they resumed their journey to the cabin near the brook far to the east. After several days, when Totsuhwa was nearing home, he was met by his dogs — each sounding the alarm of approaching riders with their barking.

Galegi was in the house but heard their voices. She thought of her husband or maybe visitors and family from the village, but she also thought of raiders. Out of habit she took down her own rifle from near the door and went to the cabin opening whistling a high-pitched birdcall as she did.

Young Chancellor heard his mother's whistle and felt it snap his mind away from his hunt. Though he had seen only eight winters he recognized the whistle and knew it could mean good or bad but seldom knew which. But even without knowing the outcome, Chancellor understood that the whistle meant to move. He did not have to rush to the safety of the house for his parents had taught him that as the shelter of the family, if enemies were coming the house would not necessarily be the safest harbor. However, the birdcall did tell him to come near and observe the cabin and main trail like a mouse and learn if it was safe to come out or hide and perhaps fight.

Chancellor's face had streaks of black mud across the bridge of his nose and beneath both eyes. It was his camouflage and war paint against the keen eyes of his enemies in today's fight — frogs. Throughout the day his steps had been slow, steady, and silent. He stayed in the cover of the dry tan reeds and tall golden grasses that lined the bank of the stream. When the unwary Chickasaw frogs were within kill range he drew back on his miniature bow and sent a sharpened stick arrow into their backs. Then he pounced like a cat, pulling his tiny knife from his waist and scalped the impaled frog. The frogs' legs became scalps in the triumphant walk back to the cabin and later, as he nibbled a tender frog's leg, Chancellor would recount the story of the Chickasaw raiders he had turned back at the riverbank.

The scrub grasses and brush were thick between the creek and the cabin. Chancellor hid easily and crept along, peeking up periodically to check his progress against the oncoming riders. He got within sight of the cabin and settled in to wait. Time passed far too slowly for the little boy in him. He immediately began to let his mind wander around the house and fight other battles.

The cabin itself was easily defended. There was no true window, but there were ports in each side for firing. There was also no true door, only a piece of wood fashioned from small trees strapped together with heavy pieces of leather as hinges. It was enough to ward off harsh winds and rain and discourage pests — animals and human.

Circling the cabin was a wide ring of open space. The ground had been cleared by Totsuhwa many years before and kept clear from the brush and trees that tried to sneak back in. This open space made movement around the cabin easier but also provided clear shooting lanes to the scrub brush line.

Beyond the scrub bushes and tall grass were groves of trees, some tended, others wild. Fruit trees yielded in season along with the hickories. The spoils of each was gathered by Chancellor and his mother and enjoyed as treats or carefully tucked away to last throughout year. Each fruit might comprise a full meal if game had been elusive or the Chickasaw frogs had run in fright.

Further away from the cabin and the small trees were the foothills that stretched into glorious dark green rolling mountains. All thickly forested, this was the home of the big game that would feed a family for weeks. Chancellor had only recently begun accompanying his father into those hills on the hunt.

There, he listened always and spoke seldom as his father relayed the method of hunting with bookends of wondrous stories of how the land and its inhabitants had come to be.

The hunting trips had planted themselves firmly in the little boy's mind and came forth now as he crouched in a thicket spying the main trail to the house. The small bow was loaded and ready in his hands as one of the dogs came bouncing down the trail toward the house. Behind it came the shuffling sounds of several horses. Chancellor looked back at the cabin and saw his mother standing in the open door. She was watching the approach of the single dog as well and gauging its actions. Already they both knew that the trail brought a friend known to the dog or it would not be wagging its tail and jogging toward the cabin like a carefree child. Still, Chancellor noticed that one of his mother's hands remained inside the frame of the door, hidden from view, and he knew that in that invisible hand rested a cocked and ready rifle.

From his vantage point, Chancellor was the first to see his father's horse come into view. The sight brought him to his feet in a flash and he was sprinting through the underbrush, into the clearing, and onto the path.

Galegi didn't have to ask who was coming. Her boy's reaction was more than enough to tell her that her husband was home safe with a wealth of new experiences, both good and bad, many of which she would never hear of. Totsuhwa's closed lips over exploits of battle and exchanges with the whites never affronted her. He would tell her the funny stories always and the dreams occasionally, but that was all. He was home safe and until he left again that was all that mattered.

Galegi's hand released the rifle and placed it back against the wall just inside the door. Before she sprinted out the door she went to a small rough-hewn shelf near where she slept and picked up the rhododendron comb. In her haste, the comb bit too deep in her thick black hair and she felt a single tooth snap. Her shoulders sagged under the disappointment as she pulled the comb out and examined the damage. She found the lone tooth, caught in her hair, pulled it out, and held it in its place in the comb. She could hold it that way for hours and it would never be what it was again.

Very delicately, like something more fragile than it was, Galegi set the comb and its broken tooth on the shelf. She took the mirror more carefully and looked at herself. The face was clean. She alternated hands in the holding of the mirror as she used her fingers in place of the injured comb to straighten her locks. Then she returned the mirror to its place by the comb and spun toward the door.

Chancellor had sprinted from his hiding place and was greeted soundlessly by one of the family's several wandering dogs. He ran by the mutt without a pat and raced down the path to his father with his bow now braced over his skinny shoulder. When he reached his father, Totsuhwa pulled up the horse and reached down with a well-muscled arm. Chancellor took a hold of it with both hands and felt himself being lifted effortlessly and swung onto the horse's back behind his father. Chancellor held on tightly and was rewarded with an arm reaching back to hold his thin leg. The gentle hand cradled the boy's leg as it held the lead of the string of horses that followed.

"Osiyo, e-do-da. Hello, Father," the boy said somewhat muffled as he pressed the side of his face against his father's back.

"'Siyo to you, my son. How are you?"

"I am good. I have been practicing too! Yesterday I took three bullfrogs!"

"Three!"

"Yes! I think they were Chickasaw bullfrogs."

"I am sure of it. They send them down the Long Man to listen at our fires." Totsuhwa smiled, but Chancellor could not see.

"I took their scalps."

"Oh? Do they hang from your war club?"

"Umm...No. Mother and I had them for dinner."

The smile grew and Totsuhwa patted his son's leg. "That was the right thing to do."

The reference to his wife took Totsuhwa's mind further up the path to the cabin. "How is your mother?"

"Fine, Father."

"Have you taken care of her as I asked?"

"Yes, Father."

"Have you done what she has told you?"

"Yes."

"With no complaint?"

This answer was less quick in growing. "I think so."

"We will soon see."

Chancellor continued to hug his father and felt the warmth of his back as the horse jostled him from side to side with each step. In his mind however, he was retracing the words and actions of the days since his father had ridden away and wondered what misdeed long since forgotten might rise up to bite a young boy. He was certain there must be one, maybe two, or perhaps a dozen. But the fear of his misplaced transgressions was pushed aside by the sound of his mother's voice as she ran onto the path.

"Totsuhwa! 'Siyo, my little one! You have come back to the one who loves you most!"

Chancellor looked around his father's waist and saw his mother coming to meet them. Her arms were already lifted high even though she was the length of several horses away. His father's arm, holding the reins, came back toward Chancellor an instant before the horse stopped. In nearly the same motion Totsuhwa swung his right leg over the horse's neck and slid from its back. Without taking his eyes off his wife, he handed the reins and the lead line to his son.

"Hold the ponies."

Chancellor took the lines from his father with no small measure of uncertainty. The animals were massive to him and he knew from past experience that his father's horse did not mind him at all. The lack of control became evident as soon as Totsuhwa began to step away. Though his father didn't notice, as his eyes were locked on Galegi, the horse with its skinny rider was walking right behind him. The other horses were more reluctant and tarried behind, stretching Chancellor between the reins of his father's horse and the taut lead line to the others.

Galegi saw the growing predicament of her son and pointed it out to her husband before he could reach her. Totsuhwa stopped and turned, bringing his horse up short in the process. Husband and wife were reunited with a quick kiss before they both concentrated on their boy.

"Trouble, son?" Totsuhwa asked.

"I got 'em."

"But for how long?"

Galegi nudged her husband to action. He placed a hand on the nose of his horse and pushed down slightly. The horse stepped backward under the increasing pressure from its master and released the tension in the boy's arms. Chancellor relaxed as his parents came up alongside the horse. His father took him down with one arm, the other occupied with the waist of his love. Totsuhwa then took the reins of his horse.

"I will take this one. You bring the string."

The family and their horses walked up the path to the cabin. Totsuhwa and Galegi kissed often and stroked one another's hair as they moved. Though there was much news to exchange, to Chancellor it seemed they talked surprisingly little. He could not yet understand that the touch of the partners' hands was communicating reassurances that exceeded the limits of language, but he knew enough to let his parents have their time. It was always this way when his father returned even if the absence was only a day.

So Chancellor trailed quietly behind his mother and father, leading the Creek horses with the dogs bounding in and around everyone. Chancellor knew that tomorrow he would fall under his father's attention and lessons that had ended nearly two months ago would now begin again.

Galegi knew only that her husband was home, probably hungry, a little unkempt from the ride, and eager to touch. Tonight in the firelight they would make love many times. First however, there was a welcoming meal to prepare.

At the cabin Totsuhwa and Galegi stepped apart and left one another dangling by a reaching fingertip. She went inside to begin the meal and he took the horses to be hobbled. Chancellor followed his father and helped him fashion temporary hobbles for the new stock.

"Tomorrow we will take these to the village for trade. If the price is not good we will ride further to the trading post."

"Mother does not like that place. She had many chances to go there with women from the village, but she would not."

"She has strong principles."

"I think she does not like the white people."

Totsuhwa smiled as he tied up the legs of the last horse. "I believe you are right, my son." He paused in his tying and looked around as if about to whisper a secret. A quick jerk of his hand motioned for Chancellor to lean close. "But she likes the presents we get her there, doesn't she?" The husband and father smiled.

Chancellor giggled like the little boy he was and looked around with his father as though his mother might hear and punish them both for revealing her secret.

When the last knot was pulled tight Totsuhwa snatched up his boy and slung him over his shoulder. The two left the horses to graze among the grasses that would hold the horses nearby throughout the night. The hobbles insured it.

When Galegi met her men at the cabin door, Totsuhwa lowered Chancellor to the ground. "I bet there is a fine meal for us, Chancellor."

"Not until you go dip yourselves in the stream. You both have the smell of a horse about you. If you come in the cabin the flies are sure to follow."

"Etsi. Mother. Awww..."

"Etsi," Totsuhwa mimicked. "We are as clean as sunshine."

"You are clean as the root of a tree! Now, get to the water!"

Totsuhwa playfully pushed Chancellor backward and took off running but not too fast. "Race you!"

Chancellor took off behind his father with his mother's words chasing him. "And wash that mud off your face!"

"It is not mud! It is war paint!"

"Wild as your father," Galegi said softly as she smiled after her two men.

The washing time at the creek turned into a game of splash and dunk. Chancellor, by design, won the race by the narrowest of margins. His prize was to be taken up in his father's arms and tossed a good distance out into the water. He floundered for breath then rallied to climb up the bank, the dried mud on his face giving way in dirty streaks. Totsuhwa knelt near the water and began washing, knowing the outcome as soon as he did.

Chancellor was suddenly quiet and stealthy, as though his father would not notice the boisterous boy gone. He crept away from the creek and made a small impatient circle to come up behind his father. In a sudden rush he plowed into Totsuhwa's back, intent on knocking him halfway across the stream. The blow was slight, but Totsuhwa launched himself into the water with a horrific splash, much to his boy's delight. The hand Totsuhwa offered up the bank in asking for Chancellor's help naturally proved the boy's undoing. Totsuhwa yanked the boy off the bank and proceeded to dunk and be dunked until the mud of the war paint and the smell of the horses drifted away down the stream.

The short walk back to the cabin was not enough to dry Totsuhwa's clothes. The buckskin pants would take some time. Chancellor, nearly naked and shoeless, would be completely dry in no time. Partway back to the cabin Chancellor climbed his father like a stout tree until he sat high on his shoulders straddling Totsuhwa's neck. His bare feet dangled down and bounced with his father's steps until Totsuhwa took a hold of them. Only then, more secured by his father's hands, did Chancellor release the death grip he had held on Totsuhwa's black and wet long hair.

Galegi heard their laughing and came away from her efforts at the meal long enough to meet them at the door.

"Let me see that face," she said as reached up and took hold of her boy's chin. "That'll do."

Then her hand released her son's chin and took up with her husband's. "And you. How is that face of yours?"

"Lonely for a kiss."

"My. You are the bold one!"

She patted the chin then moved her hand to his hip and slapped the wet pants. "Get into some fresh clothes."

"These will dry."

Galegi's hand ran across the front of his pants and momentarily pressed into him, unseen by her son. "Change. And put on your red shirt."

The subtle tease widened Totsuhwa's eyes. "Yes, Mother. I will."

"See that you do." And Galegi went back to her work. She never knew the exact day her husband would return from his ventures and so had little prepared. She had saved the best chestnuts she had gathered and would make a tasty mash of corn, squash, and beans that she would serve with strips of dried venison. She would set a shallow bowl of cornbread mixture near the fire before the preparations moved any further and by the time the meal was ready, served, and finished, there would be fresh cornbread for dessert. Over it all would be hot tea, it too brewing by the cooking fire. Dinner would be taken out of doors as was nearly all their meals. The cabin could be dark and smoky from the fire so the family, like most of their Cherokee neighbors and friends, ate outside.

Sleeping was much the same. Unless the weather was very poor — extremely cold or raining, they chose to sleep outside, even when the doors to their homes were but twenty feet away. Totsuhwa and Galegi liked the fresh breezes of the night air and the smells that rode it. The wind came down from the hills at night and carried the sweet scents of the woodland pines, the rhododendrons, and the countless wildflowers. The sounds of the night — crickets, the night birds, and even the prowling creatures — threw sounds across the dark valleys and down the gentle hills to the ground around the cabin. And most magnificent of all were the stars and the moon. Totsuhwa and Galegi spent more nights than they could remember lying next to each other in the light of the moon and a thousand twinkling stars, speaking softly of their love, their family, and their plans for the next day and beyond.

Tonight was just such a night. They ate the simple meal leisurely. Totsuhwa sang a song thanking the Spirit for his safe return and for the protection of his family in his absence. Galegi gave the same song in praise but sang it louder and with such feeling that the depths of her love could not be mistaken. For his part, Chancellor worked hard at remembering the songs but lost a verse or more as he sat in awe of these glorious people who happened to be his mother and father.

After the bread, served straight from the clay tray Galegi had constantly rotated near the fire and before more tea, Chancellor's eyes began to droop. His mother held his head on her lap as she sang other pleasant songs. Before many refrains he was asleep.

Totsuhwa moved him away from the fire a short distance then laid him on a blanket Galegi had thrown down. His mother unfolded a second blanket over the skinny frame of the boy and tucked him in. A gentle kiss on his forehead from both parents and the boy's day was done.

Standing next to him nearly brought forth a speech from Totsuhwa about the changes the nation was making and how they would affect the sleeping child. Galegi sensed the dreamy wonderings in the stare of her husband's eyes. To break off the concerns, she kissed him. In the kiss she tugged at the red shirt until it gave up and came out of his pants. She held the bottom hem and backed away, pulling an easily led husband to the darkness a considerable distance from the fire. As the couple knelt in the grass Totsuhwa took off the red shirt. He spread it beneath his wife and laid her down across it.

Galegi was lost in a kiss until she felt the shirt protecting her from the ground. Her body tightened as she raised up from it. "This is not a blanket for the grass."

"No, it is a blanket for you," Totsuhwa said as he kissed her tenderly.

"I do not want to mark it."

"A little scar is good. It will be a memory for the shirt. And one for me when I wear it." And he kissed her again.

————————————

"When the game is near, we will get a bat's wing for your stick," Totsuhwa said as he tossed the ball to his son. Chancellor's hands were quick and the basket of his stick snapped out and plucked the ball from the crisp and cold winter air. He spun with the momentum of the catch and released the ball toward his father like a whip.

"Is there magic in a bat's wing?"

"Do you not see how he flies? He is quick and cutting in his moves. He will give his speed to you. Like he used in the first ball game."

"I remember it. It was the birds against the animals. The bat wanted to play with the four-footed animals, but they would not allow it because he was so small. The bear and the deer said they would easily win and the birds were concerned. Then the bat crawled up into the trees to ask the birds if he could play for them. They felt sorry for him and said yes but had to make some wings for him."

"From what?"

"A drumhead?"

"Very good."

"So they made him some wings and he won the game. He has been a flying animal ever since that day."

"Well done. The drumhead was from the groundhog. And the birds also stretched the skin of te-wa, the flying squirrel, and he too helped the birds win. Do not forget that."

"Yes, Father."

Totsuhwa caught the ball and sent it back, this time in a hard line bounce over the ground. Chancellor had to run to head off the rocketing ball and Totsuhwa saw he wouldn't reach it.

"Sorry, son," Totsuhwa said as an early apology.

In his run however, Chancellor had dropped his hand to the very tip of his stick's handle. He lunged for the passing ball and caught it in the far reaches of the wicket as he fell. The stick and its prize were drawn up beneath him as Chancellor rolled with the falling catch, came up to his knees, and threw the ball back to his father, all in one motion.

"Sorry for what?" Chancellor said puzzled.

Totsuhwa caught the ball and looked with surprise at the boy who was becoming a man.

"You liked that roll, Father? I will teach it to you if you study hard."

"You will teach me?"

"If you study," Chancellor laughed. "Now throw a little harder. I am not a child."

Chancellor was right. He was still a boy and was lean, but the awkwardness of youth was already behind him. He was growing stronger and grew in height as quick as the corn. As Totsuhwa tossed the ball, only slightly harder, he considered his handiwork running before him.

Chancellor was agile and quick, of foot and mind. He was a very capable hunter and fisherman compared to other boys his age and unafraid with the courage of youth — a blind courage that told him he would be young forever. The boy's hair was ramrod straight, exactly like his mother's, and Totsuhwa noticed that Galegi kept Chancellor's hair the same length as hers, a bit long for a warrior but alright for a boy and alright for this mirror of his wife.

Totsuhwa saw other likenesses of Galegi as well. The boy had the strength and kindness of his mother — a different strength than the power to pull back a bow but equally as potent. It came as a steadiness — a constant unwavering attachment to family that Totsuhwa knew he lacked. He loved them, would fight for them, die for them, but there was that strange part he had always reserved for himself, not out of selfish want but protection. Somewhere deep in his mind was that same echoing reminder that those he had loved had always left him — Father, Mother, Ama Giga, and Tsi'yugunsini.

He had avoided a wife for many years under the guise of his work as a shaman. The truth in his heart said doing so would keep him away from the hurt he would feel when the wife and family would be taken by the Raven Mockers. Galegi had come to him late in his life and he loved none before her. He took her but the deep love he now harbored for her had been slow in coming.

The first days were filled with the passion of a man and a woman. That grew to respect and fondness. Later it was sincere admiration and the early blossom of love like the sprouts of a strong cedar. They had been together through many seasons yet only in the last few winters would Totsuhwa dare say that he truly loved her. His fear of the Raven Mockers overhearing his words and coming for his wife had died as the love had grown. Today, in the rhythmic catch and release of the ball with this young man, he was reminded of the many steps he had taken to insulate himself from a pain that he now was certain would never come and he felt regret for days lost and feelings unspoken.

With each toss of the ball Totsuhwa considered again the number of times he had ridden away from the family for as many varied reasons. When battle called he rode, as he hoped Chancellor would but hoped all the same that he would not be called to do so. There were other times, many of them, when lesser fights took him away when he could have let other men go.

There were those endless month-long treks across the mountains in search of medicines that he might have found in a day's ride. Hunting trips that could have ended quickly had he taken the first deer, but instead, consciously or otherwise, he'd let the animal slip away and prolong the hunt. And there were the sojourns of spirit that took him into the high mountains and deep back valleys for weeks of fasting and prayer. The refreshment he found in these respites was welcomed and sometimes needed. Sometimes.

As he concentrated on other things, a slightly errant throw skipped by him.

"Should we get the tail of tewa and fix it to your stick, Father?" Chancellor jabbed.

Totsuhwa smiled and jogged off after the ball. When he scooped it up and returned he was still smiling but it was a considerably more devilish smile. As he trotted back to his place he cocked his stick and whipped the ball out of his basket with a vicious snapping motion. The ball whistled with amazing speed aimed directly at Chancellor's head. In self-defense the boy raised his stick and ducked to the side. The ball tore into the basket and pulled Chancellor to the side with its momentum.

His eyes were wide. He looked into his basket, partly pleased that he caught the ball but mostly amazed at the speed with which it had traveled. Then his wide eyes looked across the grass in front of the cabin to his father, now smiling wildly.

"Hey, son? I think we can let tewa keep his tail. Do you agree?"

Chancellor ran up to his father and laid his stick with the ball still in it at his father's feet. "You are still the teacher."

Totsuhwa admired the respectful play, even if it were only play and he took the boy's shoulders. "I may still be able to teach you many things but do not dismiss your abilities so quickly. There are things I learn from you and your mother that no one can see. For these things and much more, I love you." And he hugged his son.

Chancellor hugged his father in return and only stopped when Totsuhwa bent to pick up the boy's stick. The pair turned toward the house, each carrying their own sticks now, Chancellor tossing the ball up to himself.

"So," Totsuhwa said slowly. "You liked that throw?"

"Almost killed me!" Chancellor ran into the house ahead of his father.

Galegi was grinding corn when her son sprinted in the house.

"Father tried to kill me!" he shouted.

For her part, Galegi scarcely nodded. "If he had tried he would have succeeded." And the grinding stone continued to pound.

Chancellor went to his mother's side and hugged her around the grinding. He spoke much softer now. "Mother, he can throw a ball faster than the hummingbird can fly."

"He is very strong."

"I think he should still play. He would if you told him to."

"I do not tell your father what to do."

"Yes, but we would win."

"Your father is a great shaman to the nation. That is his gift. He likes to watch you play."

"But I cannot throw so hard! No one can!"

Totsuhwa entered the cabin, and the conversation stopped. "Go on. You can talk about me if you wish," he said as he leaned his stick in a corner.

"We were not talking about you," Galegi said quickly. "I was just asking Chancellor to collect some wood for me. The night wind will be cold. I would like a fire inside tonight."

"Yes, Mother," Chancellor said as he hugged her again then jumped across the room and out the door.

His footsteps had just faded when she spoke again. "He thinks you are the greatest player. Your throw moves as quick as a hummingbird."

"He said this?"

"He did. You know how he sees you."

"I will try not to disappoint him."

"You never disappoint anyone. You think you do but it is only you who thinks these things."

"I have not disappointed you?"

"Of course no!"

"Our cabin is small and we have few horses and stock."

"We could have more if you would ask the allotment a shaman deserves, but you give your medicines for free to—"

"To those who have nothing to give."

She stopped, reminded herself that she agreed entirely, and moved on. "I have all I want and more." She set the stone grinder down and walked to her husband. "I have a love in my heart and in my house. I have a child to care for and a husband to care for me. What I get from one, I give to the other. And so it goes. These are the things that make a woman happiest."

She hugged him, kissed his cheek, and went back to her stones. He watched her walk and gradually followed. From her side he watched the stone work in her hands and the hard corn turned to powder. His black eyes never left the grinding as he talked.

"Galegi... I have left you alone many times since we came to this cabin together."

"You have the business of the people to attend to. I have always understood."

"Yes. I know. You have always understood. But, I sometimes... I often stayed away."

The unique and special love that carried a man and a woman through decades of mountain peaks and valley floors came up from Galegi's heart. She knew. She had always known. And nestled beside the knowing in her mind and heart was a waiting-want that someday this time would come. She heard the confession in her husband's halting voice, the begging to be forgiven, and the desire to start anew after so many years.

Had they been years wrought with pain, she would have taken him in. But the years had been beautiful. She had felt love grow around her as sure as his arms. Love had been seeded and grown in her belly until Chancellor now ran as a young man. The trinkets and charms he brought her, the medicines and prayers when she was sick. The way he tucked the buffalo robe around her when he thought she was asleep. The years had been wondrously loving around her.

To him they had been void of that part of himself that he had held in abeyance as a blanket against an impending frozen wind. These things she had known since the first days. Today, at just this moment, Galegi felt the blanket slip from his shoulders. He was holding it out to her there in the cabin, trying to reassure himself that he would be warm without it. Though the process was part of the healing, she loved him too much to have him standing before her so bare in his emotions.

"Shhh," she whispered as the stone fell from her hands and she took him up in her arms. "I have heard your words through your fingertips when they dance with mine. And I have felt the door between you and the world."

"I have tried to leave it open to you."

"Do not be afraid of the door. I am not. You think that having a door has served you well. It may have been so. I have not walked the trails you have walked so I will not say. But if you throw the door open I will see that no harm comes to you. Is this what I hear in your voice?"

"It is."

Galegi smiled. "For a man who lives from words of songs, rites, and prayers, you know few today."

Totsuhwa smiled back at this woman in his arms. "I am sorry, Galegi — for my words of a child. And I am sorry for the time I have lost us."

She kissed his face and rubbed his nose with hers. "We have a lifetime yet to erase those days."

"I love you, Galegi. I will not go away any more."

She pushed back only a little in feigning objection. "We need to eat!"

"Yes. Then my hunting will be done in three nights."

"And if there is no meat in three nights?"

"We will eat beans every day," he said laughing.

Chancellor broke into the room as the laughter turned to a kiss sealing the new covenant. Chancellor set the wood down noisily just inside the open door but didn't interrupt his parents. Instead he went to his father's rifle and picked it up as he sat down against the wall. His hands examined each nuance of the weapon with great attention to its details as though it was the first time and not the thousandth that he had done the exact same thing.

When the kiss waned and ended in smaller and smaller flicks of lips across adoring faces, Chancellor felt it safe to interrupt.

"Father, can we go hunting tomorrow? I want to shoot your gun."

"You have a bow."

"Yes, but I think it is time for a gun."

"You do?"

"You may use mine," Galegi said. "I am no hunter."

"That is true, Mother. Do you wish to give me your gun?"

"You may use it. If it likes the way it is treated, perhaps it may accept you."

"Thank you, Mother."

"Do I have a say in my house?" Totsuhwa said as though he had been completely disregarded, as nearly he had.

"Yes, of course," Galegi said as she began pounding the corn again. "If you would like to go with Chancellor on his hunt, you may. But carry your own gun. Chancellor and I do not want you to use our rifle. You are too big. It may not like you."

"Hmmm...You are one of those funny people."

Chancellor had set his father's rifle down and was examining his mother's smaller weapon. "This is a fine gun," Chancellor said as he held the rifle out in front of him and shook it. "I will take a deer with it tomorrow."

"We do not need a deer tomorrow," Galegi said as her husband wetted his finger and stuck it in the corn meal.

"I need to practice taking a deer for when we do need one. I can sell the hide in the trader's store. Tomorrow I will kill a deer." And he brought the gun to his eye and aimed for a shot.

"Chancellor, you know better," his mother said sternly.

"What if I give the meat to people in the village?"

"The season has filled their homes," his father said forcibly. "Take what you need when you need it. Do this only. And always give something back. Have you forgotten these things already?"

"No," Chancellor said as he jumped around the cabin with the gun still to his eye. "But I am a hunter. A hunter hunts. Tomorrow I will hunt."

"Tomorrow you will help me in the corn."

"Mother! I am a hunter not a farmer! The corn is for women."

"And young boys too anxious to grow."

"I am already grown!"

"After a hunter I suppose you will think yourself a warrior."

"I will. After I kill enough deer, I will go against the Creek or the Chickasaw or the Shawnee and fight them."

"Why?" his father interjected.

"That is what you did."

"You will do something just because I did?"

"Yes," Chancellor said proudly as he puffed up his skinny chest.

"Then you will help your mother with the corn tomorrow as I helped Ama Giga when I was your age."

"But I want—"

"That is enough talk," Totsuhwa said and the subject was closed.

The cabin remained quiet for several minutes as Chancellor dejectedly walked his mother's rifle back to its place. He would fetch water before dinner and eat quietly as the gloom of his life rode around with his steps. His mother and father respected the presence of their boy's despair and spoke little. When supper was complete, Galegi went to the garden to already begin collecting the foods that would make up the next day's meals. Totsuhwa accompanied her there then yelled for his son.

"Chancellor!"

The boy, still stung by the thought of farming and all but reluctant to enter the garden today when tomorrow would come soon enough, appeared around the corner of the cabin and plucked at a few tall weeds growing there.

"Yes, Father?"

"Come with me."

Totsuhwa left the garden that Chancellor continued to avoid. The boy walked around the patch of earth that would shackle him with the sun of the next day and fell in alongside his father as the two walked through the clearing to the framing woods. Just inside the trees, Totsuhwa's eyes began to search.

"What are you looking for?" Chancellor asked hesitantly, still trying to be withdrawn from his father's orders regarding his hunting.

"I have need of cedar, but I do not believe there is any nearby. Have you seen any in your playing?""

Chancellor began to search through the trees for the familiar dark red bark. He didn't care for the word "playing" any longer to describe his activities but was loathe to correct his father.

"No."

The exploration continued for some time. Chancellor purposely moved off in a direction away from his father and searched not too heartily for the red wood. The sun was only a sliver above the furthest hill when he heard his father calling for him. He jogged through the trees to his father's voice. He found him kneeling at the base of a tree, his hands running delicately through a group of short plants.

"Are they cedar?" Chancellor asked as he looked down at the plants.

"No, they are rattlesnake's master. They are dying in the cold now. We will take a few of their roots."

"What do you use it for?"

"Snakebite. The weather is turning cold. The snakes will be collecting in their dens for the winter. Every year someone comes upon a nest and wish they had not."

As he explained the uses of the rattlesnake's master, Totsuhwa's hands dug in the dirt around plant. He pulled up a few sections of the tuber and snapped them off from the main root. He left the hole open and put the roots to the side. He loosened a very small deerskin bag from his belt and opened the slip-knotted top. Inside was a fistful of small white beads. He took two and carefully placed them in the hole where the bulbs had been withdrawn.

"Thank you for your medicines," he said and he pushed the dirt in over the roots of the plants. "It is important, son, to always give back. If you do not, if you take and take, the plants will one day not show themselves to you. One day you will look for them because you need them — perhaps you have been bitten by a snake — and they will hide from your eyes. You will have become like the whites who only take then cry out when they are bitten because there is no medicine. Do you understand?"

Chancellor felt the message of the plants tug at his wanting to kill a deer. He tried to hold back and offer some resistance, but his father was right, as he always was.

"Yes, I see."

Totsuhwa stood up and carried the roots in one hand and the small bag of beads in the other. "Then come and see this." He walked only a short distance through the trees back in the direction of the cabin until he came to another clump of the same type of plants.

"Do you see these plants?"

"Yes. They look like those you dug."

"They are. Now come." Again he only walked a short distance closer to the cabin. "Do you see these?" he said as he pointed out still another group of the plants.

"Yes. Father? If you knew these were here, why did you pass them by to gather the others?"

Now Totsuhwa's tone changed from teacher to father. He put his hand on his son's shoulder and looked into his eyes. "Because that is how it is done. It has always been so. But I do it not just because others have done so. I do it because it is the right way. By passing the two growths, I make sure there will always be rattlesnake's master when the people have need of it."

He hesitated to let the words reach the bottom of Chancellor's ears.

"Now, my son, my son who I love, do you understand this?"

Rather sheepishly, Chancellor answered, "I do."

Totsuhwa lifted his son's chin. "Be proud, Chancellor. You have learned a great thing today. And in learning it you have become greater. All the things we learn make us what we are and what we will become. Many men live a lifetime and never understand life. They live and die in ignorance. You, because of today, will live as a wise man."

Totsuhwa pushed the roots and the bag into his son's hands. "Spend some time with the earth and the plants, son. Then put the roots near the door to the house to dry. Bring the beads with you in the morning. Ahwi will wait until we call him. Tomorrow we hunt for cedar."

The father left the son with the roots and the beads, the plants and the earth, to study on them and the things he had just learned. Chancellor did think about the rattlesnake's master. And he thought about the giving back for as long as he could, but it wasn't long at all. He put the roots and the beads in his own pouch on his waist and began thinking other thoughts. Before his father had reached the cabin, Chancellor was darting through the trees chasing unseen deer, Chickasaw warriors, and white soldiers.

Darkness came to find Totsuhwa and Galegi already asleep in the cabin. A small fire was burning inside on the floor near the open cabin door. The smoke from the fire filled the upper reaches of the tiny house then puffed out from beneath the header of the door when the cabin ceiling was full. The couple was sleeping on the floor well beneath the smoke but still warmly affected by the heat of the fire.

Chancellor had chased his unseen prey until after the sun had set. Reassured the land had been cleared of raiders, he crept into the room as quietly as possible. He went to his place along the far wall, leaving the fire between him and the door in the event a brave Chickasaw might have followed him home. He put his small knife, point first, into a small crevice in the wall just a foot or so off the floor — a very handy spot to quickly retrieve it if need be.

His blankets were already spread for him compliments of his mother. As he stretched out he felt the clumps in his pouch and recalled the dirty roots and the white beads. He pulled the bag from his waist, took the roots out, and laid them on one side of his bed nearer the fire to dry and put the tiny bag of beads on the other against the wall.

The sounds of the night were muffled by the cabin walls and the crackling of the small fire. Chancellor thought he probably should have put more wood on the fire, but he was already to bed and had no intention of righting his oversight. The blankets grew warm. Soon he was far too comfortable to move even if he had reconsidered.

The dancing light cast by the fire stabbed his mind. Looking through the diminutive blaze Chancellor could see out the cabin's open door. The shadows created by the flames took the form of the Chickasaw warriors. They had followed him!

He stared through the fire and propped himself up on an elbow to see. The minor change in perspective was enough and the warriors vanished, but when he lowered himself back to his blankets they returned. His eyes went to his father, the family protector. He was asleep, or seemed to be so, and his rifle, hatchet, war club, and knife were leaning against the wall, inches from his head as they always were. His mother's rifle was there as well. Chancellor knew that both weapons were loaded and cocked in case of an emergency such as this.

He pulled the blankets up tighter around his face and his hidden hand slipped out from beneath, reached up slowly, and quietly pulled the knife from the wall. He held it beneath the blanket, staring through the fire at the taunting Chickasaw.

The fire was dying. When it came to its end the Chickasaw would attack. They would be coming. There would be a horrific fight. Somehow he would overpower them and save the family. The room grew darker, but it wasn't the death of the fire. Chancellor's eyes were abandoning the imaginary fight before it began. In a moment he was asleep.

The boy's eyes opened in what seemed to his mind to have been just a few seconds. They focused a bit slowly and their attention was drawn to his mother unrolling dried meat from a cloth bundle. The fire that had exposed the Chickasaw and apparently kept them at bay throughout the night was burning brightly again, warming the cabin and a clay urn of tea that sat next to it. His own bed was warm and comfortable and he nestled into it and pulled the blankets up further around his face and delayed the start of the day.

His father however, had different plans. Totsuhwa had already picked up the roots of the rattlesnake's master that had been pushed nearer the fire in the night. He was outside at first light stripping the fibrous mixture apart to help it dry. When prepared it would ease a snakebite and even prevent a bite if a piece of the root was carried in one's mouth.

When the tubers were ready to dry again, Totsuhwa called to his son.

"Chancellor? Are you ready?"

Of course he knew the boy was still wrapped in his blankets and not inclined to get up just yet. Galegi knew it too and went to the hot urn and poured two cups of tea. She took one to her son along with some cornbread from the night before and dried meat.

"Chancellor. Your father will want to leave soon. Have some tea and breakfast to wake yourself. I will slow him with his own breakfast while you chase the sleep from your eyes." She left the breakfast on the floor, then brushed the straight black hair from his face and kissed his cheek. "Do not go back to sleep. Your father will be ready."

When his mother retreated beyond the fire through the doorway, Chancellor snuggled into his blankets for one more minute of comfort. The minute's passing was hastened by the smell of the tea and the presence of the meat and bread. A lone hand left the comfort of the blankets behind and carefully picked up the tea. To drink would necessitate propping himself up on an elbow. This was the first true move at getting up and was the difficult beginning of what would prove a difficult day.

With the encouragement of the warm tea Chancellor threw back his covers and sat upright. He took the bread and meat and began to nibble between sips of tea. The tea was momentarily returned to the floor as he pulled the blankets back around his legs to repel the cool morning air for a few extra minutes. As Chancellor ate in his bed, Galegi was standing with her husband as he did likewise outside.

"Will you be gone many days?"

Totsuhwa looked out over his tea. "You are thinking of my new promise?"

Galegi dropped her eyes and said no even though she was.

"We will be back tomorrow."

"So quickly?"

"I could stay away longer if you would like."

She playfully swatted his backside. "Do not think about it!"

He nearly spilled his tea as he grabbed for her but she was quick and his effort not too fierce, so she easily dodged him.

"When you come home you will have to be quicker if you want to catch this prize."

"You are a bold woman."

"That is why you love me. I will prepare something for your walk."

As she stepped toward the house, Totsuhwa snatched her arm and spun her until he had the arm delicately pinned behind her back and he was pressed tight against her. "You are wrong. I love you for your tender heart, as soft and fresh as new blades of grass."

"Thank you," she answered softly as she kissed him.

He released her then swatted her on the rump as she again moved toward the cabin. "And you are not so quick you cannot be caught," he said.

Totsuhwa finished his breakfast as he walked around his cabin. The smell of the air told him that soon they would be into winter. Last night's chill was only the cold months knocking at the door. He told Galegi that he would be gone just overnight today, but he knew that with the next full moon he would have to go on a fall hunt. The family would need provisions. The hunter in him also realized that the hunt, even with an accurately placed shot on the first deer, might take several days. The game that had once been so thick could be scarce, even for someone as well versed in the ways of the woods as he. For this scarcity he could thank the white men who built homes where it suited them and the white soldiers who tramped through the nation by the hundreds, killing and eating everything they found.

The consideration upset him as it always did and he wanted to move. Even though today and tomorrow would be spent hunting for cedar he was suddenly anxious to get started, perhaps before the trees themselves grew scarce under the tramping of white boots.

"Chancellor! We will leave now!"

Totsuhwa gulped the last of his tea and bread. He stuffed the meat in the cheeks of his mouth and sucked on them, but the swelling reminded him of the white men's habit of doing so with tobacco and he didn't care for the association. So he roughly and partially chewed the dried meat and swallowed it whole. A few last drops of tea and he was ready to go.

"Chancellor!" he called again, more anxious than the first time.

Instead of the boy, Galegi appeared in the door. "What is it?" she said, purposely buying her son more time to finish his breakfast.

"What do you mean?"

"Why are you in such a hurry? Is the cedar running away?"

"It may be," he said and he picked up his bow, the quiver already across his back and walked away.

Galegi turned back into the cabin and brought Chancellor to his feet. "Finish your breakfast afoot. My chief has a bur beneath his blanket for some reason. Follow close but stay behind and let the trees ease the anger or despair or whatever it is that troubles him from his soul. After a few minutes in his woods he will be whole again."

"Yes, Mother. I know Father and what he needs."

"He is changing, but it may come slowly," she said as she pressed a satchel of dried meat and cornbread into his hands for the trip. "Now go with him and have a fine day. I will see you tomorrow and you will tell me the things you have learned."

Chancellor ran through the door, shoving the last piece of breakfast in his mouth and throwing a blanket around his shoulders as he passed. Before he had sprinted across the clearing to his father who was nearing the trees, Galegi was in the door yelling to them both.

"Totsuhwa! Look for distai'yi, the devil's shoestring. Bring some to me for my hair!"

Her husband looked her way and nodded from afar.

Chancellor turned slightly but did not stop running. "I will find it for you!"

All three members of the family then went their ways. Galegi retreated to the cabin for a short while then went to her large garden and continued the preparation for cold weather that would take her several more weeks. There were more fall vegetables to be taken from the ground — the late squashes mostly — who now lay in scattered bunches at the ends of withering vines throughout the large patch of tilled soil. Later she would rake the vines and turn them into the ground to feed the earth for next spring's seeds.

Chancellor followed his father by several paces, heeding his mother's advice until he deemed the quiet trees had worked their magic. When he felt they had, he came up closer.

"Father? Mother wants the devil's shoestring, distai'yi. Why does she want this?"

"For her hair."

"Why for her hair?"

"The roots are strong. She will make a wash with them for her hair. Then her hair will be strong."

Chancellor laughed.

"Would you like to collect some for your hair as well?" Totsuhwa asked. "It is long like your mother's."

"No, I will not wash my hair with women's potions."

"Your hair is long."

"Do you think it is too long for a man, Father?"

"I do."

"Then I will cut it."

Totsuhwa was pleased with his son's quick reaction but thought instantly of his wife. "Good. But we will talk on this with your mother before we put your hair to the knife. She takes pleasure in it and I like to see her happy."

"Yes, Father."

The trees had done their part, but they were greatly aided by the thoughts of Galegi and her happiness.

"We should collect the devil's shoestring for you anyway, even if it is not for your hair," Totsuhwa said as he walked deeper into the woods.

"Why?"

"The same wash your mother makes to toughen her hair will toughen your legs and arms before a ball game."

"This is so?"

"I would not have said so otherwise."

Chancellor was impressed, as he always was with his father's knowledge of the plants and their medicines. As happened most times he would talk little on this overnight trip and learn much. That was to be his plan and he stuck to it well. Totsuhwa pointed out plants and trees and herbs in their hours-long walk, and Chancellor took it all in and remembered as much as he could — replaying the plants, their names, and their uses over and over in his mind with each step.

They ate the dried meat and bread for lunch without stopping and rested only long enough to drink from a stream they forded. At the stream Chancellor noticed that his father was not carrying any water and asked about it.

For the first time in the long walk Totsuhwa examined his son critically. "We have covered many hills and valleys already today and you have not noticed this? That is not good. You are keener than this."

"I was studying on the plants."

"You must do many things at once, Chancellor. In battle your enemies will come at your front, your back, and your sides at the same time. Be observant. Notice the small things. When they come for you, see the small things. See what weapons warriors carry in their belts and if scalps hang from them. This will tell you who is most dangerous and needs to be killed first. Do not hear their war cries. They are only the screams of diving falcons. It is the talons that cut, not the noise."

Chancellor found himself scanning his father now very closely for any other things he may have missed. The bow was in his hands without an arrow. They were in a full quiver on his back riding next to a single blanket rolled and tied tightly with a loose cord holding it on his broad back. His medicine pouch hung at one side and on the other was his knife. A polished war club of dark wood was stuck in his leather belt. His pants were long and still a little dusty from sleeping on the floor. He also wore a shirt of tanned leather with no sleeves and no decorations.

When Totsuhwa saw that the examination was complete he put his hand on his boy's shoulder. "Water would be extra weight we do not need to carry. We will be gone just one night and there are streams along our way. And the cold is coming. We will not want for water like we do when the sun pulls it from us."

The pair began to walk again. Chancellor was put off some by his father's rebuff at not noticing the absent water, but he put it aside and tried to remember his plants and their lessons. After a considerable time had passed, Chancellor left the plants and remarked on the enemies he would one day face.

"Father, why do warriors shout when they attack?"

Totsuhwa did not have to think long on the answer. "Many men are made afraid by loud noises. They are not afraid of a wolf or the panther until it growls. For the animals, these are meant as warnings to leave them be or as a signal to us to prepare to fight or prepare to die. In their growls we hear them tell us to summon the Spirit so He is near to take us to the West.

"As warriors we may do this for the same reason, but it is more likely that our cries are meant to frighten. When you are afraid, you do not move. For a moment your body will freeze and think only of the fear and not of what it should do. In that moment is when most men will die. This I have seen many times."

"You have killed many men, Father?"

"You know I have."

"Are you ever afraid?"

"Never. There is no room for fear in a warrior's heart. If fear lives there the heart will not beat for very long."

"Do I have fear in my heart?"

"You may but only because you are a pup. When you have grown into a wolf and your teeth and long and sharp, fear will have left you."

Chancellor was following behind his father throughout the conversation. He reached up and felt his teeth with a thumb and forefinger, testing their length and sharpness. They seemed rather flat and dull.

"When will I grow teeth like a wolf?"

"The teeth are inside you — in your heart and in your mind. You will feel them grow as your skill and confidence grows."

"When will that be?"

"Perhaps spring. Or a few more winters. Only the Spirit knows for certain. Each man comes of age in the Spirit's time."

"How old were you when you had wolf teeth?"

"I was very young."

"Younger than me?"

"Younger than you."

Chancellor was stilled by the thought. Totsuhwa felt the disappointment behind his back and tossed his son a rope to cling to.

"But my teeth came in crooked for a time. Not so straight as yours will be. I had no father to teach me until I was older than you are now. Until then I had only Ama Giga. She taught me the medicines and the ways of the people, but she could not teach me how to fight and hunt. These things I learned from my father, Tsi'yugunsini, when I was nearly a man. All that prevented me from a life with bent teeth was his teachings. You have the benefits of beginning your lessons at a younger age. Your teeth will come and they will come straight and true to you. Your mother will see to these things as will I. Do not worry."

So it was the lessons of life mixed with lessons of medicines on the walk deep into the woods of the Tsalagi. The plants continued to present themselves to the shaman and he in turn presented them to the boy. They kicked out a deer just as the sun began to set and stopped only long enough to listen to its crashing escape. When the quiet returned to the forest they moved on until the light was nearly gone. Only then did Totsuhwa suggest a camp.

They ate the rest of the meat and bread and drank from a nearby stream as before. The night was cooling quickly, so they set up a small fire as Totsuhwa tested his son's recollections of the plants and their uses. Chancellor held his own and his father was patient.

"But we did not find the devil's shoestring for Mother's hair," Chancellor said over the cracking of kindling for their fire.

"No, we did not. Perhaps tomorrow. Will you know it when it shows itself?"

"I will."

"Then what will you do?"

"I will thank the first two and pass them by."

"Good."

The conversation teetered around other plants and medicine for a time, but after the largest log had caught sufficiently Totsuhwa lay down on the ground nearby and went to sleep suggesting his boy do the same. Totsuhwa needn't have made the suggestion. Chancellor had mimicked his every move all day and this would be no exception. In the darkness, beneath the rising plumes of glowing embers dancing up from the flames, the father and son went to sleep. Totsuhwa fell off quickly, but Chancellor, busied by thoughts of all he was trying to commit to memory, was held awake for some time. Soon however, the day's trek tugged at his eyes and he followed his father into the arms of sleep.

A thousand miles to the southeast a large regiment of soldiers was trying to do the same. The soldiers' descent into slumber was not to be accomplished so easily if at all. Encircling them as they lay covered from head to toe in layers of blankets despite the warm night of the deepest South were hordes of ravenous mosquitoes. They lit on the blankets, smelling the flesh just beneath, and penetrated through the wool like daggers into the men's skin. With every bite each soldier jumped and swatted the spot, but in doing so opened the door for the dead insect's kin to float beneath the covers and feed without being impeded by the wool blanket. Then the soldier would reach down his back or scratch at his arms after one more invader had been squashed. But the mosquitoes would eventually win by sheer number and the restless night would end with the soldier's skin riddled with small swollen blotches.

The bugs made no distinction for rank. A buzzing gang of the bloodsuckers hovered over the prostrate form of General Jackson as he struggled for sleep like the common soldiers around him. He had the single advantage of anyone in his company with a fine mosquito mesh he placed on top of his blanket as another measure of defense. It worked against some, but still others crept in unguarded crevices and folds in the blankets and bit the general with a fury driven by starvation for blood, not unlike the man they dined on.

There were other noises in the darkness besides the buzzing of invisible wings to keep the soldiers awake. Fires, fueled exorbitantly high and smoky to ward off the mosquitoes, were beacons to the Seminole warriors the soldiers were in search of. Eyeing the fires at night, the Seminole could gauge their pursuers and stay ahead or behind or to the side of them at will. Or they could lead the soldiers into swamps that had no end or ambushes that left the men prey to legions of hungry alligators. And when they wished to, the Seminole, cloaked by the night, attacked in spurts of fives and tens that Jackson and his weary men took to be hundreds.

The sentries surrounding the exhausted camp wrapped themselves in their blankets against the mosquitoes and stood in the smoke until they choked. Then they hurriedly made their rounds and hustled back into the smoke. Some however, didn't return from their circles around the slumber-seeking encampment. If a marauding alligator didn't reach them first they would be found the next morning with their throats slashed open by a razor-sharp Seminole blade and their bodies saturated with an infestation of bug bites. Their rifles and side arms would be gone along with the blanket they had leaned on for protection.

In the early stages of Jackson's campaign against the Seminole these midnight murders inflamed the soldiers and they drove forward without need for further encouragement. But now, months into what had become the pursuit of ghosts, the bodies only served to dishearten and discourage troops that could shoulder little more. And unlike the early days, Jackson had to all but use a whip to entice his men after the enemy.

Although it was now deep in the fall, the relentless Florida sun broke feverishly over a flat horizon signaling the beginning of another day's drudgery. A few of the men began to stir. Most however, felt the relief from the night insects that had been driven away by the sunlight and tried to sleep. Jackson was up though and expected his men to do likewise. There was no reveille, no resounding triumphant horn, to welcome the day and rouse the men to life. The smell of coffee, brewing at the hands of a stalwart few, was the only call.

"Have our scouts returned?" the general asked an underling lieutenant.

"The Creek have not returned and our own scouts are just heading out now, sir."

"Just heading out? Why we should be pulling out ourselves! I'd like to see us get a good ten miles in today."

The lieutenant shifted uncomfortably. "Sir, the men are bone weary. It's damn near impossible to sleep with the bugs. They're about to go mad. I feel it myself, General."

"Think I don't? But by God I'm up and ready to march."

"Yes, sir, but perhaps the general would be better served by a few more hours' rest or perhaps another day or two — just to get our wits back about us."

"Two days! Well you're damn right about one thing, Lieutenant. You have lost your senses! In two days there won't be a redskin in two hundred miles of here."

"I don't think there is one now, sir. We've marched through swamps an alligator would avoid, and all we've got to show for it a regiment of sick men. Sir, I'm afraid if we push on too far too fast we won't have a fighting man standing when and if we do find the Seminole."

"To hell with what you think, Lieutenant! To hell with it!"

Jackson's outburst was drawing attention. Passing soldiers slowed their steps to hear and see what would happen next. As others held back, a grizzly sergeant fell out from the pack and approached the arguing officers.

"Beggin' the general's pardon, sir," he said as he roughly pulled a beaten cap from his unkempt head. "The lieutenant there is mighty mistaken 'bout one thing. That being that there ain't no Seminole 'round these parts. The boys just found one of our sentries over yonder," the sergeant said as he motioned not fifty yards from where Jackson had slept. "Throat's been cut from ear to ear." The old man paused as Jackson eyed the spot from a distance then the sergeant continued. "Hair's missin' too."

The declaration had the effect intended. "Were you aware of this, Lieutenant?" Jackson asked.

"No, sir," came the slow answer.

The general's hands slipped behind his back. He turned and walked away from his junior officer and the sergeant and away from where the dead sentry lay collecting flies. The sergeant turned toward the soldiers still collected nearby and gave them a hearty thumbs-up to which the men all smiled and moved on but with a livelier gait.

"What was the purpose of that, might I ask, Sergeant?" the lieutenant asked despairingly.

"Means pack your shit, sir. We're headed outa this goddamn swamp."

"What makes you say so?"

"I've been trapsin' around this country on Jackson's heels for better than ten years and I ain't never seen him look like that. Never."

"Look like what?" the lieutenant asked as he abandoned the sergeant and began watching Jackson weaving slowly through the sprawling disjointed camp.

"Beat."

The word brought the officer's attention back to the old man. "Not hardly. Not by a long shot."

"Bullshit. I mean...beggin' the lieutenant's pardon, sir. We ain't made no headway in these swamps and you know it, sir. This is Indian land. No white man wants this ground anyway. What are we even doin' down here?"

"The Seminoles harbor runaway slaves. That's possession of stolen property, Sergeant."

"So we're up to our asses in bugs and gators to run down a handful of darkies?"

"That's the law."

"You go back to Virginia or wherever the hell that fella layin' out there missing his scalp is from and tell his kin he got hisself kilt over a runaway."

As the sergeant turned to leave, he nearly ran into General Jackson. He fumbled his cap, bent, and snatched it up from the ground and stepped around Jackson who watched the sergeant with apparent curiosity.

"Sorry, General Jackson, sir. Didn't hear you come up on me like that."

"Sergeant," Jackson said solemnly. "Gather up a few of your men and bury the sentry. Bring his effects to me — and I mean everything. Do you understand?"

"Yes, sir. General, sir."

"I'll tell his family myself how it was he happened to die — 'kilt over a runaway,' was how you put it. Is that right?"

"Them was just words, General. I—"

"See to the sentry, Sergeant."

"Yes, sir. Won't be easy though. Turn three spades of dirt and you're in water. Chances are the gators'll get to him right off."

"Chances are," Jackson repeated slowly. "But do it just the same."

"Yes, sir." The sergeant saluted.

Jackson returned the salute as he spoke. "Then pack up, Sergeant. You too, Lieutenant. As soon as the burial detail is completed we'll be pressing on. The Seminole were obviously here last night. Can't be far ahead now."

The sergeant walked away and motioned to a few men nearby as he moved off in the direction of the body. When the soldiers came near he passed on his thoughts. "Not to worry, boys. I seen what I seen. We ain't long for these swamps."

The lieutenant was closer to the subject. "We're moving ahead, sir?"

"That's what I said."

"Sir, you know the Seminole. We can't track in these conditions. Don't know where to start. Can't fight them when we do find them. The undergrowth is so thick—"

"If you can't lead your men, resign your commission and I'll find someone who can."

The lieutenant didn't respond.

"Anything else, Lieutenant?"

"No, sir."

"Then proceed with your duties and make short work of it."

Jackson's camp was still rubbing the sleep from its eyes by the time Totsuhwa and Chancellor had been on their way for hours. They discovered several fine growths of the devil's shoelace and made note of where it was so they could gather some on the trip home. They only stopped once to devour a bag of beans Totsuhwa had carried and drink beside a trickle of a stream. Not long after, Chancellor spotted the first object of the pilgrimage — a cedar standing surprisingly alone in the middle of a clearing in the woods.

When the boy followed the reddish cragged trunk upwards with his eyes he realized why little else grew nearby. The height of the great tree and span of its branches captured all the available sunlight. Any lesser tree that tried to grow nearby would starve to death before it took root.

As Chancellor stood staring up at the tree, his father walked by. "This way," he said as he pointed through the forest to the distinct reddish bark of another cedar deeper in the woods. The scene repeated itself until a third tree, even larger than the first was found.

Totsuhwa approached it quite tenderly. He placed both hands on the trunk and lowered his head as though to pray. His hands didn't move, didn't feel the split and ragged bark, but they caressed the tree just the same. Totsuhwa mouthed a song of thanks for the tree and its strength and asked that a twig of its great power be passed to him for the good use of the Real People. When the shaman felt the echo of reply to the appeal resonate through him he removed his hands from the tree and patted it as you would an old dog.

Chancellor had come up slowly on his father and had waited until the two old friends had silently spoken. "It is a beautiful tree," he said with respect for the expression on his father's face and in his hands. "It must be very old."

"It is. And very wise."

"A tree can be wise?"

"This one can, yes. It has a history and with history comes wisdom. It is the same with people."

Chancellor looked up at the treetop as though a bit confused by it all. "What is the history of this tree?"

"It is more the history of the tree's tribe. Like the history of the Tsalagi is your history. Many, many winters ago when the Tsalagi were a young people there was an evil priest among them. He did many bad things to our people and our land but was powerful and difficult to stop. In time his attention faded and as it did the strength and bravery of a warrior grew. The warrior tried to kill the priest, but he would not die. The people tried many ways. Death was afraid of the evil in him. After many such tries the warrior cut off the priest's head and still he did not die."

Chancellor's eyes were wide. Totsuhwa began to walk around the tree as he continued, crouching occasionally to pick up small twigs and branches that had fallen from the great cedar.

"The warrior eventually climbed this great tree and hung the head of the priest in the highest branch. The tree was strong and held the head fast and the blood began to flow from it, and with the blood came the wicked priest's life and he died. The tree was stained with the blood and its family remains stained to this day. The power the cedar took from the priest's blood, it turned to good so that as long as there were trees like this it could give back to the Tsalagi to make up for the evil of the priest."

Totsuhwa bent to pick up more branches. Chancellor snapped a small piece of bark off the trunk and looked at the underside. It was brighter red than the weathered outside and he ran his fingers over it then looked at them to see if the blood color had come off. It hadn't. "The tree is good to us now?" he asked.

"The tea from its young branches has many uses and the smoke from them goes from the land right to the home of the Everywhere Spirit. Certain things must never be made from its wood and other things must always be made from it. And apart from the smallest twigs, it is never to be burned. This you must learn."

Chancellor held the piece of bark and began gathering pieces like his father. They collected different sizes, lengths, and ages of wood from the floor of the forest until they had a bundle perhaps as big around as Totsuhwa's arms could reach. He knelt on the pile to compress it and pulled a thin rope from his pouch. With Chancellor's help he slipped the rope beneath the bundle, over the top again and tied it up tight. When he stood he held his hands to his face and smelled the fine cedar scent of the wood. Chancellor duplicated his father and breathed in the freshest scent he could imagine.

"That is a gift itself, is it not so?" Totsuhwa asked.

"It is a pretty smell. Mother would like it in the house."

"Tomorrow it will smell like this and she will smile."

Both grinned at each other and the praise Galegi would heap on them for bringing home the fresh scent of the cedar. Chancellor was still smiling when Totsuhwa walked away to the base of the tree where he knelt and began digging, using his open hand as a spade. Before a small hole was finished, his father called to him.

"Chancellor, bring the white beads." And the air went out of the boy's lungs. Before he could move, let alone reply, as he had neither the beads nor an answer, his father finished his own thoughts. "We must leave a gift for the tree in exchange for what we will take."

Chancellor's mind raced down a single path. He recalled now his father's words from the woods two days before as he was handed the bag of white beads and the roots of the rattlesnake's master. "Spend some time with the earth and the plants, son. Then put the roots near the door to the house to dry. Bring the beads with you in the morning."

Chancellor had done neither thing. The roots were dried inside by the fire, and the beads — the beads were still in their bag, still knotted at the top, and still against the wall of the cabin where he had slept. They were probably wrapped beneath his blankets he figured, trying quickly to find an excuse as to why he had forgotten them.

The hole was ready and Totsuhwa turned slightly to look for his boy. What he saw was instantly clear to him. He stared for only a moment and the disappointment rained over his face. He didn't speak, but instead turned back to the hole he had dug and silently filled it in with his dirty hands.

Chancellor took a very tentative step toward his father's back as he began to plead. "Gaest-ost yuh-wa da-nv-ta. I am sorry."

"Tla-o-s-da. No good."

Now Chancellor took another step. "Father, forgive me—"

"It is the tree who you owe."

"Then ask the tree to forgive me. I am sorry. I put them near my bed and we left in such a hurry that I jumped up and ran out the door after you."

"This is my fault?"

"No," Chancellor said as he dropped his head. "It is mine."

Totsuhwa was already up from the hole. He snatched up the bundle of branches and began untying the rope.

"We cannot take the wood?" Chancellor asked.

"We cannot."

"But we have traveled—"

"We have no gift to leave."

Chancellor ran through everything on his person and came away with nothing. Totsuhwa was gently spreading the twigs and branches around the tree as they had been.

"Mother will be disappointed about the smell."

"As am I," Totsuhwa said as he tossed aside the last of the sprigs.

"I am sorry, Father."

"I know you are, son," Totsuhwa said as he stopped and looked at the boy. "But it is wrong to take and not give. You have forgotten something important today. When you are the man I know you will become, you will remember something else though — something more important than beads and cedar wood."

Chancellor thought as he stared at the ground and the short grass starved by the great tree. Before he could muster an answer or breathe a comment that might somehow return him to grace with his father, Totsuhwa stepped out from beneath the tree and headed home.

"There is no more work for us here."

They walked along at a brisk pace for the rest of the morning. When Chancellor's stomach signaled to him and his father that it was time to eat, Totsuhwa offered another suggestion — one that Chancellor could not refuse.

"Let us run for a time." And Totsuhwa began to jog along slowly without waiting for an answer.

What began as a lope "for a time," evolved into a training run that lasted several hours. The pace was not fierce, but it was steady, and after several miles, Chancellor began to flag. His father, who seldom lost track of the boy, noticed the wilting and slowed for a time then began to walk. Chancellor rammed his hands on his hips to relieve his chest and breathed as deeply as he could without alerting his father that he had been ready to fall.

Midway along the respite they stopped at a stream and drank. Some berries provided a little nourishment and the walk continued. As the sun was nearing the horizon the run began again. This time it would continue until the woods had fallen completely dark. Chancellor blindly stayed on his father's heels — darting with the large shadow before him in hopes of avoiding the obstacles his father seemed to avert so easily. After what seemed like endless hours Totsuhwa stopped and Chancellor ran into him in the dark.

Totsuhwa caught him from falling. "You would like to keep running?"

Chancellor tried to breathe normally but was hard pressed to do so. "If you...want to...rest, I can wait."

The father's smile was hidden in the dark. He was still stinging from his son's forgetfulness but impressed just the same with his owning up to it and his acceptance of the punishing run, which was exactly what it had been.

"We will rest for a short time here then move on before the sun wakes."

Chancellor's answer came as the hurried unfurling of his blanket and an even quicker descent to it and to sleep. Sleep's embrace was tight and complete in moments but was rudely shaken off. He

opened his eyes that were nearly stuck together and saw the looming shadow of his father kneeling nearby rolling his own bedroll up
into a tight bundle.

"We will race the sun to the mountains. Come quickly."

Totsuhwa was off. Chancellor scrambled from beneath his blanket part out of obedience, but also out of a strong understanding
that to dawdle would mean to be abandoned there in the cold dark
of the far early morning. He wadded his blanket as best he could
and tied it up as he sprinted to catch his father's step.

The trip home changed little from the evening before. They
drank from passing streams and snatched a few late-blooming
and mostly drying berries from plants along their way, but they
never officially stopped again. The run angered the sore muscles in
Chancellor's worn legs. There was limited talk and even diminish-
ing thought as he became increasingly tired from the combination
of running and little to eat. His father, or Chancellor himself for
that matter, could have hunted up a meal, but it was plain that
Totsuhwa wanted to be home and Chancellor was in tow as surely
as if he'd been tied.

When the terrain became more familiar Totsuhwa walked
again. By the time the valley that held the cabin was in sight it was
late in the afternoon and the day was cooling. Chancellor had his
breath but was terribly hungry. His mother wouldn't have a meal
ready, unsure as she always was of when they would return, but he
knew she would put something together quickly and the thought
made his mouth water and his stomach grumble.

As the pair broke through the last stand of trees and into the
clearing that embraced the cabin they excited the dogs who barked
ferociously at first then began to yelp as pups who were thrilled
to see their masters return. As always Galegi heard the barking,
relaxed immediately when the sound changed and grabbed her clay
pot and set it full of water near a fire burning softly in the simple
mud and stone fireplace. She had corn already ground and immediately set out to prepare a meal.

At the opposite end of the rough table on which she worked sat
the small bag of white beads she had found when she straightened
Chancellor's bed. As a mother and wife she knew the anguish the

presence of the beads still in the house must have caused her men beneath the shade of the tall cedar, but also as wife and mother she understood that it was better met at the front door, acknowledged then put aside. She wouldn't inquire about the trip or how much cedar was discovered or even if they brought her some of the devil's shoelace. She would leave it all out in the forest between the two except for the pouch of beads, which had to be handled, bounced in Totsuhwa's hand and then put away for the next trip. Then they would eat and rest and tomorrow would begin another brighter day.

Galegi was as much a shaman in her own home and with her family's internal interactions as Totsuhwa was shaman to the nation. Her husband's actions were accomplished as though she had scripted them. He walked in, hugged his wife and kissed her face then Chancellor took his place. While mother and son kissed and she stroked his long hair, Totsuhwa picked up the beads, was assured of being seen by his son as he weighed the bag in his hand then put it away in his large medicine pouch. Nothing else was ever said of it as a family, but when Chancellor went to sleep, with his dinner nearly still in his mouth and the sun still just above the horizon, Galegi pried the story from her husband as a wife might and a mother should. They discussed it all and were in agreement on both the lesson learned and their empathy for the sadness in their boy.

The couple slept outside though it was fast approaching the cool weather of the deep fall. They slept wrapped in each other's arms and found the warmth there comforting. Their passion heated them both until almost an hour later when Totsuhwa threw back the blanket and sat up. The steam was rising from his sweaty body and the cool air refreshed him. Galegi however, screamed in offense to the sudden rush of cold air and begged him to return to her side. He laughed, she chastised him, and they coasted away to sleep surrounded by a warm damp blanket and the gentleness of their love.

Normally the first light of day would have snapped Totsuhwa's eyes open, but he felt the strain of the previous days and nestled closer to his wife and pulled the blanket over his eyes. When the day was in full swing and the sun, weak and tired as it was from a summer of hard work, was edging near the top of the trees, the couple stirred. They each looked toward the house to assay their boy's position and condition.

"He ran with my every step," Totsuhwa said.

Galegi answered by pushing herself into him roughly and rolling her husband to his back. They made love with physicality far distant from the romantic affair of the night before. She bit his shoulder roughly in the final throngs and he pulled her hair back to expose her tender throat. His teeth caressed the veins pulsing in her neck and bit her only enough to show her his presence and what he could do. Then their muscles relaxed, they fell into softer arms, gentler kisses, and enjoyed together the soft cool breezes of the fresh day.

Unknown to the lovers, Chancellor was not asleep in the cabin. He was not in the cabin at all. As his parents loved away the morning Chancellor was already hard afoot across the mountains, pressing on toward the devil's shoelace and the great cedar tree, the bag of white beads jangling in his hand with every stride. He had woken early, shaken by something inside that begged him not to sleep. In the cool darkness of the cabin he realized his parents had slept outdoors. Their absence gave him the opportunity and that was all he required as the incentive had been planted deep within from the moment beneath the tree when he realized he had forgotten the offering. In the emptiness of the cabin he was able to fumble to his father's medicine pouch and take the beads. He also rolled up his blanket, neater and tighter then when he had first set out, took what food he could carry and slipped into the woods well removed from the sleeping figures near the cabin.

It would take the day and a night with little sleep before Chancellor was again under the arms of the great tree. He had made better time, unencumbered by lessons and whipped by the disappointment he had seen in his father's eyes. The sticks and branches he collected were the same ones his father had scattered and he tied them in much the same fashion. Then he dug out the soft dirt from the recently filled hole at the base of the tree.

He opened the small pouch and poured a few of the white beads into his hand. There were three at first and he shook the bag until another rolled out. Chancellor looked at the size of the tree and the large bundle he had gathered. The bag tapped against his hand again and three additional beads joined the number already in his hand. One rolled free of the undersized outstretched palm and made a jump for the hole in the ground, but Chancellor set the bag aside, picked up the wayward bead, and placed it again in his palm with the others.

"I do not know all the words, great one. Here are seven of the white beads. Seven gifts, one for each clan of my people." Chancellor placed a bead in the hole his father had originally dug as he recited each clan name.

"The Paint. The Deer. Bird. Wolf. The Bear. Blue. And the Wind. Thank you for these gifts I carry away today, and thank you for the help you give to the Tsalagi."

When the last bead was in the hole Chancellor slowly and reverently pulled the loose dirt over them and raked the ground with his fingers until the space where they were was invisible. He stood up slowly and wiped his hands on his loose buckskin pants. Then he looked up at the tree and touched its skin as his father had. He thought briefly about the head of the wicked priest hanging from the top most branches but then pushed away from it and the tree.

The walk back would be slower. He would have to contend with the bundle of wood and he would stop for the devil's shoelace for his mother. It would take another day or so to get home. His parents might worry, but what he had done was right. He felt it in his heart and the heart shared its feelings with his tired legs and encouraged him on.

In the interim, his parents had found his bedroll missing. Galegi had a few anxious moments thinking her boy had run away because of the embarrassment of the forgotten beads, but Totsuhwa went immediately to his medicine pouch and when he found them gone, they both realized what was happening.

Galegi began to suggest Totsuhwa go after their boy but reconsidered and agreed as soon as her husband said no. This was something Chancellor had chosen to do and he would have to see it through by himself. To go out and meet him, to help carry the bundle, would defeat the penance the boy had placed on his own head. It was best he come home tired and alone but with the gifts the tree had given to him along with the return of his pride and dignity.

A day later, when a bone-weary hungry boy staggered into the camp with a load of cedar wood and devil's shoelace, it was plain that the pride and dignity of his parents and his people came with him.

The season quietly advanced on the cabin, the village nearby, and over the entire nation. Harvesting was completed, and the pace slowed. During the days, hunting trips were planned for the winter and later, stories, myths, and legends were passed on around fires that burned bright long into the cool evenings.

Further to the south the nights were cooler as well, but not enough to pacify General Jackson's soldiers or lengthen their stay in the swamps of the Seminoles.

The renewed push into the heartland of the Seminole had been short-lived, just as the old sergeant had suggested. Another week of wading hip deep through muck and mud, chased by mosquitoes, snakes, alligators, and their own prey day and night was enough.

Jackson reluctantly called a halt to the pursuit. At first he hid the defeat by suggesting the Seminoles had outflanked his army and ordered a retreat to catch the conniving redskins. But that veil parted quickly. Sentries were placed only for the army's protection, and scouts were no longer sent out. Soon, spirits began to rise as the men neared the northern border of Florida.

As the camp began to breathe again, freed from the stifling heat and humidity of the swamps, Jackson, instead of showing his own relief, began to fume and place blame.

"Damn men. Not even men," he said to a tin cup of whiskey and no one else as he muttered inside his tent while outside soldiers were lifting their voices to bleating banjos. "Singing. Goddamn if they're not singing. Defeated and still they sing. And whipped by savages." He stopped long enough to refresh his cup. The bottle hit the edge of the cup too hard but came away none the worse for the wear.

"Damn Indians. All over the country. Gotta get rid of them. Hiding out in the swamps like a bunch of goddamn animals." His fist abruptly slammed the table and startled the cup and bottle. "And I couldn't catch 'em! Goddamn it all!" Then he listened again to the singing outside. "I'd have killed them if I had real men with me. Not this bunch. Piss-poor scouts. Not a good one in the bunch. Them Creek too. They didn't do a goddamn thing. All related to them Seminole is why. Should have brought them Cherokee down here, goddamn ungrateful bastards. If they'd a come, I'd of cleaned that swamp free of them Seminole. Cherokee made me look bad. Goddamn Cherokee."

In the firelight outside the general's tent, a group of soldiers were doing a square dance. The ones playing the women sashayed with great enthusiasm, and the men playing men bowed deeply to their corners. The banjo strummed, and the dancers danced, and all the soldiers, tired of fighting unseen enemies, relaxed and talked of cooler weather, sleep without bugs, and home.

The old sergeant was reclining with a few others near the edge of the fire and the square that held the dancers.

"Old Hickory's mad as hell!" he shouted, laughing over the plinking of the banjo strings and the shouts of the dancers. "Goddamn woe to any poor sum bitch Indian he happens to run into twix here an' the Ohio River!"

1775   1790   1806   1814   1818   **1821**

I n the mountain valley of Totsuhwa and his family, preparations
were underway for a hunt. Chancellor cleaned and polished his
mother's rifle until it glowed in his hands. It was more his than
hers after taking his first deer with it two years before, but he still
called it hers out of respect and the comforting tie it represented to
his mother. He rubbed the nicks and scrapes in the stock until most
disappeared entirely. The others he continued to labor against, not
knowing that they represented the maturity of the rifle, the battles
it had fought, and the deer it had brought down.

His father cleaned his own rifle with much less polish and more
attention to the firing mechanism. And while both attended to
their guns, Galegi wrapped up what remained of the family's dried
meat. It was the last of the venison of the last deer and would fuel
the hunters on their return for more. They were not out of food
nor did they have abundance. It was the right way. With the meat,
Galegi packed some nuts and a sizeable amount of ground corn. She
also tucked in some tobacco for her husband and a few dried straw-
berries she had set aside as a treat for Chancellor.

By the time the bundle was ready and the guns cleaned the
shadows outside had grown long. Totsuhwa was ready to go and
Chancellor even more so, but they would wait and leave with the

morning light. Tonight Totsuhwa found no anxiousness to go. Those days had passed with the last seasons. Instead he would linger, though Chancellor annoyingly paced, and sleep in the arms of his wife once more. Morning and the departing would come far too soon for the man who at another time would have been blown away by the slightest breeze. Now even the harsh wind of hunting for food could scarcely rock him from his love.

Later, in the darkness of the cabin as the small family settled in to sleep beside the dying firelight, Totsuhwa spoke to his son. "For the hunt, we will only use the rifles. I want to see what your practice has left you. Even if ahwi lies down for you on the first shot I want you to reload as if the Creek Nation was coming for that long hair of yours. Understand?"

"Yes, Father."

"We will leave our bows here for your mother." In the dark Totsuhwa playfully squeezed her. "If ahwi comes near she may have his skin stretched by the time we come home."

"Mother cannot draw our bows. They are too strong for her."

Galegi was instantly up on an elbow peering over her husband through the flickering light at her son. He felt her stare and chanced a look in her direction. Her black eyes were sharp and not too playfully fierce. The black hair that shined like his own framed her face.

Chancellor squeezed deeper into his blankets. "Now that I think, Mother, you are strong. You could shoot my best arrow into the mountains from our door."

His mother settled back into her blankets as Totsuhwa laughed. "That was an important lesson, Chancellor. One you must learn over all else. Blacksnakes are beautiful, fast, and friends to us. But if you grab their tail they will bite you."

"I see so."

Totsuhwa hugged his wife and laughed quietly a few more times. In minutes the trio was asleep.

At first light Galegi was up making breakfast. Chancellor rolled from his blankets at the sound of her steps and perched himself near the door, rifle in hand, checking his knife in his belt.

"Father, I am ready," he ordered.

Totsuhwa rolled lazily in the blankets, still smelling of the warmth and breath of his wife. He looked up at his son, armed to the teeth, and smiled. "Relax, my son. The game will wait for you."

"But I am ready."

"I see so."

"And the deer are ready to fall under my rifle."

"Shhhh," Totsuhwa said in a whisper. "Do not say this or think of them in that way. They will hear you and sense your coming. They may hide from you. You must go into the forest as a friend."

"But I will kill them. How can I be a friend who kills?"

"Go into the mountains as a friend and they will come to your steps so you may eat and feed your mother. That is what they will do for you as your friends. Do not think of them as your prey or as an enemy to be hunted like you may the Chickasaw. The ahwi do not feel this way. Neither should the hunter."

"Yes, Father. But can we go?"

"Do you see your mother preparing our breakfast? Do you want to insult her and leave her food standing?"

Chancellor didn't answer but set his mother's rifle against the wall near the open door next to the finely crafted bow his father had made for him the winter before. He went to the rough-hewn table on which Galegi worked and stood waiting.

"Do not be a rude son," his mother said sharply. "Go bring your horses to the front of the cabin for your father. Fetch some fresh water and bring wood for the fire."

Chancellor spun away and dashed out the door. His footfalls betrayed how aggravated he had become at the waiting.

Totsuhwa and Galegi looked at each other. Her brow was wrinkled at her son until she caught her husband's eye. Then they both broke into smiles.

"He is always so excited to hunt with you," she said.

"Not now. He is out bringing up the horses, fetching wood, getting water—"

"He is doing what his mother told him — being a good son. Not peering at her fixing a meal like a vulture sitting in a tree."

"He is a good son. We have done well."

Totsuhwa threw off his blanket then turned to roll it up as Galegi continued with her breakfast. Her hands stopped in the mixture of ground meal and she glanced again across the small room to her husband. He had his back to her and was tying off his bedroll for the trip.

"Little One?" she said hesitantly.

Totsuhwa finished his tying then spun on his heels and looked at her a bit puzzled. "What does my wife wish?"

"Why do you say so?"

"You call me 'Little One' when a wish is right behind it."

"Not so."

"Do you have a wish before I go? We will have to hurry before Chancellor comes back if you want to...warm the blankets again."

"You are a bad man! Behave before I take a switch to you."

"I was mistaken." He smiled again. "I will be serious. What is your wish?"

Galegi was quiet and thoughtful as she kneaded the corn flour. "Our boy. He is growing fast. He will be a fine man. I see you in him often."

"And I see you."

"Yes, yes, we have thrown a fine colt, Totsuhwa, but I have had a thought. A thought you will think foreign to me and perhaps even bad of me."

Now he stood and moved to the table. "I cannot think bad of you. Ever."

"Wait until you hear my thought." She paused again when the dough had been folded over several times in her hands. "Chancellor will be a fine man, but I see and hear things, even from our home. Things I did not see before. This is not the same world you and I were born into. He will become a man, and a fine one, but one who must deal with things that you and I have been able to escape."

Totsuhwa saw the end of the conversational journey. "You mean the white people."

"You are smart," she said smiling as she nudged him with her hip and her hands busied themselves again with breakfast.

"What are your thoughts of the whites?"

"You know my thoughts of the whites, Totsuhwa."

"Yes, and I am glad not to be one!"

"Smart and funny."

"But you have a new thought now?"

"I think we would be helping our son if we sent him to the school near Echota." The words came out fast and all in one breath as if she had hesitated they might stop of their own accord.

Galegi's hands slowed then stopped entirely. She did not look up from her work to her husband for another moment, recognizing that she may have suggested a horrible thing. In another moment she realized that her once dreaded thought was being received with at least a measure of consideration. Encouraged, she continued.

"Their language is important to trade — to trade without being cheated. And their talking leaves. I once thought it a dark magic, but I see its purpose. They make marks and their kind can tell the other's thoughts. It is near wondrous."

She carefully measured her husband before taking up once more. "My thought is that I want Chancellor to have these things to protect himself from the whites and to use them to protect his people as he grows to a great shaman like his father." This was said as the final convincing stroke for herself as much as Totsuhwa and it was followed by one last pause. "Please tell me how you feel on such things as this," she said stoically as her hands began their work again.

Totsuhwa was hesitant to reply but mostly out of surprise. He listened once more to the words as they echoed in his mind to be certain his ears had not tricked him. When he was sure of what he had heard he began to think about his answer. Galegi and he both shared a distrust and dislike bordering on hate of the white men, but they had come to see the tools they had as useful. Perhaps there were other useful things as well.

"I too have thought of the talking leaves," he said. "My mind tells me that it may be useful, as the needles you sew our clothes with and the metal for blades."

"Those are my thoughts," she answered as breakfast took shape.

"Chancellor would have an advantage in trade as he learned the white man's leaves and mastered their tongue. I know that the words I understand have helped me many times. To know them all would be good for him."

"And the people."

"And the people," he echoed. "But there are many things to be learned from the whites that cannot help anyone, especially a young boy who aches too much to hunt and forgets offerings for cedar."

"That was a long time ago and the same boy retraced the steps of his father and made right the wrong. And his rifle leans there against the door while he fetches water for his mother."

Totsuhwa turned away from the table and went to the doorway. The heart of the father opened and new reasons spilled out against his wife's radical thoughts. He was not looking for Chancellor outside the cabin specifically but he saw him in his mind's eye. And in his mind the boy was just three feet tall and scrambling for his father's lap.

"He would have to stay near the school."

Galegi immediately went to the doorway and hugged her husband from behind. "I know you — tough, strong fighter. And I fear what you fear. We do not have to decide today. My thoughts are only food for our minds to consider."

"It is some distance away."

"Our legs are strong," she countered.

Totsuhwa breathed deeply. Somewhere inside he remembered when he had passed through the crossroads that told him he need not fear that family and love would leave him. Now his son might be doing just that. He wrestled some and danced some with this notion there in the doorway, supported by the comfort of a woman's arms that themselves would feel the emptiness of a son away from home.

"Not today," she said again as she eased him back inside. "We will think on this some more. Come and eat before you leave me."

He did as directed — the tall, powerful man in the prime of life, being led to the table by a small hand that came from a strong love. The comfort in her touch immediately dissuaded him of any of the old fears and as he reached the table the die was cast for Chancellor's future.

"He will go."

"I think it is a good choice, Totsuhwa," she said, in both support and acknowledgment that the decision had been his.

While the words yet echoed, Chancellor came into the doorway with fresh water in one hand and wood in the other, much of which was haphazardly tucked up under his arm. The wood began to spill from his arm as he protected the water. In a hurried dash, he made it to the rough fireplace before the bulk of the wood tumbled to the floor. He jerked and spun to get the wood to fall in one direction while keeping the wooden water bucket upright. When the fracas ended, he held the water out to his parents. "I did not lose a single drop!"

"You could have made two trips," his mother suggested as breakfast took shape on the table.

"Oh, no," Totsuhwa said. "There is no time. We have a hunt to go on!"

Chancellor nearly danced as he set the water aside, straightened the wood, and coaxed the quiet fire to life. Galegi raised her eyes and watched her husband as he watched their son. She knew that the anguish over the decision she felt in her own heart was magnified in the man who not so long ago had come to grips with the fear of abandonment. She saw Chancellor poking the fire and missed him already, but she began to wonder if perhaps her timing had not been good for the man she loved most in the world.

Later, after the last bite of breakfast had been swallowed, Chancellor leaped across the room and took up his mother's rifle, which would be his for the next several days.

"Do-da-ga'go-v-i, goodbye, Mother!" he shouted as he disappeared out the door leaving both his mother and father behind.

"Chancellor!" Galegi called.

The boy appeared in the door as though in slow motion. He didn't ask why he'd been summoned.

"Carry your food or go hungry."

Chancellor's shoulders slouched hard as he trudged across the room. He picked up the bundle of food Galegi had carefully wrapped in an old but clean cloth. The tight parcel would sustain him and his father for three days. It would be supplemented by what the route would offer and would insure Galegi her men would sleep each night with her food in their bellies.

Chancellor's return for the food was naturally not the only reason for his recall. Though a little downtrodden at having been called so sharply, he knew he owed his mother a hug and more. When he took hold of the bundle, she took hold of him. She hugged him tight and rubbed his back as though to ease away in advance any ache the hunt might cause.

"You will bring me back a fine deer?"

The harsh words were instantly forgotten. A broad smile of intended accomplishment exploded across Chancellor's face. "A big one! Enough to last the whole winter. Oh, shhh! We shouldn't speak of ahwi."

"You remembered," Totsuhwa said as he picked up his rifle.

"Go with your father and do not return until there is plenty of meat on your back."

The boy hugged her as a thank you as much as a goodbye. He pulled away and she pulled him back and kissed his cheek. "Do you know I love you?"

"Yes, Mother," he answered, impatient to begin the hunt.

"And you will make me proud to be your mother? So I can walk through the village and people will point to me and say, 'There is the mother of Chancellor'? Today, tomorrow, and all the days to come?"

"I will make you proud."

"And you will be a good boy in the process?"

"I am not a boy."

"That is true. You will be a fine man in the process?"

"I will."

"Good. Now go get some meat for our table." And she swatted him on the rear.

Chancellor took two steps away and stopped. "Mother. You do not spank a hunter before he goes into the woods. I think it is bad luck or something. If it is not, it should be."

Galegi tried to frown. "I see. I will be more careful in the future."

"Thank you," her boy answered, all grown up, or at least trying to be. He went to the door again, slower now and stepped through it, carrying the food and his mother's rifle. "See you in a week or so, Mother. Maybe more," he said from outside the cabin. "We might have to go the edge of the nation and back!"

Galegi turned to her husband who answered the question in her eyes before she could ask it.

"We will be back in three days, maybe less." He hesitated only long enough to sidle up close to her. "I remember my words. Three days is enough for him to hunt. We will go again when the geese have all passed and the trees are asleep."

"Good. Three days then." And she kissed him.

The kiss was returned, yet there was little passion behind it. Like his son and despite all his fresh words and thoughts, Totsuhwa did feel the pull of the mountains as a hunt came near. He would be back in three days as he had promised, but now he was ready to go.

As he turned from his wife's embrace she swatted him on the backside like she had her son and like the boy, Totsuhwa stopped and turned.

"It will counter the bad luck I put on our young hunter," Galegi said matter-of-factly. "I believe that is the way."

"And I believe you are a greater teacher than I will ever be."

"Why do you say so?"

"Because I learn new ways to love you with each day. And each day, it pleases me more. I will speak to Chancellor about the white school as we hunt."

Galegi smiled the smile of a woman who had love in her heart and her home. There was comfort even in the leaving of the two men she adored. They would soon return and be by her side all the days of her life.

Totsuhwa stopped in the doorway. "Three days."

"Three days," came the echo from his love. And Totsuhwa walked out of the cabin.

Chancellor stood with the horses, packed and ready to travel. His father did not speak but took the reins of his mount from his son and swung effortlessly onto the horse's back. Chancellor had to pull hard on his horse's mane and jump at the same time. He squirmed to right himself but was quickly seated and ready. Totsuhwa had already begun to move off and Chancellor's horse followed automatically as did the family's dogs until a harsh word from their master turned them back toward the cabin.

Before the riders had cleared the open space and entered the forest, Galegi appeared in the doorway of the cabin. Both her men were keen for the hunt — Totsuhwa from memories of past wants to escape, seasoned now with the continued training of Chancellor, and her son pressing ahead into manhood. Preoccupied by their thoughts, neither looked back as Galegi faintly held up a hand to wave goodbye.

The remainder of the day slipped by in a quiet routine. Galegi busied herself with her home and garden in anticipation of winter. The season would not be long or fraught with the bitter winds she had heard tales of from the Shawnee and Iroquois far to the north, but still there were preparations to make against the ending yield from her garden. What plants had already given up against the cool nights were pulled and the soil tended to make ready for next spring's plantings. She labored this way for most of the day and by late afternoon she was ready to spell herself.

"Perhaps," she thought. "I will go into the village and see if what I have heard is true."

There had been much talk over a spinning wheel that had reached the remote town. Others in the nation had been spinning thread and making cloth for some time, but these were mainly in the larger towns closer to the white man's influence. The isolated settlements, like the small collection of homes a brisk walk from Galegi's cabin, would be the last to accept this gift. Spun cloth was a good thing most said and she was prone to agree.

There had been a story, she recalled as she worked, wherein the Creator gave the Cherokee a book and the white man a bow. The Cherokee traded the book for the bow and thus never learned the things the book could teach. He became instead a wonderful hunter and warrior and flourished while the white man studied the book in a far-off place. Now, it would seem, the time had come when the white man's studies were ready for harvest. And if the Cherokee could share in the harvest, as he had shared the secrets of hunting with the whites, he should do so. With this thought in her mind she considered again the notion of Chancellor going to the white school. Totsuhwa had not disagreed. He was too wise and saw the benefits as she did. Somewhere in the hunt she hoped her husband would be able to get their son, full of enthusiasm for hunting and rifles, to understand the importance of learning the white talk and the way of their talking leaves.

The late afternoon sun was casting the first long shadows of the early fall nights when Galegi thought again of going to the village. A few more dead plants to uproot and she would be off. She would stop at the stream to wash the dirt from her face and hands then drift into the town just before the sun set so she could see the spinning wheel.

The dogs were about her and the cabin. Two older dogs lay nearby warming themselves in the weakening sun casually watching their master's wife from time to time. A yearling dog pranced through the grass of the clearing between the cabin, the garden, and the tree line. Neither Galegi nor the older dogs paid him any mind — that is, until he ceased to bounce and froze pointing directly at the edge of the trees.

When he stopped and didn't make a sound it was as if he had shouted to the others. The ears on the senior members of the pack jumped to attention and pointed at the tree line. Their ears pivoted like a human's eyes and searched for the sound that had brought the younger dog up short. When they found it their intense eyes followed and brought them very slowly to their feet.

Galegi took instant notice. The dogs signaled that something, or someone, was out of place in the world of the cabin. She stopped her work and strained to see into the trees as the dogs began to move away from the cabin and into the clearing, crouching low to the ground using the inborn hunting skills their Cherokee owners mimicked. The two older dogs vanished into the taller grass before Galegi could make out what had drawn their attention, but in another moment the form of a young buck deer materialized from the trees.

Galegi relaxed as the dogs, hunting now, grew tenser. She watched the deer, its own nose testing the air, move quite brazenly into the open field. He walked with a purpose and Galegi recognized that he was following the scent trail of a doe. Because of his distraction he had wandered close to the cabin clearing, oblivious of what might wait there.

"The hunters are looking for you in the mountains," Galegi said with a smile. "And you come here instead. You are very wise, ahwi. I hope you are as fast as you are wise. If they can, my dogs will run you until you can run no more. They will come to you from downwind. Be quick, ahwi. Be quick."

As Galegi had said, the older dogs were circling to get downwind of the buck. The younger dog, so pleased with himself for finding the deer first, quivered at the thought of the chase but did not move otherwise. He would try to wait until the others made the attack.

Galegi watched from her garden. The older dogs were invisible to her, but she knew where they would make their move. The young dog, to his credit, stayed frozen while the deer boldly strutted into the trap, thinking only of the scent of the doe. Her trail led very near the young dog and when the quarry was nearly on him he could hold himself in check no longer. He was uncertain how to attack but sprang up in the air like a deer himself and rushed the startled buck.

The other dogs raced in as the deer dropped his rack of antlers and sprinted. He was at full speed in three strides with the old dogs coming fast behind his flashing white tail. The young dog dodged the sharp antlers by inches. As the rush of the buck cleared him, the others drove past the beleaguered youngster. The yearling pup immediately joined them in the pursuit and a race to the death was on.

Galegi saw the first attack and the sprinting deer, which veered through the field and back into the trees. In a heartbeat all three dogs broke from the field themselves, hot on the freshest of trails.

"It will be close," she said as she bent to pick up the litter and debris from the summer crops.

In a few minutes she had finished the last row for the day. The dogs had covered nearly the first mountain range in pursuit of the deer that continued to run hard and her men were almost a full day's ride to the west. No person and no animal was there to hear the words from the white man that crept silently around the corner of the cabin.

"That was my deer," he said in English.

The solitary gardener twitched, startled by any voice, but instantly given over to fear when her ears relayed the English. Galegi did not move now and only stared at the man who had startled her. He was big - far heavier than her Totsuhwa but much shorter and fatter. His face was a mass of an unruly and filthy beard that mixed with his long tangled hair until it was hard to tell where one ended and the other began. There was an old buffalo hide draped over his shoulders with a length of dirty rope tying it tighter to his protruding waist. Beneath the rope were the tools of his trade — a large ugly skinning knife in a tattered sheath, a few small pouches for gunpowder and tobacco, a tomahawk with a carved dark wood handle and at least two black-haired scalps. One hand carried a big bore rifle meant for the deer and on the other hand his fingers twitched as if anxious to begin something as yet unclear, but sinister.

"That was my deer," he said again, this time in a broken mixture of Cherokee and Shawnee as he pointed to the trees with the twitching fingers.

Galegi pressed her fear to the side and bent to pick up the dead plants she had just dropped. She took her eyes off the man by his account but secretly she was watching every move, trusting that her apparent disinterest and lack of fear would dissuade the deer and scalp hunter from making any moves toward her.

"If that is your deer why do you not track him?"

"Your dogs run him off."

"He will not go far."

"I'm figuring you owe me for what your dogs done."

"I am sorry the dogs have spoiled your hunt. I will fix you a meal for what you have lost," she said as she took a step toward the cabin only to see the rifle come up to the man's waist and level at her with both his hands.

"Not so fast."

Galegi stopped and looked at the big hole in the barrel of the rifle.

"Maybe I'll take my pay in something other than grub."

"And maybe my husband will come out of the cabin and slit your throat like a pig!" She wished for the words back, but she had challenged the man and it was too late.

"Ain't nobody in that cabin. I checked her out before. Let's you and me head on up in there and see what else you got. You know, to pay me for losing of my deer."

Galegi didn't understand all the words but knew enough of them to follow. Even if she hadn't understood at all, the barrel of the gun motioning her to move was explanation enough. Very slowly, watched by the big hole in the barrel of the rifle, she stepped out of the garden and around toward the front of the cabin.

When they neared the open doorway both her and the white man heard a shout from the facing tree line fifty yards away.

"Connie! What you got?"

"Come up! I got us another one!" he said in English.

While Galegi stood prisoner outside her own door, another man dressed as the first but thinner, rode up from the woods leading a riderless horse.

The gun held Galegi fast by the cabin until the second man arrived and dismounted. He looked at Galegi quickly as he fastened the horses to the log the family often used as a seat. He pulled his rifle from its scabbard and walking cautiously in the direction of the cabin door.

"She the only one 'round?" he said as he looked into the cabin and waited for his eyes to adjust.

"She's it," Connie answered. "But she'll do."

"Where's her kin?"

"Don't know. I scared up a deer and was tracking it. Her dogs run it off. Figure she owes us."

The second man turned from the doorway and spoke to Galegi in the same broken language mix the first had used. "Where's your man?"

"Fishing," she said as she pointed toward the stream.

"That's a lie. We just come up along the stream. Ain't nobody there."

The thin man went inside and began to rummage. Galegi took a step toward the door but the rifle stopped her. The sound of things being tossed about came from the cabin and Galegi began to fume.

"My husband will be back with his brothers. Then you two will pay with your livers for going in my house!"

"C'mon, Pany," Connie said. "I can't make it all out, but she said her men are on their way."

The thin man came to the door holding a bag of ground corn, some tobacco, Galegi's mirror and comb, and Totsuhwa's red shirt. "They ain't comin' back jus' yet. There ain't no guns in here, just a couple a bows against the wall. Want 'em?"

"No," Connie grumbled. "Let's go."

"I figure they's off on a huntin' trip," Pany continued. "We could probably hole up here for days." He carried the things to his horse and tucked them in his saddlebag except the shirt which he unceremoniously tossed to his partner. "This here's too big for me. Fit you though. Mighty nice for Indian work."

Galegi, not with enough speed to force a shot at her, forcibly walked to the horses and ignoring the one called Pany, began to take her things out of his saddlebag. "These are mine."

Connie stared at her defiance but Pany merely stepped aside, pulled up the butt of his rifle and clubbed her in the back of the head. Galegi went down, unconscious against the horse.

The animal scampered to the side, frightened by the falling woman and allowed Galegi to fall headlong to the ground. Both men looked down at her, still confused by her actions as though trying to decide if she were brave or foolhardy.

"She dead?" Connie asked.

Pany rolled her over with the toe of his boot then bent down near her. "She ain't dead. I didn't whack her too hard."

"Good. Let's get her tied and back with the others. Her men are off huntin' all right, but who knows for how long. And be mindful of your tracks. If they get back soon, they'll like to be trailin' us."

Pany stood and pulled a long rope from his saddle as he looked around nervously. "Hopefully we'll be long gone before they get back. There won't be no trail then. Gimme a hand, Con."

The men threw Galegi over the back of Pany's horse like a bag of seed. "Tie her good and tight," Connie said. "This one's a fighter. I can see it."

Galegi was shaken back to consciousness by the jostling gait of a horse. It was a few minutes before the pain in her head eased enough for her to make sense of where she was and what was happening. She came to realize that she was bound, hand and foot, tied and slung head-down over the back of a horse. Beneath her she could see the horse's hooves working their way through the short grasses of a trail. In time she made out the sounds of the stream over the trudging of the horse and moved her throbbing head enough to see the boot and leg of Pany seated in the saddle in front of her. She began to struggle against the ropes that held her, not realizing Connie was riding behind.

"She's coming around, Pany."

"How's that?"

Galegi heard the words but did not understand them. She knew only that she had to get away. The ropes did not budge; however, Pany's calf was close to her head. She lurched to get within reach then buried her teeth through his pants just above where she thought his boot would end.

"GODDAMN!" Pany screamed. He jerked his leg up and brought Galegi up with it. The shifting weight would have tossed her from the horse had not her jaw been clamped on Pany's leg. His boot was caught in the stirrup and held him while Galegi clamped down harder.

"Leave go, bitch!" Pany screamed again as he punched Galegi in the face while loosely holding the reins. His horse bolted and sent Galegi off the side. She felt the flesh in Pany's leg give way as she was thrown to the ground.

As soon as she hit she was up and trying to run, but the ropes wouldn't permit it. Connie insured she couldn't run by ramming her with his horse and sending her sprawling. In her tumble she rolled further near the stream. With her hands tied behind her back it was impossible to do much, but as she lay in the taller grass she forced her arms down the back of her legs and pushed herself through, effectively bringing her hands, still bound, up in front of her. They stopped at her ankles and began tearing at the ropes.

Connie was busy laughing at Pany who was busy himself trying to corral his horse and get a look at the bite on his leg. This gave Galegi the few seconds she needed. The ropes eased up on her ankles and she kicked them free. Like the crouching dogs earlier in the clearing, she set out low through the grass toward the water, biting at the rope on her wrists as she moved.

Pany had pulled up his pants and seen the bite that had penetrated his pants and his skin. Blood was trickling from the nasty rip when he began to look around the trail for his attacker. "Where is that filthy bitch?" he said as he spun his horse around.

His partner was still laughing but began to urge his own mount ahead through the grass. "Dumped on her head over here somewhere." In three strides the horse and rider came across the loose rope lying in the grass.

"Slipped her harness, Pany! Come on!"

Galegi heard the horses crashing through the underbrush behind her. She would have to make it across the stream and hide in order to have a chance. Then she would circle back to the village and rally the people. Her hands remained tied, and it hampered her running. She used her teeth yet again and tugged at the ropes until they began to loosen. Torn between stealth and breakneck running, she worked through the scrub trees until she was at the water's edge. At the same moment the rope gave way and began to loosen from her wrists. In doing so it tangled her feet and sent her stumbling, too loudly, into the stream.

"She's made the creek!" Connie yelled as he immediately spurred his horse out of the trees and into the stream some distance below where Galegi had entered. Right away he saw her hurriedly wading through the waist-deep water, still trying to free the rope from her wrists and legs.

"Pany! Over here!"

Pany heard but so did Galegi and she rushed across the stream as fast as she could. The water held her up more than it did the horse however, and soon Connie was between her and the bank. Pany dove his mount in from the opposite side and she was trapped once again.

While Connie maneuvered his horse back and forth to keep Galegi from the shore, Pany came on from behind. Galegi heard the splashing of the horse and turned to see the fire in Pany's face and the rifle coming up. "Bite me, you goddamn whore!"

"Pany, no!" Connie shouted and jumped his horse deeper into the water until he came between Galegi and his partner. Now the rifle was pointed at him. Galegi had no one between her and the bank now, but was leery of stepping out from the protection of Connie's horse. Minus the shield she was certain Pany would kill her on the spot.

"Outa my way, Connie! Goddamn bitch is gonna pay for what she done to my leg!"

Connie tried not to laugh, but a chuckle erupted even though he was facing down an angry man with a gun. "Okay. Okay. Make her pay, but don't kill her, you damn fool. Know how much tradin' goods we can get for her? Pany, take a hold of yourself! We've got three grown women and a sprat girl. We get them to the auction block and we won't have to trap, or hunt, or mine for a year or better. Now use your goddamn head!"

Connie spun the horse quickly, reached down, and snatched Galegi by the hair. The long wet hair made a nice hold for him as he quickly wrapped his hand around it. He kicked his horse and dragged Galegi from the water and up the bank by her head. The pain made her reach up and half claw, half hold Connie's arm to keep from having the hair ripped from her scalp. When they got up on the bank, Connie dismounted and jerked her head around until he could get a good look at her pretty face. Then without a word he pummeled her back into unconsciousness. By the time Pany reached the shore Galegi was motionless in the grass and Connie was breathing hard.

"Goddamn, Pany, if she ain't a hellcat," Connie said as he licked the blood from Galegi's scratches on his arm and hand.

"Bitch!" Pany said as he kicked her, his leg still smarting badly. He recoiled from the kick more than the oblivious Galegi and grabbed his calf. Connie watched him curiously as he rolled up his pant leg until they both could see the round-shaped gash left by Galegi's teeth.

"Better slap some pitch on that, Pany. She got you good. I've seen horse bites prettier than that."

"Bitch," Pany said as he kicked again, this time with his good leg.

"Easy there. We got to have enough of her left to sell."

"Hell, ain't no one gonna want her. She's wild as a mountain cat."

"She'll come around. They all do eventually. Fetch me a stout stick. We'll pin her arms back. That'll take some of the sass out of her."

By the time Galegi woke again she was completely trussed up. Her arms had been pulled back and a two-inch round stick three feet long had been placed between her elbows and her back. Her hands were tied again, this time in the front, but the stick prevented any movement. A second rope tied her ankles but more like a set of hobbles so she could walk. A third rope ran from the hobbles up her back to the stick. She could stand and walk but she couldn't use her hands, kick, or run. And a thin rough piece of leather through her mouth, fastened at the back of her neck and on down to the stick, made sure she couldn't bite. Most of the binding was Connie's, but the bit in her teeth was Pany's idea. When it was done he shoved her to the side.

"Now let's see ya get loose of that, ya whore."

Galegi was waking up with the shove. As before it took some time before she understood where she was and what had happened. Somewhere in her mind she had begun to think the capture had been a dream and was still thinking this when the men pulled her to her feet and said, "Walk!" in their butchered Cherokee. Hurt badly, she moved ahead like a tied cow, oblivious to what was waiting for her but too crushed to resist any longer — at least for now.

A few miles away lay the temporary camp of the kidnappers. Another man, younger and clean shaven by Connie and Pany's standards, waited, watching over two women and a young girl. The girl and one woman were Shawnee, the other, a Creek. All three had their hands tied behind their backs, their feet hobbled, and their necks tied to trees. Each had only enough play in their leashes to lie down.

The guard, Niak, was a half-breed Creek who looked more white than Creek and passed for the same. When the other men arrived, towing Galegi between them with ropes tied to the stick, Niak was annoyed.

"That don't look like no fresh meat to me," he said as he looked at the bruising already showing on Galegi's face.

"Oh, she's fresh all right," Connie said with a dirty smile, "but if you decide to take a poke you better knock her out first. She's got a mouth full of choppers and she knows how to use them. How's the leg, Pany?"

"Shut your fat mouth, Connie. Before I crack you like I did this bitch."

Connie just laughed. "Here," he said as he tossed the rope tied to Galegi at Niak's feet. "Tie her fast. A ways away from the others. She's a might coarse yet but she'll settle. Mind you watch her close. She ain't one to play with."

"Pretty thing though," Niak said as he picked up the lead rope and escorted the still swooning woman to a nearby tree.

"She is that," Connie continued as he got off his horse. "But go easy if you go in for a poke, like I said. We had to rough her up some already. Don't know how much she can take just now. Be better if you throw it in that Creek bitch yonder. She's been pretty easy to get along with."

Galegi sat beneath a tree trying to clear the pain and confusion from her head. She looked at the other women and the young girl and guessed the girl to be about Chancellor's age. Then in her haze she drifted off to semi-consciousness amid thoughts of her boy.

He was riding behind his father through the mountain passes and valleys that were showing the signs of the cooling weather. Galegi's rifle lay across his forearm and was nestled close in the crotch of his arm and snuggly against his waist. Chancellor found he looked down at it often and when a wayward leaf fell against it he brushed it away, or when he bent to ride through the hanging limb of a tree he covered the gun to protect it from the scratching branches.

When the riders entered a long clearing Totsuhwa spun his horse around once and came up alongside his son. The two rode on side by side and talked easily about the day, the hunt, the love of their wife and mother, and the training Chancellor was continuing to receive. Totsuhwa quizzed him on a great many things and he did well with his answers. The names and uses for plants came to mind easily and there were no true mistakes and only a very few omissions.

"You have the mind of your mother," Totsuhwa said. "You remember things I have shown you. That is a good thing. You have done well. Your mother and I are very proud."

Totsuhwa hesitated some and Chancellor let him. He anticipated the beginning of another great lesson but never would have considered the road that was about to be laid out.

"My son, your mother and I have spoken on a thing. You have learned much of our ways. There are other things I cannot teach. There are things your mother can not teach."

"If you and mother cannot teach me these things, I do not need to know them."

"In the time of my grandmother, Ama Giga, and my father, Tsi'yugunsini, what you say was true, but today it is not. There are other lessons to be learned to protect a man and his family from harm. When I was like you, Ama Giga taught me the ways of the people and the power of the medicine which has been protected by the clan. Then my father taught me to hunt and how to fight our enemies. He made my bow like I have made yours and taught me how to make the arrow go straight to the heart." Again he paused and again Chancellor let him, his patience this time brought on by a growing confusion as much as respect.

"Chancellor, today there is more to learn than the use of medicine for the people and to shoot a bow."

"Yes, today I have a gun!" Chancellor said emphatically as he adjusted the rifle in his hand and held it up in front of him.

"You do, and it will serve you well, but there is another weapon your mother and I want you to learn to use."

Chancellor ran through the arsenal he had known in his short life. He even scanned his father for a peek at something new. He saw his father's knife, war club, and the rifle resting across his thigh. There were medicines he had heard of that could kill as easily as heal, but he knew of these already. Perhaps there was something else.

"Is it a powerful weapon?"

"It is."

"What is it and how can I learn to defeat my enemies with it?"

"You must go to the white school."

"Why there? Do they have this weapon?"

"They do. It is in their talking leaves."

"I do not understand."

Totsuhwa pulled his horse to a stop and Chancellor did the same. "Son, the whites have their own words. I know some of these words, but they have many I do not know. It is important for you to learn these words of theirs."

"Yes, Father..."

"And more important is the way of their talking leaves. You must learn to understand them. This is something I know nothing of. Nor do most of our people. There are a few fine young chiefs like Major Ridge and John Ross who have studied these things and can speak from the leaves, but they have white blood and I have a fear in my heart for the nation under their control. They want to be accepted by the whites and live as brothers. These are good things, son, very good. The Tsalagi do not look for war with the whites, but war comes in the tracks of the white men's boots. It is not the moccasin trail of the Real People.

"I have had many visions on these things, Chancellor. The way of our people will be covered with stones. There are difficult times ahead — hard winters and swarms of locusts coming over the mountains. There needs to be full-blooded Cherokee men who can interpret the leaves and the white words and tell the truth to the nation without the influence of trinkets and promises. Your mother and I wish for you to be such a man."

The boy was in awe of his father's eloquence and of the confidence he and his wife placed in their son. The rifle did not appear so important in his hand now.

Totsuhwa encouraged his horse and the two riders began to move ahead. Chancellor rode along quietly and thought about the things his father had just imparted to him. Finally the boy spoke, as stoically accepting as a man but with a few questions from the heart of a boy.

"I will have to move away to the school."

"That is so."

"Away from you and Mother and our cabin?"

"It is not so far."

"How often can I return home?"

"When your learning time permits."

"That time may be small."

"It may."

"Can you and Mother come to the school?"

"To see you? I think it is permitted."

"Will I have my horse?"

"I would say yes."

"My bow?"

"We will say yes to them if they ask us."

"Mother will need her rifle."

"She will keep it clean for you."

"Are there white boys there?"

"I would say yes, but I do not know."

"Will I be the only Tsalagi?"

"No, I have heard that many are sending their sons to such schools."

"Not sons from our mountains, I do not think. All of the boys from our ball games live here. None go to these schools."

"That is true, but it may change. You will be the first. It is good to be first."

"Yes, it is good to be first," Chancellor repeated.

The conversation trailed off as the horses continued. They would not talk of the school again until that night around a small fire. Most of the questions were repeats of ones asked earlier on the trail, but Totsuhwa spoke as if they were new, though in truth he didn't know most of the answers. He slept uncomfortably that night, troubled by some of his answers for the boy headed to the white school and an occasional ripple of trouble in his mind of which he could not find the cause.

Galegi slept only a little. She had been lashed to a tree, seated upright. Connie had given her some water the night before and had left the strap out of her mouth. It helped only a little. Her arms were numb, her face was swollen, and her head throbbed.

It was nearing daybreak and she was staring into the remains of a small fire when her eyes finally came into their own again. She saw Niak had taken the Creek woman to the edge of the camp and was grunting on top of her while Connie appeared to sleep and Pany pawed through the spoils of the day before. He held Galegi's mirror close to his face and began to trim his hair and beard with a knife.

Her eyes focused but were surrounded by pain. Her head throbbed front and back from the blow of Pany's rifle butt and the smashing of Connie's fists. One eye was swollen nearly closed and her jaw hurt, but she began to watch the man at the fire holding her mirror. He was having trouble holding the mirror in one hand and trying to cut his hair with the other. Finally he placed the mirror precariously on his forearm and pulled his hair tight with one hand and cut it with the other. When the cut hair gave way the arm jumped back and the mirror fell. When it hit the ground it cracked in a straight line across the glass.

"Damn it all..," Pany muttered.

Galegi saw the fall and heard the crack. "That is mine, you dog!" she screamed.

Pany stood up slowly. "What'd you say?"

Galegi was quiet, not understanding.

"Connie, what did that bitch say to me?"

"Shut up, will ya? I'm trying to get a little more shuteye. You best do the same. We gotta move out soon enough unless you want her kin liftin' your hair."

Pany ignored him and took a few steps toward Galegi. "Niak. Niak! D'you hear what this squaw whore said to me? What'd she say?"

Niak propped himself up slightly from the Creek woman. His face was sweaty and glistened in the firelight as he smiled.

"She said the mirror is hers and she wants it back. And you are a worthless, scrawny dog, and a bitch dog at that. She wants to know how many pups suckle at your tits."

Connie laughed beneath his blanket by the fire.

"She said all that?"

"Damned if she didn't," Niak said as he returned his attention to the Creek woman.

Pany took a step back and picked up the mirror before he headed for Galegi. He felt the pain from the bite in his leg as he walked. It reminded him that he owed the Cherokee woman something. He looked back to check on Connie and Niak. Their attention was elsewhere.

Pany held the cracked mirror out to her and said in his broken Cherokee. "This yours? You want it?" he said as though teasing a child with a gift or a dog with a piece of meat. "Here. Take it," he said as he held it close only to snatch it away time and time again.

Galegi tried to reach for it with her tied hands, but the stick at her elbows across her back and the rope from her throat to the tree stopped her. She quickly realized the game however, and backed up so slightly and slowly that Pany, in his fervor to torment, never noticed.

For his part Pany began to dance around with the mirror, admiring himself in it selfishly. "Woowee! Ain't I pretty! Think I'm pretty, Miss Indian bitch? Think so?"

"Shut up, Pany," Connie grumbled.

Then Pany shoved the mirror down the front of his pants and rubbed it against his crotch. "There, missy, how you like your fancy mirror now?" he said as he humped the mirror. In a flash he pulled it out and put it down the back of his pants. "How 'bout now? Still want it back?"

Now both Connie and Niak were looking at the carrying on of their partner.

"Pany, shut up and get some coffee going," Connie chided. "Dad blamed fool. She don't understand a thing you're sayin' anyway."

"By God, she might not but she's learnin' her place, now ain't she? She knows now that we take what we want and that's that!"

When he took another step closer to punctuate his declaration, he ripped the mirror from his pants and held it in Galegi's face. For an instance she saw her swollen reflection. She didn't move until Pany dropped the mirror away from her face and still squatting, turned slightly to the others.

"See there? She seen she ain't so pretty anymore and it shut her up. Knows now I'll slap a beatin' onto her if she sasses me!"

Galegi pivoted a quarter of a turn until the stick across her back lined up with Pany's chest. Before the slave trader recognized he'd been lured too close to the flame, Galegi lunged. The stick jabbed Pany hard with its blunted point and sent him sprawling. Behind him, both Niak and Connie roared in laughter at the thud of the wood and Pany's involuntary groan. Even the other women, who had not smiled in days, felt themselves doing so again.

But Pany soon recovered. "Goddamn, bitch!"

"Hold on, Pany," Connie said as he began to get up, though still laughing.

Pany was too close to be stopped by his partners. However, the same could not be said of Galegi herself. She had brought the stick back around behind her and stood as erect as possible with her head bowed by the rope running from her neck to the tree. Even tied she was facing Pany straight on. She knew what he'd do. When he rushed at her she threw herself up and sideways and cracked the end of the stick flat against his face. This time Pany went to the ground hard. Connie fell back to his bedroll in hysterics and Niak rolled off the Creek woman holding his stomach as he doubled up, naked from the waist down. The young Shawnee girl broke into outright laughter until the other woman urged her to be quiet.

Pany stumbled and fell again as he tried to stand. His brain was rattled and unsure which way was up. He struggled to stand and fell again, like a drunk, as his companions screamed in laughter behind him. The last time he stayed down. He waited there on his hands and knees for his mind to gain a sense of itself.

Galegi waited as well. She realized that the man would eventually get up and come at her. She receded against the tree that held the line to her throat, breathed heavily, and braced for what was to come.

Connie and Niak were having trouble breathing themselves. Their laughter had been so intense their eyes were full of tears and their stomachs ached. Even if they understood what was about to happen it was doubtful they could have prevented it.

Pany struggled to his feet and staggered across the campsite. It was another moment before his head and eyes were clear enough to let him move with any measure of precision. He took a step toward Galegi and her tree but his failing head diverted him off course. He stuck his leg out quick to brace himself and felt the pain from the bite in his calf. He didn't need any more incentive to attack but received it just the same.

Two more lumbering steps and Pany was at Galegi again. This time he was wary of the stick. She swung it around as before but he caught it and spun her with her own momentum until he was behind her. Pany was still off balance from the crack to his face and both he and Galegi went to the ground. Niak and Connie laughed again but not as hard. The Shawnee girl did not laugh at all now and the woman nearby held her tight.

The rope around Galegi's throat was choking her as it stretched to the tree. Though she tried to kick and claw, the stick and her bindings made it easy for Pany to toss her around until he was seated on her chest. Galegi tried to scratch at his crotch but the effort was too little to ward off the crashing of Pany's fists into her face. Consumed by the excitement of the fight the first blows only served to stun her. By the time the second and third rounds of punches began to land, Connie was scrambling for Pany himself.

Niak yelled as he tugged at his pants and tried to stand. "Pany! Go easy!"

But Pany continued slugging with all his strength — over and over — brutal, wild, and vicious. His knuckles were already bloody as Galegi's face began to give way. Badly bruised from Connie's punches the day before, she was ill prepared for another beating. Even if she'd been fresh and strong it was unlikely the fragile bones of her delicate face could have weathered the onslaught. She felt the punches land and the cracking of her cheeks. Her teeth snapped at their roots. Some fell down her throat while others flew from her torn lips as her head was wracked from side to side with the pummeling. The light bones around her deep dark eyes collapsed and she could no longer see the fists, the man, or the shimmering first light of early morning coming through the trees above him. All that remained was a faint whitish glow.

There came the sense of a rushing movement across her head — a blurring sound and motion she could not really see but that the last of her senses told her was there. A popping noise inside her head only she could hear was echoed by the cracking of bones that everyone in the camp understood.

Connie dove and his bulk ripped Pany off the battered woman. His weight rolled them both away from Galegi as Niak scrambled across the camp to her. While Connie pinned Pany to the ground, Niak fell to his knees beside Galegi's bloody face and started to touch it as though it was hot.

"Oh my God," he said. "Her face is near gone."

The half-breed Creek was about as right as he could be. The beating was so severe and her ability to resist so limited, she was unrecognizable as a woman. One eye had been punctured by the splintering bones nearby. The fluid from it ran slowly out and down the shattered face, leaving a trail through the blood. Her jaw and nose were so misshapen that it was difficult for her to breathe. Though completely knocked out, a convulsive reaction to the gore in her throat made her involuntarily cough and she spit blood and chips of teeth on Niak's face.

Connie sat up on Pany only enough to deliver a harsh backhand across his face. The slap shook Pany from his rage enough to stop him and Connie instantly got up and went to Galegi. She was beaten as bad as any man he had seen killed. He looked at her for only a few seconds then turned and shook his finger at his partner.

"She's dead, you goddamn sonofabitch!"

"She ain't dead. She just coughed some," Niak said.

"Oh, she's dead all right," Connie continued as he menacingly took a step toward Pany. He looked back at Galegi and moved his quaking finger from the man on the ground to the bloodied woman. "That's your share, Pany! That lump a shit right there is your share! I ain't losin' no money over your stupid bullshit! You get what you get off a third of that little girl yonder. Niak and I are splittin' what comes from the Shawnee and the Creek. But not you. You hear me? That bitch there is dead."

"She ain't dead," Pany said now as he slowly got up and went back to view his handiwork.

"Hell she ain't! Might as well have thrown three hundred dollars gold right in the goddamn river!"

Pany nudged her with his toe. Galegi didn't move.

"She's gone," Niak said as he got up and wiped the blood from his face and began fastening up his pants. "Damn, Pany."

"To hell with her. And to hell with you," Pany said as he walked away from Galegi and began wiping his own blood and hers from his knuckles.

"And to hell with you!" Connie screamed. "I goddamn well mean it, Pany! You don't have no stake in them other women. You kilt your share!"

Pany spun around. "She ain't dead yet, Connie!"

"Might as well be! Look at her! Ain't got no face! Even if she does come to—"

"Which she won't," Niak said.

"Which she won't. She can't travel. How do you expect to get her to the auction block? Carry her three hundred miles? And what do you reckon she'll fetch with her face mashed in like that? Goddamn," Connie said as he moved by her and continued his diatribe. "I can see she lost at least one eye. You suppose she'd fetch a fair price with a hole in her face where an eye used to be?"

Pany walked over to the Shawnee woman who still sat pressed against the young girl. He ripped his knife from his waist and the girl screamed. The woman tried to cover the girl as Connie ran for his rifle. But Pany merely grabbed the woman, flipped her, and cut her wrists free. He swiped at the line that fastened her to the tree, caught it, cut it, and tossed it down.

"Go clean up the woman," he said in broken Shawnee.

The woman hesitated and looked beyond Pany to Connie, holding his rifle.

Now Pany snatched up the rope and jerked it and the woman's throat with it. "You hear? Go tend to her!"

"Don't make her do your dirty work," Niak said. "Why don't you nurse her if you're so worried about her?"

"Shut your mouth, breed," Pany threatened as he pointed at Niak with his knife.

Niak pulled his own. "Whenever you're ready. I'm no woman tied up on her back."

Pany took a step, but Connie stepped in between them with the rifle. "First one of you fools makes a move with them skinners and I'll blow you to hell."

Everyone froze where they were. "Now, Pany. Put that knife away. You too, Niak. We still got a lot of miles to cover. There'll be other villages between here and the block. I reckon we can get us another one or two. But, Pany, she's still comin' out of your cut. Understand?"

"I don't give a good goddamn—"

"That's fine too. Now get packed up. We gotta get on out of here."

"How about the Cherokee?" Niak said as he motioned to Galegi.

Connie walked over and looked down at her. The only movement was the early morning flies that had begun to collect and gorge themselves on the blood. He brought the rifle barrel up and pointed it at her stomach. He pulled the trigger.

The report sent a shock wave through the camp. Though everyone except Pany had been watching, they all jumped at the unexpected blast from the gun. Galegi's body lurched on the ground and settled back slowly. She never uttered a sound. The gun had been fired at such close range the muzzle flash caught her clothes on fire and they smoldered for a moment before they were extinguished by blood.

Forty miles away another gunshot went off and Chancellor dropped a deer with his mother's rifle.

Connie turned away. "Let that be a lesson to you," he said in Shawnee to the other women. Then he looked at Pany and Niak as he spoke in English. "And you too. Let's go."

The woman Pany had cut free walked over to Galegi and knelt beside her. She touched the shattered face with one hand and the smoldering bullet wound with the other. There was a slight rise and fall of Galegi's chest. The woman slowly took up two handfuls of grass and dirt and pressed them into the hole left by the bullet in

Galegi's stomach. The dirt turned to mud with the blood, but the bleeding eased. The Shawnee then pushed the hair back off Galegi's brow and began to sing a soft song for the dead to help the woman she did not know find her way to the West.

Niak was collecting his things and tying them to his horse. He listened to the woman's mournful song as he retrieved the Creek and placed her up on another horse. Connie came up with the young girl and easily set her on the same horse behind the Creek woman.

Pany packed as well but had heard enough singing. He went to the Shawnee, grabbed the length of cord that still hung from her neck and jerked it. "Shut up, you! Get a goin'!" he shouted as he motioned toward the horse the Creek and young girl sat on. "Niak, fasten this bitch to them others," Pany ordered as he pulled his knife again. "I can get something for this scalp anyway."

Pany reached down and lifted Galegi's limp head by her hair. Before he could set his blade against her forehead, the Shawnee woman jumped on his back and the two of them tumbled over Galegi to the ground.

"Goddamn it," Connie muttered. "That is enough!"

He marched to Pany who was locked wrist to hand with the Shawnee. The knife was closing in on the Shawnee's throat though she held him with surprising strength. Connie stemmed the tide in the woman's favor by dropping his rifle and grabbing Pany by the collar and the back of his pants. He snatched his partner off the woman and tossed him ten feet or more.

"You ain't learned nothin', have you?" Connie spit. "Now get on your horse."

Pany pointed at Galegi then shook his knife at the Shawnee woman. "You're next, bitch! You're next!"

"Touch that one, Pany and I'll kill you. I swear to God I will kill you dead. I ain't losin' no more money because of your foolishness. Now, mount up! Sun is up near solid. I want to put a few miles between us and that squaw's cabin."

Connie marched up to the Shawnee and took the rope off her neck. He retied her wrists in front of her and took her to his own horse. A longer rope was lashed to the short one around her hands and Connie carried one end up to his saddle. He heaved himself onto the horse and began riding out of the camp and away from Galegi.

Pany and Niak got on their own horses. Niak held the lead line of the horse that carried the two captives. As he fell in behind the walking Shawnee woman and Connie, he chided Pany. "You had a tougher time with that one, didn't you? Little different when they're not tied up."

"Shut your face, breed."

Niak just laughed and the line of horses, women, and white men slowly vanished into the woods leaving Galegi oblivious to the world, lying on the forest floor, bound and bleeding.

Chancellor's deer had been given a drink and a prayer of thanks to accompany it to the Darkening Land. Afterwards it was cut and prepared for the trip home. Chancellor would have liked to postpone the return trip and lingered in the woods — perhaps take a second buck — but his father was ready to once again be in the comfort of his wife and their cabin. He slung the deer over the back of Chancellor's horse behind his son, tied it fast then nearly leaped onto the back of his own mount.

"Your aim was true today, my son. You have made your mother proud. When we return she will make a feast for you from the meat you bring to our cabin."

"She will be proud?"

"You have become a fine hunter. Remember the things you have learned these days. Yes, she will be proud."

"I will remember."

The pair rode off, back toward the east and their cabin, only a day's ride. They would stop and sleep back in their own mountains but would be home shortly after the first light. Totsuhwa was happy. "Three days," had been the last words Galegi had said to him. "Three days." And three days it would be.

Thoughts of Totsuhwa's wife dominated his mind while the carcass bouncing behind Chancellor reminded him of his wondrous accomplishment. By his reckoning the deer could have easily been a Chickasaw warrior, decorated and ablaze with feathers and fresh scalps, charging him with a polished tomahawk when Chancellor calmly brought him down with a single shot. His trophy would be a scalp instead of a deer hide and he thought of how it would be to scalp a man. Perhaps his first scalp would be from a white man, but either way Chancellor wanted it to be a big and fierce man fighting for his life. The image so consumed him that he was surprised when his father stopped to make a quick camp for the night.

"We will be off the ground before the sun is on us. If you value your deer lash a rope through the bones near its feet then hoist it into the trees. This will protect it from the smaller animals, but the wolves and bears may come when they smell the meat. Sleep with one eye on your deer. Once you have taken it, it is your responsibility to protect it and see that it gets back to your mother. You also owe ahwi safe passage. Understand?"

"Yes. I will put it in the tree."

Chancellor did as his father had directed and cut a hole through both hind legs of the deer. He ran a rope through the holes and tied it fast then tossed the other end over a high branch. He tugged on the rope, but the deer's body resisted and only its hindquarters lifted off the ground. Without a word, Totsuhwa came alongside his son and helped pull the fresh meat well into the tree.

No thank you was offered or expected for the strong hand on the rope. For Totsuhwa it was enough to be pleased with his son for his effort that day and for Chancellor he was more in love with his father than ever before.

When they settled beside a small fire to sleep, Chancellor softly whispered to his father the words of a son, not a warrior or hunter. "Thank you, Father. Thank you for today."

"You are welcome. Now go to sleep as a boy and wake as a man."

Neither could know how fitting those words would be.

When the morning sun began to peek over the mountains, it came upon riders separated by miles and sentiments nothing could measure. Totsuhwa and Chancellor had lowered the deer from the tree at the first hint of daylight.

Several valleys away, Connie had also kicked the sleeping legs of Pany and Niak to life and had his packed train moving through the woods still following the stream up the valleys.

"Ain't we backtrackin'?" Pany yelled up the line of horses to Connie who was leading the way.

"We are at that," Connie yelled back. "Just enough to toss those Cherokee off our trail. We'll ease into the creek now and move along for a mile or so then cut back across the mountains."

Following his own directions, Connie coaxed his horse down the bank into the knee-deep water. The animal didn't resist and the one behind followed in short order. In no time the entire line had resumed its form in the stream. The water brushed away their tracks as soon as they were made or so they hoped. Connie had used the same trick when he had left the country of the Shawnee to the north after snatching the woman and girl. But the trick hadn't worked then and it wasn't working now.

Two miles passed slowly with the horses sloshing along, slipping on the rocks occasionally and kicking up flumes of water with their front hooves on each step. When Connie had convinced himself that he had outsmarted another tracker, he urged his horse out of the water and went straight into the trees for several hundred yards then turned toward the east.

His ragtag followers stayed in line throughout. When the turn had been made and the sun shone on Connie's face as it continued to rise in the eastern sky, he turned and hollered back at Pany.

"We've got miles of trail now. A few weeks of ridin' through these mountains are all that's between us and the auction blocks. We're way east of the Cherokee and I doubt anyone even knows that squaw is missin' yet."

"Yeah, but we headed right back north toward them goddamn Shawnee in the process." The shouting debate continued as the horses walked along.

The Shawnee woman heard a bird's cry — a bird that would not normally cry at this time of the new day. She caught the eye of the young girl behind her, tied up on the horse, and smiled.

"Forget them," Connie laughed. "We snatched that pair weeks ago. They gave up on them by now — probably blamed the Iroquois. Hell, I ain't known a Shawnee yet who could find his own ass if he used both hands!"

Pany was still laughing as the Shawnee arrow slammed into Connie's chest and ripped his heart wide open with a jagged piece of flint stone. From behind, neither Niak nor Pany could see the arrow or the second and third that followed in frightening succession. Connie didn't have time to issue a warning apart from leaning over in his saddle and turning slightly as though to look for help from behind that was not going to come. Only then did Pany and Niak see that something had gone wrong with their leader's plan of escape.

Connie's face was contorted, strained by shock as much as crushing pain. As he leaned forward he snapped off the shafts of two of the arrows in his chest as a fourth screamed from the trees behind him and buried itself in his hunching back as his horse ambled on. He never felt it hit but immediately lost control of his limbs and fell from the horse.

The Shawnee woman launched herself to the horse that carried the other captives. She reached up and took hold of the rope that ran to the girl who was still looking around innocently as she tried to figure out what was happening. With a vicious jerk, the Shawnee woman pulled the girl forward toward her, off the horse, and to the ground. In a flash the woman scrambled over her, effectively shielding her from the exchanges she knew were coming.

The Creek woman was slower to respond but followed the Shawnee and dove from the horse into the underbrush. Now there was no one between Niak and Pany and the Shawnee warriors who had been pursuing them for weeks.

Half a dozen arrows silently exploded from the trees. Each one hit Pany but none instantly fatal. In defense, both he and Niak pulled up their rifles and fired blindly into the trees, hitting nothing. With the rifles empty, the Shawnee warriors broke from the woods in a screaming horde that made the horses bolt. A swarm of Indians ran up each horse like ants on an enemy and dragged the horses over and the men with them. The horses immediately scampered back to their feet without their riders.

Tomahawks and knives flashed in deeply tanned hands above the masses of attacking Shawnee. Niak shouted in Creek and the attack against him stopped for the moment. Pany was not

so fortunate and had Niak known the torturous fate intended
for him in the Shawnee town several days' ride ahead, he would
have opted to die with Pany right on the spot. Behind him, Pany
screamed his last and then Niak was beaten into unconscious
submission. When he woke he would find himself naked, bound
even tighter than Galegi had been fastened, but in the same
manner with a stick linking his arms behind his back.

Connie and Pany bodies were also stripped naked. Their
genitals were hacked for their atrocities against the women and
to show others in the afterlife what they had done. All their
clothes and possessions were tied on their horses or summarily
taken as private trophies by members of the vengeful Shawnee
party. The Shawnee woman also enjoyed the spoils and discovered Galegi's mirror and comb and took them for herself.
Totsuhwa's red shirt was claimed by a warrior who immediately
put it on and marveled at the fine thread. Others in the band
lifted the scalps from Connie and Pany while others cut their
arrowheads from the bodies. When the butchering was completed the bodies had been cut in a hundred places. The only
portions that were intact were the strikingly white bare feet of
the men who had fancied themselves prosperous slave traders.

The clean white feet collected little attention from the fall bugs.
The cooler weather kept their numbers down, but soon the remaining insects gathered on the wounds. And as the flies feasted the
Shawnee mounted their horses and rode quietly toward the creek
to wash the blood from their hands and weapons and drink before
heading to the north and home.

Miles away Totsuhwa and Chancellor were riding triumphantly to their cabin. They would have been home a sooner
but Totsuhwa had purposely diverted their track out of the
mountains into the far end of the village. They did not stop but
ambled along slowly, permitting Chancellor to show off his prize.
While the men raised their hands or merely nodded in approval,
the younger boys raced along Chancellor's horse and patted the
deer's legs and sides. They chattered like giddy children, but
Chancellor rode in near silence, content to absorb the praise

behind the face of a staunch hunter. Totsuhwa nodded back to the men, the proud father, but surreptitiously looked through the faces of the women for Galegi. If she had been in the village, someone would have brought her out to see the trophy of her son.

Once near their cabin the dogs sprinted out barking to meet them but ran sideways over the scents of Pany and Connie's horses. The dogs had fumbled around the smell of the men at the cabin for most of the night after they returned from their unproductive pursuit of the deer, but were tired from the chase and soon abandoned the new scents and curled their tails over their noses to sleep. Now they rushed out to meet their masters and sniffed at the legs of the deer that hung from either side of Chancellor's horse.

When the barking dogs did not bring Galegi to the door of the cabin, Totsuhwa's eyes darted back and forth from one corner to the other, expecting to see his wife appear from either side as she came from her garden chores. When she did not, a feeling he had never felt before ran up his chest like the flush of a fever and he pulled up his horse. Chancellor saw his father's horse reined in and stopped his own, immediately setting aside the glory of his deer at the sight of his father's face.

"Father, what is it?"

"The dogs barked when we came in, did they not?" Totsuhwa said slowly as his hands adjusted the rifle in his lap.

Instinctively, Chancellor felt for his own rifle and looked down at the firing mechanism. "Yes, Father. Why?"

"Then where is your mother?"

Chancellor glanced around rather casually. They were still seventy-five paces or better from the cabin. Totsuhwa looked at his home as if he'd never seen it before, studying it for signs and answers while Chancellor looked at everything and nothing all at the same time.

"Maybe she is at the stream or the village."

"No. The dogs would be with her."

Chancellor started to smile. "Maybe she is playing a game. Maybe she—"

"Shhh!" Totsuhwa said sharply. He looked around the cabin and at the woods then down at the dogs still sniffing the deer. He pointed to one corner of the cabin and motioned for

Chancellor to ride in that direction. "I will meet you at your mother's garden. Be wary."

"What is it?"

"I do not believe your mother is here," the great shaman said almost in a choke as he rode off slowly toward the opposite corner of the cabin.

Chancellor was left sitting on his horse. He hesitated, caught off guard by the words but more so by the tone in them. He had never heard his father's voice tremble. Something was terribly wrong and though he didn't know what it was, he rode toward the back of the cabin as his father had directed.

Totsuhwa swung out wider than his son and Chancellor reached the back corner of his side in advance of his father. But as soon as he cleared the corner and saw the empty garden, Totsuhwa and his horse raced around the corner. The horse was stopped in a spin as Totsuhwa turned him immediately back toward the front of the cabin, holding his rifle out away from his body.

"There are tracks from a white man on this side! What do you see?"

Chancellor had been so bent on seeing into the garden he never looked at the ground. Now he looked down and around but saw no tracks on his side of the cabin. "None here!" he choked as his heart leaped into his throat.

Totsuhwa took off to the front of the cabin and Chancellor followed his father though it would have been closer to turn around and go back the way he'd come. When he came around the front he rode up on his father's horse. Totsuhwa had jumped from its back, rifle in hand and raced into the cabin. He was only in there long enough to see that it had been ransacked and Galegi gone.

When he came from the house his eyes were scanning the ground for tracks. "Two white men," he said as he snatched the reins to his horse and vaulted onto its back. He spun the horse again until it came broadside Chancellor's. Totsuhwa jerked his knife from his waist and slashed at the ties that held his son's deer. When the rope gave way to the razor-sharp knife, Totsuhwa effortlessly flipped the deer off his son's horse to the ground. "We have to move quickly. Stay close and have your rifle ready. Can you pull the trigger on a man now? Like a true warrior?"

"I can."

The words had just started from Chancellor's mouth when Totsuhwa began to trot away from the cabin, watching the ground with every stride. The dogs began to follow, but their master turned them back with a scream that sent them cowering toward the cabin.

Totsuhwa followed the rough tracks of the kidnappers' horses with relative ease. In minutes he was at the trampled grass near the stream where Galegi had bitten Pany's leg. He saw where the two horses had split up and sent Chancellor after one while he tracked the other. Both eventually led into the stream. Chancellor was immediately grateful when the tracks converged again as he was unsure of what to do if he came across a white man, especially one that was holding his mother.

His father was several yards ahead urging his horse from the creek. When Chancellor arrived he too saw the matted grass where Connie had knocked his mother out and bound her with the stick.

"They are a day or two ahead. That is all. The grass is trying to stand again. Do you see it?"

Chancellor examined the grasses and knew from his hunting that his father was right. They immediately moved off on the trail. Though there was urgency in his voice, Totsuhwa spoke calmly about the trail and what he was seeing. Forest litter disturbed with the steps of the horses made a neat trail to his practiced eye. Chancellor could see it plainly too. In the silence of watching the ground behind his father's horse, Chancellor heard a confusing question for his father ringing through his head and out his mouth.

"Father? Why would mother go with white men?"

Totsuhwa gave little thought to his answer as he watched the signs of the trail. "Your mother was made to go."

Chancellor was quiet for a moment and thought about what he just heard and what he knew happened to lost children in the woods and brave warriors taken prisoner by the Chickasaw and the Creek. "Is mother all right?"

"Watch for the signs, son," Totsuhwa said with little thought. "And ask Adanvdo, the Everywhere Spirit, to keep her safe until we can get to her."

Suddenly the reality of what was happening struck the boy. He was no longer stalking frogs along the creek bank. And even the deer that now lay in the dirt of the white men's boot prints seemed a distant memory that mattered for nothing. He was chasing live men, hard men, who had taken his mother prisoner and the tiny arrows meant for frogs — the thin sticks that often flew in crooked paths — had become the rifle jostling in his hand. Chancellor was afraid, but the fear gave way to a heartbreaking concern for his mother and it kicked all his years of training onto a higher plain he had never felt before.

He would follow his father's lead at every step, careful not to make a wrong move and endanger his mother. H was ready to fight and kill and die like a warrior and more so, like a son fighting for the life of his mother. Chancellor grit his teeth hard, squinted into the trail of the white men and squeezed the stock of the rifle. Someone would die today under his hand and rightfully so. His heart pounded in his thin chest but his mind and body were under complete control.

After a few hours of hard riding the overnight camp of the trappers-turned-slave traders was ahead. Totsuhwa could smell the smoke from an old fire hanging in the wind and knew he was close. He didn't slow as the trail and smoke told him that he would find their camp empty.

The ground of the camp was still trampled flat and the fire pit had ceased to smolder but still formed a black hole at its center. The eyes of a hunter scanned the camp from side to side with each step of his horse until he saw Galegi lying on her side, her back to him, with the stick still tied between her arms. Her long black hair was tangled in the debris of the forest floor, but he knew instantly that the still form was his wife.

Totsuhwa whistled, kicked his horse, and the animal bolted. He never attempted to rein it in as he raced up to his wife. Instead he flung himself from the horse's back and stumbled headfirst into the ground near Galegi. As he scrambled on his hands and knees to his wife, Chancellor rode up slower, so consumed by disbelief that he stayed on his horse as the animal stopped.

Totsuhwa recognized the stick and arm binding mechanism immediately and pulled his knife as he got to his wife. He reached over her to slash the bindings on her hands before he really looked at her face. But when the bindings gave way and he ripped the stick from her arms without thinking, the pain of the sudden release on Galegi's cramped arms woke her from unconsciousness with a stifled cry.

Chancellor jumped at the sound.

His father touched the bloodied swollen face and whispered, "I am here, Galegi. I am here."

Her face was a mass of dried blackened blood. Totsuhwa brushed at it and began the pick away large pieces from her mouth that had nearly frozen her lips together.

"Little... One...," she mumbled.

He could scarcely understand. "Shhh. Rest. I am here."

Chancellor dismounted and went up opposite his father to stare at the woman who, though dressed like his mother and with her hair, was unrecognizable to him.

"Be still and rest," Totsuhwa continued as his hands came away from her face and dove into the medicine bag that rested on his hip. "I have what you need."

Galegi fumbled haltingly with her hands until she found his. "No... Save the medicine...for children." Her voice, coming around splintered teeth and through a broken jaw, was all breath and not her own.

"You are a foolish girl," Totsuhwa said with a slight but very anxious laugh. "I have plenty."

Galegi used the last of her strength to squeeze his hands though hers were numb. "There is no time. I knew...I knew you would come. I have waited."

"I am here." And Totsuhwa waited for the instructions.

"Where is our son?"

"He is here."

A weak hand struggled to reach up and Totsuhwa guided it to Chancellor.

The boy was almost hesitant to take it as the woman below it was so grotesque. The muffled voice worked its way through the shattered face and called his name. Even in the hideousness of the sound was a mother calling to her only son.

"Chancellor?"

"Yes, Mother? I am here," he said as he took the cold hand and crouched beside his mother's broken body.

"The white school? Has your father...has he told you of my dream for you?"

"Yes, Mother." Tears welled in the boy's eyes.

"You will go?"

"I will go." The tears burst forth and trickled down his cheeks.

"Remember where you were born and your people...Teach the ways...of your father...to your children and tell them..."

Galegi's voice trailed off until it was indistinguishable from her shallow breathing.

Her husband finished her thoughts and her words. "He will teach our grandchildren and they will teach theirs."

Totsuhwa wanted to say that she would see it all, but he could not bring himself to say the things both he and Galegi knew were not true. He touched the mass of dried blood and mud on her dress, understood instantly that someone else had tried to stem the bleeding as Galegi's hands had been tied, and wondered what had happened.

Galegi knew her husband's mind and took as deep a breath as she could and offered what her strength allowed. "Two white men and a Creek. Slave traders. Connie, Pany, Niak. They have other women..."

"Shhh," he said as though it was not what he wanted to hear.

She weakly patted his hand as she knew him too well until the hand immediately fell away. Her strength was gone. The will to live, which had held her just to the east of the Darkening Land of the Dead until she heard her husband's voice and felt his touch, slipped from her tired grasp. Her shallow breathing stopped.

"Galegi, my child. Fight to stay in the light. Time will heal you. There is much I can do, but you must fight to stay. Do not give up, little girl."

She did not answer and there was no hint of movement in her hands.

Chancellor still cradled his mother's motionless fingers, but reverently passed them to his father. Totsuhwa took his wife's hand from his son and looked over to his boy. The great warrior's own eyes were wide and filling with tears while his strong hands began to tremble.

"Your mother is asleep now. We will let her rest."

Chancellor watched as his father placed the hand across Galegi's breast and then crossed it delicately with the other deathly still hand. Totsuhwa patted the hands enough to hold them in place. "Sleep, pretty girl. When you wake—" but his words choked to a stop.

Chancellor touched his father's hand over his mother's and felt the shaking in them. He squeezed them slightly and patted his father's hands as the husband had patted the wife's. The two stayed that way for some time, neither speaking, just touching each other's hands and the cooling skin of Galegi. Each wiped their faces on their shoulders, unwilling to take their hands from the woman they had loved and who had loved them.

For Chancellor, his mother was dead, and he knew it. The body before him — disfigured, broken, and dead — was not his mother. He imagined scenes of the woman he knew in his mind and cried, knowing that she would no longer be in their cabin or touch him like only a mother could. The tears were a steady stream now and he let them run. He no longer knew what to think, say, or do.

Totsuhwa's tears were controllable. A few fell at first but were pushed from his eyes by an acknowledgement of his own shortcomings. He had failed this woman who loved him. He had left her alone often, far too often, and now, his abandonment of her had cost her life. Her death was on his hands, on his head, and his shoulders were not broad enough to carry the weight.

"So many times I have failed," he reminded himself softly. "The payments for medicines that could have eased your burden. The journeys I have confessed. Now I have let you be taken."

Deep in his mind Galegi whispered to him, but her words could not fill the widening cracks of self-torment and guilt.

Instead, her voice was swallowed up whole by the cavernous moans of a man dying within. The soft voice that forgave all and remembered nothing but love was enveloped by a screaming discourse of disdain for himself and what he had done, how he had failed. The gaps in his mind exceeded those in his heart, and the world passed from color to shades of gray interrupted only by quick flashes of pitch black across his darkening mind.

Chancellor, still holding his father and his mother's hands, felt the grip of Totsuhwa move from quivering to tightening. The move was gradual, like freezing water, but soon Chancellor's fingers felt the pinching and his eyes widened. He tried to gently ease from the clasp of the mass of hands, but he was caught. His attempt to pull away grew stronger until he reached for his father's white knuckles with his free hand.

"Father!" he shouted and Totsuhwa's head snapped toward his son.

The grip eased only enough for Chancellor to free himself. He stared through the blurriness brought on by his remaining tears and saw a blackness in his father he had never witnessed before. So many times when his father had been on the verge of travel, Chancellor had seen a faraway look in his father's eyes. Of late, he thought a change had come over him, but just now he realized that a bleak coldness had come with a vengeance and he wondered how a man whose love lay dead beside him could flash eyes so black and empty while his own young eyes were still bathed in tears.

Totsuhwa stood and looked down at his wife. He looked at his boy who still knelt beside Galegi then bent quickly and picked up his wife's limp body. Her hands stayed fixed across her breast, and her legs dangled loosely off her husband's thick arms. Totsuhwa hefted her as gently as he could, and some life returned to his eyes as he spoke.

"Bring your horse. You will take her home."

Chancellor stood and stepped off toward the wandering horses on legs grown numb. He had only taken a few steps when he stopped and caught his father kissing Galegi's battered face and burying his cheek in her long black hair. Chancellor came back. While his father held her, the boy brushed the streaks of black hair, some loose, some matted and bloody, from the battered face he could not recognize. When the last strand was in place as best he could make it he looked up at his father.

"You will go and find the white traders?"

"I will go." As he spoke Totsuhwa's eyes stayed locked on his wife's disjointed face.

Chancellor looked again at his mother and brought in a deep breath that would push the words from his throat.

"Father. I will go with you."

"There is no time. You will take her home and tell the news to those in the village."

"No. I will go with you."

Only now did Totsuhwa's eyes come away from his wife. "You must tend to the needs of your mother."

"I must tend to the needs of her killers!"

Chancellor's voice was stronger than it had ever been. His father heard the fresh power and was stymied by the weight on his heart of the body in his arms. Still, he tried. "There is no time. I cannot wait for you."

"Mother will wait. She will wait here for our return."

Now a rush of impatient anger came in Totsuhwa's voice. "Would you have the wolves drag her to their dens for their pups?"

"No," came the quick reply and Chancellor immediately pointed up in the tree his mother had once been tied to. "Mother will wait for us. We will bring back three scalps and carry them home with her and she will sing our praises in the West."

Totsuhwa held his arms out straight and Galegi's body with them. "This is not ahwi! This is not an animal!"

"I know this!" Chancellor screamed as he started again to cry. "But I must go with you. Go ahead if you think you must, but I will take her home then race to catch you and if I lose the trail I will ride on forever, looking for it always and finding it never. I will not come back to this place because I would be ashamed."

Totsuhwa's arms relaxed, and Galegi's body came back nearer to him as Chancellor continued, much quieter. "They are three. You may have use of me."

Totsuhwa turned toward the tree and looked at the height of its nearest branches.

"The trail grows colder, Father," Chancellor said.

Totsuhwa stared only a moment longer. "Then give your mother your hands."

With tremendous care, Galegi was passed up the tree until she was set upright on a stout limb a considerable distance from the forest floor. Chancellor tossed up his bedroll and his father draped it over Galegi's head and body.

Totsuhwa then delicately tied a rope around her waist to the trunk of the tree before climbing down. He could not bring himself to look back up into the tree but instantly went for his horse.

Chancellor followed and crawled up on his own animal but found himself staring back at the hooded figure resting in the tree. The sight was eerie and awkward and brought to mind the playful woman who had been replaced by the dead figure on the limb.

Totsuhwa had caught his horse and was on its back. As he rode by his son at a trot, searching the ground for signs, he spoke softly yet forcibly. "There is no time for tears now." And he pushed off into the woods ahead.

Soon the trail turned back into the stream. Totsuhwa spun his horse around then pushed on into the water. "Wait," was all he said, and Chancellor held his mount on the bank. His father examined the stones of the creek bottom until the depth and murkiness of the water prevented it. Then he urged his horse on over to the opposite bank and up and out of the stream. He rode back and forth on the edge of the creek several lengths of the horse in each direction. Then he rode back to the spot where he had crossed over and called to his son.

"Ride up that side and look for where they came out!"

The boy's heart raced. He knew the trail was less than a day old. He might come upon the traders any moment or they upon him. The grip on his mother's rifle tightened as he moved it out into a ready position. He found himself searching the trees around him for the enemy as much as he surveyed the stream bank for signs.

Two miles ahead the Shawnee war party was resting at the creek side and washing the blood from their weapons. Connie's scalp was hanging from the belt of a warrior called Root who was crouched beside the water washing his face and drinking. The Shawnee woman who had been rescued came up and stood beside him.

"The Creek woman asks what is to become of her. What are your words?" Root did not interrupt his washing. "She will come with us and be of our people. Will she do this as a sister or a slave?"

"I have told her this already and she will come as a sister. The one they call Niak. He is a Creek as well. Will he come as a brother?"

"No," Root said. "He will be given to you and your women to be punished when we are home again."

"This is as I had hoped."

Root dipped his hands in the stream again as the woman paused in her leaving and turned back to him.

"There was a Cherokee woman with us last night."

Only now did Root's attention come away from the water. As he stared, the woman continued.

"They killed her this morning. She had a warrior's spirit. She would have been powerful in her village. I believe her people will be coming for her."

Root looked away from the woman and around the stream banks on both sides as he stood to his full height quietly and cautiously as though he was already being watched. "We are in the land of the Cherokee," he said.

"She was a strong woman and very fierce. I think her man will be the same."

Instead of heeding the warning, Root took the words as an affront. "The strongest Cherokee is weaker than the weakest Shawnee!"

The woman turned away. "Do what you will, but I have been a slave already. I do not want to be one again. They may have a war party twice our number out for her even now. I would like to move on."

As the woman continued away Root called to his warriors. They talked for some time then several began retracing their steps through the trees toward the spot where they had ambushed the white traders. In a short time they had taken up hiding spots all around the naked bodies of Connie and Pany.

Chancellor had found the signs — trampled grasses trying to stand again and dried mud from horses' hooves. "Edoda! Father! Here!"

Totsuhwa heard his son and plunged the horse into the stream. Not far away, the waiting Shawnee heard Chancellor's voice as well. They silently moved through the trees until the dead men lay between them and the boy's voice. A few took up positions to the sides and prepared to catch the Cherokee in a crossfire while another sprinted silently back to the stream bank to get Root.

By the time Totsuhwa and Chancellor raced onto the scene of the killings, a dozen Shawnee warriors had planted themselves in a wide, but neat half circle around the bodies. They had left a gap on the trail of the dead men for the Cherokee to enter the snare as they tracked the slave traders.

Driven by his pursuit of the men that had killed his love, Totsuhwa did not notice what had occurred in this place until the loop of the snare closed around him and his son. Chancellor did not realize it even then. He stared down from his horse at the mutilated bodies and looked to his father for answers. Totsuhwa was already eyeing the trees for the safest retreat.

"Come quickly," he said as he turned his horse away from the bodies and back the way they had come but as had happened to Connie on this exact spot, it was too late. Arrows were already in the air.

The difference however, was that Totsuhwa was expecting them. His ears picked up the faintest of whistles and he dropped down flat on his horse. Several arrows passed within inches of his back where he had sat upright a split second before. Only one hit its mark — an errant launch that buried an arrow head so deep in his left thigh that it stuck in bone.

Fortunately, Chancellor had been ignored in the first wave as the Shawnee had all concentrated on the well-muscled warrior and had overlooked the skinny boy. This gave him the slimmest of chances, but even that chance evaporated in the rush of screeching tomahawk-wielding Indians that ran at him from the trees. Over their heads came a second round of arrows, but the shouts and rushing of the Shawnee spooked the horses and the uncontrollable bouncing of the horses made Totsuhwa and Chancellor difficult targets. A single arrow cut the edge of Chancellor's right shoulder while Totsuwha's horse, rearing against the onslaught, caught two arrows deep in its own chest.

"RIDE!" Totsuhwa screamed at his boy as he slid from his horse. The lurching animal had made it impossible to draw a bead on the enemy with his rifle, but once on the ground the barrel was up and rock steady.

The nearest Shawnee to Chancellor may have heard the report of Totsuhwa's rifle, but if he did, it was the last thing he heard. The ball struck him flat against the side of his head and propelled the opposite side of his face off and into the air. Yet in his death came the signal that Totsuhwa's rifle was temporarily empty, and the living Shawnee assailed him ferociously.

Chancellor saw the Shawnee warrior's head explode and his own rifle came up toward the warriors that were rushing toward his father, but he could not return the favor. As he struggled to hold his horse still enough to aim, a Shawnee brave leaped up on his horse until they were nearly both equally astride the frightened animal. The horse bucked at the sudden weight and the rifle went off harmlessly in the air.

Suddenly hands were all about him and Chancellor felt himself being ripped from the horse's back. The empty rifle was torn from his hands. The last thing he saw was a war club descending and his world went black.

A foggy sight, blurred at the edges, awaited Chancellor when consciousness slowly shook him. He was lying on his side in the grass, not far from Pany's hacked body. There was a buzzing in his head and he came to feel a tight cramping in his arms and legs. Inside of a few moments, he realized he was tied tightly, hand and foot, with his hands behind him bound close to his ankles. As he blinked away the fog and looked for something to orient himself he saw his father, also lying in the grass, only a dozen feet away.

Chancellor's eyes cleared, and he saw a large fly crawling down the back of his father's arm. He followed it and waited for his father to brush it away. When the insect stopped at his father's elbow, Chancellor saw the stick braced between his father's arms, just exactly as his mother had been pinned and his heart skipped a beat as he thought his father must be ready to die as well. The bug stopped and Chancellor found himself concentrating on it. As he watched, the vermin began to bite and burrow into the flesh of his father. When there was no reaction it confirmed in his young mind that his father and mother were together.

As a fresh tear came to blur his vision again he began to hope that he too might be with them soon. When given the chance he would force the Shawnee to send him to his parents in the Darkening Land where he would never again complain about gathering wood or fetching water.

Chancellor could hear the Shawnee talking amongst themselves as his brain came back to life. He understood a great deal, but some of the conversations were blurred by an ache in his head and words of a language different than his own. Through his eavesdropping he learned that the hostile warriors were planning on taking their captives home — the boy to be raised as a man or die and the Cherokee warrior to be tortured. If they were to torture the Cherokee warrior, his father must still be alive though it appeared otherwise.

Chancellor squinted hard and focused solely on his father. There was breathing — he could see it now. The broad back moved ever so slightly. The movement restored his strength and he began immediately to plot escape and revenge with his father at his side. The sight of a Shawnee warrior passing nearby wearing the red shirt his mother had made before he was born kindled the growing fire. He tested his bindings secretively. They were sound, but the time would come and he would be ready.

Without seeing how, he was lifted partially off the ground and set upright. He faked a drowsiness much more severe than he felt and watched around him with falsely drooping eyes. He saw his father kicked easily, slapped smartly, and roused back to consciousness and set upright as well. Then the apparent leader of the Shawnee war party, one called Root by the others, came near his father and slapped his face harshly.

"You have killed a fine warrior today, Cherokee dog! For this you will pay with the skin of your eyes! Our women will cut off your fingers and show them to you and peel the flesh from your bones like a snake sheds its skin."

Totsuhwa's head had been low but it came up slowly and inadvertently showed Chancellor the beating he had already endured. The boy cringed at the sight of his father's puffy jaw and eyes and was instantly reminded of the same swollen features on his mother's face. But Totsuhwa was still strong and though clubbed and tied would never bow.

"You have your women do all your work?" Totsuhwa said.

Root's knife flashed in the sun, and he grabbed his captive's hair, yanked it back and exposed Totsuhwa's throat. Chancellor could see the pulse of his father's heart beating strongly in the bulging veins that pressed outward from the sweaty neck.

"Edoda!" Chancellor yelled as a gut reaction to an inevitability he could do nothing to stall.

But the word did just that, though the sinister knife only changed the focus of its attention. Root released Totsuhwa's hair and wandered casually toward the boy who realized that his cry had in all likelihood deepened the pitiful circumstance he and his father had stumbled into.

Root looked from Chancellor to Totsuhwa and back again several times. "Your boy," he said pointing at Chancellor with the knife. "Perhaps there is another way to burn your eyes. Would you like to see the stomach of this little one spilled out on the ground like the guts of a deer? That would redeem the life of my warrior."

The Shawnee chieftain reached Chancellor and snapped his head back and put the knife to his throat, mirroring how he had held the father just moments before. "A life for a life," he said as the knife coiled back to strike.

"Tecumseh will frown if you kill the boy!" Totsuhwa yelled.

Root held the knife back and pointed it at Totsuhwa. He scowled at the bound Cherokee warrior. "You do not even speak the name of such a great Shawnee chief. After this cub bear is skinned, your tongue will pay for its crime!"

"Tecumseh! Tecumseh! I will say the name! And when I die, at your filthy hands or as an old man in the hills of my people, Tecumseh will welcome me to the Darkening Land. He waits there even now with my father, his brother. Though they did not share a mother, they were brothers against the armies of the white men. Their spirits will come for you if you harm their grandson. These are things even the ignorant must know."

Root took a tentative step toward Totsuhwa and spoke in a voice equal parts intrigue and confusion. "The great Tecumseh would only call one Cherokee brother. Who was your father?"

Now it was Totsuhwa who hesitated. A part of his warrior's heart did not wish to see him spared for the name of another when his own weakness had left him and his son beaten and tied like dogs. He looked at Chancellor and saw in his face, framed by the too-long flowing black hair of Galegi, the eyes of his wife and they begged him to reveal the heritage that would save them.

"Tsi'yugunsini," he answered.

Hushed breaths of the name flittered through the Shawnee, and they looked at each other for an assurance that they were still safe.

"How was he called by the whites?" Root pressed, albeit lightly.

When Totsuhwa did not answer quickly enough, Chancellor shouted the name and saw the Shawnee recoil at the sound.

"DRAGON! He was the Dragon."

The Shawnee fell back further and their eyes glanced into the trees above and around them.

Root advanced to Totsuhwa, still holding the knife but at his side. "This is true? You call the Dragon 'Father'?"

"I do."

Root looked around at his warriors, some of whom still had wide eyes and scanned the trees as if an enemy they could never defeat was about to explode upon them. "The Dragon had a son," Root continued. "He is known to our people as a powerful shaman. Tecumseh carried his name back to our people when he last met with the great Dragon. I know his name. How you are called?"

"Totsuhwa."

"That is the name," Root said as he looked back to Chancellor. "And this is your son, the grandson of Tsi'yugunsini?"

"He is," Totsuhwa answered proudly.

The knife moved slowly toward Totsuhwa's bindings but hesitated and came away. Root returned to Chancellor and cut him free.

As Chancellor rubbed the life back into his wrists, Root spoke clearly to him, "Stay here. Do not move." Then Root walked slowly back to Totsuhwa and crouched down in front of him.

"I will free you, Totsuhwa, son of Tsi'yugunsini," Root said. "And your son will live." Then he motioned to the dead Shawnee Totsuhwa had shot. "But there is a debt to be paid."

Totsuhwa did not move.

"And it is now known to me," Root continued. "That the white men killed a woman. Your woman. The wife of Totsuhwa and the daughter of Tsi'yugunsini. We have taken your revenge for you. Another debt you owe."

"It is one I would rather have collected with my own knife and the knife of my son."

"Perhaps. But the debts against you have grown and they will be paid."

Totsuhwa spoke again, more clearly, offering but not pleading. "Take my horse and rifle and give it to the family of the dead Shawnee. It is a fine rifle and the horse is strong."

Root got up and walked around the camp to where a warrior held the Cherokee horses. He looked at the underside of Totsuhwa's animal and touched the blood trickling from the arrows that dangled from the horse's belly. "This animal will die and your rifle is already in the hands of my men. Life is counted against life. This is something even the ignorant must know."

Hearing his own words used against him caused Totsuhwa's muscles to tighten against the bindings, but he was temporarily powerless even though he understood clearly what was about to happen. He would not give it away by looking at his son but instantly began to feel the same ripping sensation in his heart that he had felt when first his father, then his mother, Ama Giga, Dragon, and finally Galegi, barely cold, had been taken from him. Totsuhwa knew plainly that the Shawnee would take his boy and he was in no position to prevent it. The black fear was back in his heart and mind with a vengeance.

As Root moved away from the horses and back to his captive, Chancellor watched, not understanding what had happened between the two men and their short exchange. It was made no more clear by Root's words to Totsuhwa or his father's reaction to them.

"You will speak plainly to the boy. If you do not make him understand he will suffer for his confusion." Root reached down with the knife to cut the ties on Totsuhwa's hands but looked at the thick forearms, sweating with veins seemingly about to pop from the tension of the ropes and he thought better of it. Instead of freeing him Root issued his final warning as he stood erect and came away leaving Totsuhwa still bound. "You and the boy live today because of Tecumseh and Tsi'yugunsini, but if you come into Shawnee land to collect what once was yours you will die.

"These words are not enough to keep you out of our villages, I know. So put this in your heart, Totsuhwa, son of the Dragon — if word reaches the ears of the Shawnee that Totsuhwa can throw a stone and make a splash in any of our great rivers, this boy will be put through the gauntlet for your crime." Root turned away from Totsuhwa but then back just as quickly. "And he will not survive it. When you come for him he will be dead."

There was a pause in the circle of men before Root motioned for Chancellor to be taken nearer his father. "Totsuhwa, great shaman of the Cherokee, speak now to the boy and make his ears hear you. Then we will go in peace and your debts will be paid. Are we agreed?"

"We are," Totsuhwa said. "But I have a request."

"I have granted you much already—"

"It is a simple thing, son of Tecumseh."

The flattery worked and Root relented. "What do you want of me?"

"Come close, my friend. It is only meant for your ears."

Root was leery of the powerful shaman but respectful and curious as well. He went close and leaned down until his ear was close to his prisoner's mouth.

Totsuhwa whispered faintly for nearly a minute as Root listened silently. The nearby warriors and Chancellor held their breath in an attempt to hear the words but they could not. After the quiet discourse Root stood straight again.

"You have lost much today, Totsuhwa, Tsalagi priest — your wife, your son, a fine horse, your rifle. What you have asked I will make so and there will be no move against it. These are the words of Root." He took one step away but turned back and pointed at the broken arrow sticking out from Totsuhwa's bloody thigh. "There is a witch on the point of that arrow. You would be wise to save your best magic for yourself."

The Shawnee chief now addressed the warriors nearby as he started to return to the stream. "Give them space for talking while you collect our brother's body. When the priest says he is finished bring the boy."

Only when Root vanished into the woods did Chancellor begin to fully understand what was happening. Warriors pushed him across the ground until he scrambled to his father. Even then he held out for a different answer.

Chancellor's questions were painted on his frightened face. Totsuhwa looked him square in the eyes.

"You will go with the Shawnee. They will not harm you."

Chancellor wanted to throw his arms around his father and never let go, but the Shawnee warriors nearby were too close and would see too much. Even in his fear, Chancellor wanted to be more man than a boy. He grabbed his father's thick arms and answered firmly, "No! I will not!"

The Shawnee slowed in their collection of their brother's body and began to look warily at the two Cherokee. Totsuhwa saw beyond his son to the warriors and his voice softened even more.

"Chancellor. You must go with the Shawnee. You must stay with them. Become a strong Shawnee warrior—"

"No!" the boy answered again. "Never!"

Behind him the Shawnee stopped their work over the body. They whispered among themselves before one left for the stream. Totsuhwa instantly knew he was going for Root.

"Listen, my son! Listen to me like you have never listened! You are a man now and a man must do many things to show he is a man." Totsuhwa motioned after the departing Shawnee warrior with his chin then looked back at his son. "When that brave returns he will be carrying a knife in his hand. He will use it to kill you before my eyes and I will not be able to stop him. Because of my father they will leave me here with his Spirit to live or die. When I am well I will travel to the land of the Shawnee to kill that warrior, Root, and all his people for taking you from me. I will kill many Shawnee, but when the sun sets my scalp will be hanging from a Shawnee lodge pole."

"No," Chancellor said weakly.

"Yes. Yes! And our whole family will be dead—"

"I would as soon be dead if I must live without you—"

"No, son. You will go with the Shawnee. Go with your head high — a proud Cherokee warrior always on the inside. You must go and live the life your mother wanted for you. Have her grandchildren. Teach them her ways."

"And yours?"

Totsuhwa paused for only a breath. "And mine."

"I should go? I must go?"

"Yes. You will always be the son of Totsuhwa. The grandson of the great Tsi'yugunsini. No matter where you lay your head at night. And—" Totsuhwa choked. "And I will always love you."

Chancellor set his mind against what lay ahead. He trusted his father and believed that to do anything short of what he said would mean death to them both. "I will go, Father. I will go. But I will see you again." Chancellor ignored the returning Shawnee and the others watching and hugged his father. "I will see you again, my father."

When Totsuhwa saw the warrior coming back from the stream, knife in hand as he had said, he shouted, "The boy is ready! Put away your knife!"

The Shawnee obeyed the Cherokee priest as readily as if the words had come from Tecumseh himself. He sheathed his knife, looked away from Totsuhwa and once again began picking up the body of the dead man.

"Go, son. Do as you are told. Do not run away. Take the training well. Be proud and strong. Remember who you are."

Chancellor stepped back from his father, who still remained bound and kneeling in the matted grass. "Remember who you are, my son."

The Shawnee had the slain warrior's body up and were moving. Three lingered behind for Chancellor, but they did not touch him. The boy continued stepping away from his father and nearer the Shawnee until he was in their midst. He looked back repeatedly as the warriors began to move toward the stream with the captive boy in an invisible tow. The trees came up between father and son until only glimpses of each other between leafless trunks could be seen. Then, in another long step he would never forget, Chancellor could see his father no more.

Totsuhwa watched his own reflection in his son vanish in the trees. When his eyes could see no more of his boy, he listened. And when his ears could hear no more of his son's steps the great Cherokee shaman lowered himself to the ground. He felt the pain in his leg of the broken arrow shaft and its flint head and pushed against it until the pain seared his mind. Totsuhwa did not cry out but ground the arrow's shaft into his leg with his own weight, a punishment for failing his wife and now his son.

The pain became so intense he nearly passed out from it but stopped short — he wanted to be awake and feel every measure of the anguish he felt he deserved. Though the weather was cool his face was bathed in sweat and his leg began to twitch, unconsciously rebelling against the self-torture. Soon tears began to mix with the beads of sweat and shortly thereafter exhaustion brought an end to the abuse.

Totsuhwa relaxed and began to cry in earnest. He could have worked out of the stick binding but found a strange contentment in staying tied, increasing the pain and punishment he saw as warranted. So he stayed on the ground, bound to the stick, the arrow still imbedded, reaching for fresh blood deeper in his thigh as a result of his pressing on it, and stayed that way until the sun shut its face from him.

Chancellor walked in a stupor. The Shawnee did nothing to physically restrain him, but Root posted silent sentries ahead and behind. If he bolted they were ready to imprison him. But it wasn't necessary. Chancellor took the words of his father into his heart and he would do as he had been told. Maybe it was the lingering effects of the war club to his head, but for some reason he had only a vague recollection of his mother's death and the separation from his father already seemed distant. Somehow he would soon awake and be sleeping on the cabin floor. Between him and the door would be the sleeping fire and the Chickasaw warriors beyond. And to the side would be his mother and father — their rhythmic breathing rising and falling in unison as if they were one and the same person.

This dream carried Chancellor for the rest of the day's walk as the troupe followed the winding path of the stream to the north, away from the Cherokee foothills and into the land of the Shawnee. When darkness began to settle around them the Shawnee made camp. Chancellor had no place and no apparent responsibility. He wandered through the quieting warriors who looked at him with wonder as they recalled the stories they had heard of their own Tecumseh and the famous Tsi'yugunsini.

The Shawnee woman who had been rescued came near and asked him to come sit with her and eat. Though he had no notion to eat, Chancellor followed her and found himself sitting beside her, chewing dried deer meat and eating corn meal bread as she talked in a language he did not completely understand.

"Your mother. She was brave. I sang for her," the woman said.

The reference to Galegi stirred Chancellor slightly but the haze of the day remained.

"You knew her?" he asked.

The woman, who struggled less with Cherokee than Chancellor did with her tongue, answered as best she could though she still lost a few words.

"Yes. I was with her and the white men." She patted his leg. "Your Shawnee brothers have killed them for what they did to your mother. They are your brothers now. And I and my sisters will be your mother when we have killed the last of the butchers there." The woman pointed across the camp to Niak, who was bound tightly and tied by the throat to a tree.

Chancellor had not even noticed the captive until the woman pointed him out. The sight of the Creek half-breed in the dying light brought Chancellor further from his dream.

"He was one of those who killed my mother?"

"Yes, and he took me and my child and the other, the Creek woman. We have all suffered by him. When we are back in our valley we will return the pain. He will hurt no woman again. Your mother will rest quietly when he is dead."

The last words played themselves over, around, and through Chancellor's head: "Your mother will rest quietly when he is dead."

The woman continued talking, but Chancellor heard little. She talked on about how the Creek woman would become a Shawnee and be a sister to her. And how he would become a son and a fine Shawnee warrior. "I have heard the men say that the blood in you is that of Tsi'yugunsini and Totsuhwa, the great Tsalagi chief and priest. You must live up to the blood that is in you from such great men. You must not attempt to return to your old home now. You must stay with us. If you leave and return to your land you will shame your people."

Once again the woman's words broke the spell Chancellor was under. "How do I shame them for wanting to return to my home?"

"You are here to pay a debt. It must be paid. You cannot leave. Do you understand?"

"My father said these things."

"Your father is wise."

There was a silent moment between the two and they each chewed a piece of the giving deer.

"My mother waits for me to bury her," Chancellor said as he choked back a tear.

"Your father will tend to her for you," the woman said.

"I will miss them," Chancellor said as the tear made its escape.

The Shawnee woman stood up and moved to a small bundle that rested nearby. She fumbled over it for a moment then returned in the near darkness. She carried an old ragged pouch that she pressed into the boy's hands. Chancellor opened the pouch and reached inside. The touch of his hands immediately told him what waited there. He pulled them out and saw again his mother's mirror and comb.

The woman covered his hands, the mirror, and comb and spoke in a mother's voice. "You will keep these special things and remember her through them."

Chancellor did not speak. He merely nodded as the woman squeezed his fingers.

Root came across the camp through the fading light. The woman pushed the mirror and comb back in the bag and Chancellor instinctively slipped the package from Root's view. The young chieftain looked down at the boy and woman and understood that a necessary comfort was being spread over Chancellor's wounds. He nudged the boy's shoulder with the barrel of a rifle to get his attention even though it wasn't necessary.

"You are called Chancellor?"

"Yes."

"Why does the blood of the great Tsi'yugunsini have a white name?"

Chancellor sharply pushed away the rifle barrel from his arm. "If we called this a flower and not a rifle it would still kill. True?"

Root was taken aback by the quick movement and the sharp wit. He stood quietly for a moment and the woman became anxious. She thought the boy carried too much of the Dragon's Cherokee blood to ever make a Shawnee and that Root might kill him and not adopt him as a brother, but those fears were pushed aside when Root squatted down in front of Chancellor. He held the rifle in front of him. In the poor light Chancellor could see the rifle was partially wrapped in a red cloth.

"What you say is true, young warrior. It is clear that the voice of a man comes from your mouth. You have taken the wisdom of your father and grandfather into your heart. That is good."

Root's voice carried a peculiar resignation he was unfamiliar with. The woman heard it in his voice as well. "Totsuhwa asked me to see these things came to your hands. To appease the spirits of the great Tecumseh and Tsi'yugunsini, his brother, I give them to you now."

Root pushed the rifle and the red cloth onto Chancellor's lap. The boy delicately unwrapped the cloth and found it to be the shirt Galegi had made for her husband. Beneath it was her rifle.

"Wado," Chancellor said in a whisper.

Root answered hesitantly as though the presentation was not totally by choice, as indeed it was not. Rather, it was brought on by the promise he had made to a valiant enemy and a fear of offending two of the greatest chiefs who had ever lived.

"Yes," is all Root said as he stood. Then Chancellor and the woman saw him smile. "Your father asked for the rifle. He did not ask for it to be loaded. In time."

Chancellor nodded and the woman smiled as well. "He will be a fine warrior for you, Root," she said empathically. "Your promise will reap many rewards for you."

"I do not think that is so. The blood of this one now carries pain. The Shawnee and the Tsalagi know that pain is a path for dreams to tread. When the visions come to him he will listen. For me, I will sleep well beneath the sky of my home and one day when I go to the West, Tecumseh and Tsi'yugunsini will welcome me there."

As soon as Root walked away Chancellor produced the bag. He took out the comb and mirror and noticed for the first time that it was cracked. He wrapped both pieces gently in the red shirt as they had been years before when Totsuhwa brought them to his wife. He slipped them carefully back in the Shawnee pouch.

"The looking glass of my mother is broken," he said.

"I have seen so," the woman answered as she pulled a blanket from beneath her and handed it to him. "But it is safe again. It will break no more. Lie down and rest now with this blanket to stay warm. We are still in the land of your fathers. Root will have no fire for two more days and the nights are cold."

Chancellor did as he was told. He set the pouch and its precious contents near his head and covered himself and his mother's rifle with the blanket as he nestled with the gun like a child with a cornhusk doll. He felt the comforting hand of the woman as she eased the blanket back and gently dabbed a sap mixture in the arrow wound on his shoulder. It was as numb as his mind. He tried to recall the day but found he could not do so clearly. It had been a dream, a nightmare, and he closed his eyes to wake from it.

Totsuhwa's eyes were opening to the dark of midnight. A quarter moon provided some light, but it was meager. The night was very cool and he woke cold. His arms and hands and shoulders were completely asleep from the effects of being tied and the pinching of the harsh stick at his back. The injured thigh was worse than asleep. It was completely numb and the severed muscles in Totsuhwa's thigh made it impossible to move the leg as he normally would. It was tied at the ankle to his other leg. He repeatedly rolled and listed to the side until he was able to use his good leg to begin the painful process of pulling the damaged limb out straight.

His eyes lolled in their sockets with the rush of pain, but it subsided to a degree when the useless leg came to rest more or less straight alongside its mate. Totsuhwa breathed deeply and rested though he knew he had only just begun. Now he was on his back, his elbows buried in the matted grasses and the arms still held captive by the rope and stick. He eased his good leg over the bad several times and threw his weight with it until he was able to launch himself up on his side with one end of the stick firmly planted in the ground. In the process however, he also rested on the broken shaft of the arrow and could feel it grinding against the bone in his leg.

He began to push down hard against the stick and slide it free. By the design of his captors, strong notches of broken branches caught his tingling elbows. He could feel the pressure against them but not the pain. A deep breath, a grunt, and the total thrust of his body weight down on the stick and the jagged notch tore through the skin of his inner elbow. The cramping stemmed the flow of blood from the new wound and the sense that he was almost rid of the stick erased the pain.

Now Totsuhwa had but to sit upright and shake himself until the stick fell, leaving just a scratch on the other arm. He eased his arms out straight in front of him as best he could and felt the blood rushing into the cramped muscles. While he waited for life to flow back into his arms he looked down at the broken arrow shaft sticking out of his leg. Even in the dark of midnight he could see its jagged end protruding from his pants, black with his own blood.

"There may well be a witch on your flint," he said to the broken shaft, "but I have battled many witches. You are not so strong." And he spit with a dry mouth at the arrow. "I am not afraid of you and your medicine is weak. I have been bound like a deer to a drying pole and still I fight to be free. Soon you will give up your new home in me and I will toss you aside. You will be as useless as wet gunpowder."

His shoulders ached but were able to move again. Slowly he began to flex his arms up and down — in little moves at first — until his range of motion returned. He wiggled his fingers and stretched them like a dog stretches in the morning until they too began to feel again. Now he brushed the ropes around his wrists gently against his face until he could feel the knots. Cautiously, as though as a test, he began to bite them. As he gained confidence that he was pulling on the right spots he bit hard and pulled with both his teeth and hands until the ropes relinquished their grip. It wasn't long before Totsuhwa was loose. He didn't throw the ropes but set them to his side. What had once been an enemy might soon be useful.

As Chancellor had done in nearly this same spot, Totsuhwa sat and rubbed the life back into his weary wrists. When they responded he began to run his fingers over the arrow in his leg. He gripped it carefully and pulled on it slightly and could feel the witch move in his leg. The strange pressure he felt inside the thigh told him that the arrowhead shape was not unlike his best hunting arrows — with backward-facing points that embedded themselves and prevented the arrow from being easily dislodged.

His hands eased away from the shaft and he touched the numb thigh gently. "Relax, leg. And you sleep well, witch. The sun will see you soon." Totsuhwa would wait until the morning light to remove the arrowhead. For now he wanted to sleep, but he wanted water first.

His hands felt around his feet until he found the knots that bound his ankles. In moments he was free. He felt around in the dark until he came upon the stick that had once held him. He

used it as a brace and with his good leg beneath him stood like a
newborn colt. He was dizzy for only a moment then hobbled off
in the direction of the stream. The wounded leg dragged and the
short length of the stick was not well suited, but he struggled
ahead. He recalled the general direction the Shawnee had taken
and before long his ears guided him to the stream.

Totsuhwa walked knee deep in the water and was about to lie
down when he realized his medicine pouch still hung from his
waist. The Shawnee had taken his knife but had left him life in the
bag. Gratefully he slipped it from his side and placed it carefully
on the bank as he stood on one foot, the injured leg nearly floating
in the knee-deep water. Now he lay down in the stream and felt
the coolness of the Long Man washing away the blood and sweat of
the day and night. He drank heavily and washed the swelling on
his face.

Prayers for his wife and son began as whispers on his lips.
While they never reached high voice they did grow until they
were clear and sharp in the late autumn moonlight through
lips that were cut and swollen. The prayers continued with
the washing until the water had done its job well. Revived but
tired, Totsuhwa pulled himself up on dry land and stretched
out on his back to sleep. His last thoughts were of his wife,
sleeping high off the ground, and his boy, somewhere far
upstream sleeping surrounded by the Shawnee or looking up
at the same quarter moon and thinking of his father.

"Sleep, my boy," Totsuhwa said as the moon slipped away above
him as he descended into a restless sleep. "Your father's arm is
around you even now..."

A buzzing noise woke Totsuhwa when the sun was a full hand
above the mountains. His eyes opened and focused on a cloudy
sky far above the still-rising sun and he listened to the sounds of
the water moving nearby. The buzzing was from flies drawn to
the sleeping body and the smell of blood. Totsuhwa brushed the
few that lingered near his head and felt the ache in his arm in
doing so. He sat up slowly and found the ache was everywhere.
The beating the Shawnee had inflicted was taking full effect and

the tears in the skin at his elbow were stiff and sore. The arrowhead was burning his thigh with its piercing teeth.

His heart however, was flowing with an anguish that overcame all the throbbing that cried out from his body. He sat in the mix of sun and clouds and flies and thought of his wife and son. His hands settled into his lap and ignored the flies as his mind replayed what his eyes had seen in the last day. Like his son, he wondered if it could have been a dream — a horrible vision brought on by a sin he had committed against a powerful spirit. The flies hovered and landed. Without thought or concern he brushed them away. In doing so he inadvertently hit the broken arrow shaft in his leg. The splintered wood wrenched the flint head and found a fresh avenue for pain that snapped Totsuhwa back to reality. Beads of sweat erupted on his face as he bit his lower lip.

The flies had found the blood at first light and were busy flittering around and feasting on the wound. Totsuhwa shooed them away, but they were not easily discouraged. To escape them he eased his tormented body back into the stream. The water worked its magic as it had the night before and Totsuhwa splashed his face and washed away the sweat. He tore his pants around the wound until he could see it clearly just beneath the surface of the water. Very carefully he stroked the flesh around the shaft of the arrow and watched as puffs of blood erupted and were swept downstream.

From his place in the stream Totsuhwa reached out of the water to his medicine pouch that had rested beside him through the night. With both hands dripping from the stream he rummaged through it carefully and pulled out small bag after bag of roots and powders. One he untied and shook half of its contents into his mouth. Then he hoisted himself from the water and spread a sizeable portion of what remained of the powder around the wound. One hand began massaging the powder into his flesh while the other set the small bag aside and went back into the medicine pouch. It came out in a moment holding two pieces of flint, one of which was the arrowhead Tsi'yugunsini had given him from the deer they had killed so many years before. He set the larger, sharper piece down and weighed the old arrowhead in his hand.

"You have lost your cutting power, my friend. The years of riding in my bag have dulled your keen edge. My own senses are this way or I would not be here as I am...and my boy would not one day take a Shawnee bride."

Reluctantly Totsuhwa put the old arrowhead back in the bag. When his hand emerged again it held a short piece of leather with deep cuts along its entire length. This he immediately placed between his teeth. Then, as though he had practiced the routine a hundred times, he picked up the remaining piece of razor-sharp flint in one hand, grabbed the arrow's shaft in the other and began to pull on it strongly, slicing with the flint to tear the Shawnee witch from his leg.

It was over quickly. Bright red blood flowed from the leg and sweat cascaded down Totsuhwa's face into his eyes and off his chin. He set the broken arrow and its flint point aside and picked up the small bag. The medicine man haphazardly shook the bag over the bloody mess until what powder had remained in the bag was gone. Once again he massaged the powder around the wound, fighting the gathering flies for the chance. Then he pulled the ragged tears of his pants over the fresh cuts and pressed down hard.

The flies were denied access to the wound but still licked at the back of Totsuhwa's bloody hands. He allowed them to do so as the powder worked in the wound and the pressure eased the bleeding. He sat there for some time like that, occasionally swabbing his face with his shoulders to wipe away sweat and flies.

Meanwhile, Chancellor was trudging further away from his homeland. He carried his mother's rifle and rode his own horse just as he had done a few days before, but the entire world had changed. The men who rode nearby did not speak to him and the woman who talked to him at night was not his mother. Yet even encased in the shock of the last days, he could sense an odd wave of respect when the Shawnee came near. They knew well their own great chief, Tecumseh, and the stories of Tsi'yugunsini's battles against the whites were already legend even in their

foreign camps. The name of Totsuhwa, the great Cherokee shaman, was also common to any man who appreciated a brave
warrior and powerful medicine. So reverence cloaked him like
an invisible blanket and the Shawnee looked at him with sideways glances and whispered among themselves.

After meals had been eaten on horseback and yet another range
of mountains passed, a single Shawnee warrior rode up alongside
Chancellor's horse. He held out Totsuhwa's rifle. "This is the rifle of
Totsuhwa. You should carry it."

Chancellor almost instinctively reached for it but stopped and
pulled his hand back. "No, my father wants the gun to be given to
the family of the man who died."

"They will not take it. The spirits of Tecumseh and the Dragon
may not be pleased. We have spoke of these things," he said as he
looked over his shoulder back at the others in the party.

Chancellor looked again at his father's rifle but heard Totsuhwa's
words in his head. He put his hand tenderly on the rifle but only to
touch it. He spoke calmly. "No, tell the family no curse comes with
it. A blessing instead."

"You will pray to your grandfathers, Tecumseh and Tsi'yugunsini,
on this thing?"

Chancellor felt the change in him. He was becoming the young
shaman his mother had hoped he would be. "I will," he said strongly
and the warrior slowly withdrew the rifle.

Now Chancellor's mind raced ahead with the wisdom of his parents and the brashness of a boy. "The same is not true of the knife
of Totsuhwa," he said plainly. "My father wished for his horse and
rifle to pay the debt, but the knife must come to me for Tecumseh
and Tsi'yugunsini's grandchildren's children."

The Shawnee only stared.

"Tecumseh and the Dragon steadied that knife in Totsuhwa's
grip. It is only meant for one hand," Chancellor finished.

The warrior spun his horse away and raced back to the small
group that had been watching from some distance. Chancellor pivoted on his horse's back and watched the man as he talked loudly
to the others. Each seemed to glance back and forth from one to
another among them as the Shawnee raised Totsuhwa's rifle in the

air and shook it. One of the men shouted at the rifle bearer and yanked Totsuhwa's long knife from his own belt. The irritated warrior kicked his horse and steered straight for Chancellor at a hard gallop, screaming with the knife held menacingly above his head.

As the horse closed in on him Chancellor was uncertain what was about to happen but took no chances and slipped from his horse, tossed his mother's rifle in the air and caught its barrel. Wielding it like a long club he waited for the racing Shawnee.

Root was in front of the straggling line of his band. When the shouting began behind him he stopped and turned on his horse like Chancellor had done to see what was causing the commotion. When his man raised the knife and descended on Chancellor, Root began to race toward the boy who now stood with feet firmly planted on the ground.

The galloping Shawnee warrior bore down close on Chancellor who responded by cocking the rifle back further, ready to crack the man when he came within reach or pummel him with the rifle butt if he dove knife first from his horse. However, all the heart-pounding preparation was unnecessary. At the last possible moment the warrior jerked the horse to a stop, so close that clumps of sod showered Chancellor's feet. He was talking so fast in Shawnee that Chancellor, nearly deaf from the excitement, understood little. All he heard was that the warrior was not afraid of a Cherokee spirit but wanted Tecumseh to rest in peace. With that, a hand, shaking from the hoof pounding of the excited horse beneath him, held out Totsuhwa's knife. Chancellor lowered his rifle and took it as Root trotted up nearby.

As soon as the knife cleared the Shawnee warrior's hand, the warrior kicked the horse again and rode on ahead. Root looked down at the knife now resting in Chancellor's hand then into the boy's eyes.

"You are quick. And courageous. And now you are armed. Does the grandson of Tsi'yugunsini think he and I will fight one day? Will you raise that knife against me, son of Totsuhwa?"

The knife brought Chancellor's eyes down but only for a moment. Then he returned a stare to the Shawnee on horseback above him. "No, Root. You have spared the life of my father. I will lay my weapons down if ever you should come for me."

Root spun his anxious horse around in a tight circle. "More wisdom from one so young. I believe you, young Tsalagi. But I also believe you will not stay in the valley of the Shawnee. Other voices, Chancellor with the white name, other voices from the spirits of both our nations call to you. In your mourning you do not hear them. They are not your mother's or father's. When you understand the dreams you will rush to them."

As Root began trotting his horse back to the lead of the traveling Shawnee, Chancellor slipped his father's knife into the belt at his waist. When the blade was settled, Chancellor looked again toward the Shawnee leader. As Root passed the disjointed column Chancellor followed him with his eyes until he came to another set of eyes staring back at him from near the front of the group. They belonged to Niak.

The captive Creek half-breed was still tied with the stick pinning his arms back and in addition a rope had been loosely tied around his neck. A young Shawnee warrior who was on a horse in front of him had been pulling him like a dog. When Root assumed the lead and the horses began to move again, the rope snatched Niak's face away from Chancellor's for the time it took him to begin walking again. Then he turned slightly as if to gauge a foe while the rope urged him ahead.

Chancellor stared back until the yank of the rope broke Niak from the stare down. Behind the young Cherokee, the Shawnee men were lingering, waiting for Chancellor to mount and join the procession. He obligingly did so but only after staring at Niak for another long moment. Once mounted, he adjusted his mother's empty rifle across his lap as well as his father's knife at his waist. He suddenly caught himself thinking that the gun may be empty and almost useless, but the knife was not. The knife certainly was not.

The Shawnee pushed hard all day and well into the evening. With each step of his horse, Chancellor made notes in his mind on the passage. When the day finally ended he found himself in valleys he had never seen. While he ate some from the hand of the Shawnee woman, he wondered how far he was from his own land and how his father had fared over the course of his first day as head of the disintegrated family.

If the boy could have seen across the mountains and valleys he would have found his father sitting on the ground in the dark at the base of a tree, his damaged leg sticking out as numb as a stick of wood. Alongside his father's sleeping form Chancellor would have seen a long pole, used as a crutch to help the wounded man get this far. And above Totsuhwa, covered in a blanket and nestled on a branch against the tree's trunk, Chancellor would have seen the form of his mother.

While the Shawnee around him quickly fell to sleep, worn down from their hard ride and relieved to be back in their own lands, Chancellor feigned sleep but lay awake. He stared up into the limbs of the trees overhead and envisioned shadows of his mother's form lit by the moon. Nearby he could hear the deep breathing of the Shawnee woman and others beyond her buried in their slumber. What Chancellor did not realize was that as he watched the moon dip in and out of the clouds across the nighttime sky he was himself being watched.

Root had lain down some considerable distance away. His own eyes were heavy from the preceding days, but he held out against sleep and watched the form of the Cherokee boy with a peculiar sense of awe. He did not know that no true blood of Tsi'yugunsini was in the boy, but even if he had, it would have mattered little. Being a son was derived more from nearness and lessons taught and learned; experiences and beliefs shared and acted upon. This was what had made Tecumseh and Tsi'yugunsini brothers and what commanded Root's respect as he eyed Chancellor.

Near Root's head were the feet of the warrior who had momentarily challenged the boy only to relinquish Totsuhwa's knife. The Shawnee chief did not realize the warrior was also still awake and neither realized the boy was the focus of the other's attention.

Chancellor looked through the darkness to Niak who slept nearly upright against the base of a tree. The half-breed Creek had remained bound to his stick for so many days that his arms and hands might never work properly again. He was also deathly weak from lack of food and water. He had been given small measures to keep him fit to travel and alive just enough to make an entertaining spectacle when tortured and killed.

Chancellor scanned the rest of the sleeping camp and found no movement, only the quiet breathing of sleeping men and women. When the moon slipped behind a cloud, he came out from beneath his blanket like a slithering snake. As quiet as that same snake, he slipped into the trees surrounding the makeshift camp — his mother's rifle in one hand, his father's knife in the other and in his mouth the small bag given him by the Shawnee woman. He was safely in the trees when the cloud gave up the moon's hiding place and the dim light showed the watching eyes that Chancellor had disappeared.

Root never raised his head, but the other warrior did ever so slightly and immediately gave away the fact that he had been watching. Though Chancellor didn't see the subtle move from the trees, Root did. Now Root was watching his own warrior, strangely content to let the offspring of so gallant a bloodline of men escape unmolested. But before the Shawnee could move to light out after the boy and before Root would have moved to stop him, Chancellor suddenly materialized back on the far edge of the camp. Both the warrior and Root settled back to watch though the brave thought he was still alone in the doing so.

Chancellor moved from tree to tree along the edge of the camp like a ghost. He timed his moves with the hide-and-seek game of the moon and the clouds. With each new ray of moonlight Root and the brave would scan the trees for a hint of where the boy was. After several long silent minutes Root came to realize that Chancellor was closing in on Niak. Several more moves followed until the Cherokee boy was behind the tree to which the lashed Creek was sleeping. Chancellor had not made a single sound the entire time.

The Shawnee warrior thought the quiet young Cherokee was going to free the other captive and tightened in preparation of moving off just as stealthily to prevent it. Before he could begin he felt Root's hand tighten around his ankle. He froze and looked down the length of his body to see Root's eyes and a calming hand silently instructing him to remain as he was.

Neither man moved apart from the warrior retraining his eyes on Niak's tree and Root's hand settling back to the ground.

Behind the cover of the tree Chancellor set down his mother's rifle as though it was as fragile as a robin's egg. He took the pouch from his mouth and set it and its precious contents of the comb and mirror, tightly wrapped in Totsuhwa's red shirt, on the rifle. His hand came away slowly and returned to the rifle and bag several times in soundless succession, each time drawing further away. This served to confirm the exact place so when the time came he could grab the gun and pouch in a hurry if it was necessary.

Root had not seen any of this and the passing time caused the Shawnee brave to shake his leg slightly to garner the chief's attention. Only Root's eyes moved, but when they had, the brave silently asked to go out after the boy. Once again Root told him without a sound, "Do not move."

Chancellor's back was against one side of the tree. He was sweating. Niak was against the opposite side — asleep. Totsuhwa's knife weighed a bit heavy in the young hand. Chancellor moved it back and forth from hand to hand and alternately tried to dry his sweating palms against his pants. Then he looked up through the trees for the moon. He could see the shadow of a small cloud approaching and a larger one looming behind. The effect would be perfect. The junior cloud would mask his move around the tree and the spray of light before the main cloud would give him the light he needed to gauge Niak completely.

When the small cloud eclipsed the moon, Chancellor breathed deeply and slipped around the tree. Root and his anxious partner saw the boy mysteriously appear in the briefest rays of light as the little cloud passed and saw a muted flash of moonlight reflect off the blade of the slashing knife. Then the larger cloud covered the face of the moon, and the young Cherokee warrior disappeared behind its cloak. Chancellor gripped Niak's hair in the dark, eased his head back with the tenderness of a mother adjusting a sleeping baby, then buried his father's broad knife beneath one of Niak's sleeping ears and cut his throat so deep the width of the broad blade was buried as Chancellor pulled it completely across the Creek's throat.

Chancellor's hand jumped from Niak's hair to his mouth and squelched any sound from the mortally wounded kidnapper. In his dreamy wakening Niak did not know to cry out until he tried to reach for the hand covering his mouth. The stick prevented him, so he tried to shake the hand free. Chancellor kneed him hard in the chest to hamper the struggle, but even the muted thump was so quiet it did not reach Root's ears.

Had Niak's hands reached his mouth he would have only found his throat lying open as the knife slashed two more times. Chancellor did not realize that blood was spraying from Niak's throat in a torrent and covering his own legs and arms. Nor did he understand that he could have released the Creek's mouth for his neck was so torn that no sound could have worked its way to the dying lips.

Weak from the lack of food and water and still caught in a dreamy state of wakening, Niak's body began to relax as a Raven Mocker crept in the wide gash in his throat. The dead man tried to kick one last time as his life spilled down his chest. Chancellor felt for the trembling legs with his foot and pinned them to the ground. Life was over for the renegade half-breed.

The Cherokee boy, schooled on taking animals in the wild, continued to hold Niak's bloody mouth until he was certain the man was dead. As he held Niak's lifeless mouth, Chancellor looked up through the trees and saw that the cloud was preparing to give way to the prying eyes of the moon. Though he would have liked to have waited longer to insure Niak could not cry out he had to move. He released the dead man's mouth slowly as though ready to cover it again at the hint of any sound. When none came he grabbed Niak's hair again. This time it was with the bloody hand of a warrior.

Absent was the tenderness he had used before to his advantage. This time he pulled the hair up and ran the knife neatly around the dead man's head. He pulled. The scalp resisted. He cut again and tugged, but it still didn't come loose as he thought it would, and the cloud was slipping away above him.

The first glimmers of moonlight shown across the camp and showed Chancellor the places his knife had missed. He cut the scalp easily and it came off in his hand as Niak's head slumped forward. A reflex caused Chancellor to look into the camp. At the far edge he saw the Shawnee brave standing holding a rifle at his side, but down. Root was gone.

Ignoring the exposing moon, Chancellor jumped behind the tree with his trophy. He shifted the scalp to the knife-wielding hand and reached for the rifle and pouch. He found them but they instantly slipped from his bloody hand. He dropped to the ground and fumbled for them with his free hand and the other which still clutched both the knife and Niak's scalp. He had the rifle and pouch in a flash and came up running, certain the Shawnee warrior was about to reach him. He sprinted low to the ground and darted from side to side through the woods in an attempt to make himself a difficult target. The moonlight was now an ally used to avoid the trees though he knew it could also lead a Shawnee bullet to his back.

In his desperate race from the pursuing warrior, who in fact had yet to move, Chancellor was making too much noise. So much so that he did not hear the running horse until it was on him. With a blow that sent him sprawling across the forest floor, the shadow of a horse and rider crashed into him. By the time he scrambled to his feet — knife, scalp, rifle, and pouch still in his bloody hands — he came up facing the bore of Root's rifle.

Root dismounted in a flurry though he knew Chancellor's rifle was empty. The freshly bloodied new warrior set it down along with the pouch. Then he tossed the scalp toward Root's feet, crouched into a fighting stance, and menacingly waved the bloody knife toward the barrel of Root's rifle.

As soon as he did, his own words echoed in his head. Chancellor stood up straight and gently tossed his father's knife on the ground between the two warriors.

The Shawnee chieftain brought the rifle up to his eye and sighted down the barrel at Chancellor's head. In his fore hand were the reins of the horse and the animal tossed its head in the darkness and jerked the rifle to the side. Root steadied it again on Chancellor's face and saw the young Cherokee lift his chin and set his jaw.

Root spoke from behind the raised gun. "Why do you toss aside your only weapon?"

"I will not fight you."

"You know you are overmatched."

"Think what you will."

"You are not afraid to die?"

"No. My mother's death has been avenged. Our clan is at peace and our world is right."

"She waits for you in the West. Your father too, no doubt."

"Yes," Chancellor said, but his chin stayed high.

Root looked at the young man he had come to admire. His hands tightened on his rifle. He squeezed the stock against his cheek, closed one eye, and aligned the sights on Chancellor's forehead. The boy did not flinch.

Root's grip lessened. His face lifted from the gun and he eased the barrel down. Chancellor understood that he was to be spared, at least for the moment, but felt he would be marched back to camp as a prisoner now instead of a would-be Shawnee warrior.

With Root's rifle resting on him, but now only waist high, Chancellor knelt as though pained and picked up his things. He stepped forward and retrieved the knife then held it openly as though ready to give it up.

"Son of the Dragon," Root said forcibly.

Chancellor saw Root in the moonlight. He had lowered the rifle completely to his side and was holding out the reins of the horse.

"I have my own horse," Root said. "Even in the dark I know him. He is a fine horse. This one is not as good, but then he is not a Shawnee pony," Root said as he turned away from Chancellor and patted the animal's neck. "He is a Cherokee."

Chancellor moved to Root's side and noticed for the first time that the horse was his own. In the moonlight, he felt Root slip the reins across the barrel of his mother's rifle.

The Shawnee was talking to the horse as though Chancellor was not present. "Go slowly through the dark away from the moon. Save your strength. When the sun awakes race toward it until you come to the hills. You will be on our land for another day. Move quickly. You will not be safe. When you reach your mountains turn to the south. Your own valleys will take you home."

Root patted the horse again and turned toward Chancellor. He dropped his eyes and crouched to the ground. Root found Niak's scalp and picked it up but did not stand. Instead he looked up at

Chancellor standing above him with the blood-soaked knife in his hand.

"You have kept your word, my friend," Root said as the point of the blade moved within inches of his face. "There are other battles you must fight. The battles to come will require the iron of your word as much as the iron there in your father's knife. Go and fight them." With that he stood and held the scalp out to the young Cherokee warrior. "For the spirit of your mother."

Chancellor took the bloody hair and saw Root step away toward the camp. After a few strides Chancellor called to him. "Root, Chief of the Shawnee people?"

The warrior stopped and turned.

"Thank you," Chancellor said plainly.

Root nodded, raised his hand to say goodbye and then turned away.

Chancellor raised his hand as well and held it up until he could no longer see Root's form through the darkness of the trees. Then he looked around him and hurriedly wiped the knife in the grass and stuck it in his belt with the scalp. He took the reins of his horse and swung himself up on the animal's back. Holding the pouch in the same hands as the reins and his mother's rifle in the other, he urged the horse through the trees and the darkness toward home.

It was nearly a full two days before Chancellor rode into the clearing where he had been taken. The day before he had caught up to the stream and washed the caked blood from his hands, clothes, and his father's knife. He had rinsed the scalp as well then rolled it wet. Soon it would be stretched on a hoop of cedar wood. Even with the washing there was dried blood along the edges of Chancellor's fingernails.

The naked bodies of Pany and Connie were riddled with holes from boring flies and bugs and something had been chewing on the fleshy part of Connie's fat leg. The cool autumn nights had inhibited the decomposition, but it would come soon enough. His horse snorted at the smell as they passed near enough to see, but they didn't stop. Instead Chancellor rode in ever-widening circles around the brutal scene in search of his father. He expected to find him, dead or alive, but there was little sign.

There was a matted patch of grass near the stream and flies in the grass indicated blood that was scarcely visible. The Shawnee arrowhead had been tossed in the arms of the Long Man. There was no sign of Totsuhwa, but hope came out through Chancellor's heels as he spurred his horse toward home. Until he found his father he would continue to petition the Everywhere Spirit for his life.

It wasn't long before Chancellor's horse stood beneath the tree where he and Totsuhwa had placed Galegi's body. She was gone. Chancellor knew his father had survived and was warmed by the thought, but he remained seated on the horse for several minutes staring up into the empty tree as the animal shifted its weight from foot to foot, anxious to move on. When he at last steered the horse toward home he was careful to not let the animal step on the spot where his mother had been found. From the horse Chancellor looked down at the bare ground and saw her there as clearly as he had when he knelt alongside her body. Now however, in his remembrance, his mother's face was unbroken and as shapely and pretty as when she had kissed him goodbye.

Chancellor didn't move very fast. He let the horse amble at its own pace as though it were wandering through a field grazing. They retraced the ground they had raced over several days before when he had helped his father track the slave traders who had taken his mother. He noticed again the spot where she had been beaten and hobbled and made a note to come here to sit and feel the strength of her spirit. Then he left the place behind, wiped a straggling tear from his cheek and continued following the stream toward home.

When he brushed his cheek, he felt a painful twinge and for the first time since the Shawnee woman had treated his wound, realized how deep the gash was. Other pains far outweighed the needs of the physical injury. But he touched it, felt his own caked blood, and thought instinctively of his father's teachings and the medicines he would use on himself. Chancellor was his father now, and as his hand came away from what would become a wide scar, not unlike the scar Totsuhwa carried on his own shoulder, Chancellor saw the wound as a symbol, his own talisman, a visible reminder of the pain he would forever carry in his heart over the murder of his mother.

He was tired, sore, and weak. His head bobbed as though he was falling asleep and his body listed back and forth on the horse. Lost in the last leg of his trip home, Chancellor scarcely noticed a faint song being sung in the distance. At first he thought his ears were conspiring to trick him, but when he recognized the refrain of a funeral song he brought himself and his senses back into focus.

The song brought the horse up short as Chancellor listened to the wailing cry. He knew the song was for his mother, but suddenly felt a tightness in his throat as he considered that the singing might be for his father as well. Maybe he was wrong. Perhaps his father had been found dead by the village and it was they who recovered Galegi. Now the songs were carrying both of his parents' spirits to the West. For the first time in well over a day he spurred his horse into a gallop as though arriving sooner would make any difference.

Totsuhwa was sitting at the water's edge on the Long Man's shoulder near the open grave of his wife. Galegi had been placed sitting upright in the hole and had already been covered with a soft deerskin and provided with gifts of corn and the other things she would need to see her through to the Darkening Land. Nearby, friends had gathered to sing and mourn. They had been here, sleeping on the ground near the grave and their shaman since Totsuhwa had stumbled into the village.

In minutes the makeshift town had emptied out as everyone pitched in to help the one who had helped them so often. Totsuhwa carried his pride above his hurt and never asked for them to do so but understood it would come regardless. And despite his pride it was clear he could not manage alone. Other men helped him on a horse and he led them back to Galegi. While they were bringing her home, others prepared the grave by the banks of the stream near her cabin. Now they sang and cried and waited for Totsuhwa to say the prayers as husband and shaman that would signal them to cover the grave and return to their own homes holding hands and touching more often, reminded by the funeral that life and love was precious.

Totsuhwa was not yet ready to wave his hand over his wife and have her cut off from him. He sat with his legs out straight in front of him, occasionally lying back to rest. Alongside rested a stout stick others had fashioned to take weight off the injured leg as he hobbled. The arrow wound was covered with a fresh poultice he had helped prepare, but his clothes were the same he had been wearing when he and his son discovered Galegi.

He was dirty except for the injured leg that had been washed by attentive hands he scarcely noticed. His face was puffy around one eye and his lower lip was split from the fighting with Root's men. The knuckles of his right hand were scabbed over from punches delivered to the jaws of still smarting Shawnee warriors who, two days before had stood over the dead and scalped body of Niak, talked softly among themselves, then led by Root had mounted up for the return to their village in the north.

Chancellor pulled his horse up on the far side of the stream directly across from the grave. He saw his father, sitting with head bowed low, and the tightness slipped from his throat. The horse began to wade across the water and Chancellor called out to his father.

"Edoda! Father!"

The sound reached Totsuhwa but was not recognized as his mind had already told him he would never hear the word again. It took a more urgent cry, closer now, to make Totsuhwa raise his weary head.

"Edoda! EDODA!"

Totsuhwa looked across the water at the horse kicking up spray. Behind the rising flume he saw his son holding up a tired hand and took the boy and horse to be an apparition. He lowered his head to the side and stared into the grave.

"You have sent a vision of our son to comfort me, Galegi."

But nearby, the men and women who were in waiting were already rushing to meet Chancellor. The young boys scampered by ahead of the rest and plunged into the water. Their rushing brought Totsuhwa's attention back to the stream and he saw the boys collecting around Chancellor's horse. Slowly, in part hampered by pain and still clouded by disbelief, Totsuhwa attempted to stand. He leaned heavily on his crude staff until hands, mindful not to lift away the shaman's pride as they took his arms, helped him to his feet.

Chancellor had stopped the horse near the water's edge in order not to walk over the swarm of people. Some of the boys were his age but now were seemingly a lifetime removed from the young man on horseback with the Creek scalp tucked in his waist.

"Edoda," Chancellor said and the clamoring crowd became instantly quiet. "I am home."

Totsuhwa teetered near the bank and held his arms out for his son. Chancellor slipped from the horse into the water and ran up the bank, still holding his mother's rifle. The two threw their arms around each other and Totsuhwa kissed the top of Chancellor's head several times and ran his hand through the hair that had been too long. He felt his wife's black silky mane slip between his fingers and squeezed his son all the harder.

Chancellor buried his face in his father's chest to hide the tears and hugged him with the rifle and a clutching hand that once thought it would never touch family again. After several silent moments the embrace eased and Chancellor ducked his head enough to slip his free hand up to his face and brush away his tears. Totsuhwa aided him in hiding the streaks in his dirty face then held him out at arms' length.

"I am saying goodbye to my wife who is leaving for the land of the dead. But I say hello to my son who has returned to the land of the living."

Everyone nodded and spoke in soft tones of their approval and offered thanks to the Spirit that had brought Chancellor home. For his part, Chancellor looked away into the grave then back to his father as he pulled the scalp from his waist.

"This is the half-breed Creek that rode with the white men. The Shawnee have been cheated of their revenge, but we have not."

Totsuhwa looked at the black mat of hair than placed a strong hand on his son's shoulder. "And the Shawnee have also been cheated out of a fine warrior, my son. Today you will take your place with the men of the Tsalagi. The boy you once were must now sleep in his mother's arms. You are a man."

The men and woman nearby came in a makeshift line and disjointed bunches to pat both father and son on the back and shoulders. The women hugged the boy and one took the scalp from his hand.

"I will stretch this for you," she said. "When your father says it is time we will dance over it and you will tell us the story."

Then the people began drifting toward their village. The boys looked back in awe at Chancellor while others bounced around the woman with the scalp to see and touch it. Before long however, they had all gone and father and son were left to stare down into Galegi's open grave. They were stoic, numb, and hurting, but empty of tears and so grateful the other was still alive, the pain of Galegi's grave before them was momentarily insulated from their revived hearts.

They did not speak and it was Chancellor who moved first. He knelt beside the grave and reached into it to touch the deerskin that covered his mother's head. He stroked it as gently as she would have brushed the hair from his eyes when he slept. He didn't speak to her as he withdrew his hand. By accident he pushed a small amount of loose dirt into the grave and he felt his heart jump.

Totsuhwa started to ease himself down beside his son and Chancellor jumped up to meet him. He helped his father sit then waited until Totsuhwa nodded. Only then did he begin pushing dirt into the grave. The fervor of the burying varied, slow at first, small handfuls dropped almost delicately, followed by larger faster, more haphazardly placed ones. Totsuhwa began to sing a mournful song for his wife and helped some with the filling but found he had no strength for it. As the grave filled to Galegi's head both pushed dirt in quickly, with Chancellor up on his knees shoving small mounds with both hands, each anxious to have the task complete.

When she'd been covered completely and the earth leveled, the tenderness returned to their hands and they groomed the loose soil. Each flicked away small stones and pieces of root and grass that took away from the smoothness of the freshly turned dirt.

At last, when the ground was tamped and caressed until it appeared as soft as the hide of a fawn, Totsuhwa withdrew his dirty hands. "Sleep, little girl," he said softly. "I will be along."

Chancellor looked from the manicured grave to his father and saw again the vacant black eyes he had first seen across his mother's body that terrible day in the woods when she died. He touched Totsuhwa's dirty hands as they rested on the ground. The desolate husband looked from the dirt of his wife's grave to his son. As Totsuhwa struggled to focus, Chancellor saw the deep blackness vanish, replaced by the love of a father for a lost son found.

"Have you eaten, Father?"

Totsuhwa shook his head no almost like a child.

"Me either," Chancellor said as he stood up and felt the fact of his statement flow through his head as though he would faint. His recovery was quick and Totsuhwa did not see it. With both hands, Chancellor took hold of his father's thick arm and helped him to his feet while Totsuhwa pushed hard against the crutch.

Once he had his father to his feet, Chancellor picked up his mother's things and began walking toward their cabin with his father's arm draped heavily across his shoulder. They stopped and looked back at the grave for only a moment as if checking to see if they were being followed then continued on their way.

Totsuhwa looked down at Chancellor's waist and saw his own knife. "Did my blade open the door for the Raven Mocker to visit the Creek?"

"It did." Chancellor pulled the knife from his waist and handed it to his father.

Totsuhwa took it gently and slipped it in his own belt. "And you also have brought back your rifle."

"Mother's rifle—"

"No. It is her gift to you."

"Thank you, Father. And I have her gifts to you."

Chancellor stopped walking, a rest Totsuhwa was grateful for and set the rifle down while he opened the Shawnee pouch with both hands. He gently pulled out Totsuhwa's red shirt and the comb and mirror. "These are yours, Father."

The husband stared at the precious shirt made by his wife's hands and his hands trembled as he took the bundle. "I thought it was gone." He held the shirt to his face to feel the love no one else could sense. When he eased it down he fingered the comb with the missing tooth and the mirror and remembered that night outside by the firelight when he had given them to his wife.

"I am proud, Chancellor. You have escaped our enemy, taken revenge for your mother and brought home the things that were stolen from us. You have done all the things a warrior would do. It is a fine showing."

Drenched in pride, Totsuhwa and his son walked on toward their cabin as the father's voice dropped low. "The Shawnee have left their mark on you. Your shoulder."

"A scratch."

"A memory."

"Yes, Father. A memory," Chancellor echoed as though the words were melting.

The sight in front of their home was grisly. Chancellor's deer which had been abandoned at the door of the cabin had been half eaten by the family dogs. Its entrails spilled out from its sides in a long line of gore. At the end of the path of guts lay a dead dog with two arrows sticking out of its back. Another dog, the young one, was dead at the deer's head with a single arrow sticking completely through its neck. The third dog was a considerable distance away at the end of a trail that indicated it had dragged itself for several minutes before dying. Chancellor recognized the arrows as his father's.

Totsuhwa felt the boy's shoulders slump at the sight of the dead animals. He looked out over the scene then stepped again toward the cabin, effectively urging Chancellor on, but the boy resisted and continued looking at the slaughtered dogs and the mutilated deer.

Chancellor was ready to ask why but his mother's voice inside his heart whispered to him to be still. Instantly, he recognized that the dogs had been killed for not protecting Galegi and that to talk about it would bring into the light the failure his father felt at not doing the same.

The pair moved past the deer carcass and the dead young dog to the cabin door, casting long shadows behind them as the sun was setting. "The men were going to take it away, but I told them no," Totsuhwa said weakly. "I will do it."

"I will help you," Chancellor said as they walked together into the cabin.

Inside there were bowls of prepared corn, beans, and meat, left by the women of the village, wrapped in neat bundles on their rough table. Fresh water was in a small bucket alongside the meal. Near the fire pit was a mountainous stack of wood and kindling and a small fire was burning.

Chancellor set his mother's rifle just inside the door where she had always kept it then guided his father to the fire and helped him sit. He brought the food and water from the table and they ate until they could eat no more. Occasionally the scent of the dead deer drifted inside, but Chancellor played the fire until it smoked enough so neither was put off by the rotting smell.

As they ate they talked of the recent past and the future.

"Will you tell me how you got my knife before you tell it at the dance?" Totsuhwa asked.

"Yes."

"Good. I want to hear how you came to be a man."

"When will the dance be?"

"When I can move without the help of this tree," Totsuhwa said as he tapped the rough crutch. "By then I will have sung enough to see your mother to the West. Then we will celebrate her reaching the Darkening Land as well as your triumph."

They were quiet for only a moment before Chancellor asked. "And then?"

Totsuhwa took a small drink from a wooden bowl. "Then you will fulfill the wish of your mother and go to the school."

"But it was white men who—"

Totsuhwa raised his hand, and Chancellor stopped.

"I know," Totsuhwa said. "It is exactly what she wanted you to learn — why these people do these things to us. She was very wise. She believed that if you could learn their way you could help protect our people. That was her wish."

"Is it your wish as well, Father?"

"It is."

"And what will you do when I go to the white school?"

Totsuhwa thought for a short while. "I will go into the mountains of my father. I will talk to him and learn what I must do."

"Will you be here when I come from the white school?"

"I will be near." He smiled. "You are a good tracker. You will find me."

Chancellor hesitated. "Do you want to go to the West with Mother?"

Totsuhwa's smile faded and he looked out the open door with a tired longing look growing across his face. "I miss her. And I came to know it too late." He looked back into the tiny fire and took another small bite of dried meat. "I thought you were taken from me as punishment for what I did to your mother."

"You did nothing to—"

"I was not here. I left her often when there was no need."

"You had taken me hunting. To teach me. If there is blame, it is mine."

"No. You were a boy then. There is no blame for children. I disappointed her many times and failed her many times. I should have had a better cabin for her. Should have killed deer for their skins to trade and gotten the things the others have to make her life easier. But now there is no reason."

Totsuhwa absently chewed the meat as his voice trailed off. Chancellor was too tired to debate and did not know what to say if he had tried. Instead he got up and pulled his parents' blankets over nearer the fire beside his father. He took what food remained and wrapped it up tight and put it and the water back on the table. He returned to the fire with another worn blanket and lay down. From his bed, he tossed a few small sticks on the fire and spoke deliberately to Totsuhwa.

"I will go to the white school and learn their way. You will go to the mountains. We will both do what we can, but Father, promise me you will not tempt the Darkening Land. Tell me you will not tease the Raven Mockers. I need you here to teach me what the school cannot. For my promise to Mother you must promise me this."

"I can only promise that I will go to the West when the Spirit calls me."

"But you will take care in the mountains as you always have done. Promise me that."

Totsuhwa hesitated. "My heart is broken, son. It cannot make promises."

Chancellor had no words to say. He nestled in the blanket and accepted defeat. His own heart hurt for the loss of his mother, but now there was another layer of pain for his father. The school was far away and Chancellor considered that he would not see his father for a long time — perhaps ever again after he departed. He knew the hollowness he had seen in his father's eyes would find a home in the mountains. Despite the turmoil in his mind and heart, the weariness of Chancellor's body soon overran his thoughts and he fell asleep.

Totsuhwa stretched his tingling leg and massaged a powerful ache out of the knee below the wound. When he finished, he heard Chancellor's deep sleep breathing and looked at his boy for some time, thankful for his safe return. As he prepared to lie down he felt his knife along his side. Cautiously, as though it was not his, he pulled it out and examined it in the cabin, now completely dark except for the fire's light. He turned the knife over in both hands then one hand began to tighten on its handle. The knuckles of the hand turned white beneath the fierceness of the grip and the knife began to slash through the air over the fire.

"Yes, my son," Totsuhwa said in a whisper as his jaw clenched as tight as his hand on the knife and the hollowness returned to his black eyes. "We will each do what we can."

The knife's stabbing slowed until it once again was passed tenderly from hand to hand. Then Totsuhwa lay down and the knife with him. It rested beside the fire while its tormented master fell into a restless sleep as new tears were drying on his cheeks.

Before his father woke the following morning Chancellor had dragged the dead dogs and the deer deep into the woods. He cut his father's arrows from the dogs and rinsed them in the creek. When the bloody memories were rinsed away, he set the arrows beside the cabin to dry in preparation of their return to their owner's quiver.

After his father woke and treated his leg, father and son had breakfast together and spent the rest of the quiet day at the grave, singing songs and offering up prayers for Galegi's spirit. Later, Chancellor and Totsuhwa washed themselves and their clothes in the stream. Then Totsuhwa cleaned and packed his wound again and worked his leg by hand to get the movement and strength back. More songs followed and the day came to a close.

The following days were spent in the same fashion. Chores were minimal, Totsuhwa healed slowly — hindered by his broken heart — and songs were sung to the West for Galegi. A new moon came and went before Chancellor took the bow his father had crafted for him and his mother's rifle into the mountains to hunt.

* * *

AHWI

I can never recall the exact moment I open my eyes each morning. It is not something I dwell on. I dwell on little and I don't truly sense why that is, but it is curious to me that I feel as though I am always awake. If not totally so certainly my senses seldom sleep. I hear in my sleep. I smell changes in the wind that seep into my nostrils even as my eyes are useless. And then they are open and I take in the world around me.

The trees overhead are losing their leaves. I have been crouched on the ground for some time, asleep I suppose, as there are leaves resting on my back settled there from the branches above. Their touch might have wakened me but as always, these things in me, these senses of mine tell me what touch, what smell, what sight or sound is a part of my place here and harmless.

Though I don't know when I opened my eyes I can see clearly and I am instantly wide awake. The ground under me is warm from my own body and my legs are curled beneath me. I am comfortable — neither cold nor warm, but there is an urge in me that stirs me to stand. I am hungry. There is no tingling in my thin legs. I stretch a few muscles grown stiff on the ground, but it is a luxury. I know I am ready, even from the ground, to run at full speed if I have too.

The forest is quiet except for my own steps on the leaves which make only the slightest sound as my delicate feet lightly press them back into the ground they were born from. I check everything so naturally. There is no sound, no movement, no smell that is unfamiliar. Nothing escapes me as I walk away from my bed of leaves. There is no hurry this morning. I know where the grass will still be greenest and it will be there when I get there.

As I walk I make very little noise. Purposefully so but it is effortless. My hooves are small, cover little ground and it is my nature to step lightly. The forest surrounds me like my own skin. I know it so well. Since birth I have traveled paths through it, following the trail of my mother and her sisters. My own sisters followed her as well and may still, but I have made my own way since my first rack of antlers began to grow. Many times they have grown and fallen off. Now they are thick and wide with sharp points as plentiful as the branches of a tree. They have grown bigger each autumn and each autumn I have used them to ward off others who venture into my portion of these woods. Especially during this time of year. In this cooling weather I flair my nostrils and curl my lips to the scent of the females and I feel my neck tighten.

The grass is still lush under the trees near the edges of the forest. The light frosts haven't reached here yet, but they will. And later snows will come. They will be light and won't last. I will see the tracks of others in the snows, friends and foes, but the signs aren't really needed — I can easily smell where they have passed.

The trees are nearly empty here along the edge of the fields as there is no protection from their own friends and the wind blows freely. As I move through the forest I casually check the ground for dying shoots and nibble what green I find. There is enough to sustain me through the short winters in these woods. From time to time I might have to stand on my hind legs to reach tender resting branches and some dry shriveled fruit that had refused to fall. Later I will reach high to the first buds of spring life. I always make do and am seldom truly hungry. The woods in my valley and these hills take care of their own. Food is still easy to find and there are more pressing things to do. I feel it in my throat.

When I reach the edge of a large open space I find the freshest grass that remains. As I eat, I continually examine the woods and open field. My ears flick to the front and back, almost involuntarily, listening for footfalls that do not belong here. My eyes see the grass then scan around me as I chew. They are always looking for movement or a shape in the trees that is not normal.

And my nose never stops. The breeze brings me the scent of everything in the forest. When the wolves enter, coming out of their rocky dens in the mountains, I smell them despite their wandering tricks. Even when I know they are here, I fret little. My speed is their enemy and I have faced them down with my antlers more than once. The young and the old are their focus, not someone strong and quick like me.

Today the wind is clear, but I remain wary. The wolves are cunning yet forthright. It is the slow ones that walk upright that I look for in the broken silhouettes of the trees. In the evenings, I sometimes raid the neat rows of corn that grow near their dens. There is usually the smell of fire nearby and it is unsettling to me, but the corn is sweet. Then there are the dogs that live with them. They often try to run me down like the wolves, but they tire quickly and do not have the strength of the pack behind them.

The breeze is fresh — crisp at times — all but empty except for the changing season on its wings. There is however, a scent in the wind that is most pleasurable. I scan the tree line of the open field for what my nose has told me is already there — a doe in heat. My ears twitch and my heart speeds up, fueled by a desire that affects me with this season. As I watch, she emerges fully from the trees and walks brazenly into the field. Soon after she does, she pauses and stomps her front feet.

She knows I am here as well. Her stomping is a challenge. Her own body wills her into the chase.

I snort in reply and she spins away in a flurry. She sprints straight across the open field — not what she would do if true escape was her plan. I bolt into her steps and easily keep her in sight and close rapidly. There is none in the forest as quick as I, even among my own kind. In a moment she ducks into the trees, careful that I am fresh behind her.

As I clear the field the teasing chase comes to an abrupt halt. She stomps her feet again, the length of a tall tree away. I snort again and curl my lip to taste her in the air. She is sweet yet raw and I tighten as though ready to fight. The feeling is nearly the same, but the fighting is now days behind me. I have driven all suitors from my woods. Now those females that reside here or come into my domain are mine alone.

As I wait and my muscles tremble in anticipation, she squats slightly and urinates. Her own legs are shaking. She is as ready as I. The scent of the urine at this special time of the year floods my senses and I am blinded by her.

I never hear the flying stick, but the bite of its teeth as it rips into my side shakes me from the lust. I jump as though stung by a bee and my would-be conquest leaps toward me as though this were part of the game.

My nose and ears find the one who lives with the short-winded dogs just as he steps from his hiding place. The movement startles the doe and she bounds away at twice the speed she displayed before. I bolt at the same moment but deeper into the heart of my woods and the safety of the tangled trees.

I am quickly out of his sight — he could never run me down — but my legs, those that have saved me so many times before, are oddly tiring. I stop briefly, almost unconsciously, as if to ask them what is wrong. Then the muscles in my side begin to throb as the rush of the moment disappears. The arrow is deep inside me. I have bled before from fights with rivals, but never like this. As I lick the spot and the dripping blood, to heal it as I have done before, the stick twists its fang and I stagger.

The pain is something I have never known before. It is intense, hot and piercing, like a slice of the sun set loose against my heart. Then as quickly it is cramping and dull, a throbbing that sucks the strength from my legs. But I must move on, deeper into the mountains and find a place to heal.

And yet after only a few steps my legs grow weary again. I am panting like a wolf who has given up the chase. It is hard to breathe and there is a numbness coming upon my side and overwhelming my legs, taking my strength as it advances. I stagger to the side, lumbering like a fawn that has yet to find his new legs. In a flash I have fallen for the first time in my life.

Stretched out flat I work to breathe. In a moment I try to rise, but my body rejects what my mind commands. After kicking some, I am upright but my legs are splayed in front and behind and I cannot stand.

What is this? I have been injured in battle. I know the taste of pain. But what is this ferociousness that has brought me to my knees? Why do my legs not respond when I call their name? Limp if you are hurt, but move. Move! For even now the hunter comes again. I smell him on the air. Run! But my body does not hear me.

He comes slowly through the forest. Glimpses of him flash between trees as he moves toward me. He is very quiet and walks not unlike myself, stepping with practiced gentle care on the ground. His bow is initially raised but he lowers it as he draws near. Finally he emerges. He crouches low and rests the bow on the ground. He is covered in the skin of my ancestors and though the weapon is between us, there is a kinship with this one.

My eyes, tight on the man, suddenly fade. Can I be going to sleep? At this time of day? At a moment such as this? Darkness comes over my eyes and recedes like clouds passing over the moon at night. I lower my head to the ground and I can see again but the clouds are not far behind. I cannot sleep now. I'll catch my breath, collect these useless limbs of mine and run. The hunter will raise his bow again, but before he is ready I will have been cloaked by my friends the trees. But not yet. Not yet. First, I'll rest. Try to breathe. Rest but a moment more. Just a moment more.

There is a smell clawing at my nostrils. I know it. It is the smell from the still ones. The ones that go to sleep and do not wake or the ones that have been run down by the wolves. It smells of blood and sweat and fear caused by running and being caught or the decay from annoying flies as they turn muscle and bone into dust. I can feel it in my nose and taste it on my tongue. My head lolls in dreamy agony as I discover the place of its birth. The scent drips from my own skin.

I try to stand and cannot even find a feeble attempt. I am so weak and so very tired. Is this what the old ones have felt as they sleep never to wake? If it is so, why does it grip me? I am young, fresh, and strong. I am the prince of these woods. I cannot go to sleep like this. Pain, yes, I know your face. Weariness and even fear, I have faced you before. But once more in my troubled mind I ask myself, what is this that holds me fast to the ground and bids me sleep when I see danger crouched before me? What is this and how did it ride on a single stick? The hunter is still watching. Perhaps he knows.

I look back, though through blurry eyes. The pain has left me. My legs and chest are sleeping already. I will join them. Just for a moment. Just for a moment I will sleep. I lower my head and lose the hunter's gaze. Do what you will, hunter. I can fight back this sleep no more. When I awake my legs will be my own again. That much I know. The sound of the forest no longer reaches my ears. That dreadful smell has no effect. My eyes are worthless and see only blackness. I have slipped off to sleep I suppose.

My spirit is now in the trees above me. I see myself sprawled on the ground and the shaft of the stick coming from my side. The hunter comes to me and crouches by my head. I hear his voice and somehow I understand the man language.

"Here, my friend," he whispers as he places fresh cool water on my lips. "This will help you on your journey. Wado, great ahwi. Thank you."

The polished curve of his bow lies beside me and reminds me of my own antlers. He is not so different than I. He is a fine warrior. Like myself. Though I am not certain what has happened to me, I know today he bested me, but I lose no honor to such a hunter.

I will go to the West. I hear the songs of others there and will join with all who call that land home. This man will come there one day and with the gifts of the West we will discuss this day. Perhaps he will explain to me what has happened. And in my ears I can hear him even now telling me how I fed his family and kept the children warm. It is not so bad. This thing. This forever sleep, if that is what this is. It is not so bad. This forever sleep. Forever sleep. Forever sleep.

* * *

Chancellor returned to the cabin with two deer — a large buck with a rack of antlers that spread wider than three of his stretched hands that fell under his bow and a second smaller one taken with Galegi's rifle. He took the smaller one to the village for the old and young as an unnecessary thank you for the people's many kindnesses. The big buck was a gift for Totsuhwa. It would be skinned and the meat hung to dry to sustain his father into the winter while he continued to heal.

Totsuhwa set about fashioning a fine bone knife with an antler handle as a gift for his son as his small knife had been lost to the Shawnee. While he worked on the knife and Chancellor cut the strips of deer with his father's blade, the two talked about a great many things. Chancellor would be at the school for as long as a year before he would travel home again. His father would take the upcoming winter to heal and hunt then trade for a horse next spring. Perhaps when he had a horse again he would go see his son, but he spoke of his duties to the village in such a way that Chancellor understood it would be something else that would keep his father away. It would be the mountains and his hollow eyes.

"When you get to the place of the school," Totsuhwa said, "ask for Chief James Vann's son. He is called Joseph. Tell him I have sent you. His father had the school built. His family has taken the white way and has acquired much gold, but he is a fine young man and will give you a place to stay."

"Yes, Father. I will take my bow for food along the way. I will leave Mother's rifle with you."

"No, the rifle is yours. I will have another soon enough."

"You will need it to take skins for trade."

"My bow is strong."

"Yes, but—"

"No. Tsi'yugunsini made the bow with his own hand. It has sent countless enemies to the West and has fed many Tsalagi. No more. Your mother gave the rifle to you. It is yours."

A month later, Totsuhwa was walking without the crutch. A short while after, he gave word that the scalp dance would be held. The village danced all night around a large fire, sang, ate, laughed, and recounted stories of battles and hunts. Galegi's spirit was praised countless times and she was exalted for her wisdom and devotion to her family, her clan, and her people.

Early on, Chancellor was pressed to tell the story of Niak's death, the telling of which he had shared with his father during their days at the grave. He told the truth and in it passed on the charity of the Shawnee woman and the kindly wisdom of Root. He praised the spirit of his grandfather, Tsi'yugunsini, for protecting him and giving him wisdom and strength. Totsuhwa was pleased and proud throughout and it did not matter that Niak had been bound and asleep when killed. The Cherokee instead praised Chancellor's stealth, courage, and wisdom.

During the celebration Totsuhwa told of how Chancellor would be going to the school and learning the white way. The dancers were quiet for a while. Then, encouraged by the wishes of Galegi and hopes for the future of the Real People, they accepted the notion of their shaman. To a person they were pleased that a young man of such obvious high caliber would represent them with the powerful yet foreign tribe.

The next day Chancellor prepared to leave. He had few possessions, apart from the rifle and his bow. He loaded his horse with a few blankets and fewer clothes while his father busied himself inside. When Chancellor mounted, his father came from the cabin carrying three small bundles. He handed each up to his son and explained what they held.

"These are medicines you will know. When you are free from study, visit the forest and maintain its friendship."

Chancellor took the package and slipped it into a pouch holding a few clothes dangling from the horse.

"This is a gift of food from the village of your birth. It will carry you for many days. Remember these people who carry you in their hearts."

"Thank you, Father. Have you saved enough for yourself?"

"Plenty, but you eat more than me." He smiled. "You are a man now but are still growing."

Totsuhwa handed up the last package. "These are your mother's things." He pressed the last bundle that held Galegi's comb and mirror into his son's hands. "I know you will say for me to keep them, but I will be hunting much. These precious things will be safer with you. Understand?"

Chancellor was hesitant to take the package as he knew that this meant his father would lose himself. If there was a tie to this world in the East, it was knotted by this old comb with the chipped tooth and the cracked looking glass. "Father, they may bring you comfort."

"No, my son. They are not a comfort. They are a reminder of my failures."

"There are no failures, Father. Not one. Mother would say the same."

Totsuhwa smiled weakly and patted his son's leg, but the time for words on the matter had all passed.

"You remember who to ask for?"

"Joseph Vann, son of Chief Vann."

"And you know the way?"

"Yes, Father."

"Ride to the north and east. The sun will—"

"I know the way, Father. I will be alright."

"And you will work hard — make your mother proud?"

"Yes I will."

After Chancellor had answered several other questions correctly for at least the third time, Totsuhwa walked alongside his son's horse down to the stream with his hand resting gently on his son's leg. Chancellor said goodbye to the grave of his mother and was encouraged again by his father's reminder that the school was her idea. As they walked away from the grave and down the trail, Chancellor had no idea that Totsuhwa had said goodbye to Galegi as well.

After a few minutes of quiet walking on the trail, Chancellor reined in the horse, leaned over, and hugged his father. There was no long goodbye and no tears. Father and son kissed and hugged again then Totsuhwa stepped back and patted the horse and his son's leg as they passed by. He stood in the path and waited until Chancellor approached the first bend. They waved at first then Chancellor pumped Galegi's rifle in the air with his fist.

Totsuhwa smiled, knowing his son would forever know who and what he was, but when Chancellor vanished, Totsuhwa's smile did as well. It would never return with any regularity just as Totsuhwa would not return to the cabin as a home. He stopped at it only long enough to collect his weapons, a few blankets, what food remained, his medicines, and the red shirt. Before Chancellor had cleared the first valley, Totsuhwa was climbing deep into the forest. Each step hollowed out the blackness in his mind until he began to run — into the mountains and away from the world.

THE END OF BOOK ONE

Look for Book 2 in the Cherokee Series

Losing St. Christopher

Chancellor's education continues as he struggles to bridge the gap between his nation and that of the New Americans while his father's world comes apart. The Cherokee Nation is fragmenting as well. Encroachment and violation of treaties leave little room between a war they cannot win and assimilation that may be equally as deadly. Chancellor takes a white wife without his father's blessing and begins his family under the harsh eyes of racism. Gold is discovered in the historic Tsalagi hills and the race is on to rid the land of all traces of Cherokee culture. General Jackson, now President of the United States, signs The Indian Removal Act which leads to the "Trail of Tears." Totsuhwa struggles with sanity as he pits his vow to Tsi'yugunsini against the salvation of a family he has all but disowned.

Made in the USA
Charleston, SC
26 November 2012